Little Miss Strange

LITTLE
MISS
STRANGE

a novel by

JOANNA ROSE

Joanna Rose

ALGONQUIN BOOKS OF CHAPEL HILL ☮ 1997

Published by
ALGONQUIN BOOKS OF CHAPEL HILL
Post Office Box 2225
Chapel Hill, North Carolina 27515-2225

a division of
WORKMAN PUBLISHING
708 Broadway
New York, New York 10003

Library of Congress Cataloging-in-Publication Data
Rose, Joanna.
    Little Miss Strange : a novel / by Joanna Rose.
        p.   cm.
    ISBN 1-56512-154-6 (hardcover)
    I. Title.
    PS3568.07633L58   1997
    813'.54—dc21   96-46817
                                              CIP

10 9 8 7 6 5 4 3 2 1
First Edition

All I would say to you, Tom Spanbauer, I can only say with my heart. And of teachers and guides, thank you Dangerous Writers, Fiction Asylum, recording angels, and reading whores. Erin Leonard and Candy Mulligan, road babes. Stevan Allred for such care. Suzy Vitello for ironic distance, in the hope that someday I'll know what that means. Of teachers and guides, Joe Knapp, who was there when I looked back. And thank you Peter Christopher, and thank you Terrence O'Donnell, and thank you Miss Zae Stineman at Hoyt Street Elementary in Saginaw, Michigan. And thank you Geneia, Sherry, Diana, Colleen, and along came Terry. Lewis Nordan for the gift of advice. Diane Jackson for you know what. The people of Powell's Books. The people of Algonquin Books. Thank you all.

for Tony Roses, with love

Little Miss Strange came out of the darkness
Danced across my head and stood under the light.

—JIMI HENDRIX

Little
Miss
Strange

1969

The front porch was a big square porch, secret behind holly
bushes where bluejays lived. There was a table and a chair and
boxes, from a washer or a dryer, sometimes a television box, under the
boarded-up window. Jimmy Henry and me lived in the upstairs apartment,
and he took care of our house for the landlady, who lived somewhere else.

Our apartment was big white rooms with big clean windows, all open
and light and full of air. My bedroom used to be a sunporch, off by itself
behind the kitchen, and I could see across Ogden Street to the Safeway
store. At night, the red Safeway sign lit up my bedroom pink.

Downstairs there were two empty locked-up apartments behind black
painted doors in the hallway, and the floor of the hallway was cold from
cold black air that came under the crack at the bottom of each door. Sometimes the boys from the alley got into the downstairs apartments through a
window out back. Jimmy Henry got mad and red when they did that, and
once he yelled at the boys that he would shoot them, and they ran all the
way to the end of the alley, yelling swear words back at him.

ONE DAY, one of the black painted doors was open wide, and I could see
all the way out to the alley, the back door wide open too, and there was
music and drifty blue smoke in the air. A lady, in the middle of the room
there, was swishing around a stringy mop, kind of singing, kind of dancing.
There was a bucket of suds and a bottle of dish soap. When the music
stopped, so did the lady, and she looked right at me.

"Who are you?" I said. "What are you doing?"

"I call myself Tina Blue," she said. "I have fled the dark heart of America, and I am hiding."

"Well," I said. "I'm Sarajean Henry."

"Yes," she said. "So you are."

SHE MOVED in, into the one-room apartment at the back of the hallway, and she painted purple and green on the walls and shelves and ceiling.

I said, "Do you think those colors go together?"

"My eyes love green," she said. "But my heart belongs to purple."

TINA BLUE set little lamps in the corners, and she covered the little lampshades with paisley scarves from her collection.

"The quality of light," she said. "Depends on the quality of the dark."

ONE MORNING Jimmy Henry had to leave early, when it wasn't all the way light yet, and he took me down to Tina Blue to wait until it was time for Free School. He knocked one knock on the black painted door, and opened the door into gray dark.

"Here's Sarajean," he said, and he kissed me on top of my head and then he shut the door behind me and his feet went away in the hall, out the front door.

Tina Blue was still in her bed, getting up from pillows and blankets. Tina Blue's bed was on the floor in the corner where the closet doors used to go across. The mattress stuck out from the corner next to a tall skinny window that looked out at the house next door, and then straight up to a triangle of sky.

She stood up and stretched her arms toward the ceiling. She had a big T-shirt of blue and white tie-dye and her hair was curly all in her face.

She said, "I don't ordinarily rise until I am called by the sun."

"I like your sky shirt," I said.

"That is a non sequitur, child of God," she said. "Choose an album. I'll make some tea."

Tina Blue's albums were lined up across a shelf, just like Jimmy Henry's albums. I looked at the albums. I looked around the room. Tina Blue clinked cups in the corner space that was back behind the door, the kitchen corner. The room was not so dark as at first. I bumped my finger back and forth along the albums and watched. Tina Blue brought cups and a flower-painted teapot to the table by her bed, a short table with curvy legs.

"What have you chosen for tunes?" she said.

I took out the album my fingers were touching and she put the album on her record player, clicked the record player on and the music started, soft ringing music, and Tina Blue stood with her eyes closed, moving her head around in like a circle.

"Good choice," she said.

She stepped back into the pillows and blankets in the bed. I stood still and straight by the shelves, and my hands stayed by my pockets.

"Come in," she said. "Take your shoes off."

I said, "In your bed?"

"That is where we drink tea in the morning, Miss Sarajean," she said.

I untied my sneakers and took them off and left them by the door. The floor was cold through my socks. I got onto the mattress by the edge. Tina Blue handed me a cup that was halfway full of tea, and she said,

"How long until school?"

"Eight forty-five," I said.

She tucked down into the pillows and blankets and sipped at her tea, and I sipped at my tea. It was sweet with honey. Tina Blue hummed along with the album, and sang, a song about a tambourine, her eyes closed. She knew all the words.

The room was full of stuff, all the shelves, all Tina Blue's stuff. A white china elephant up high on a shelf glowed like a ghost elephant, and the dark got lighter and lighter. A long leafy plant turned into a snake, then a giraffe, then a shirt hanging from a chair by the table. I sat very still, breathed very still. Tina Blue stopped humming and singing. Her teacup was empty. She had a round dark freckle on her neck, and a shiny silver ring on her hand.

When she woke me up with a little shake, the tea honey taste was still in my mouth. I got out of pillows and blankets, on the cold floor, sock feet. I put my on sneakers without tying them and opened the door, shut it behind me, out the front door to Ogden Street.

Saint Therese Carmelite was two straight blocks away, the sidewalk straight, the street lined up straight, so all I had to do was walk, like I always walked the two straight blocks to Saint Therese Carmelite, where I went to Free School in the basement.

Tina Blue's room felt all around me like it was one of my boxes on the front porch.

THERE WERE seven other kids who went to Free School in the basement of Saint Therese Carmelite, and only one was a girl, Lalena Hand. Lalena Hand had crinkly red hair and a vest with long fringes that she let me wear. Lalena Hand said since we were the only girls at Free School we were best friends, and had to tell all our secrets to each other, like the tattoo her daddy's new girlfriend Kate, or maybe Katie, had on her butt, and me stealing a purple peace symbol keychain from the store.

There were different teachers at Free School. Sometimes it was Fern, who made plant hangers, or the guy who played songs on a zither, or Lady Jane, who had long blond braids and mostly sat with us in a circle and we all held hands, being one in spirit. The boys at Free School hated spirit circle. John Fitzgerald Kennedy Karpinski picked his nose so no one would try to hold his hand.

In spirit circle we all took turns telling something new about our life trip.

IN SPIRIT CIRCLE I said, "I am Sarajean Green now."

"Far out," Lady Jane said, and smiled all sleepy all around spirit circle.

Lalena yanked her hand away from my hand and she frowned, frowning like with her whole self.

Lady Jane said, "Now don't be a bummer, Lalena. Sarajean, can you tell us a story about Sarajean Green?"

Lalena crossed her arms across her chest, not looking at me, just frowning. Lady Jane hummed.

I said, "The quality of light belongs to purple."

Lady Jane smiled just at me. Her eyes had tears.

Lalena said, "It's Sarajean Bullshit."

The boys all started laughing, the way they always laugh when Lalena says swear words, and I had to start laughing, the way I always laugh when everybody else laughs. Lady Jane hummed with her eyes closed and tugged on her braids. Lalena's cheeks got two pink spots and she wouldn't look at me.

I whispered to Lalena.

I said, "I'm really still Sarajean Henry."

She stayed all frowning. She kicked Lady Jane, and Lady Jane stopped humming and opened her eyes and smiled all around spirit circle.

She said, "I was Ruby Tuesday once upon a time."

And she taught us the song.

THERE WERE eight houses between Saint Therese Carmelite and my house. From the sidewalk in front of Saint Therese Carmelite I could see my holly bushes. I walked home from Saint Therese Carmelite by watching my holly bushes.

Right next to Saint Therese Carmelite was a dirty yellow house with no yard, just the house walls right up against the sidewalk. Then a white house that did have a yard but no grass, just dirt. There were five different kinds of doorbells on the green door of the white house. There was a big brick house on the corner, with a fence and smooth grass and a sign that said KEEP OUT.

Then came Tenth Avenue, and the WALK WAIT sign, which was the first sign I ever learned to read. There were hardly ever cars on Tenth Avenue. Tenth Avenue went just a little way down to the church parking lot and DEAD END.

My block of Ogden Street was green, white, gray, gray, tan, and then my house, dark red. There was no other color on my house, even our front door was dark red.

Usually when I got home from Free School I stayed out on the porch. There was a certain kind of being quiet in our apartment in the afternoon. It was different than late at night quiet. Jimmy Henry would be sitting in his chair by the upside-down applebox table. He would be smoking Marlboros, and he would look up and say, "Home so soon?"

Then he would get up out of his chair like his butt was stuck on it. He would go in the kitchen and open the refrigerator door for a while and ask me if I was hungry.

I never said yes or no or anything, and Jimmy Henry would cut up apples or make cheese and crackers and the quiet would go away. I didn't like making the quiet go away. I always stayed out on the front porch for a while first.

Jimmy Henry quiet wasn't very different from Jimmy Henry when the quiet went away. He was quicker when it was not quiet, flipped his matches into the ash tray on the applebox table. Quiet, his long hair would hang in his face and I couldn't see his eyes.

Sometimes I stayed in my bedroom. Sometimes I heard Jimmy Henry talking, not to me, just to the quiet, no words, just talking.

After Tina Blue moved in downstairs the quiet was different. There was music in the quiet, Tina Blue's music, coming up through the floor. Tina Blue played her albums a lot, sometimes the same song over and over. The black painted door to her purple and green apartment stayed mostly shut.

LALENA WANTED to know about Tina Blue.

"I want to come and see her," she said. "Is she pretty?"

"I don't know," I said. "She wears long skirts."

Lalena said, "I bet her and Jimmy Henry are balling."

Lalena told me all about balling once.

"A guy has a dick, see," she told me.

She showed me secret pictures from a magazine of grown-up naked guys with long red dicks sticking out. Jimmy Henry didn't have one of those like that, I would have seen it. His blue jeans just had a zipper in front. Whatever Lalena said about balling I didn't count Jimmy Henry. Besides, Jimmy Henry didn't have a girlfriend, and girlfriends were the other part of balling, besides a dick.

"Nope," I said. "Tina Blue is just the new downstairs neighbor is all."

JIMMY HENRY'S alarm clock went off every morning of Free School, ringing in his bedroom. Then barefeet sound coming out to the kitchen floor and stopping to light the fire under the teakettle with a wooden match from the red box.

Jimmy Henry opened my bedroom door and he said, "Who's in there sleeping?"

He said that every morning.

He came in and sat on my bed and he said, "It's time to greet the day." That's what Jimmy Henry said after who's in there sleeping.

I sat up in bed and kept my eyes closed, bumped my face into Jimmy Henry, his clean T-shirt smell, his breathing in his chest. His arms went around me and he said, "Braids or barrettes?"

Then I would have to decide how I wanted my hair. Jimmy Henry pulled his fingers through the tangles, and then the hairbrush, slow sleepy morning hairbrushing, long down my pajama top.

"Braids or barrettes?" Jimmy Henry would say. Jimmy Henry said it was good to start the day with a decision. He said his decision was to get out of bed.

BREAKFAST WAS cinnamon toast and peppermint tea at the kitchen table with the bench built into the wall. I was squirting honey out of the honey bear's hat into my peppermint tea when Jimmy Henry said, "You have to go over Lalena's after school."

"Before I ever come home?" I said.

I didn't like to go anywhere after Free School. I had to come home and check on my boxes. I had to be with Jimmy Henry and the quiet.

"I have to go to Colorado Springs," he said. "I'll be back around dinnertime. I'll come and get you."

He took my toast plate and put it in the sink.

I said, "Why can't I go with you?"

"I have something to do," he said.

"Doing what?" I said.

He said, "I'm just helping some guys is all."

He took the honey bear out of my hands. My cup was almost running over with all the honey I squirted in there.

I said, "I can just come home and wait."

"No," he said. "You'd be all by yourself."

I said, "Why can't I wait at Tina Blue's?"

"No," he said.

I drew lines with my finger through the cinnamon sugar that was spilled on the table.

"Why not?" I said. "I could wait for you down there."

"I already asked Lalena's mother," he said, "Please, baby."

He said, "I didn't ask Tina Blue, and it's too early to wake her up and ask her now."

No music coming up through the floor.

Jimmy Henry said, "Get your coat. I'll walk to school with you."

"I hate my coat," I said.

I blew away the cinnamon sugar.

"Why do you hate your coat?" Jimmy Henry said, picking up my tea mug, crunching in the cinnamon sugar on the floor.

"I've hated that coat all my life," I said. "It's orange."

"You want to wear my coat?" he said.

Jimmy Henry's coat was his big army coat. The army coat had a beautiful horse patch on the sleeve.

"Okay," I said.

He went in his room and got the army coat.

"Arms out," he said.

I stood up and stuck my arms straight out, and Jimmy Henry put the army coat on me, one arm at a time. He got down on the floor on his knees, his clean T-shirt smell right next to me. He rolled up one army coat sleeve until my hand stuck out the end, and then the other sleeve too, rolled up almost to the horse patch. When he stood up, there was cinnamon sugar on his knees.

AFTER FREE School Kate-Katie was waiting outside Saint Therese Carmelite.

"Bitch," Lalena said to me.

Lalena said that about her daddy's old girlfriend too.

Lalena and Kate-Katie and me walked to Lalena's green house on Corona Street. Lalena lived in her whole house, upstairs, downstairs, no apartments, and there were other people, different people every time I went there. Her father, Sammy Hand, who she called Daddy, her mother Margo, who she called Margo, and sometimes her big brothers, Robbie and John, who she called jerks. Kate-Katie lived there now too.

Lalena's daddy sat in his chair, smoking, just like Jimmy Henry but noisy. He yelled when we came in the door.

"Well, I'll be damned, it's them girlies," he yelled. "Hey, girlies."

Kate-Katie kissed him on his cheek and kept on walking into the kitchen. Lalena went to the stairway, pulling me by my arm.

"How's that Sarge doing, Sarajean girl?" Lalena's daddy yelled. He meant Jimmy Henry. Lalena's daddy called Jimmy Henry Sarge sometimes.

"He's fine, Daddy," Lalena said, and she kept going, pulling me up the stairs by my arm.

Lalena's room was dresses and shoes and hats and other stuff, on the floor, on the mattress, the chair, the doorknobs. The closet door was open and the stuff all on the closet floor and all the hangers were empty.

"Okay," Lalena said.

She dropped her coat on the floor. Then she took off her shirt and pants, and she had on just her underpants and her purple socks. I sat on the mattress on the floor and Lalena messed around in different piles of stuff. She put on a shiny pink pajama top that went almost to her knees.

I said, "That looks good with those purple socks."

She got down on her knees and looked under some blankets, and she pulled out a purple scarf. She tied the purple scarf around her middle. Then she tipped the chair until all the clothes on it dumped off, most of them on me.

"Hey," I said. I kicked a fuzzy sweater up into the air.

Lalena put the chair in front of the dresser with the mirror, and she climbed up there, up on the chair, up on the dresser in front of the mirror. She turned around in a circle and bowed.

"Beautiful?" she said.

"Beautiful," I said.

"Wear anything you want," she said.

She climbed down off the dresser and jumped off the chair. The chair tipped over. Lalena went into the closet.

"Here," she said, and she threw a red cowboy boot out of the closet, and then another one. She came out of the closet backward, yanking on a long piece of twisty leather.

"You can be an army girl," she said. "That coat can be your army dress."

I took off my pants and shirt and put on Jimmy Henry's army coat over just my underpants, the insides of the army coat on just my bare skin.

"Beautiful," I said.

"Beautiful," Lalena said. "Okay."

I went after her out the door, the red cowboy boots on the wooden stairs going down loud. Lalena's daddy was still in the front room, and Robbie and John were in there. I followed Lalena to the kitchen doorway.

Margo was cutting up potatoes at the sink. Kate-Katie sat at the table stringing beads onto a long string. Lalena went and pulled back a chair from the table and sat next to Kate-Katie. She picked up a glass by Kate-Katie's elbow and drank out of it, made a face, drank again.

"Sarajean's an army girl," Lalena said.

I stood still right by the kitchen doorway.

Margo said, "If you use saffron instead of salt, it purifies your aura."

She turned and took the glass away from Lalena and set it back down on the table.

"Don't drink that wine, sweetheart, it's not good for little girls," Margo said. "Saffron vibes with Mercury."

She turned to the sink and started cutting up potatoes again. Lalena smiled at me, a big stupid smile. Kate-Katie kept putting pink beads, one at a time, onto the long string. Lalena picked up the glass with the wine, got down from the chair, and she walked by me out the door.

Kate-Katie said, "Mercury vibes, huh?"

I followed Lalena as far as the front-room doorway and I stopped there, and Lalena went like a dancer into the middle of the front room. She danced around holding the glass with the wine up in the air.

"Hey, soldier," she said. "Love you twice five bucks."

Lalena's daddy looked at her.

"Get your little ass out of here," he said. He said it quiet.

Lalena stood in front of his chair. She drank the rest of the wine out of the glass, and then she dropped the glass onto the rug and it rolled under her daddy's chair. She danced around in a circle, and when she was by her daddy's chair again he reached out and caught the long end of the purple scarf, pulling the scarf untied, pulling it off. Lalena ran out, past me, through the doorway. The pink pajama top came out behind her like angel wings, and she ran up the stairs.

Her daddy looped the purple scarf around his neck. I stayed right by the door. I didn't want to make any noise in the red cowboy boots. I waited right there by the door until Jimmy Henry came to take me home.

ON SATURDAY mornings we cleaned our apartment, me and Jimmy Henry, and washed our laundry. The clothes went into a pillowcase, and the towels and washcloths too, except for one washcloth. Then I took off my sneakers and climbed into the bathtub still wearing my pants and shirt. I turned on the water, with the plug left out, and poured Ajax around in the bathtub. Then I washed the bathtub with the last washcloth and rinsed the Ajax away with the red-handled pot Jimmy Henry used for washing hair. Being in the bathtub with clothes on was the best part of Saturday.

The worst part was trash. My job was to empty the little trash can in the bathroom into one of the big trash cans. The big trash cans were lined up alongside of the boarded-up old garage in the alley. To get there was down the stairs and out the front door, and I usually looked in my boxes on the way, in case any paper blew in there or anything. A long skinny sidewalk went between the houses, with bright green moss growing along the edges. The sun never got in there, just rain or snow or dripping. Halfway was the tall window next to Tina Blue's bed.

The sky up over the skinny sidewalk was a long stripe of blue. Tina Blue was there, in her window, leaning her head on the windowsill, her arm like a pillow.

I said, "Hi, Tina Blue."

She didn't answer, didn't look down from looking up at the sky.

"Hi, Tina Blue," I said.

She looked around, finally looking down at me.

I said, "What are you doing?"

She said, "I am contemplating the perfection of the view."

"We're cleaning house," I said.

She looked at me for a while, and I held the bathroom trash can out for her to see, and then she closed her eyes and laid her head back down on her arm like a pillow, her fingers dangling over the edge of the windowsill.

A porch went across the back of the house for the back doors of the two downstairs apartments. There was a purple curtain in the window of Tina Blue's back door, and a green chair on the porch next to the door, and a scraggly fern sitting in the chair. The other door didn't have a window in it, but there was a window right next to the door, a little window with newspaper taped on there, old newspaper turned brown. The backyard didn't have much grass.

The big trash cans were next to the garage, three of them, big and dented. The trash cans looked like they had never been any color at all. I held my breath whenever I got near them, pushing one big metal lid up with one finger, just enough to dump the bathroom trash in. Then I ran until I was far enough away to breathe without the smell, back to the skinny sidewalk.

Tina Blue's arm was still there, her head still on her arm like a pillow, her hand dangling out the window. She didn't look down. She wasn't looking up at the sky. I couldn't even see any of her face. Her fingers moved a tiny bit, and then I saw her silver ring, and I heard it land with a sound on the skinny sidewalk and there it was, Tina Blue's silver ring in the mossy corner of the skinny sidewalk. I looked up at her, all I could see was her curly brown hair, and I went to the corner and picked up her ring, closed my fingers around the cold circle of it, and ran out front and onto the porch.

I set the trash can on the top step and went inside my washing machine box. I sat very still and listened, and the cold ring turned warm inside my hand. I opened my hand out flat. It was a spoon ring. There were flowers in a little bunch on the part that used to be the handle of the spoon. My stomach felt like it was laughing. I put the ring into the front pocket of my pants, where it made a bump, and I could feel it, on my leg. I crawled out of my box. I got the bathroom trash can and I went in the front door as quiet as I ever was. The black painted doors were shut. Tina Blue's door was shut. I tiptoed up the stairs, into our apartment and into the bathroom and shut the door like I had to pee. Then I took the ring out of my pocket. It was way too big, even for my thumb.

"Hey, baby, you ready to do laundry?"

Jimmy Henry was in the kitchen, right outside the bathroom door. The ring jumped off my finger and rolled on the bathroom floor. I got down and grabbed it before it could roll behind the toilet and I put it back in my pocket and Jimmy Henry knocked on the bathroom door.

"You in there?" he said.

I opened the door.

"Hi," I said.

My face was hot and my hands were hot, and there was still the feel of the ring on my pointer finger, on my thumb, and the bump of the ring in my pocket. I pulled down on my shirt.

Jimmy Henry said, "Let's hit the Laundromat. Here's your jacket."

We went out the door, Jimmy Henry first, carrying the pillowcase of our laundry, down the stairs, past the black painted doors, past Tina Blue's door, me carrying the red coffee can with our laundry soap, out to Ogden Street.

The sun was bright on everything, bright on the coffee can, bright on the metal buttons that Constanzia at Someone's Beloved Threads sewed on my jacket, buttons all down the front of my jacket and one button on the pocket on the front over my heart. I touched the bump on my leg. I unbuttoned the little metal button on the heart pocket. Mostly I held on to the coffee can.

When we got home there was music in Tina Blue's. Her door stayed shut.

I kept Tina Blue's ring in my pants pocket all day, rubbing on the bump of it. I didn't take the ring out until bedtime. Then I put it in the front button heart pocket of my red corduroy jacket, buttoned the metal button, folded the red corduroy jacket up on the chair by my bed.

SUNDAYS WERE different. No alarm clock, just Jimmy Henry waking up. I was already awake when his bare feet came into the kitchen. I was still in my bed and my red corduroy jacket was on my chair. There was no music coming up through the floor.

"Who's in there sleeping?" Jimmy Henry said.

That part of Sunday was not different.

Jimmy Henry looked in.

He said, "You're already awake."

I said, "I know."

He came in and sat on my bed. I sat up and he put his arms all around me. I twisted around to where I could see my red corduroy jacket on the chair.

Jimmy Henry said, "French toast?"

He didn't say braids or barrettes, because of Sunday.

"Okay," I said. "I'll get dressed now."

Jimmy Henry went back into the kitchen, and he left the door open a little bit. I closed it a little bit. I got dressed in my blue-striped overalls, my truckers. Lady Jane called overalls truckers, because they were for trucking around, and then she would sing. I put on my red jacket over my truckers. I unbuttoned the button and looked, silver flowers down in the heart pocket, and then I buttoned the button back up. I went out in the kitchen and got into the bench. Jimmy Henry looked up from mixing yellow eggs in the glass bowl with a fork.

He said, "Cold?"

"No," I said, leaning my elbows on the table, leaning on the table, leaning on the bump in my heart pocket.

Jimmy Henry said, "Got your jacket on."

"I know," I said.

I said, "This is my favorite jacket, you know."

He dripped vanilla into the eggs.

After breakfast on Sundays was when Jimmy Henry brushed my hair. On Sundays he just brushed my hair loose, no braids, no barrettes. On Sundays, Jimmy Henry brushed my hair for a long time, brushing and brushing. He was brushing my hair when music came up through the floor.

He said, "Want to go visiting?"

I said, "Go visiting where?"

"Tina Blue," he said. "We'll bring her coffee."

"Tina Blue drinks tea in the morning," I said. "In bed."

"Okay," Jimmy Henry said. "Tea."

He took the apple teapot from the shelf over the stove, and he took the box of rose hip tea from the cabinet, and the round teaball from the silverware drawer.

"Maybe we shouldn't," I said.

"Why not?" he said.

I smooshed leftover pieces of French toast around on my plate, swimming them through the syrup. When the kettle whistled Jimmy Henry poured tea water into the apple. He squirted in honey. Then he picked up the apple by the smiley worm handle. He looked at me.

"Okay," he said.

I said, "Okay."

I slid out from the kitchen table and walked after him out of the kitchen, looking at his back pocket of his blue jeans in front of me.

"Wait," I said, and I went back in my bedroom. I took off my jacket and folded it up on the chair. Then I went back out.

"Okay," I said.

The hallway was dark, the doors were all shut.

"You knock," Jimmy Henry said.

I knocked one knock.

"Louder," he said. "She's got the music on."

But the door opened and there was Tina Blue. No rings on any fingers. Jimmy Henry said, "We've come to call."

Tina Blue said, "So you have."

She wore a silver bracelet with bluish green stones. She had dangly red bead earrings.

We went into the painted apartment and Jimmy Henry set the apple teapot on the curvy table by the bed. Tina Blue turned the music down, and she was kind of smiling, not at me or Jimmy Henry, kind of just smiling at the record player. I looked around, looked at the white china elephant up on the shelf. Looked at the windowsill.

"And some for you," Tina Blue said. She gave me a mug. I took it and stood still, looking down into the pink tea.

"You can sit, baby," Jimmy Henry said.

I sat down on the floor.

Tina Blue laughed and sat in her bed. Jimmy Henry sat in the big chair. Tina Blue was smoking a pink cigarette, and she got up and gave the pink cigarette to Jimmy Henry, even though his Marlboros were in his T-shirt pocket, and she took a hairbrush from the shelf by the white elephant, a hairbrush with a wooden handle. Then she sat back into her bed and scooted back until she was by the skinny window, and she started brushing her long curly hair. Jimmy Henry watched her and took little puffs of the pink cigarette. Tina Blue closed her eyes.

She said, "I don't know."

"Tina," Jimmy Henry said.

She brushed her hair, long slow hairbrushing. The music stopped and the record player clicked a bunch of times and the record started to play again.

Jimmy Henry said, "Why don't you brush Sarajean's hair?"

"You already brushed my hair," I said.

Tina Blue stopped brushing her hair, her eyes still closed.

"Come here, Sarajean," she said, her eyes still closed.

I sat still on the floor.

Jimmy Henry stood up and put the little end of the pink cigarette in a dish on the shelf by the white elephant. He reached his hand down to me.

"Come here, baby," he said. "Let Tina Blue brush your hair."

I set my tea mug on the floor and got up. I put my hand in his hand.

"Wait," I said.

I undid my sneakers and took them off. Then I got onto the bed, into the pillows and blankets, in front of Tina Blue, close enough to look out the tall window if I leaned over there a little bit. I turned away so Tina Blue could brush my hair like Jimmy Henry wanted her to. After a minute she did, slow, soft. Careful. It almost tickled. Jimmy Henry sat back down in the big chair. It stayed that way for a long time. Jimmy Henry sitting in the chair. Watching. Tina Blue brushing. Me sitting still.

When Tina Blue stopped brushing I got off the bed right away. I went and stood by Jimmy Henry and nobody said what to do now. The record stopped and clicked a bunch of times and started again. Jimmy Henry got up and clicked it to off. Tina Blue opened her eyes.

She said, "Where do we go from here?"

She said it kind of like singing.

Jimmy Henry picked up the apple teapot and he didn't say where we were going. He opened the door and we went out into the dark hallway. I ran up the stairs. Jimmy Henry came up the stairs slow steps behind me.

The Sunday newspaper was in the kitchen, so I got it and spread the funnies out on the front-room floor. Peanuts had Woodstock in it. Li'l Abner had Daisy May who was beautiful. When Daisy May was sad, she cried stars.

ON MONDAYS Fern was the teacher at Free School. Fern lived on my street, Ogden Street, in a brick building past the Safeway store, on the corner of Colfax Street. Fern was tall and skinny and her fingers were like that too. She liked to make braids.

"Trinity," Fern said.

I always had my hair in barrettes when it was Fern at Free School, and she braided my hair into tight little braids called French braids, Fern's bony fingers making skinny braids that went tight all along the side of my face. Her plain white face close right by mine, braiding. On Mondays when Jimmy Henry saw my hair after Free School he liked to say, "You have macramé hair."

Macramé was something else about Fern. She braided rope in long fancy braids and tied in beads and shells, sometimes feathers. The long braided pieces twisted together at the ends, with a long tassel, so a plant could sit there and hang from a hook by a window, and that was macramé.

Fern sold her plant hangers on the sidewalk on Seventeenth Avenue, in front of Bead Here Now. She laid all the braided hangers on the sidewalk, and people would come walking along and buy the hangers instead of walking on them.

She had a long beaded necklace of wooden beads that clicked when she walked. There was a silver cross hanging from it. I liked walking by her because of the clicky sound.

At the end of Free School on Monday Fern said, "I'll walk you home."

Fern almost always said that at the end of Free School on Monday. We walked on Ogden Street, yellow, white, brick, KEEP OUT, WALK, WAIT, green, white, gray, gray, tan, my house, red.

Tina Blue was walking up to the door with a Safeway bag.

I said, "Hi, Tina Blue."

"That's Tina Blue," I told Fern.

"That's Fern," I told Tina Blue.

"Yes," Tina Blue said. "So it is."

Then Fern touched my French braids, and she looked at my face, her face looking down at my face.

"'Bye," I said. "Thank you for the French braids."

Which is what I always said to say goodbye to Fern on Mondays after Free School, and she went away up toward Colfax Street, the clicky sound of her beads coming back to us. Tina Blue watched until Fern was past the Safeway store.

Then she said, "Come in for tea. I have wafer cookies."

I said, "Should I go get Jimmy Henry?"

Sometimes we had wafer cookies instead of dinner, right out of the box, if Jimmy Henry was especially sleepy on the couch.

Tina Blue said, "How about just you and me?"

"Well," I said.

"Okay," I said.

We went past my boxes, into the front door. Tina Blue went first, straight to her black door. I didn't shut the front door until Tina Blue's door was open in the dark of the hallway.

She put the grocery bag on the big table and went over in the kitchen corner and lit the fire under the teakettle. She got out two mugs and put them on the table, and she sat down, in one of the table chairs, not in her bed. I sat in the other table chair, by the grocery bag.

Tina Blue said, "Is Fern your teacher?"

"Sometimes," I said. "It's different teachers at Free School. Next year it will be regular first grade, with just one regular teacher."

Tina Blue said, "Who are the other teachers at Free School?"

I said, "Lady Jane. Sometimes Lalena's mother, Margo."

She said, "Margo?"

"She makes cookies," I said. "No-bake granola cookies. Not good cookies. Not like wafer cookies."

"Is Lalena your friend?" Tina Blue said.

"Yes," I said. "Best friend. Because we're the only girls."

Tina Blue stood up and got a little wooden box from the shelf by the white elephant. She got one of her pink cigarettes out of the box, and lit the pink cigarette with a match and blew a puff of smoke out into the middle of the room.

She said, "So, you have lots of friends?"

"Lalena mostly," I said.

"I hope we can be friends," I said.

"You're a grown-up," I said.

"What about Jimmy Henry?" she said. "He's a grown-up. Isn't he your friend?"

"No," I said. "He's Jimmy Henry."

Tina Blue poured tea in our cups. Then she sat back and smoked the pink cigarette until it was down to a tiny end, and she got up and put the tiny end into the little dish on the shelf. She sat back down.

I said, "Don't you have other friends who are grown-ups?"

She sipped at her tea, looking at me over the edge of her mug.
She said, "Family of man."

She didn't say anything else. She didn't say anything about the wafer cookies. After a while of Tina Blue just looking at me over the edge of her mug, I said, "I have to go now."

"'Bye," I said when I got to the door. "'Bye."

I shut the black painted door behind me and ran up the stairs, in our apartment. It was quiet and bright and Jimmy Henry was in his chair. Tina Blue's ring was in my pocket.

IT WAS late, way after bed, and it was late night pink in my bedroom. There was knocking on a door downstairs, and Jimmy Henry went down there. I was almost back asleep when there was music at Tina Blue's. I was all the way asleep when Jimmy Henry came back. I woke up when he came in the front door of our apartment. He turned off the lights in the front room. It was quiet all over our house.

WASHER BOXES were best. Refrigerator boxes were too big. Television boxes were too small, smaller than they used to be.

Now there were two washer boxes on the porch, one old, one new. Both of the boxes faced my table, which was at the end of the porch, by the railing. The back of the boxes was all you could see from the front door. There used to always be one box facing the door, so I could see, in case of visitors. Now the inside of my boxes was secret, so I could be in there, secret. It was the best place to take Tina Blue's ring out of the heart pocket. I would hold the ring in one hand, then the other hand. I put the ring on each finger, one finger at a time. I set the ring down on the floor of the box, right next to me. I set the ring in the very back corner of the box. I sat in the new washer box, and the ring sat in the old washer box, and I looked around the corner at the ring, Tina Blue's silver ring, sitting in the big box all by itself.

MARGO LIKED to buy food at the big wooden food store on Seventeenth Avenue instead of Safeway because of farm workers. Lalena and I got to have dried papaya, but besides the dried papaya there wasn't much stuff in the wooden food store that was really food, like Jimmy Henry's food that he bought at Safeway, bread and cans of soup and bacon and frozen broccoli.

The Saturday of the short red truckers was a special Saturday even before we went to Someone's Beloved Threads. It was going to be Memorial Day weekend the next day, and Margo was buying stuff for a picnic in Cheeseman Park. All the people from Denver Free University were going to be there, and all the kids from all the Free Schools, like my Free School, everybody having a big picnic in Cheeseman Park. The grown-ups were going to sit in one big circle in the grass, and all the kids were going to sit in the middle of the circle in a peace symbol design. It was going to be beautiful. Telling about it made Lady Jane cry because of beauty.

Me and Jimmy Henry walked to Lalena's house after lunch on Saturday. It was too hot to wear my red corduroy jacket, so I had to leave it at home, folded up on my chair, with Tina Blue's ring in the pocket. Walking to Lalena's house was sunny and windy, and Jimmy Henry stopped at the corner of Twelfth Avenue and Corona Street to look at the Rocky Mountains.

Jimmy Henry said, "Always look at what's far away, so your eyes will remember how to see far away."

Jimmy Henry always said that at the corner of Twelfth Avenue and Corona Street, on the way to Lalena's house, when it was a sunny day and we could see the Rocky Mountains.

Lalena's daddy was sitting on their porch. Jimmy Henry went and sat by Lalena's daddy, and Lalena's daddy said to me, "Them girlies are back in the kitchen."

The house was big and empty between the front porch and the kitchen. Lalena sat at the big table by Margo. Margo was filling up her string shopping bag with folded-up brown paper bags, and she had on her straw hat. Margo's straw hat was wide around with painted blue stars on top. Kate-

Katie sat on the windowsill, drawing designs in the air with the smoke from a stick of incense.

"Okay," Lalena said when she saw me.

She jumped off the chair and jumped right in front of me and spread her arms out wide.

She said, "This is my Memorial Day outfit."

Lalena's Memorial Day outfit was a long dress that had big blue and white stripes going up and down. The dress tied around her neck in long red ribbons.

Lalena's said, "Beautiful?"

I said, "Beautiful."

Margo said, "Okay, who's on the bus?"

Margo always said that. We never rode a bus to Seventeenth Avenue. We always walked.

We walked on Corona Street and then we walked on Colfax Street. Colfax Street smelled like the food from the Mexican restaurants, and people walked fast, and cars drove by fast. We turned when we got to the big church. Margo liked to walk by the big church. It was a white church, with tall white towers and a sleeping angel above the doors. There was a black fence all around the white church, a curvy black metal fence. After Margo looked at the white church, looked at the big wooden doors and the sleeping angel, and looked up at the white towers, we turned the corner and walked on Logan Street, where it was houses again for two blocks and then Seventeenth Avenue. Seventeenth Avenue was the best street. Down Seventeenth Avenue one way was Bead Here Now. We turned the other way on Seventeenth Avenue to go to the wooden food store, walking under a Frisbee game. Gandalf was there. Gandalf was a big mostly black dog. Gandalf always caught the Frisbee, and he always had drool.

The stores on Seventeenth Avenue had people living upstairs. People were in the windows up there, and the people in the windows waved and yelled and talked to the people on the sidewalk. The stores were all connected, and in between the stores were doors leading up to where the people lived. Margo stopped to talk to the guy who sold *Cripple Creek* newspapers out of his bag and Lalena and I went and sat on the bench under the window of Together Books. Together Books was decorated inside for Memorial Day weekend.

I said, "They put their flag upside wrong."

Lalena stood up and looked at the flag in the window, turning her head sideways, then turning her whole self sideways.

"Upside down," she said. "It's upside down."

Margo started walking away on the sidewalk, and Lalena and I went after. When we got to the wooden food store we went to the dried papaya box and got out two long orange pieces of dried papaya and went back out on the sidewalk, to sit on the square gray sidewalk stones. The sidewalk was cool on my butt.

Lalena said, "You have to get a new outfit for Memorial Day."

I said, "What kind of outfit?"

"A flag outfit," Lalena said. "Lady Jane said everybody should wear flag stuff. You need a special new outfit, like this outfit."

She rubbed her hands up and down on the stripes of her new long dress. Sitting down like we were, Lalena's new striped dress covered all of her legs and her feet.

She said, "We'll ask Margo if we can go to Someone's Beloved Threads on our way home. We'll find something really beautiful."

When Margo came out of the big wooden door of the wooden food store, Lalena said,

"You promised we could go to Someone's Beloved Threads after the food co-op."

"I did?" Margo said. "Well, okay. But you can't stay and try on everything in the store. I have to get home and start bread."

Someone's Beloved Threads was the most beautiful store on Seventeenth Avenue. There was a flower box with rows of flowers, purple and pink. Last summer, Constanzia's grown-up boy, Erico, grew tomatoes and sunflowers there. The doorway of Someone's Beloved Threads was painted with flowers and vines and at the top was a yellow sunface that looked like Constanzia's face, and Erico's, except yellow instead of brown. Inside Someone's Beloved Threads was dark and crowded with clothes, clothes hanging along the walls and clothes hanging from clotheslines in the middle, and big boxes of clothes on the floor. The boxes were best. Lalena and I would pull the clothes out of one box, looking for good outfits. We piled all the clothes back in when it was time to start on a new box. We tried stuff on. Sometimes we lost the clothes we had on to begin with, so we wore different outfits when it was time to go home.

Today Constanzia was sitting behind the counter at her sewing table, which is how it usually was. When we came in, she got up and said, "Just at the right moment do I see Sarajean Henry."

She held up the short red truckers. They were beautiful. The short red truckers were just like regular overalls, but instead of regular blue jean stuff, they were red. Instead of long bottoms, they were shorts. Short red truckers. Somebody had patched a big blue star on the pocket on the front. I took off my pants and put on the short red truckers. Lalena kicked my pants into the corner. Constanzia did up the straps on the short red truckers, hooked the straps on to gold snaps, and there was a gold snap on the pocket at the top of the blue star.

Constanzia said, "Muy bonito."

That meant beautiful in Mexican.

I said, "Gracias."

That meant thank you.

"How much?" Margo said.

"Out of the goodness in my heart," Constanzia said.

That meant free.

Lalena and I ran out of the shop and it was cool air on my underpants. I wanted to run all the way home. We walked.

THE NEXT day was Memorial Day weekend. I got up early, way before Jimmy Henry's alarm clock, and I put on the short red truckers, with Tina Blue's ring in the pocket under the blue star, and I snapped the snap at the top of the blue star.

After breakfast we got ready to go to Cheeseman Park. Jimmy Henry had two six-packs of beers. Lalena and I were going to get bottles of pop. I was hoping for potato chips too. When we asked Margo if we could have potato chips for the Memorial Day picnic, Margo said, "I have to draw the line somewhere."

Jimmy Henry sneaked two bags of cherry candies into the bottom of his backpack, so I wasn't too worried about what Margo would bring to eat. Margo made stuff like rice with lumps of stuff and pieces of plants. Sometimes nuts. Usually raisins. Jimmy Henry and I put all our stuff on the kitchen table. There was his backpack with the secret cherry candies and the beers. He put his extra Marlboros in there, and his sunglasses. Jimmy Henry put his sunglasses in his backpack instead of on his face because I didn't like his face with sunglasses, so he never put them on until the sun. He put the Frisbee in the backpack. He put our blue squirt gun in the backpack.

I said, "The squirt gun?"

Jimmy Henry said, "Margo said bring it."

I had my own bag for my own stuff. My bag was a special bag that Fern made for me out of her old cutoffs. The legholes were sewn across, and she braided a macramé strap. I put crayons and colored pencils in there. Jimmy Henry had his red bandanna around his head, so I put my red bandanna in my bag. I put the purple peace symbol keychain in there too, so we could all remember how to be inside the circle. I had two dimes in my bag too. Jimmy Henry always gave me two dimes.

"A candy bar and a phone call," he said.

Jimmy Henry put his backpack on his back. I looped my cutoff bag around my neck. I put my hands in the big side pockets of the red truckers, blue star right in front, a little bump in there at the bottom of the star.

Jimmy Henry said, "Sneakers."

"I thought I'd leave them here," I said.

"Sneakers," Jimmy Henry said.

I went in my bedroom and got my sneakers. I came back out carrying them.

"On the feet," Jimmy Henry said.

I sat down on the kitchen floor and put my sneakers on my feet. Then we walked down our stairs. There was no music at Tina Blue's. It was hot out on the sidewalk. It was even hotter when we got to the Safeway parking lot and no trees. The Safeway store had flags all across the front, and all the flags were right side up.

We turned up the hill past the Safeway, walking slow on the sidewalk. Jimmy Henry smoked a Marlboro while we walked. He puffed a big puff of smoke and then walked right through it. He didn't put his sunglasses on his face. I sang for a while, while we walked. I sang, "Oh, bandanna, oh, don't you cry for me."

After a while Jimmy Henry sang too.

At Cheeseman Park the sidewalk ended into grass all the way across for a long way. There was a little curvy road and some big trees and mostly grass. There were people on blankets and people with Frisbees and balls and dogs. I held onto the strings at the bottom of Jimmy Henry's cutoffs. He started to walk into where all the people were. I stopped.

"Maybe we could have our picnic here," I said.

"We have to find our friends," Jimmy Henry said.

I looked at all the people all over the grass.

"I don't think so," I said.

"Well, here," he said.

He picked me way up and put me on top of his shoulders. He held me on my knees.

He said, "Can you see our friends now?"

"No," I said, between laughing and laughing.

Jimmy Henry said, "You just watch from up there."

The grass was full of dandelions. I was as high as a yellow Frisbee that went flying by us. I could see all the way across Cheeseman Park to where the buildings started again. Jimmy Henry squeezed my knees where he was holding on.

We found Margo and Kate-Katie and Lalena's daddy and Lady Jane and Fern and everybody. All the kids from Free School and the kids from the YWCA Free School and the Thompson Street Community Center Free School. There were lots of Free Schools. There were lots of kids.

Lalena was wearing her Memorial Day weekend dress with the red ribbons tied around her neck. Her hair was all over, brushed loose, fuzzy bright orange.

"We all have to go sit in the circle and be a peace symbol," she said. "Then we get pop and stuff. After the peace symbol."

People were starting to sit out in the sun, on the grass, sitting in a big circle. Kids were standing around with other kids and sitting around and there were ladies by the kids saying, "No, here. Sit there. Over there. Over here."

Lady Jane was in the middle of all the kids and ladies, telling kids to sit in different places. Fern was in the middle too, sitting in the grass. I took my cutoff bag off and put it down by the big tree, and Lalena and I went and sat by Fern. Fern was picking dandelions and laying them in the grass.

"Look," she said.

She picked up one dandelion and held the long stem part out for us to see. She poked her thumbnail through so there was a long hole in the stem and white wet stuff dripped out. Then she took another dandelion and put the long stem of that one through the hole in the first dandelion stem. The two dandelions were hooked together. Fern made another hole and put another dandelion stem through that hole and then three dandelions were hooked together.

Lalena and I started making holes in dandelion stems, hooking the dandelions stems together, making holes, hooking them together. Our fingers got sticky from the stem juice. It was a dandelion rope. Fern went along on her knees in the grass, showing other kids how to make it work.

Jimmy Henry stood under the big tree with some guys, smoking Marlboros, leaning on the tree. I held the dandelion rope up for him to see, but his sunglasses were on his face.

People were starting to sing. Lalena and I sang. We both knew some of the words. We both knew the main words. Everybody knew the main words. The music of singing got louder when it was time to sing those words. Lalena and I counted five tambourines, except I said we shouldn't count John Fitzgerald Kennedy Karpinski, since he had his mom's tambourine and didn't bang it right, didn't even bang it in time with the main words. There was a lady with a guitar. I couldn't hear the guitar at all, since I was on the other side of John Fitzgerald Kennedy Karpinski.

Margo was by the big tree where Jimmy Henry was smoking Marlboros. She had a milk bottle and she was making yellow Kool-Aid.

I said, "Did you find out about potato chips?"

"Not for sure," Lalena said.

Lalena was making a long dandelion rope, letting it pile up into a dandelion rope pile next to her on the grass.

People were driving their cars slow on the curvy road that went around Cheeseman Park. One man driving one of the cars leaned out of his car window while he was driving and he took a picture of all of us sitting in the circle on the grass. A pickup truck guy yelled out. Fern stopped making dandelion ropes and looked at the road.

"Never mind," she said.

Lalena said, "Never mind what?"

"Just never mind," Fern said.

"Redneck, right?" Lalena said.

Fern said, "Lalena."

"Redneck or straights, right," Lalena said.

"Lalena," Fern said. "Be kind. Be generous. Be better than them."

Lalena looked at me and made her stupid face.

"Yeah," she said. "And do unto others."

"Family of man," I said.

Lalena snorted, which made me laugh, like I always laugh when Lalena snorts.

I said, "I'll be right back."

My butt felt wet from sitting on the grass. My knees were green. I walked over to the big tree, and Jimmy Henry put his sunglasses on top of his head. He leaned on one side of the big tree and Lalena's daddy was leaning on the other side of the tree. Lalena's daddy had his sunglasses on his face. They were both smoking Marlboros.

Jimmy Henry said, "Time for a bottle of pop?"

"Okay," I said.

He got a bottle of pop from the white cooler box and he opened it with the opener on his keychain. He got a beer out of his backpack, and he put the other beers into the white cooler box, except one for Lalena's daddy. Margo filled up a paper cup with yellow Kool-Aid. Jimmy Henry got our blue squirt gun from his pack and he gave it to Margo. She pulled out the little white squirt gun cork, and she poured the yellow Kool-Aid into the blue squirt gun. The blue squirt gun turned green. She stuck the little white squirt gun cork back in.

"Give it to Sarajean," Jimmy Henry said.

He said, "Take it out to the circle. See if Lady Jane wants a squirt. Or any of the grown-ups that want some, you get to squirt it into their mouth. Be sure to tell them it's Margo's Kool-Aid."

Margo said, "No Kool-Aid for kids."

"Okay," I said.

"I mean it," Margo said in her serious voice that she didn't use very much. "Don't you squirt that in any kids' mouths."

I aimed the squirt gun at Jimmy Henry's mouth.

"Not me," he said. "I don't do Margo's Kool-Aid."

I set my bottle of pop in the grass next to my cutoffs bag and went back to my place in the circle next to Lalena and the big twisted pile of dandelion ropes.

"This is our blue squirt gun," I said.

Lalena said, "That squirt gun is green."

"It's green because of yellow Kool-Aid," I said. "Yellow and blue makes green, remember?"

Lalena took the squirt gun and shook it, looked at it, shook it.

"You can't have any," I said. "Just grown-ups, Margo said."

"Electric," Lalena said. "We'll make it a cord to plug it in, look."

She stood up and pulled her dandelion rope out from the dandelion rope pile. She walked away, pulling the dandelion rope along with her until a long dandelion rope was pulled across the grass. Then she wrapped the end of the dandelion rope around the handle of the squirt gun, mashing some of the dandelions, so that the dandelion rope was hanging from there. It was beautiful. We walked over to Fern.

I said, "Want some Kool-Aid in your mouth?"

Fern said, "Did Margo make that Kool-Aid?"

"Yes," I said. "In the milk bottle."

"None for me," she said. "And none for you either. Ask Lady Jane."

We squirted Kool-Aid into Lady Jane's mouth.

"Far out," Lady Jane said. "Today my name is Lucy in the Sky with Diamonds."

I said, "A special Memorial Day weekend name?"

"Just for today," Lady Jane said.

The dandelion rope dragged out behind us. Lalena squirted until the squirt gun was empty and blue again, and we went back to the tree to fill it up. The dandelion rope was getting shorter. Margo dripped the last of the Kool-Aid into the squirt gun and the squirt gun turned green again and she gave it back to me.

I said, "Let's go squirt Lady Jane again. She'll say far out again."

"You mean old Lucy?" Lalena said. "What a weirdo name."

We walked back across the grass. The singers in the circle were singing, and then the singing stopped, a few voices at a time, until the only voice left singing was John Fitzgerald Kennedy Karpinski. Then he stopped too.

Lalena said, "Pigs."

She was looking at the road that went by the edge of the grass. A black and white police car was there, stopped at the edge of the grass.

I said, "Not pigs. Fern said don't say pigs."

"Pigs," Lalena said.

"Brother Bacon," I said. "Fern said to say Brother Bacon."

The police guys walked up to the tree, and Jimmy Henry and Lalena's daddy stopped leaning on the tree and stood up straight. They both had their sunglasses down on their faces. Margo put the empty milk bottle in the grass. The police guys walked past Margo and the empty milk bottle, walked to the big tree and stopped.

Lalena went, "Sh."

She went some tiny tiptoe steps toward where the police guys were, toward the tree.

I said, "No," in a whisper.

She said, "Sh."

I went right behind her. She stopped a little way behind the police guys.

One of them said, "There's some patriotic Americans out here today, boys."

The other one said, "It is boys, isn't it?"

The first police guy took Jimmy Henry's Marlboros out of his T-shirt pocket. The police guy looked at each Marlboro and then dropped it on the grass until all the Marlboros were lying on the grass. There were a lot of people around us, watching us, watching the police guys look at Jimmy Henry's Marlboros. The singers in the peace symbol watched. The pickup truck guy drove by on the road.

Lalena's daddy said, "America."

He said, "Vietnam . . . my buddy . . ."

He said, "Officer, you are looking at patriotic Americans."

Lalena turned to me and she said, "Brother Bacon, you are looking at patriotic Americans."

I said, "Sh."

She whispered back at me.

She said, "Squirt him in the butt."

I said, "Squirt the police guy?"

"Just in his butt," she said. "Look at that fat butt. He won't even know."

I aimed the squirt gun at the police guy's fat blue butt.

"Go on," Lalena said.

The squirt didn't go anywhere close by the police guy's butt. I saw Jimmy Henry. I saw Jimmy Henry see me. Jimmy Henry took his sunglasses off his face and frowned right at me. Then he smiled at the police guy. I put the squirt gun into the side pocket of my truckers and turned back to the circle, just seeing my sneakers on my feet. I kicked one sneaker off hard. I sat back down at our same place in the circle and Fern's feet came over by me in the grass.

I said, "Leave me alone."

Lalena said, "What's the matter?"

"Just shut up," I said. "Now I'm in trouble."

"You never get in trouble," Lalena said.

Fern said, "Why don't you give me the squirt gun?"

I put the squirt gun into her reaching-down hand.

"It's okay," Lalena said. "They're leaving. The pigs are leaving."

"Lalena," Fern said.

The black and white car drove away along the curvy road.

Then Jimmy Henry and Lalena's daddy left, walking away out of the park.

There never were any potato chips.

A bee got in my bottle of pop and drowned.

When it was time to go, Jimmy Henry still wasn't back and some of the people were going home out of the park.

Margo said, "You come on with us."

Fern said, "You can come with us, Sarajean."

Margo said, "Jimmy Henry is probably over at our house."

I walked back to Corona Street, walking behind Margo and Kate-Katie and Lalena. Jimmy Henry was there, asleep on the couch at Lalena's house.

Lalena's daddy was asleep in his chair. They didn't wake up, and I slept in Lalena's bed with her. She went to sleep and snored little snores for a long time.

DANDELIONS GREW all over my backyard, and it was hot back there, and not too many bees. Lalena and I sat in the tall weeds behind the ivy tub, in the little bit of shade from the sumac tree, making dandelion ropes, and Tina Blue's back door opened and there was Tina Blue.

She leaned in the doorway with her eyes closed, with the sun shining right on her face. She had her wooden hairbrush in her hand. She didn't open her eyes and see Lalena and me behind the sumac tree, behind the ivy, in all the tall weeds.

Tina Blue had a swishy purple top with beautiful purple ribbons dangling from her neck. The sleeves were long and big, like purple wings, lacy and see-through to her arms. Her skirt was made from blue jeans and patches.

I leaned over close to Lalena's ear and I said, "That's her."

Lalena whispered back. She said, "Why is she standing there with her eyes closed?"

I said, "She likes to have her eyes closed."

Tina Blue touched her neck with the wooden hairbrush. She brushed the hairbrush on the bare skin of her neck, down her shoulder, up to her neck again, up and down. Then she went back in. Shut the door. Never opened her eyes.

Lalena said, "Fucking stoner."

I said, "Fucking stoner?"

"Fucking stoner," Lalena said. "Fucking stoner fucking stoner."

Lalena said it again, over and over, fucking stoner fucking stoner, until it was so funny we both started falling over, falling down in the dandelions saying fucking stoner fucking stoner.

☮

WHEN IT was hot and summer out I stopped going to Free School. Jimmy Henry said who's in there sleeping, but I was usually already awake, early, the sun coming in my window, on my face, in my bed, and on the red truckers folded up, Tina Blue's silver flower spoon ring under the blue star, snapped into the pocket.

Sometimes after I got dressed I got back in bed and hugged my pillow. It made me sleepy again, back in bed with the red truckers on and Tina Blue's ring in the blue star pocket and hugging my pillow against the bump of it.

It was granola for breakfast almost every morning, with bananas for me, with coffee for Jimmy Henry. I didn't have to eat the granola all the way to the bottom of the bowl, but I had to put the bowl in the sink. After breakfast was in the sink we walked outside without shoes. We walked to the corner across from the Safeway store to the yellow metal newspaper box and I put the nickels and the dimes in. Jimmy Henry opened the little door on the front of the metal box and he got a *Denver Post* from the stack of *Denver Posts* inside there. Then he let the little door bounce shut and it locked, and we walked barefoot back to our house. Jimmy Henry usually went back upstairs. I stayed on the porch. I got the funnies.

Sometimes Jimmy Henry came back downstairs with his coffee in his cup. He drank coffee and smoked Marlboros on the top steps of the porch. Making smoke rings. Flipping his cigarette butts in a swoop out into the street. Quiet but not too quiet. The bluejays screeched a lot right there in the holly bushes, and sometimes people came over, and Jimmy Henry would get up and say come on up.

I was coloring Brenda Starr's hair with yellow, which didn't look blond, it looked yellow, and then I heard Kate-Katie's green Volkswagen, which always sounded like roller skates. Lalena's daddy was driving, and Kate-Katie was in the front seat and Lalena was in the back seat. They all got out, and Lalena had her shoe box of colored pencils and crayons, a whole shoe box full.

Lalena's daddy said, "Hey."

He stomped his feet on the steps like there was snow on his shoes, like it was winter, not summer.

Jimmy Henry said, "Come on up."

Lalena's daddy and Kate-Katie and Jimmy Henry went in the door and then their feet went up the stairs. Lalena walked over to me at the table and dumped her shoe box upside down on top of the table.

She said, "Fucking carrot juice."

Most of the colored pencils and crayons stayed on top of the table, rolling around, some on the floor. The pink pencil rolled off the edge of the porch and under the holly bushes, which is where there are spiders. Lalena didn't see the pink pencil go under the holly bushes.

Lalena always got in a bad mood when Margo made carrot juice. Lalena wouldn't drink it. John Fitzgerald Kennedy Karpinski said carrots made Lalena's hair orange. I gave her the Daisy May part of the funnies.

When Kate-Katie and Lalena's daddy came back down the stairs, Kate-Katie came over to the table.

She said, "I think Brenda Starr is a redhead."

Lalena said, "Shut up."

Lalena's daddy said, "Margo will come after you later, Lalena girl."

They got in the Volkswagen, and the Volkswagen drove away.

Lalena didn't color. After a while she went and sat in one of my boxes. The boxes were lined up facing away from the door. After a while I went and sat in the other box.

I said, "What do you want to do?"

"Nothing," Lalena said.

The sun was shining on my face, and I laid down and closed my eyes a little, for rainbows in my eyelashes. When I closed my eyes all the way it was bright orange. The door opened behind us. Banged shut. Sandals across the porch, down the stairs, away on the sidewalk. Lalena stuck her face around the side of her box and whispered.

She said, "That was her."

"Tina Blue," I said.

Lalena got out of her box. Her feet went to the porch steps, and then they came back. She stuck her face in my box.

She said, "She's gone."

"I know," I said. "I can tell."

I laid back down and closed my eyes to the sun. Lalena got in my box next to me and whispered at my ear.

She said, "Let's go in there."

"In where?" I said, whispering back.

"In Tina Blue's," she said.

"We can't," I said, not whispering.

"Sh," Lalena said. "Why not?"

"We'll get in trouble," I said.

"You never get in trouble," she said. "She won't know."

"Jimmy Henry will get mad," I said.

Lalena got out and went to the front door, opened it, and went in. She came back out.

"It's not locked," she whispered at the back of my box.

I crawled out.

"Your pink pencil went under the holly bush," I said.

She went to the front door and stood there, looking at me, and then she went in. I went after, into the dark of inside. Lalena went first and opened Tina Blue's door a tiny crack, and she looked back at me. Then she went in, and I went in.

It was dark inside Tina Blue's apartment. It was quiet. The bed was messy and full of blankets. I shut the door behind me and stood still, looking around in the dark. Lalena went over to the table. There was nothing but a glass there. She went through the door to the bathroom. All Tina Blue's stuff, her albums lined up across the shelf, the white elephant, the little wooden box.

The skinny window by the bed was closed down and a green and purple striped cloth was hanging there. The blankets all smelled like new laundry. I got on the bed on my knees and across to the window, pushed the striped cloth a little bit away and looked out, down to the skinny sidewalk between the houses. I unsnapped my blue star pocket and took out Tina Blue's ring and set it on the windowsill. Silver flowers. I put it back in my pocket and snapped the blue star.

Lalena came back out of the bathroom and she went to a little dresser with four drawers. The top drawer was open, and Lalena took out a lacy undershirt.

"It's beautiful," she said.

I said, "I don't think you should look in the drawers."

I climbed back across the pillows and blankets, climbed back out of the bed.

Lalena took out some pink underpants with flowers.

"Beautiful," she said.

Then she took out a little blue painted box. There was a little click when it opened.

"Come on," I said. "I'll get your pink pencil back."

Lalena said, "Look."

The blue box had balloons inside. Balloons tied with knots, two red balloons, one blue.

"So what," I said. "Balloons. Come on."

"Balloons," Lalena said, "Ha. Fucking stoner."

She clicked the little blue box closed. She put the box back in the drawer, and she put both hands in the drawer and wiggled her hands around in all the underpants and things.

Jimmy Henry's feet walked across the ceiling.

"Come on," I said.

We tiptoed out, shutting Tina Blue's door as quiet as we could shut it. Nothing, not Jimmy Henry coming down. Outside on the porch was bright again, and noisy from bluejays and from cars and being back outside. I laid down on my stomach at the edge of the porch and quick grabbed Lalena's pink pencil.

IT WAS raining, big thunderstorm raining, and Margo and Lalena and I ran home from Cheeseman Park all wet. We ran on the sidewalk splashing. My sneakers got completely wet. Lalena's hair was sticking to her shoulders and sticking to her face in all red squiggles, her face mad, her whole self mad. Goosebumps on all her arm freckles. We ran up onto my front porch out from the big raindrops. Margo opened the front door and stopped there looking in. I looked around her while I took my wet sneakers off my feet.

Tina Blue's door was open, and Jimmy Henry was sitting on a box in there. I went past Margo, through the dark hallway, to Tina Blue's doorway. Jimmy Henry sat on the box in the middle of Tina Blue's apartment with a piece of paper, holding it.

Tina Blue's apartment was empty. No albums lined up across, no books. No white china elephant. The little curvy table was gone and there was no blanket, no pillow, just plain striped mattress stuff with old mattress stains. The little dresser against the wall had all the drawers sticking out.

"Is she gone?" I said. "Did Tina Blue move out?"

Jimmy Henry's hair was down hanging over his face, over his eyes. Lalena went over to the little dresser and she looked in the top drawer.

"Empty," she said.

My bare feet made wet bare feet prints from the door to Jimmy Henry sitting on the box. Margo came over to Jimmy Henry and took the piece of paper out of his hand.

"What does that piece of paper say?" I said. "Does it say goodbye?"

Margo gave it back to him.

"Yeah," Jimmy Henry said. "It says goodbye."

He folded it into a long square.

The purple and green striped cloth was gone from the tall skinny window and the window was all foggy and wet inside. There was a lopsided heart drawn into the fog on the window, and the heart was dripping down.

"Did she draw that heart on the window?" I said.

Jimmy Henry didn't say yes and he didn't say no. He looked at the lopsided heart on the window.

Lalena said, "Tina Blue doesn't draw very good hearts."

Margo touched Jimmy Henry on his arm.

She said to Lalena, "Come on, sweetheart. We have to go."

Margo and Lalena left.

"What's in that box?" I said, kicking at the box Jimmy Henry was sitting on.

"Books," he said. "Her books."

He stood up. Tired.

"Let's go have macaroni and cheese," I said.

I pulled on his shirt and pulled him away from the box of books. Pulled him to the door. We went out in the hallway.

"Aren't you going to shut the door?" I said.

He shut the door.

Upstairs in our apartment all the lights were on and the windows weren't foggy. There was our stuff everywhere. Jimmy Henry went to his chair and sat down.

"Do you want your coffee cup?" I said.

"No," he said. "We'll fix macaroni and cheese."

I went in my bedroom. The pink of the Safeway sign was all in the parking lot because of the rain. I took Tina Blue's ring out of my pocket and put it on the windowsill. She left it here. She left without it.

I dumped my crayons out on the top of the dresser and I put Tina Blue's ring inside the crayon box. The crayon box was too skinny and the ring made a bump in there. I put the crayon box in my first drawer under all my socks and underpants.

Jimmy Henry was still sitting in his chair. Not smoking Marlboros. It was quiet all over our house except for raining outside. I opened the bottom kitchen cabinet and got out the big pot for macaroni water and put it on the counter without banging. The dishtowel drawer was the drawer to stand in to reach the macaroni and cheese box. I was standing in the dishtowel drawer when Jimmy Henry looked up out of his hair. I shook the blue and yellow macaroni and cheese box at him.

"I can make macaroni and cheese, you know," I said. "If you turn on the fire."

Jimmy Henry kind of laughed. Kind of hiccupped, kind of laughed.

1972

On the second day of third grade, Miss Rinaldi's class, Lalena turned around from her seat in front of me, Hand, Henry, alphabetical, and threw up on my desk. We both got sent home, me to put on clean clothes, Lalena to be sick. A safety patrol guy named Russell from sixth grade walked with us to my house from Thompson Street Elementary. Russell wore a white safety patrol sash and he had a badge because of honor. He held onto our hands, me on one side, Lalena on the other. When we got to my house on Ogden Street, Russell took my key from my hand and he opened the front door. He put the key back in my hand.

Lalena said, "You can just leave us both here."

She said, "My mother is supposed to pick me up here after her shift at the food co-op. Then she'll take Sarajean back to school."

Russell left. He never said a word all the way home holding our hands, one of us on each side of him, and then he left.

I said, "When is Margo coming to get you?"

Lalena said, "She's not."

"Oh, great," I said. "You're staying here at my house and I have to change my clothes because of your throw-up and go back to school by myself."

Lalena hopped on each stair behind me going up.

"That guy had wet hands," she said.

There wasn't very much throw-up on my clothes. I put on my baggy cut-offs and my Cripple Creek sweatshirt. Lalena sat flopped in Jimmy Henry's chair and looked at old funnies.

"So let's just stay here," she said.

"We'll get in trouble," I said.

"When Jimmy Henry gets home we'll say how we both got sick," she said.

I said, "Did you throw up on purpose?"

"Did you want to sit in Rinaldi's class all day?" Lalena said. "You know she's the queen bitch of homework? Daddy's girlfriend Sasha? Sasha had Rinaldi when she was in third grade. Sasha said Rinaldi is the queen bitch of homework."

"Oh, great," I said. "You want to skip school on the very second day?"

The window that looked out between the houses was partway open and sunny. I drew my finger through the dirty dust on the glass, a straight line across the middle of the window. I drew another line down through the middle of the first line, like four windows.

I said, "If you ever throw up on me, or on my desk, or on anything of mine, ever again, then we're not friends anymore."

Lalena said, "What if I'm really sick and it's accidental?"

"Then it won't be okay," I said. "But we can still be friends."

It was the middle of the day, just like the middle of every day all summer, until yesterday. But in just one day that was the first day of school, it was different.

Lalena hopped out of the chair and hopped to the refrigerator.

"Just walk normal," I said.

She opened the refrigerator door and stood looking in. Cheese, bacon, leftover pea soup in the pan. Milk. I got the crackers out of the cabinet.

Lalena said, "Let's go to the Safeway store. You got any money?"

"You have money," I said. "I saw your money. You have a dollar in your pants pocket."

"I know," Lalena said. "I just wanted to know do you have some too."

If Lalena knew how much money I had, one dollar thirty-five cents, she would add my one dollar thirty-five cents to her one dollar and say that's how much we can finger. Lalena said fingering. I said copping.

"So how much?" she said.

"Dollar thirty-five cents," I said. "But I'm probably not copping anything today."

Lalena figured that if we just stole however much we had money for then we could always just fake like we forgot to pay in case we got caught.

It was hot outside. Too hot for my Cripple Creek sweatshirt, so I took off my sneakers and set them on the front porch step. I took off my socks and put one sock inside each sneaker.

"Okay," I said.

Lalena said, "I'm probably getting peanut butter squares."

"Oh, great," I said.

Peanut butter squares came in a red and yellow wrapper with a drawing of a weird little girl on there. The wrappers never came off right and stuck to the candy.

"I'll peel them for you," Lalena said.

At the Safeway parking lot we walked along the edge on the little parking lot curb, so the black paving stuff wouldn't be too hot for my feet. Lalena was good at walking on the curb. Even with her sneakers on Lalena never fell off the curb.

The automatic Safeway doors rushed open and the Safeway smell rushed out, and the floor was cold smooth tile.

Honey bits, fruit jellies, peanut butter squares, chocolate rolls. I picked up a pack of honey bits and looked at the wrapper. Ingredients. Address. A drawing of a smiley bee. Nothing else. Sometimes there was a special offer on the back, but it was usually something stupid like "Send Away for Fifty Baseball Cards Today Kids."

Lalena was looking at peanut butter squares. The chocolate rolls were next, same price, three for a nickel. I counted out fifteen chocolate rolls. We moved down the candy aisle and Lalena picked up a pack of yellow gum, which was my favorite gum. Her favorite was green gum.

"I'm getting this for you," she said. "To make up for getting throw-up on you."

"Right on," I said.

"Don't say right on," she said.

She moved on to the candy in little bags.

"Butterscotch kisses," I said.

"Spearmints," she said, pulling a bag of spearmints off a long hook.

"Okay," I said.

We went to the checkout counter, me first. I opened my hands full of candy onto the counter and I said, "In a bag please."

I gave my money and got my bag full of candy, and then Lalena put her candy on the counter and she said, "In a bag please."

We had to say it like that so the lady wouldn't put all our stuff in the same bag.

Back out into the hot, along the edge of the parking lot, into the cool under the trees on Ogden Street. Lalena pulled a licorice whip and a caramel sucker out of her back pocket and put them in her bag. We walked back to my house, peeling and chewing and sucking, and went around back on the skinny sidewalk, cool and dark in there in between the houses. Past the tall skinny window that looked into painted green and purple inside. To the backyard. The sumac tree was bright red and only tall purple flowers were left in the grass, little fringy flowers on tall stalks poking up, looking like stickers but not. We both lay down in the grass and weeds by the ivy tub next to the sumac tree. With my eyes closed it was birds far away, and peanut butter.

Boys' voices were out front, and feet ran in between the houses on the skinny sidewalk. I opened my eyes and looked straight up at jagged red leaves and blue with clouds and purple flowers leaning over me. Whispering, boys whispering on the back porch of the two back doors of the two empty apartments. A window opened. A window shut. Quiet.

"They went inside," Lalena said, whispering in the grass next to me, peanut butter smell.

I said, "They're going to get in trouble."

"They went in that window with the newspaper," Lalena said.

I said, "Sh."

Lalena said, "Come on."

She went on her knees in the grass holding her bag of candy in her teeth. She crawled through the grass to the skinny sidewalk and then popped up onto her feet around the corner there. I crunched up my bag to put it in my pocket. Noisy paper. Then I crawled through the grass too, to the skinny sidewalk, and stood up in the damp cool cement air, out of the hot dust and buzz of the backyard, out of sight of the back porch. I leaned close to the edge of the house. No boy voices. I peeked. Empty backyard, flat porch along the house.

"Come on," Lalena whispered.

Back out front, my sneakers were still on the top step. The sun was shining right into the old refrigerator box under the boarded window.

"They're right in there," I whispered.

We went and sat next to each other, cross-legged in the box.

Lalena said, "What are you going to do when they come out?"

"They'll probably go out the alley," I said.

"What if they come out the front door?" she said.

"Nope," I said. "That hallway door doesn't open. Locks with a big lock."

It was quiet and sunny in the box, listening.

"What do they do in there?" Lalena said.

"I don't know," I said. "Get high. Leave stuff laying around. Jimmy Henry has to go in there and clean it up sometimes."

"Do they smoke grass?" Lalena said.

"I don't know," I said. "I never went in there. I saw in the back door once is all. It's dirty in there. I hate it when those boys go in there."

Lalena said, "Sh."

She crawled out of the box and her feet went to the front door. I held my breath for a minute and got out and went to the front door behind her. Inside I stood with my back against the door, the doorknob in my hands behind me, not letting any door noises happen. The hallway was dark but our door at the top of the stairs was open and light from up there made white stripes through the railing onto the wall of the stairway. The stripes of light stopped halfway down. We were down at the bottom in the dark.

Lalena went to the first black door and got down on her knees and looked under the door. Then she got up and snuck back over to me and we went out again, into the refrigerator box.

"Well," I said. "What did you see?"

"I saw a guy's feet is all," she said. "Black hightops."

Lalena and I loved black hightops.

I said, "Just one guy's feet?"

Lalena said, "Just one guy's feet. No talking."

After a while she said, "What do we do now?"

"What do you mean?" I said.

"About those guys in there?" she said.

"Nothing," I said. "They just go away."

"When?" she said. "How long do they stay in there?"

"I don't know," I said.

Those boys in there. Being home on a school day. Miss Rinaldi for third grade, queen bitch of homework. Giving me a bad mood.

"Let's go over to Seventeenth Avenue," I said.

"Let's wait," Lalena said.

I went and sat on the top step. I put my sneakers on without my socks. Blue sneakers. The next sneakers I got were going to be black hightops.

A window slammed out back. Then it was quiet.

"See," I said. "They're gone."

I tied my shoelaces and untied them. I wiggled my finger down to a chocolate roll in the bag in my pocket. Lalena got a peanut butter square out of her bag.

She said, "Well?"

"Well what?" I said.

"Come on," she said. "Let's go over to Seventeenth Avenue."

I tied my sneakers.

"Don't want to?" she said.

I untied them.

"Good," she said. "I have a better idea."

She picked up her bag of candy and hopped on both feet down the porch stairs and went around back. I followed. My shoelaces stayed on okay, untied, and the little end things made a little clicky sound, clicking around untied.

Lalena went across the back porch to the newspaper window. I stopped at the corner of the house at the end of the skinny sidewalk.

"Nope," I said.

Lalena looked around the backyard. The ivy tub. The sumac tree. Garage. She walked over to where the trash cans were lined up at the side of the garage.

"I'm going out front," I said.

Lalena took one of the trash cans by the metal handle on the side and she dragged. The trash can scraped on the gravel and through the weeds. She stopped at the porch.

"Come here," she said.

"Nope," I said. "I'm going back out front."

"Help me get this onto the porch," she said.

"I hate those trash cans," I said. "They stink."

"Please," Lalena said.

Lalena hated to say please. She said it like it was a secret.

I went and took the trash can by its other metal handle and we lifted it onto the porch. Lalena bumped the trash can across the warpy wood to the newspaper window. She climbed up, on top of the trash can, got to her knees and stood up, holding her arms out like a tightrope walker. She looked close at the newspaper window. She looked into each corner.

"I'm going out front," I said.

Lalena poked at each corner of the window. She pushed at the top half of the window, and when she pushed there, the top half slid down and banged. It was the way in. The bottom half was stuck. The top half came down. Opposite of how it was supposed to be. She looked in there.

"Yuk," she said. Her voice came from inside.

She climbed onto the windowsill and then she went through the top half of the window, one leg at a time.

"Come on," she said.

I said, "I'm going back out front."

Lalena jumped down from the window. Disappeared behind the newspaper. I heard her feet land on the floor.

"Come on," she said from inside.

The trash can sat there, dirty, dented, stinky. It wobbled when I climbed on. The windowsill was splintery. I walked my hands up the peeling paint sides of the window to standing and I looked in at Lalena through the open top half. She stood in a square of light, looking up at me.

"Come on," she said, "Climb over."

It was one room. No other window except the boarded-up one. A kitchen counter stuck out in the middle of the room, but no stove or refrigerator. Everything was brown except for red corn chip bags all over the floor, all one big linoleum kitchen floor, and across the middle of all the linoleum was a long black crack with the edges curling up. Everywhere was dark with dust.

Bits came sprinkling down on me, paint bits, dirt bits, probably spiders, me climbing through, and a long splinter stabbed out at me, stabbing me in my leg, and when it stabbed I had to jump down into the square of light. I landed on my butt and started to cry. I pulled up the baggy edge of my cutoffs and looked at the stab and round red drops of my blood dripped on the linoleum.

Lalena got down in front of me.

She said, "Does it hurt?"

"I didn't even want to come in here," I said. Not crying.

It didn't hurt too much. It was up above where my leg was tan from summer, where my leg was white, by my underpants.

I wiped at the blood with the sleeve of my sweatshirt and I stood up, holding my sleeve against the stab so it wouldn't bleed on my leg. I didn't want any more of my blood to get on the floor. I wanted to wipe up the round red drops of my blood on the floor, it was too shiny and red to be on that floor. And I wanted to pee.

"Can we go now please?" I said.

Lalena said, "Can we come back?"

"We can't even get out," I said.

There was no trash can inside. Lalena looked all around, walls, ceiling, me. My blood on the floor.

"Quit crying," she said. "It's alright."

"It is not alright," I said. "We have to get out and I'm bleeding. You call that alright?"

Lalena walked around the room. She stopped at the kitchen counter and she pulled out one of the drawers, all the way out. She brought the drawer over and stood it on its end under the window. I went first, Lalena kneeling, holding the drawer straight up. The splinter in the window stuck out, long and sharp, old wood with no paint color, except at the very point that was red and wet. I snapped the splinter off and threw it out the window and I climbed out onto the trash can. Then Lalena came out. She turned and pushed the top half of the window back up. It slid back down.

"It won't stay up," she said.

I said, "I'm going upstairs."

She said, "We could just leave it."

"Yeah, and Jimmy Henry will know," I said.

Lalena pushed the window up again. She stood there on top of the trash can, looking at me, holding up the window. She let go. The window stayed shut. She jumped off the trash can and when she landed on the porch the window came slamming down open again.

"Shit," she said.

She climbed back up on the trash can. She pushed the window partway up and stopped for a second and then she slammed it up with a loud slam. It stayed shut. She climbed down from the trash can, and she slid the trash can across the porch carefully, watching the window. I went upstairs.

It was hard to see the stab, down and inside my leg. I wet a washcloth and wiped at it. The washcloth came up smeared pink. I wiped a little more, and it hurt there, just when I wiped. The edge of my underpants got wet from the washcloth, and the blood on the sleeve of my sweatshirt was dark. Lalena sat in Jimmy Henry's chair. She had my splinter, holding it up, looking at the sharp point where my blood made it red.

I said, "What have you got that for?"

"It didn't seem like you should just leave it out there," she said.

My candy was still in my pocket, and I just lay down on the couch so I could just eat it.

MOST OF my stuff is pretty good, but the keychain is pretty junky, a purple plastic peace symbol. I always leave the keychain out of the shoe box until last, to throw it away, and then not, and I put it back in the shoe box with my other stuff.

The shoe box stays down here in the purple and green painted apartment, in the top drawer of the little dresser. All my best stuff is in the shoe box. The shiny pink scarf I got from Margo's drawer. The little square book called *The Prophet*, so small it fit in my pocket at Together Books, small and square with a drawing on the front of a guy that looks like Jimmy Henry. The silver spoon ring I got from the hippie girl that used to live here, Tina Blue. The purple ribbon with the silver heart attached that Jimmy Henry threw away in the trash.

Mornings in summer were best, when Jimmy Henry always sleeps late. Now sometimes on Sunday mornings, now that it's the school year, I come down to the painted apartment and sit in the corner where it used to be the closet, on the mattress, next to the tall skinny window. The windowsill is painted thick on old wood with dark beautiful purple, and the walls all purple and green, and in the morning the colors get lighter, and greener, and more purple. Tina Blue had two favorite colors, purple and green. She said her eyes love green and her heart belongs to purple. Lalena always has two mothers, Margo and whoever her daddy's girlfriend is.

Sometimes I come down to the painted apartment when Jimmy Henry's friends come over. Sometimes guys come over and just stand by our door in our front room, just stand there quiet. I leave like I'm going to go hang out on the front porch and sometimes the guys leave pretty soon after. If it takes a long time and they don't leave, I sneak into the painted apartment.

I never told Lalena about the painted apartment, about ever coming in here.

THE FIRST day of snow was early, only in September. Hot like summer the first two weeks of school and then it was completely winter. Jimmy Henry said it was going to be a long cold winter. He said he knew because the bluejays in the holly bushes were making a big fuss all the time, being noisy and fighting with the sparrows.

The first day of snow started during the night, and then morning was all quiet everywhere. The sky was plain white and big gray snowflakes falling straight and heavy down. I held my hands over the toaster until toast came up, and then I sat at the kitchen table with toast and grape jelly, watching how the gray snowflakes in the sky turned to white snowflakes in between the houses.

Jimmy Henry in his room, his belt buckle from his bluejeans clunking on the floor. A match. Sometimes he smoked his whole first cigarette in his room. Sometimes he came out before I went to school. I got up from the table and got a wooden stove match and scraped it across the stove. I turned on the gas and poked the match at the burner, and the stove wooshed into fire. I put the kettle there to make instant coffee for Jimmy Henry in case he got up before I went to school.

My army coat with the patch was on the hook in the closet and my boots for over my sneakers were on the floor. I left my boots there.

The kettle was almost going to whistle. I turned off the fire and went through the front room to knock on Jimmy Henry's door. One knock.

"'Bye," I said.

"Yeah, baby," Jimmy Henry said from inside his room.

I said, "I made coffee water."

"Yeah, baby," Jimmy Henry said.

Our apartment door clicked a little quiet click into the dark of the hallway, cold around me going down. Outside the front doorway was bright white gray. Ogden Street was a white street with black lines in the middle from cars. I went out to the sidewalk, making feetprints. My breath was big puffs. Snowflakes landed on my sleeve, snow coming down through the air from higher up than the tree branches, higher up than our house. The front windows upstairs were the windows of Jimmy Henry's bedroom. The curtains were pulled across shut.

The key to the painted apartment stayed in the top pocket of my army coat. That was where I found it. It looked just like my other key that opened our door at the top of the stairs.

Inside the painted apartment was dark and beautiful, big snowflakes coming down outside the tall window. I left my sneakers by the door and got on the mattress, wet socks from snow through my sneakers, cold toes curled up under me. After a while Jimmy Henry's feet came down the stairs, across the hallway, out the front door. Then the snow and the whole house were absolutely quiet. On the low roof of the house next door dark green clumps of moss were getting round white tops of snow, dark green, bright white.

The window out back banged and then nothing. No feet sounds or talking from inside the other apartment. After a while of not hearing anything I tiptoed to the door. My wet socks left half feetprints on the floor. Toe prints.

The hallway was dark, and I didn't breathe, down on my hands and knees on the cold floor, looking under the other door. A boy with long dark hair sat on the floor in there, leaned back against the counter. A candle was on the floor in front of him. The candle flame was tall and white. I didn't see the boy's face. I saw his hands, held out to the candle flame, like he was trying to hold the white light around the candle.

I went back into the painted apartment, back on the bed, feet under. I took off my army coat and curled under it and listened for the boy to go away. A long time later he went away.

It snowed all morning, still snowing when Jimmy Henry came back in and went up the stairs. Cold came through my army coat to where I was warm underneath. The end of my nose was cold. My legs were stiff getting out from under me, standing up. My sneakers were still wet. I carried them upstairs.

Jimmy Henry was in the kitchen making hot water in the kettle.

He said, "You're home early."

"Stomachache," I said, putting my army coat on the bench of the table, my sneakers on the floor.

Jimmy Henry looked at me.

"Better now," I said.

He laughed. It was a short choky sound.

I said, "Why are you laughing?"

"Because you're a little truant," he said.

"I don't know what that is," I said.

He said, "A truant is a little girl who doesn't want to go to school."

He poured hot water into his cup and the coffee smell came up.

I said, "Can I have some of that?"

"It's coffee," he said.

"With sugar," I said.

He didn't say yes and he didn't say no, and he got down another mug.

I sat in the bench. Jimmy Henry put the two coffees on the table and he sat across in the chair. He pushed his hair back away from his eyes, and it fell over his eyes again. The kitchen was kind of dark, and I got up and turned on the switch, and the light came on bright and yellow. I turned it off.

"We need a candle," I said.

"A candle," Jimmy Henry said.

"For our table," I said.

He said, "There's probably one in that bottom drawer."

The first drawer had all our forks and spoons and eating stuff. The second drawer had dishtowels and rags from old T-shirts. The bottom drawer had all different things in there. Rubber bands and matchbooks and the can opener. Safety pins and shoelaces and a nutcracker. Pencils and a burned potholder and a tennis ball in a plastic bag. And a candle. A yellow candle. The candle wouldn't stand up by itself on the table. It fell over. Jimmy Henry picked the candle up and held the bottom end over the fire of a match until wax dripped on our table, yellow wax on painted blue. He stuck the bottom end of the candle into the squishy wax drips, and the candle stood up straight. He lit another match and lit the candle. The candle flame started out small and shaky, and reached up between me and Jimmy Henry. I put my hands out, like I was holding the light. My fingers were lit up pink.

DOING HOMEWORK was at the kitchen table, with all my books stacked up in order, and usually Jimmy Henry sleeping on the couch. Science was the best homework. In third grade, science was learning birds. Birds had air in their bones so they could fly. Hummingbirds were the smallest birds. Pelicans were the biggest. Bluejays were the second biggest.

Thompson Street Elementary was three blocks after turning the corner of Saint Therese Carmelite, walking by myself. One morning almost there John Fitzgerald Kennedy Karpinski was kneeling down by the curb. I was going to walk past him and pretend he wasn't there but he said, "Hey. Lookit."

Under the back of a car there was a bird, a round gray pigeon sitting on the street. The pigeon's wings were spread out like he was going to fly away. His wings were gray and white, with different colors shining over them, silvery green and purple, like oil in a puddle. When I got near the pigeon it flapped one wing, flapping around in a circle under the car. Then it stopped and it looked at me with its one silver eye.

"He's hurt," said John Fitzgerald Kennedy Karpinski.

The pigeon flapped some more and then it stopped. Its round feather chest puffed.

"He's got a hurt wing," John Fitzgerald Kennedy Karpinski said. "And also he's probably scared."

"Come here, pigeon," I whispered. I reached out my hand and the pigeon flapped around in a circle again.

"You can't touch him," John Fitzgerald Kennedy Karpinski said. "He'll just do like that, trying to get away. I guess he'll probably die."

"What if we caught it," I said. "And put it in a box."

"He'd still probably die," John Fitzgerald Kennedy Karpinski said. "Then you'd have a dead bird in a box. You could bury him in the box."

He picked up his math book and his blue sweater from the curb.

"It's almost late you know," he said.

He walked away on the sidewalk. The first bell rang, and I walked away backward, watching the pigeon under the car until I couldn't see it anymore.

Miss Rinaldi called on me in spelling, and I didn't know what word we were on.

At recess, Lalena wanted to draw on the playground with chalk.

"No," I said. "There's a pigeon, under a car, with a hurt wing, and it can't fly," and I started to cry.

Lalena looked at my crying.

"It's okay," she said. "Pigeons always die. There are lots of pigeons."

"They do not always die," I said. "This pigeon wants to fly but its wings just flap in a circle on the street."

"It's okay," Lalena said, "There's pigeons all over."

"I hate you," I said.

I ran outside the playground fence and ran back on the sidewalk, all the way to where the pigeon was this morning. There was no car. There was no pigeon. I sat down on the curb.

"Sarajean?"

Fern, from Saint Therese Carmelite, was standing right there by me. She sat down next to me.

"What's wrong?" she said. "What happened?"

"A pigeon," I said, crying all over again. "It was right here and it was probably going to die and not fly away, just fly around in a circle on the ground, but it's gone now."

Fern put her arm around me and pulled my face in to where she was warm and she smelled like incense. She put her other arm around me and my nose was running, getting all over in between the buttons on her coat, blue buttons with anchors on them.

"Well, you know what I think?" she said. "I think pigeons go to heaven. Don't you think? All animals?"

"It couldn't fly," I said. "Its wing was hurt."

"You don't have to fly to get to heaven," she said. "Jesus just takes you there when you die. Otherwise how would people get there? We don't have wings."

I couldn't wipe my nose, it was too runny, and I couldn't get my hands out of Fern's arms around me. I looked out of Fern's coat, up at the sky. No pigeons. No clouds. In pictures of heaven, Jesus and the angels were always were always sitting on the clouds.

I said, "Where does heaven go when there aren't any clouds?"

"It's always there, somewhere," Fern said. " I guess you can only see it if you die. It's the good part about dying."

"Come on," she said. "Shouldn't you get back to school?"

My legs didn't feel like standing up, even after we were standing up. Fern put her warm fingers on my face, and her eyes had tears. She had a light blue scarf that was holding her long brown hair back in a ponytail, and she pulled the scarf out of her hair. She wiped my face with the scarf, wiped each of my cheeks.

All the kids were gone from the playground. We got to Miss Rinaldi's class and I walked to my desk. Fern whispered to Miss Rinaldi. When Fern left, Lalena turned around to me.

"Okay, class," Miss Rinaldi said. "Open your science books. Turn around, Lalena."

☮

WALKING HOME from school by myself, by the spot where I thought the pigeon was, where Fern and I sat on the curb, I couldn't tell if it was the same spot.

At home, Jimmy Henry was lying on the couch. He opened his eyes and then he sat up, rubbing his face with his hands. I put my books on the applebox table and sat down next to him on the couch. The couch was warm under me. Jimmy Henry lit a cigarette and leaned back, leaned his head on the back of the couch, and blew a long cloud of cigarette smoke up into the air. I leaned back onto him. His chest breathed under my head. The cloud of cigarette smoke floated in the air, and the smoke from the cigarette in his hand curled up.

AFTER CHRISTMAS Lalena's daddy moved in with his girlfriend Sasha because Sasha was pregnant. He moved out of the big house on Corona Street. Margo and Robbie and John all stayed there like before. Sasha's apartment was in the top of a big house on Seventeenth Avenue. Lalena and I went there when all of her daddy's stuff, like records and clothes and stuff, was in boxes on the floors in different little rooms. One little room was Lalena's for when she went there.

She said, "I get to live here now."

"When?" I said.

"I don't know," she said. "Just sometimes."

We were in their new front room, which wasn't really in the front, sorting the albums out alphabetical, for a two-dollar reward from Lalena's daddy. A dollar each.

"So you have two places to live?" I said.

She said, "Sort of."

"And you have two mothers?" I said.

She said, "Sasha's not my mother."

"But Sasha gets to tell you what to do if you're at this house," I said. I handed her an album. "Here, that's a *D*."

"It looks like an *O*," Lalena said. "Anyway, I don't have to do what she says."

I said, "But you have to do it if Margo says it?"

"Not really," she said.

"So what's the difference?" I said.

She said, "Difference of what?"

"Of Margo and Sasha?" I said.

The stacked-up records fell over and skidded on the wood floor.

"Sasha is Daddy's girlfriend," Lalena said.

"And Margo is your mother," I said.

I stacked the records up again, all neat.

"Yeah," Lalena said. "Margo used to be Daddy's girlfriend once. Before. A long time ago. When they used to ball."

"Well," I said. "Jimmy Henry never has a girlfriend. Who do you suppose my mother is?"

"You don't have one," Lalena said.

Sasha yelled in from the kitchen.

She yelled, "Lalena, come here and help me for a minute."

"You're lucky," Lalena said.

JIMMY HENRY made sandwiches for supper.

He said, "Peanut butter, or peanut butter and jelly?"

"I don't know," I said. "Jelly, I guess."

I said, "Did you have a girlfriend?"

Jimmy Henry looked at me instead of jelly and then at jelly.

"Yeah," he said. "Not in a while, though."

I said, "Who?"

He said, "No one you'd remember, I guess."

I waited the rest of the way for my sandwich, and then I got out of the bench and took my sandwich into my room and sat on my bed. Jimmy Henry came in the doorway with his sandwich and he said, "You mean like your mother?"

My face buzzed looking at my sandwich, white bread, red plate, purple jelly leaking out. He came over by me and sat down on my bed and ate his sandwich for a while and then he said, "Is that what you meant?"

I said, "I don't know."

"Yeah," he said. "Well, she had to go away."

"You mean like up in the mountains?" I said. "Or away like to California?"

"Nobody knows," he said. "She just went away."

After a while he got up off my bed and went in the kitchen and ate the rest of his sandwich while he made coffee. He made us both coffee with sugar.

I SAID to Lalena. "I had a mother who had to go away."

"Oh, yeah?" she said. "What's her name?"

"Nobody knows," I said. "She just had to go away."

LALENA'S NEW house on Seventeenth Avenue was tall and pointy on top, three stories high. There were five apartments in the whole house, and Lalena's new apartment was up in the pointy part. The ceilings in Lalena's room were slanty to the floor, and there was a little window down low, where the wall was a triangle between the slanty ceilings. Way down out the window was Seventeenth Avenue.

The stairway going up and down to all the apartments was splintery wood and saggy in the middle of each step, and squeaky on each step, like slow breaking.

There were two apartments on the second floor. One door was old wood, and the other door across from it was painted shiny yellow, with knobs and buttons and lights painted on like a cartoon. There were two other apartments on the bottom floor, by the street door, plain wooden-door apartments, and then outside was four cement steps down and Seventeenth Avenue.

Lalena sat on the top of the four steps, and I sat next to her, in the sun.

It was cold, cold in the air and cold in the cement, cold except where my leg in my blue jeans touched her leg in her blue jeans.

A hippie Mexican guy and a regular hippie guy walked by us on the sidewalk and didn't look at us, just walking. A regular lady walked by and said hi. A guy and a hippie girl went on the other side of the street. The hippie girl had a big pregnant stomach.

Lalena said, "That's what old Sasha will look like pretty soon."

"Fat as that?" I said.

"Yup," she said.

"And then you'll have another brother, or maybe a sister?" I said.

"Yup," Lalena said.

"And then all three plus you get to live here?" I said.

"Yup," Lalena said.

"Quit saying yup," I said. "Do you hope it's a sister?"

"Nope," she said.

"You want another brother?" I said.

"Nope," she said.

She looked away past me on Seventeenth Avenue, and then her daddy came up, walking big on the sidewalk, big hiking boots and a big army coat that was open to his T-shirt on his stomach. Lalena's daddy had big hair too, hair that stuck up on his head, and big eyebrows. When he got to in front of the steps he stood there, standing on his feet far apart, holding a Safeway bag.

He said, "Sasha up there?"

Lalena said, "Yup."

He came up the four steps and sat on the other side of Lalena. He got an apple out of the Safeway bag. Lalena looked straight ahead, across Seventeenth Avenue.

He said, "Want an apple?"

Lalena said, "Nope."

He leaned out and looked at me, polishing the apple on the shirt of his stomach.

"Apple?" he said.

"Nope," I said.

He got up again.

He said, "Sasha in a good mood?"

Lalena said, "Don't know."

He went in the front door and his feet went up inside the stairs.

After a while my butt got too cold to stay sitting and I got up.

"Let's go somewhere," I said.

Lalena jumped off the top step, all the way down four steps, landing easy on the sidewalk. I went down each step.

People walked on the sidewalk slow, walking like summer, looking in windows, standing around. Lalena's new house was on the block between Logan Street and Grant Street. Right next to Lalena's house there was a store of just beer and pop and bottles of wine and maybe gum. There was a telephone in there too, and the store was open all the time. The sign said BILL'S and PEPSI and OPEN ALL THE TIME.

After Bill's Pepsi store was Uncle Sam's Attic. Uncle Sam's Attic was all army stuff, like my army coat, and a row of boots going across under the front window, boots like Fern's boots. The guy in there had a long beard all the way down on his shirt. There were a bunch of guys in there, and the beard guy always sat behind the counter and talked to them. All the guys had army coats.

I said, "Do you think that guy is Uncle Sam?"

"Uncle Sam is just a guy in old school books," Lalena said.

She said, "Your army coat is best, because of that patch."

"That guy has a lightning patch," I said. It was a jagged lightning streak on a red and blue patch.

The next place just had boards on the front, and spray paint on the boards of peace symbols and PEACE and FUCK. Even the door was boards across.

Lalena said, "If you could write on here, like if you had some spray paint right now, what would you write?"

I looked at all the stuff that was already on there. There was a good drawing of President Nixon, only his head, with a big X on it.

Lalena said, "Sasha sucks dick."

"You would write that on there?" I said.

"You'd probably write 'Sarajean loves Jimmy Henry,'" she said.

"No," I said. "If I had a boyfriend, I think it would be Peter Pan."

"Peter Pan?" Lalena said. "You mean like in the story *Peter Pan*?"

One design was a peace symbol all colored in to look like planet Earth.

"He could fly," I said. "Plus he didn't have a mother."

"He couldn't really fly," Lalena said.

"Well, in the story then," I said.

She said, "You'd have a boyfriend that was just in a story?"

"Just shut up," I said.

After the boarded-up part there was a way back to the alley, a brick sidewalk with holes from bricks gone and trash and trash cans all lined up, and the backs of the buildings on Sixteenth Avenue.

Lalena went back on the brick sidewalk.

The alley was crooked bricks all oil black and the backs of all the buildings. Little metal stairs went up five steps to a metal door. Lalena went up there, and each step bonged like music. She climbed onto the metal railing and sat there, her arms folded across her chest. Her feet bonged on the metal railing. On the Logan Street end of the alley a car went by and besides that there was just us.

Lalena said, "Perfect."

She said, "Let's get some cigarettes and come here. Every Saturday."

I said, "Oh, great."

THE NEXT Saturday we walked past Uncle Sam's Attic and a guy said, "Hey."

A hippie guy.

He said, "Where'd you get that coat, kid?"

He said, "Where'd you get the First Cav patch, kid?"

"It's her dad's coat," Lalena said.

"Who's your dad?" the hippie guy said.

Lalena said, "Jimmy Henry, so fuck you."

Then she took off running up Seventeenth Avenue, and I ran after her, running hard on the sidewalk, across Logan Street without looking, and the next block and the next, all the way to Someone's Beloved Threads, and we ran inside.

I said, "Why did you say fuck you to that guy?"

I couldn't breathe from running. Lalena looked out through the clothes hanging across the window.

Constanzia was behind the counter by her sewing machine.

She said, "Mis angelitas." Little angels.

"Hi," I said. "Lalena lives here now. Sometimes. Three blocks away, down there."

Lalena was still watching out the window.

Someone's Beloved Threads always smelled a certain way, like I couldn't remember something. It was all clothes hanging across, colors of clothes all mixed in together, hanging long and beautiful, my hands were always in the hanging stuff.

Constanzia standing up behind the counter was not much taller than Constanzia sitting at her sewing machine. She was not very tall or very big, not much taller than Lalena, and Lalena not much taller than me. Constanzia had long black with gray hair that she braided, sometimes in two braids, sometimes one long braid. One long braid today.

"Can we braid my hair like your hair," I said.

Sometimes she braided my hair. Not Lalena's. Nobody was allowed to touch Lalena's hair, except her daddy was allowed to get out the snarls.

Constanzia said, "I have something especially beautiful. This is not good for anything except to be especially beautiful."

Along the back wall was stuff in boxes and clothes hanging. Constanzia's Mexico sandals, even in winter, on her feet in socks, going *sh sh sh,* she went into a dark corner and pulled a box from under there. She dumped the box over on its side and it was all silky heavy piles of thready old window curtains. The stuff was shiny gray and darker designs of leaves or something swirling in the threads. I pulled out a big piece and wrapped it around me. Parts hung in shreds.

"Beautiful," I said.

Lalena turned from the window.

She said, "What?"

"Look," I said. "Especially beautiful stuff."

We got all wound and wrapped up in the curtains. It was dusty in the air under the lightbulb in the ceiling.

Lalena said, "Superman."

I said, "Princess Tiger Lily."

We piled all the curtains in the corner and wrapped up in the pile until we were hidden. Being under there got hot. I got out of the pile. Lalena opened up a peeking hole.

She said, "Where are you going?"

"It's hot," I said.

I put my army coat on the floor and kicked off my sneakers and I dug back into the pile, all the silky curtains on my bare T-shirt arms. Lalena wiggled and wiggled and her arm reached out and threw her coat on the floor. Her arm reached out again and threw her blue jeans by her coat.

I said, "Are you in just your underpants?"

She wiggled her hand through to my arm. The door of the shop opened and banged shut, and I didn't move or breathe until it was Mexican talking, Erico, Constanzia's grown-up boy.

"It's just Erico," I said in a whisper.

Erico's feet went around the store, not all the way to our corner, talking Mexican to Constanzia. He said madre. Mother. Erico was telling his mother a story, her not talking back to him, just Erico's nice Mexican voice, and Constanzia laughed.

Lalena's hand was on my bare skin with her fingers almost tickling the inside of my elbow. She was rocking easy, just a little bit, in all the curtain stuff.

☮

RIGHT ACROSS from Lalena's house was the Lair Lounge. We sat on the step of the Lair Lounge looking across at Lalena's house. Lalena's window was way up. The window right under Lalena's window had colored lights.

"Who lives there?" I said. "Where those colored lights are?"

"Never saw anybody yet," Lalena said. "They play their records all the time."

Then it was Lady Jane, in the window of the colored lights.

"Lady Jane," I said.

Lalena said, "What?"

"From Free School," I said. "Lady Jane. In that window."

Lalena said, "Lady Jane?"

I waved my arm. Lady Jane went away inside the window.

Lalena said, "I remember her. Lady Jane? That was her name?"

"Usually," I said.

The street door opened and Lady Jane came out. I waved again and she called hey and then she ran across the street, her long straight blond hair blowing.

I said, "Hi."

Lady Jane was already talking, so I waited until she wasn't and then I said, "Lalena's new house is up there now."

"Sometimes," Lalena said. "My new house sometimes."

I said, "Is your name still Lady Jane?"

"Usually," she said. "So what's up with Jimmy Henry?"

"Nothing," I said.

"You still live there?" she said.

"Yeah," I said. "On Ogden Street."

"And Sammy is Sasha's old man now?" she said.

"Yup," Lalena said. "Sasha's going to have a baby."

Lady Jane said, "Far out."

Lalena said, "If I live there sometimes then we all get food stamps."

"Far out," Lady Jane said. "Bread not bombs."

Lalena said, "Right on."

"Well, I have to go to work," Lady Jane said.

She walked away up the sidewalk.

Lalena said, "What a weirdo."

I said, "You said right on."

"Come on," she said.

I HELD my cigarette between my two fingers, my first and second finger, my fingers sticking out straight. I touched the burning end to the frayed bottom of my blue jeans, one thread, and a tiny bit of orange burned up the thread.

"Jimmy Henry knows," Lalena said.

"Knows what?" I said.

She blew cigarette smoke out her nose.

She said, "He knows your mother's name."

"He said nobody knows," I said. "He said she just had to go away."

Lalena said, "Right. He was balling her, and they had you, and he didn't even know her name? Like he didn't even know his own girlfriend's name?"

"You think you always know everything," I said.

"Did you ask him what her actual name was?" she said.

"He said nobody knows," I said. "He said she just had to go away."

"Yeah, well, that doesn't make sense," she said. "I bet she died and he just doesn't want to tell you."

I said, "You always think you know everything."

"You're not even smoking that cigarette," she said. "Look, do like this."

She smooched out her lips and touched them to the filter part of her cigarette. Lalena had freckles even on her lips.

"Do it," she said.

I stood my cigarette up on its end on the metal railing and it stood there smoking, the smoke curling up. In the sunlight I could barely see the orange of where the fire was. Lalena tapped her foot on the railing and my cigarette fell through the metal stairs to the alley bricks, still smoking up at us.

"So," she said. "You should just ask him her name."

"You have freckles on your lips," I said.

"I do not," she said.

LALENA'S NEW house went door, kitchen, front room, bedroom, then Lalena's little room, all in a row. The bathroom was off to the side of the kitchen, looking out over the alley.

Sasha said, "It used to be a sunporch."

Lalena's new bathroom was the best room. It was pink, and a long bathtub on animal feet was under the windows. The light in the ceiling was pink too, Sasha had climbed up on the toilet and changed the regular lightbulb to a pink lightbulb. If it was dark outside, with no light from the windows, the pink light made the bathroom quiet and far away from even the kitchen. The dark pink light made my eyes in the mirror someone else's eyes, and I stared at my own face until my stomach jumped.

We had been out in the alley. We liked to sit on the metal stairs until it was completely dark and then not move or say a sound. It was like being invisible. It got really cold being invisible.

Sasha looked at Lalena's bright red fingers, because of Lalena hating mittens. She looked at me.

"You guys are nuts," she said. "Aren't you freezing? Here, take a bath. Then I'll fix you some dinner."

She turned on the pink light and she turned on the bathwater and the hot water came up in clouds. Sasha poured bubbles out of a tall bottle, and the smell was wet leaves and old flowers. She went back in the kitchen and Lalena shut the door.

"She's so nosy," she said.

She took off her shirt and started to take off her pants and she said, "Don't look."

Lalena got down in all the bubbles right away. I got in one toe, whole foot, other toe, other foot, knees, and then my butt, real slow. The water was hot, the best way of bathwater, so hot I couldn't do it all at once, and goosebumps like cold wooshed on my stomach and arms.

The music from the record player was a woman singing high, like a sad song, and the close-by clunk of Sasha's boots in the kitchen. Sasha sang all the words to all the sad songs.

Lalena yelled out, "Do you always have to sing?"

Sasha kept singing. Not very loud.

Late at night I woke up a little bit. The light was on in the front room on the other side of the big bedroom. The light went dark and I closed my eyes back into the pillow. I dreamed that Lalena's daddy came and carried Lalena away in his arms like she was a princess in a pink light castle.

ON SATURDAYS and Sundays I stayed in bed a little while, deciding on an outfit. My new best outfit was swishy red bellbottoms and a long white Mexican blouse that used to be Margo's.

The blouse went down to the knees of the red bellbottoms, and the sleeves went down to the knees too. There was elastic in the cuffs and I pushed the elastic up over my elbows so that each sleeve went down just as far as it was supposed to.

I opened my window for a while, leaning out. Cold and sun. I put on my army coat and went out into the kitchen. The refrigerator had milk, and old carrots, and a bowl with chicken noodle soup from last weekend. Mustard and ketchup and an empty mayonnaise jar. There were potato chips in the cabinet, and I took them into the front room.

It was dark in the front room. A long piece of blue cloth with designs of India was hung up across the windows. The blanket on the couch was curled up into a nest and Jimmy Henry's big white socks were on the floor. They went all the way up to my knees when I put them on. Jimmy Henry's door was closed and the India cloth made everything dark blue, Jimmy Henry's white socks, even the potato chips looked blue. I folded the top of the potato chip bag down as far as the rest of the potato chips and put it in my coat pocket. My sneakers were under the applebox table. I carried them down the stairs and sat on the top step to put them on.

The only store open on Seventeenth Avenue was Bill's Open All the Time Pepsi Store.

Five buttons went in a row at the side of Lalena's front door. I pushed the top button. The stairs inside stayed quiet. Sometimes the buzzer didn't work. I sat down on the step and took out my potato chips. No one came and no one came and then it was Lady Jane, on the sidewalk in front of me, in the sun that was all on her hair.

She said, "Hey, there."

"I'm visiting Lalena," I said.

"I don't think anyone is home up there," Lady Jane said.

I said, "Maybe the buzzer doesn't work."

She said, "It's freezing out here."

I said, "Does the buzzer get frozen?"

Lady Jane said, "Want to come in and have bagels?"

She put her hand in her pocket and took out a long tassel of keys and beads and a bell.

I said, "What's that?"

"It's my keychain," she said. "I bought it at Bead Here Now. Isn't it pretty?"

"No," I said. "Bagels. What's bagels?"

Lady Jane said, "Jewish donuts."

Lady Jane's apartment was crazy inside. The walls were all shiny yellow just like the hallway door. Little round windows were painted on, with fish looking in, and an octopus, and little bubbles going up from their mouths. The real window was the one with the colored lights, by the table of where the kitchen part was.

Lady Jane didn't wear army boots or hiking boots or even sneakers. Lady Jane wore wooden Dutch-girl shoes, and she just stepped out of them backward. Then she was just in her red socks and her Dutch-girl shoes stayed by the door.

She cut the Jewish donuts in half, and she put each half in the toaster.

When they came up she put on butter and gave me both halves. She put two more halves in the toaster, and while they were toasting she put on a record, kind of loud weird singing and a harmonica, and then she sat across from me at her table by the colored lights. It got warm enough to take off my coat. Lady Jane smiled a lot while we ate the donuts, and she danced in her chair at the table while she was sitting.

She said, "So, Sarajean, tell me a story."

"I don't know a story," I said.

"Everyone knows a story," she said. "A story is just who you are at that particular moment."

"Well, I'm just Sarajean Henry," I said.

She said, "Sarajean Henry, huh?"

I said, "Do you think Lalena is there yet?"

She said, "You can go knock if you want."

It was dark up the stairs to Lalena's door, and my knocks sounded loud and empty. I went back down to Lady Jane's yellow door, which was open, and she was dancing all around in there.

She said, "Like to dance?"

I said, "I don't think so."

She kept dancing around, and I stayed standing by the yellow door. When the music stopped she said, "Dancing is just another way to tell a story."

Another song started, and Lady Jane went away around the floor, all her beads around her neck jingling and clicking. She danced up on her toes and around in circles a lot, her skirt going around, her long hair going around. I was getting warm and sleepy. The record came to its end and stopped.

Lady Jane said, "Now will you dance with me?"

"I can't dance like that," I said.

She said, "We can dance anyway you like. Here. We'll slow dance, like olden times."

She put on another record and the song was slow, like one of the sad songs when Sasha was singing. Lady Jane took my hands, one of my hands in each one of her hands, her warm fingers wrapping around my fingers still cold. She stepped a big step back and pulled me with her. She stepped a wide step sideways and with two smaller steps I caught up. We went in slow circles like that around the yellow room, turning and turning, so that sometimes it was the fish and octopus looking in at us and sometimes it was the colored lights and mostly I watched Lady Jane's red socks to see where they would go next. At the end of the slow song Lady Jane let go of my fingers and clapped her hands above her head and then she bowed to me and her long blond hair touched the floor. I sat down on her bed and pulled up my Jimmy Henry socks.

Lady Jane said, "See, you can dance. Dancing is just moving to the music."

I said, "You said dancing is just another way to tell a story."

"Well, it is," she said. "It's both."

I hate it when things are both. Like two-fourths and three-sixths both being one-half.

Lady Jane said, "Want to dance some more?"

I said, "Can we have some more of those donuts?"

We ate donuts, and Lady Jane made tea in a white teapot shaped like an elephant. The tea came out his trunk. She lit a long stick of incense and stuck it in the crack in the middle of the table so that the smoke, strawberry, floated around between us.

She said, "So, what do you like to do, besides eat bagels and not dance?"

"Read," I said.

"What's your favorite book?" she said.

I said, *"Peter Pan."*

"Second favorite?" she said.

Little Women. Nancy Drew. Five Little Peppers and How They Grew.

I said, "I don't know."

She said, "I'll show you my favorite book."

On a tall shelf by the door was a big book covered in dark leather and designs all in the leather. Lady Jane brought the book to the table. She wiped crumbs off the table with the long edge of her skirt and she moved the tea cups to the middle and she set the big book down in front of me. Loopy gold letters said *Birds of the World* on the front.

"Go ahead," she said. "Open it."

The book squeaked when I opened it, like the squeaky steps of the house. The inside of the cover was beautiful paper made of swirly colors, gold and red and brown. The first page was empty, dark white paper, and then the next page was thin and see-through, thin tissue paper. After the tissue paper page was a big photograph of an old man and under, in fancy swirly letters, John James Audubon, his name.

After that every page was a bird in all beautiful colors of feathers and branches with a bird name at the bottom in beautiful writing. Every picture was sky and tree and one bird each. Every bird in the world had its own page.

The sun on the table was on the Lady Jane side when I first opened the *Birds of the World* book. When the sun was shining right onto the pages in front of me, Lady Jane said, "It's time for me to go to work."

She put her finger on the name of the bird on the page. Pileated woodpecker. Big and black and white, and a red head, his crest.

Pileated woodpecker. She put the *Birds of the World* back up on the shelf, and she went in the bathroom. The incense stick was all burned down to a curly ash. The elephant teapot was empty. Lady Jane's leather beaded keychain was on the table next to her empty cup. The longest string of leather had a bell in the shape of a tiny silver owl. The bell barely made any noise at all, it was so tiny. I untied the knot that held it on there. I put the keychain back on the table. I put the owl bell in my pocket.

Lady Jane came out of the bathroom, and she put her coat on and she put the keychain in her coat pocket.

She said, "You can come back and look at birds whenever you want."

"Okay," I said.

"And maybe dance," she said.

"Maybe," I said.

LALENA SAID Lady Jane was an acid head.

"Fucking acid head," she said. "That's what my daddy says. Fucking acid head."

I said, "She taught me how to dance like olden times."

Lalena said, "Big deal."

"She has a beautiful book of all the birds in the world," I said.

Lalena said, "Big deal."

"She gave me a bell," I said.

Lalena said, "Big deal."

"Just shut up," I said.

The metal stairs in the alley were sunny and not windy. We had to stay outside because Lalena's daddy was sleeping. I lit a match and when the match went out I touched the hot end to a hair on my arm. The hair turned into a little frizz and made a smell up close.

"Let's go over your house," Lalena said. "I'm freezing."

It was dark inside the front door, going up the stairs, dark that made me want to whisper, dark that made me want to be perfectly quiet going up the stairs.

"Sh," I said.

I pushed open our front door into the light and warm, and Jimmy Henry standing there leaning by the kitchen doorway. He turned around when we opened the door.

"Hi," I said.

"Sarajean," he said. "Damn."

There were some guys in there, in the kitchen, two guys maybe, sitting at the kitchen table.

One guy said, "What is this Henry? Kindergarten time?"

Jimmy Henry said, "Go on back outside. You can come back in a little while."

He looked back in the kitchen, he looked at me. I stopped. Lalena pushed in behind me.

"It's fucking freezing out," she said.

One of the guys in there said, "You want to talk China white or you want to play mommy?"

"What are you doing?" I said. "We're going in my room. What do you mean go back outside?"

Jimmy Henry said, "Damn it."

He leaned heavy against the kitchen doorway, rolling down his shirt-sleeve, and he said, "Go on outside."

Then he turned in to the kitchen and leaned over the sink and threw up in the sink.

Lalena said, "Uh-oh."

"What uh-oh?" I said. "What's wrong? What are you doing?"

Jimmy Henry turned on the water in the sink and he said,

"Damn it, Sarajean, get out of here."

He threw up some more in the sink.

Lalena pulled my arm, pulled me backward out the door.

"Come on," she said.

She pulled me out the door to the top of the stairs, and then she reached behind me and shut the door.

"What did he do that for?" I said.

"Are you crying?" she said. "Quit crying."

She started down the stairs.

"Come on," she said.

"Where?" I said. "I don't want to."

She grabbed my sleeve of my coat.

"Come on," she said. "We'll go in that place downstairs."

"Why?" I said. "Why is he all mad? I didn't do anything."

"Come on," she said. "You can't hang around when they're shooting up. It bugs 'em."

She went down, out the front door, and I went behind her, around back on the skinny sidewalk. Lalena went out in the yard to the garage and dragged one of the trash cans across the grass, and I stood there, at the end of the skinny sidewalk. I wiped my nose on my sleeve of my army coat.

"Come on," she said.

She bumped the trash can up on to the porch, over to the newspaper window. She climbed up there and banged her fist at the top of the window. The window slid down, and she caught it before it banged.

"Quit crying," she said. "There's nothing to cry about."

She climbed in and stood on the windowsill inside, looking out at me. I went over there and climbed on to the trash can, all stinky and dented and wobbly under me.

"I hate these trash cans," I said.

Lalena jumped down inside the apartment and I climbed through. I jumped down onto the floor.

"I hate it in here," I said.

I sat down on the floor under the window. Lalena sat down next to me. She said, "Listen."

Mumbly guy voices, and their feet coming down the stairs.

"They're leaving already," she said.

Jimmy Henry's voice was out there. After the feet were gone off the front porch Jimmy Henry called out, "Sarajean? Lalena?"

He was by the front door, out on the porch.

I said, "Sh."

"Yeah," Lalena said. "Fuck those guys."

Jimmy Henry's feet went back up the stairs.

"Want to go back up there?" Lalena said.

I said, "No."

"We can go over my house," she said.

"No, we can't," I said.

She said, "My other house, my Corona Street house."

I said, "No."

"Aren't you cold?" she said. "We can't just stay here, can we?"

I said, "I don't know."

Lalena said, "Well, okay, maybe we can. Are you crying again? Quit crying."

She took out the pack of cigarettes and held her hand out to me.

"Matches," she said.

She lit one of the cigarettes, and I took the matches back.

"We could probably go up there now," she said. "He said in a little while."

I lit one match and it burned, curling down orange and then black. I dropped it on the floor when the hot touched my fingers again, and again, lighting matches until there was a little pile of curled black matches on the floor between my legs.

When the matches were all gone Lalena said, "Let's go."

She smashed out her cigarette on the floor next to the pile of matches.

I said, "Where?"

She said, "I don't care. To get some more matches."

She put the old drawer on its end under the window and stood there, waiting, holding the drawer for me to climb first.

Outside it was late afternoon winter dark, and cold.

I said, "Okay, I'll take you some place secret, but it's a secret."

We went around front and into the front door.

I said, "Sh."

The key of the painted apartment was in my army coat pocket, like it was always in my army coat pocket. I unlocked the door of the painted apartment.

Lalena said, "God."

She said, "It's beautiful."

She said, "It's just like when that hippie girl used to live here."

"Tina Blue," I said.

She walked along the wall, looking at the painted shelves, touching her hand along the purple and green. I pulled out the top drawer of the little dresser just enough to reach my hand in and get a candle and the box of stove matches. Not enough for Lalena to see my shoe box.

She said, "Why doesn't anybody live here?"

She said, "I'd live down here if I was you."

The candlelight reached up to the purple ceiling. No sound of Jimmy Henry up there.

"So those guys up there," I said. "They were shooting up?"

"Looked like it to me," Lalena said. "They puke when they shoot up."

I said, "What is that? Shooting up?"

"It's needle freaks," she said. "That's what Margo says, needle freaks. I don't know, it's getting high."

She took out the pack of cigarettes.

"Like smoking joints?" I said.

"No," she said. "I think it's different."

"Like acid?" I said.

"No," she said. "I think it's different."

I said, "Different how?"

She lined cigarettes up on the floor end to end.

"I don't know," she said. "When it's joints or acid they're always laughing and being stupid or fixing something to eat. When it's needles they don't want you to be there. And then they just sit around."

Lalena made triangles with the cigarettes on the floor. The candle burned tall and long, until it was the only light there was and it was dark outside.

"I guess I'll go," Lalena said.

She put all the cigarettes back into the pack.

"I have to go home," she said. "Want to come over?"

"No," I said.

"Well," she said. "I think we should hang out in here. I mean sometimes, you know?"

"Yeah," I said. "Well, be quiet. Going out, don't slam the door."

She left. Didn't slam the door. Out the front door, not slamming the front door.

Our whole house was quiet around me and I sat on the mattress watching the candle flame. Not crying. It was cold and my face hurt from crying. I finally blew out the candle flame and it was completely dark until my eyes could see in the dark, the outline of the tall skinny window and the mattress on the floor. I put the candle back in the drawer.

Quiet in the stairway.

Quiet in our front room.

Jimmy Henry's bedroom door stayed shut.

IN THE morning Jimmy Henry was sitting at the kitchen table. I looked away from his face, at the refrigerator door, at the countertop, at the up-high cabinet door.

He said, "I'm sorry."

I went back in my room and shut the door and stood still, stood in the middle of the room, looking at the door.

"Sarajean?" he said from right outside there.

He opened the door and I turned away from his face. He came in and sat on the bed in front of me and I turned around so he couldn't see me again.

"I'm sorry I was mean," he said. "I'm sorry."

I said, "I don't want to talk to you."

He reached out and pulled me to him, and he was warm in his flannel shirt, but his hands were cold, and my hands were cold. He was holding his breath inside his shirt, and he let it out and he said, "I'll make us some breakfast?"

I said, "I don't care."

I said, "Are those guys your friends?"

"They're just some guys is all," he said.

His shirtsleeve arms were all around me, not holding, just around me.

"Are they coming back?" I said.

"Well, I don't know," he said.

I pulled away from his arms.

"Is it needle freaks?" I said.

"Look," he said. Breathing out.

"You shouldn't say that," he said. "I won't let them come over any more okay?"

"I don't care," I said.

THEY DID come over. I could tell. They came over when I wasn't there, and after they came over there were ripped up balloons in the trash, red, yellow. Junk. Lalena said that's where they keep their junk, inside balloons. Junkies, she said. I picked the balloons out of the trash and saved them in my drawer under my T-shirts.

I CAME home from school, and Jimmy Henry was lying on the couch, his T-shirt bluish white in the dark of the front room. I went past him into the kitchen. There was a yellow balloon, not in the trash, just on the counter. Not ripped up. I touched it with one finger. Lumpy inside.

Jimmy Henry sat up, rubbing his face. His hair was all tangled. I put my hands in fists in my pocket.

Jimmy Henry said, "Home so soon, baby?"

"Junkies were here," I said.

He stood up, and I didn't look in there at him.

He said, "Huh?"

"Junkies," I said louder.

He came in by me, behind me.

He said "Shit," and he picked up the yellow balloon, his arm reaching past me. Red sores on the white inside of his elbow.

"You shouldn't say that, Sarajean," he said.

"Why?" I said. "What is it?"

"Damn it," he said, like whispering, like crying, and he went in his room.

"HE SAID those guys wouldn't come over anymore but they do," I said.

"Liars," Lalena said. "All junkies are liars. That's what Margo says."

"They lie about shooting needles?" I said.

"Everything," Lalena said. "Margo says they lie about everything. Remember when he wouldn't say about your mother's name? Liars."

She said, "It doesn't matter."

SASHA HAD her baby in the summer, a girl baby named Dylan Marie. Dylan Marie was always sleeping in her baby bed. When she wasn't sleeping her eyes kind of rolled around. She smelled nice like baby powder and bad like diapers.

Lalena said, "She stinks all the time."

Sasha sat next to Dylan Marie's baby bed and watched Dylan Marie sleep. She would touch Dylan Marie on her round head where there was soft fuzz. Sometimes Sasha just leaned her head on the baby bed railing.

She would say, "You girls go on outside and play."

Sasha sang her sad songs quiet now, just to Dylan Marie.

MOSTLY WE stayed outside on Seventeenth Avenue. It was hot and people hanging around and people in windows and music. It was best just sitting on the front steps.

We got a box of broken colored chalk from some people moving out and we drew the front steps in paisley. It took all day on a hot day. We paisleyed all the sides and the fronts and all the flat parts of the steps, big flat paisleys that went from one step down to the next and over the edge onto the sidewalk. Lalena drew the paisleys. I filled them in. By the end of the day there were colored chalk footprints going in and out and away on the sidewalk, and a guy took a picture of the steps, all paisley.

LATE, OUT on the steps, the sky would get dark orange. Later the sky got black and Lalena had to go inside, or sometimes Margo came, and her and Lalena walked back to their Corona Street house. Sometimes I stayed all night with her. Sometimes I walked home by myself.

The long sidewalks along the streets were different sidewalks at night, the trees leafy in the wind, and shadows of leaves blowing on the sidewalks under the streetlights. People were inside their windows in the light or there was the jumping blue light of television.

The Safeway corner was all lit up, and I walked along the edge under the trees, looking at my front porch. Sometimes Jimmy Henry would be sitting there, and I could see the orange dot of his cigarette in the dark. The only part of him that moved was the white arm that held the cigarette up, or sent it flying into the street and land in a splash of sparks.

"Junkie," I would whisper. "Liar."

Sometimes he sat there until the parking lot lights went out, late. When he went in, and then the lights in the front windows upstairs went dark, I went in too.

1973

Cross-stitch, running stitch, chain stitch, French knot, lazy daisy, satin stitch. Constanzia taught me embroidery. Round hoops fit one inside the other, catching the cloth straight and tight. The embroidery thread popped through the tight cloth behind the needle, three strands of embroidery thread pulled apart from six strands that came gathered in a skein instead of on a spool, a skein held together with a gold paper band that said sky blue number sixty-eight or rose red number twenty-two.

On the cement floor, next to the sewing machine table, all the colors of skeins in a box next to me, I sat and made long designs and round designs and flower designs and leaves. My butt got cold and my fingertips got sore and pink and I was invisible when people came in to buy or sell their stuff. Constanzia got up and stood at the counter, her long skirt down next to me, her Mexican sandals next to me, and she talked to people like I wasn't there at all.

After school late afternoon was best, long quiet times of no people. Constanzia sang the words to Mexican songs that went along under her sewing machine. Lightbulbs in the ceiling made spots of light around, lighting up hanging colors of clothes.

I said, "Can I live here with you?"

Constanzia said, "What about your poor sad papa?"

"No," I said.

"Not him," I said. "Just me."

She didn't say yes and she didn't say no.

When it got all the way dark outside, and it was time to turn around the sign that said CLOSED inside and OPEN outside, so that it said OPEN inside and CLOSED outside, I put on my army coat and I said, "Buenas noches." Good night.

I walked down Seventeenth Avenue to Lalena's house. The windows there were all dark, Lalena's window and Lady Jane's window, no lights. The door of the Lair Lounge opened across the street and music came out for a second, then the door closed and the music went back inside. Lights on in the houses and stores up the street and down the street made yellow squares on the sidewalk.

There were people inside Bill's Open All the Time Pepsi Store, a guy talking on the phone inside the phone booth in there. The guy in the phone booth talked and laughed and talked. When he was all done talking he came out of the phone booth door and out to the sidewalk, and he went away up Seventeenth Avenue whistling a song. And then Lalena came past the guy walking away.

"Hey," she said.

"Are you going home?" I said.

"Home where?" she said.

I said, "I don't know."

She said, "Well, there's no one home at Corona Street."

"Here neither," I said.

Lalena said, "Good."

I said, "So where do you want to go?"

She said, "I don't care."

We walked along the sidewalk, walking in and out of the squares of light. Together Books was open, all the lights on, and a kind of bald on top guy with a bushy black beard was reading to a bunch of people sitting on the floor. I looked through the O of TOGETHER.

"Lalena."

Lalena's stepbrother John stood there with his coat unbuttoned, breathing from running.

"Look," John said. "I got to find your dad."

"Not home," Lalena said.

John said, "Margo's busted."

"Wow," Lalena said. "Busted?"

"Look," John said. "You guys go over Sarajean's house. Stay there. I'll find out what's going on."

Lalena said, "I'll just stay here and wait for Daddy."

John said, "What if they're busted too? Just do like I say, okay?"

He turned around back up Seventeenth Avenue.

"Wow," Lalena said. "I wonder if they took her away in a cop car and a siren?"

"Wow," she said. "Fuck."

When we got to my house, when we got inside the front door from the porch, Lalena looked at the door to the painted apartment.

She said, "Let's go in there."

"I don't have a key," I said. Liar.

Jimmy Henry wasn't home. I turned on lights in the front room, in the kitchen, in my bedroom, almost all the lights. Lalena sat on the couch with her coat on.

"Well?" I said.

She stared at the top of the window.

I said, "Want a baloney sandwich?"

Lalena kept staring at the top of the window, like there was something there, which there wasn't.

I said, "Want something else?"

She didn't say yes and she didn't say no. I went in the kitchen and got out baloney sandwich stuff, mayonnaise and bread. Lalena came in by me.

She said, "What if they make me go to Juvie?"

"I don't think so," I said. "That's for kids that get busted. Not for kids when their moms get busted. I don't think."

Lalena stood next to me, me making baloney sandwiches, her watching the top of the cabinet door, like there was something there, which there wasn't.

I said, "You're just staring at stuff. It's kind of weird. It's kind of creepy."

She said, "I wonder how long I'm supposed to wait."

"I don't know," I said. "Want this baloney sandwich?"

"Does it have pickles?" she said.

"No," I said. "Baloney and mayonnaise is all."

She pulled her baloney out and licked the mayonnaise off. She put the baloney back between the breads and took a bite. She didn't chew.

She said, "What if Jimmy Henry's busted too?"

I said, "No."

Then she chewed.

Jimmy Henry's bedroom door was shut, like his bedroom door was always shut. I opened it, into the dark. Light from the streetlights came in at the top of the curtains, lighting up the ceiling. Lalena followed me in there, into the smell of laundry, old laundry, old cigarettes. She turned on the light switch. The stuff messy on the dresser top was nickels and pennies, a coffee cup, a hairbrush, a cigarette pack twisted into a bow, a brown envelope printed with blue letters in the corner, "Veterans Administration."

Lalena pulled open the first drawer. Tangled-up white socks and thick red winter socks. The second drawer was different colors of T-shirts piled in there. The third drawer was a pair of brown corduroy pants folded up at the knees. I had never seen Jimmy Henry wear brown corduroy pants.

"Come on," I said. "Jimmy Henry's not busted. He's just not here."

Lalena pulled a white envelope out from under the brown corduroy pants. It said "Jimmy Henry" on the front in thin, loopy letters.

"Come on," I said. "Leave that stuff alone."

The bottom drawer was just Jimmy Henry's green zipper army bag, all flat and empty.

I hit the light switch on my way out the door, making the room dark behind me, and went back in the kitchen, sat in the bench, picked up my baloney sandwich. Lalena sat across from me. She had the envelope, from under the brown corduroy pants, from the third drawer.

The front door opened, and I took the envelope and stuck it under my butt.

"God damn it," I said.

Jimmy Henry came into the kitchen.

I said, "Lalena has to stay here. Margo's busted."

Jimmy Henry kind of looked at the counter, like he was thinking about having a baloney sandwich.

"I know," he said.

I said, "She has to stay here. In case of Sasha and her daddy being busted too."

He picked up the mayonnaise jar, like he was reading where it said mayonnaise.

"That's okay," he said. "They didn't get busted."

Lalena said, "As long as I don't have to go to Juvie."

Jimmy Henry said, "Well, everything will be okay."

He put the mayonnaise jar back down on the counter. Then he went in his bedroom and shut his bedroom door.

I pulled the envelope out from under my butt.

"What did you take this for?" I said.

"What's in there?" Lalena said.

"Probably none of your fucking beeswax," I said.

Lalena followed me in my bedroom.

"You're going to get me in trouble," I said.

"You never get in trouble," she said. "Just open it."

It was a piece of paper folded up. Scribbly, looping writing like on the envelope, old, almost invisible writing.

Take care of my daughter now, Sergeant James Henry. Call her Sarajean Henry and teach her to fly.

Christine Jeanette Blumenthal

"Christine Jeanette Blumenthal," I read the names.

Lalena said, "See, I told you he knew her name."

She said, "Blumenthal. What a weird name. I never heard of anyone named Blumenthal."

She said, "Teach her to fly, what's that supposed to mean?"

"Just shut up," I said.

Loopy letters.

My daughter.

I said, "What should we do now?"

"Nothing," Lalena said. "We just wait and see what happens to me is all."

The paper fell back into its three folds. I put it back inside the envelope. My mother's writing on the outside of the envelope.

"Are you going to sneak it back in his drawer?" Lalena said.

"No," I said. "No."

Christine Jeanette Blumenthal. Sergeant James Henry. My daughter.

LALENA'S DADDY came over the next day, Saturday morning.

"Stupid bitch," he said. "Fucking potheads."

He said it a bunch of times, and then him and Lalena left. I watched them walk away, past the Safeway. Jimmy Henry made coffee, the smell coming into my bedroom.

He said, "Want some breakfast?"

I said, "No."

My breathing fogged up the window. I wrote NO on the window with my finger, and the NO and the little cloud of fog faded away. I breathed on the window again, and I wrote LIAR, and then the cloud and the letters faded away. I shut my bedroom door and took out the envelope, took out the piece of paper. "Christine Jeanette Blumenthal." "Sarajean." "Sergeant James Henry." Written-out words, three people that were me and Jimmy Henry and my mother. My mother. My mother.

ON THE way home from school I cut through the alley, along the boarded-up garage doors, three in a row, the Dumpster painted with spray paint FUCK YOU and STOP THE WAR, the high metal fence of ripply metal with dark streaks of rust, into my yard.

The sumac tree was fall orange and yellow, and dark maroon seed things sticking up. The asters were done, just straggly stalks leaning, but there were dandelions around the ivy tub, dandelions still blooming tall and yellow, the ivy dying back. I set my books on the ivy tub and I sat down, leaning, the splintery curvy side through my sweatshirt. I picked one long dandelion and looked close into the tall yellow of it. I worked my thumbnail through the stem, stem juice like white glue all under my thumbnail. I picked another dandelion and stuck its stem through the hole in the stem of the first dandelion. Again. Again. It was a long dandelion rope soon, and I got up out of the grass, to maybe loop the dandelion rope around the edge of the ivy tub, or maybe hang it in the sumac tree. But the door was open.

The door into the dirty apartment with the old newspaper covering the window. The door was open just a crack.

Looking at the door, I laid the dandelion rope down careful, left my books sitting on the edge of the ivy tub, and I walked through the tall grass, stepped on the wooden porch quiet. I pushed the door open with my fingers, and it squeaked, and it opened, into dark yellow light inside.

A long-haired boy in a jean jacket sat on the counter that stuck out into the middle of the room.

He said, "Sergeant Henry's little pet kid."

I stepped inside the door. He was a Mexican boy, Mexican-colored skin. Black hightops.

"Get tired with making daisy chains?" he said.

"Dandelion ropes," I said.

He took a pack of Kools out of the top pocket of his jean jacket, and he shook one Kool up from the rest and took it between his lips so that it dangled there, like about to fall out of his mouth. He took out a little box of matches, same pocket, wooden stick matches that rattled inside the little box. He lit a match, holding the match inside his hand, so that it looked like a secret, looked hard to do, made his Mexican skin bright for a second. His eyelashes were long, like a girl's. He puffed the cigarette into being lit, and then he flipped the match, in a high swoop, across the room. It landed on the linoleum with a tiny smoke. He looked at me, through a cloud of cigarette smoke, and he squinted one eye at me over the dangly cigarette in his mouth, and he said, "Want one?"

"What?" I said. "A cigarette?"

"No," he said. "A match. What do you think?"

"No," I said. "Why would I want a match?"

He lit another match, holding the cigarette in his teeth, lighting the match behind his hand, flipping the match, still lit, across the room. The match went out when it hit the wall, leaving a little tail of smoke, where it hit the wall, and he watched me watch it.

I said, "How old are you?"

He looked about as old as me.

I said, "You always come in here."

He looked around the room, not at me.

I said, "Why are you here?"

He said, "Why are you?"

I said, "I live upstairs."

"Then what are you doing down here?" he said.

I said, "You're not allowed in here, you know."

He put his hands in the pockets of his jean jacket, smoking with just his face.

I said, "What's your name?"

He pulled his legs to underneath him so he was sitting cross-legged on the counter, all in a cloud of cigarette smoke.

I said, "Why do you come in here? It's dirty."

The boy was kind of smiling, or else cigarette smoke was getting in his eyes and looking like smiling.

I said, "You know who you look like? The Cheshire Cat. You remind me of the Cheshire Cat."

I said, "How long are you going to stay here?"

The boy said, "Where's the old man?"

I said, "What old man?"

"What old man you think?" he said. "Sergeant Henry."

"Oh," I said. "I don't know. I just got home. He's not usually home yet. How come you say 'sergeant'?"

The boy took his hands out of his pockets, and he took his cigarette out of his face, and he tapped the long cigarette ash onto the floor.

He said, "You going to run and tell?"

I said, "I don't think so."

He hopped down off the counter, and came over by me. He was small. He seemed like as big as me. He went past me, opened the door and said, "See ya."

He walked out across the porch boards, through the grass, past the ivy tub, my books sitting there, and he stepped over the dandelion rope strung out on the ground.

"Hey," I said. "What's your name?"

The boy didn't turn around, kept walking toward the alley, and he said, "Hey, man, I'm the Cheshire Cat."

He turned into the alley, around the corner of the garage. Soap and something else stayed in the air, and curls of cigarette smoke.

DOING HOMEWORK at the kitchen table, and Jimmy Henry lying on the couch, maybe sleeping, but maybe not, and the porch boards out back sounded out old wooden squeaking. I held my breath for when the newspaper window would bang open. Jimmy Henry would get up from lying on the couch and get mad is what would happen next.

"Orville made the first piloted flight in a power-driven plane at Kitty Hawk in 1903," I read, reading loud off the top of the page of my social studies book. "December 17, 1903."

Quiet downstairs. Quiet in the front room. I went in and looked over the back of the couch. Sleeping.

I tiptoed down the stairs. I peeked under the door. Four feet. Black high-tops. I tiptoed back up the stairs and back in the kitchen, listening, looking at the fuzzy picture of Orville and Wilbur Wright, and no noise from downstairs.

THE PAINTED front of Someone's Beloved Threads was all peely paint and old wood showing through. The sun at the top of the door was losing its sunface around the edges.

"Erico," I said. "I think you should paint again, on the doorway part."

Erico stopped hammering on the door, where he was hammering up plastic to keep the wind out. He stopped hammering and looked at me.

"On the sun," I said. I pointed up. "The sun needs a new face."

Erico looked up, where I was pointing, where the sun was still smiling but not shining like it used to shine, with all fiery sun streaks reaching out around it.

I said, "Don't you think? Look at its face."

Erico looked at me. He looked at the sunface. He looked at his hammer and started hammering again.

"Erico," I said. "Don't you want to paint a new sun?"

Erico stopped hammering again, and he turned around to me where I was standing on the sidewalk.

I said, "You can hardly tell its a sun anymore."

Erico bent at his knees like about to sit down in front of me. His knees cracked.

He said, "How come I got this work to do, and you want to paint pictures on the door? Why is that?"

"I don't know," I said. "You can't see it anymore."

Erico had a black mustache and no beard. His face was right at my face, and his black eyebrows went scrunched across the top of his nose. He had a kind of big nose.

He said, "Where is your little friend Lalena?"

"Who?" I said. I loved the way Erico said Lalena.

"Lalena," he said.

"I don't know where Lalena is," I said, trying to say it that way. "She's not at home."

Erico said, "Don't you have any other friends to go play with?"

"No," I said.

He stood up tall again, and his knees cracked again, and he started hammering again.

I said, "We could make the sun a catface. Did you ever hear of the Cheshire Cat? I know this other kid that's a Mexican kid. He says his name is Cheshire Cat, which is just because I said that. Is there Alice in Wonderland in Mexico?"

Erico stepped to the side and opened the door.

"Go find Constanzia," he said. "See does she have something for you to do."

I went in, and Erico's hammering started again. It was bright outside and dark inside. Constanzia was in her big chair, behind the counter, where she liked to take her catnaps. Her eyes were closed.

"Constanzia?" I whispered.

Constanzia's wrinkly face smiled. She didn't open her eyes, just smiled in her sleepy wrinkled-down face.

I pulled out the box from under the counter, skeins of embroidery thread and the hoops. I pulled a long thread loose from a skein that said sungold number seventeen.

"Sungold, Constanzia," I said. "I'm going to make a sunface with this thread. It's sungold number seventeen. And you can ask Erico to paint on the sunface outside too."

"I think he will," I said.

"If you ask him," I said.

"Since you're his mother," I said.

BOXES AND boxes of clothes. Outfits and scarfs and big squares of cloth. All Lalena's stuff and all Margo's stuff, all in boxes and stacked into Lalena's little pointy room on Seventeenth Avenue.

Lalena said, "I get it all now."

I said, "What about when she gets out, or home, or whatever it is?"

Lalena said, "I'll give it back."

"Where are your brothers going to live?" I said.

Lalena said, "By their grandma in Fort Collins."

"Is that your grandma, in Fort Collins?" I said.

"Nope," Lalena said. "My grandma lives in Ohio or Iowa or like that."

"What about your other one?" I said. "Don't you have two grandmas?"

She said, "There's just one. She's mean. She doesn't like Margo 'cause she thinks Margo is too much of a hippie."

I said, "Are there any grandfathers?"

Lalena said, "Nope."

The window in the triangle wall was covered with frost designs, and we couldn't see out. The radiator hissed and clanked warm. Dylan Marie was sleeping in her baby bed, and Sasha was making soup and singing in the kitchen. The soup was onion smell. Lalena and I had to stay in her room and be quiet, or go outside and be cold, so we were being pretty quiet. Quiet enough to hear Sasha singing.

Lalena had on a T-shirt and cowboy boots and underpants. She was putting on different outfits from Margo's boxes, trying on outfits and taking them off and trying on other outfits, but there was no mirror.

"How is this embroidery shirt?" she said.

"Is this paisley top a beautiful dress?" she said.

"Yuk," she said. "Pink and yellow plaid."

There were pieces of see-through white cloth like a bride's dress. Cut up blue jeans with pieces of bandanna sewed on. Silky dark pink stuff with tiny white stars. I laid pieces on the mattress, and all on the floor like a beautiful rug, and all on the boxes, so the boxes were like fancy chairs.

One piece had parrots, with green and red wing feathers and yellow head feathers. I folded the parrot cloth and put it in the corner of an empty box by the door.

When it was time for soup in the kitchen, Lalena and I sat at the table and had bowls. Sasha went into the big bedroom with Dylan Marie.

"To suck," Lalena said.

Sasha fed Dylan Marie from her titty. Lalena said boob. We didn't get to watch.

The kitchen was tall yellow walls and dark yellow cabinet doors and no windows at all, and counters all around the yellow walls. The counters were red. There was a Grimm's fairy tale about yellow and red. An evil dwarf kidnapped a princess, and he poisoned her with red wine and yellow wine so he could chop off her finger and steal her gold princess ring.

Lalena smashed up crackers, so many crackers that there was a pile of them sticking up in the middle of her bowl. I smashed my crackers on the table and scooped them into my bowl. I blew all the crumbs left on the table across to Lalena, and the crumbs stuck in her hair.

Sasha said, "You girls quiet down in there."

Lalena's daddy came home, up the stairs in big footsteps, and then in the door of the kitchen.

"Girl," he said. "What you got all in your hair? You been out in the snow?"

He tugged at Lalena's hair, and then he went into the bedroom. Lalena got up and went into the bathroom to look at the cracker crumb snow in her hair, and I got up and went over to the counter to get more crackers, for more soup.

Through the front room to the bedroom, Sasha was in her rocking chair, but Dylan Marie wasn't sucking. It was Lalena's daddy, down on his knees in front of Sasha. He was sucking on Sasha's titty, and his hand was on her other titty, grabbing, and her shirt was wet, and her eyes were closed.

I held my breath and sat back at the table.

When Lalena came back, I said, "Let's go outside after this."

"Too cold," Lalena said.

I said, "Let's go to Constanzia's."

"Too cold," she said.

"Lady Jane's," I said.

"That freak," she said.

Lalena's daddy came back in the kitchen. I looked at soup and cracker crumbs and the wooden table. Lalena's daddy splashed soup in a bowl and dropped the big spoon on the stove, clank, like the radiator. He stood by the stove, standing on the edge of where I wasn't seeing. The soup in my bowl was green celery, orange carrots, blue bowl, white noodles. Onions that were no color. Lalena smashed more crackers.

I said, "Want to go outside?"

She said, "Nope."

I got up and went to the kitchen door, to the wooden hooks where all the coats were, where my army coat was. I looked at the coats on the hooks and my army coat and not at Lalena's daddy and not through the front room to the bedroom. I took my army coat off the hook.

Lalena said, "Where are you going?"

"Don't know," I said.

It was dark outside the door in the hallway. My breathing came out of my nose in a whistle. The floor of inside Lalena's kitchen squeaked from feet in there, and I went down the stairs.

There was music from Lady Jane's, by the yellow door, a long song of bells and singing. The song ended, and I tapped my fingernail on the door. Lady Jane opened it, opened the door wide, and she bowed like a lady, and she said, "Look who's here."

"It's me," I said.

Lady Jane said, "Come on in, me."

She had on a long white T-shirt and blue kneesocks and a yellow joint in her fingers. She went and sat at the table and set the yellow joint on the edge of the table. Her blue jeans were hanging on the back of the chair. She took them, and she stuck her blue kneesocks feet straight out and pulled on her blue jeans, both legs at once. The music started again, more singing, more bells. Lady Jane stood up and zipped her blue jeans and then she went over to the shelf under *Birds of the World* and turned the music down to not so loud.

She said, "What's up, child of God?"

"I don't know," I said. "What does that mean, 'child of God'?"

"Like family of man," she said. "Hippies maybe. Maybe like we're all flying through the universe on the spaceship Earth together."

She said, "I have to get ready for work."

I said, "Okay."

She put on another shirt over her long white T-shirt, a light blue shirt like blue jeans, and flowers embroidered up the front by the buttons. Blue flowers, and pink and yellow leaves.

"I know embroidery," I said. "Constanzia taught me."

Lady Jane said, "Far out."

She pinned her sleeve with a safety pin. No button.

"I make leaves sometimes," I said. "I make them green."

Lady Jane started singing, a different song than the record, louder than the record, she sang,

> "Green leaves was all my joy,
> Green leaves was my hearts delight,
> Green leaves was all my love,
> And who but my lady green leaves."

She looped long beads around her neck, clicking beads, all colors of beads.

"Okay," she said. "What are you up to now, lady green leaves?"

"I don't know," I said. "Where do you have to go to work at?"

"At Celestial Tea Palace," she said. "It's a café."

"Oh," I said. "Are you the waitress?"

Lady Jane said, "Yep. I am the waitress."

She picked up her yellow joint, smoked on it, and put the end in a little white plate on the table.

"And you get to eat all you want?" I said.

"Yeah," she said. "Pretty much. It's a good gig. I'm into my solitude right now, so waitressing is my humanity hit."

I said, "Solitude?"

She put on her coat.

"So," she said. "What's Jimmy Henry up to?"

"I don't know," I said. "He goes and does stuff at other houses, like our house but for a different landlady."

"Oh," Lady Jane said. "So he has a real job these days?"

I said, "I don't know."

She pulled a blue stocking cap down over her head, almost to her eyes.

"Funny things, jobs," she said. "Sometimes you just feel like having one. Are you going up to Lalena's?"

"No," I said.

"Where are you going?" she said.

"Nowhere," I said.

"Well, come on, Nowhere Man," she said. "I'll walk you partway there."

She pulled out the plug of the colored lights, and we went out the yellow door into the dark hallway and down the squeaking stairs, Lady Jane singing all the words to the "Nowhere Man" song.

Outside it was gray sky and tiny icy snow bits in the air. I pulled my hands up inside the sleeves of my army coat.

Lady Jane said, "Don't you have a hat?"

"No," I said. "At home."

She said, "Don't you have some gloves?"

"I have some mittens," I said. "At home."

She said, "Is there a scarf at home too?"

I said, "No."

Lady Jane walked loud in her Dutch-girl shoes. We went as far as Clarkson Street, and she stopped.

"I go this way," she said.

Away from Colfax Street, away from toward my house.

"Okay," I said. "'Bye."

"'Bye," she said. She pulled a long piece of hair out of the side of my mouth.

"'Bye," I said.

Her Dutch-girl shoes clonked away on the sidewalk. She turned around once and waved at me, and walked some more, until I couldn't tell which was her and which was maybe just some other person on the sidewalk.

☮

CONSTANZIA SAVED all the bird stuff for me. A big square that used to be a skirt, one long edge hemmed up neat, the other long edge still puckered and thready from where the waistband used to be, and all light green and blackbirds flying across. A baby blanket covered in little smiley birds with blue eyes and long eyelashes. A long square of old curtain with peacocks in shining bright green. When I got the piece of parrot cloth from the box in the corner of Lalena's room, I took it home hidden under my coat.

It was cold in the purple and green apartment, even with all the candles set in a row, lit, shining. I spread the green peacock cloth on the mattress. I folded the skirt piece of blackbirds across the dresser top so the ends were even. Lying on the mattress, on the green peacock cloth, and the purple light of candles all on the painted walls, and I got all sleepy and warm. Cars going by on Ogden Street. Bluejays. My arms inside my shirt, warm bare skin, my hands down in between my legs, cold hands, warm legs, purple, green, shiny green peacocks.

Jimmy Henry came home, front door, feet up the stairs. I folded up all the pieces of birdcloth, folded them into the bottom dresser drawer. My shoe box of stuff in the top drawer, and candles, and the box of wooden matches. Two drawers in between, still empty. I went out, locked the door, went up the stairs.

Jimmy Henry was in the kitchen.

He said, "Hey, baby."

I didn't say anything, and he didn't look at me. He was pulling apart slices of bacon.

"I thought I'd fix a little dinner," he said.

"Oh, yeah?" I said. I smelled toast.

"Well, yeah," he said. "BLTs, okay?"

"Yeah," I said. "BLTs are okay."

"Hey," I said. "BLTs R OK, get it?"

He looked up from laying bacon in the pan.

"All letters," I said. "No words. Talking with all letters, no words."

The bacon started to pop in the pan.

He said, "You're pretty smart, aren't you?"

My face went all flat, and I didn't know where to have my hands.

"Well," I said. "As and Bs. That's pretty smart."

"Keep an eye on that bacon for a second," he said.

He went in the front room, to the closet in the corner. He was inside the closet door when the toasts popped up, and I laid them on the counter by the mayonnaise jar, and put in two more pieces of bread. He came back into the kitchen holding a blue book, and he handed the book out to me. A big blue book. Inside a gold circle on the cover was gold writing that said *Webster's New Collegiate Dictionary*.

He said, "That should be for you, I guess."

A big, heavy, blue book.

His hair hung down, over his eyes, and he turned to the stove and wiggled the bacon in the pan. I put the *Webster's New Collegiate Dictionary* on the table.

I opened it up to C. "Collegiate: of the nature of a college, or body of colleagues, or a civil or ecclesiastical office."

I turned ahead to E. "Ecclesiastic: of or pertaining to the church; not secular."

"Secular: of or pertaining to the worldly or temporal."

"Temporal: of or pertaining to the sides of the skull behind the orbits."

Jimmy Henry put a BLT on the table by the *Webster's New Collegiate Dictionary*.

"So," he said. "What did you look up?"

I said, "I'm not sure."

I closed the *Webster's New Collegiate Dictionary*.

"Thanks," I said. "For the dictionary. And for the BLT."

He picked up the dictionary with only one hand, held it up with one hand, looking at the gold circle of words on the cover.

"You can have them," he said. "All those books in that box in the closet. There aren't any kid books in there."

He set the dictionary down on the table.

"Thanks," I said.

After the BLTs were gone, and Jimmy Henry went in on the couch to look at the *Denver Post*, I opened up the cover of the dictionary. Inside the front cover, on the first white page, it said "Tina Blue," in thin loopy letters.

All those books from her shelves, rows of books up by the white china elephant. Jimmy Henry sitting on the box after Tina Blue was gone. Those books. Maybe the white china elephant was in the box too, a white china elephant like Lady Jane's white china elephant teapot that poured tea out of its trunk.

Lady Jane. I looked up "Solitude: state of being alone; loneliness." Lady Jane was into her solitude thing.

I turned the pages back through the Ss, not looking up words, just hearing the whispery sound of the pages. At the beginning of S a perfectly flat blue flower was there, a violet maybe, or a tiny blue pansy, thin as paper, dry as the page. There was a little ink star there, on the page of the flower. A little blue ink star next to "Sarah: wife of Abraham, mother of Isaac." I closed the pages over the flower, over the star, and carried the dictionary into the front room. Jimmy Henry was asleep and the *Denver Post* was fallen on the floor, so I took the dictionary, the flower inside, the star page, into my room. I put the dictionary on top of my dresser. The gold words *Webster's New Collegiate Dictionary* went up and down the back edge, and I could see the words from my bed, until I turned off the light. In the pink Safeway light, the dictionary was only a black square on top of my dresser.

THERE ARE eleven Blumenthals on the page in the phone book. I fold the glass phone booth doors to shut, so I am inside the phone booth, inside Bill's Pepsi market, and I stack my dimes on the little shelf under the phone hanging there.

I drop one dime in, and then another, and the dimes sound like they are dropping far away. I dial the first number, and count four buzzy rings, each buzzy ring ringing inside my chest. A guy voice says, "Hello?"

"Hello?" I say. "Is there a lady there named Christine Jeanette Blumenthal?"

"Nope," the guy says. "Wrong number."

"Well," I say. "I am Sarajean Henry."

The guy says, "This is the Blumenthals, but there isn't no Christine lives here."

I say, "Do you know me?"

The guy says, "You got the wrong number."

"Okay," I say.

"Never mind," I say.

" 'Bye," I say.

Click.

I put the phone back up on its hook, and I draw one straight line through the first Blumenthal in the phone book. I drop two more dimes down into the slot and dial the next Blumenthal.

At the end of all the Blumenthals there are three Blumenthals not crossed out because of nobody answering their phone ringing. Of all the other Blumenthals that did answer their phone, nobody knew Christine Jeanette Blumenthal and nobody knew Sarajean Henry.

I put the last dimes in the top pocket of my army coat, in where they jingle with the key of the painted apartment. I put the pencil in there too, so I can come back and dial the other three Blumenthals that I didn't cross out.

IT WAS too rainy for recess to be outside so we stayed inside. We were allowed to stay in our classroom, and no teacher, but there were monitors, Katy Carmel, who was bossy, and Bruce Baxter, who was fat. Or we could go to the gym, sit on the bleachers, watch kids play kickball. Dodgeball wasn't allowed. The other fourth-grade girls sat by the wall, by the bathroom door, going in and out of the bathroom, brushing their hair.

John Fitzgerald Kennedy Karpinski slammed the ball into the bleachers where Lalena and I were sitting.

Lalena said, "Polack."

John Fitzgerald Kennedy Karpinski came over to get the ball. His T-shirt was hanging out. His blue jeans drooped around his skinny middle and covered up his shoes with his bellbottoms.

"Polack," Lalena said.

"Ha," he said. "I'm named after a president. Not a whore in a song."

He bounced the ball away.

"Whore in a song?" I said. "What does that mean?"

Lalena said, "How should I know? He doesn't know anything."

She yelled, "Whoever heard of a president named Karpinski?"

After school it was still rainy. We went to Lalena's house, and it was just Lalena's daddy there, at the kitchen table, drinking a beer, looking at the *Denver Post*.

I said, "Let's go visit Constanzia."

Lalena said to her daddy, "Where does my name come from?"

Lalena's daddy burped a loud beer burp. I kept my coat on.

He said, "That's a song."

Lalena said, "What song?"

"Margo loved that damn song," he said.

Lalena said, "Is it a song about a whore?"

Her daddy laughed.

"Yes, it is," he said and he grabbed her and pulled her close to him and put his big face by her face.

"A song about a damn whore," he said, and he kissed her a big smacky kiss on her cheek.

Lalena punched his arm, and he laughed loud, and he said, "Margo loved that damn song."

Lalena stomped away from him, out of his arm holding her, into me, out the door. Her daddy laughed at the ceiling, and I went out the door after her. She was still stomping, all the way down the stairs.

She stood outside there, looking out at Seventeenth Avenue, and the rain, her hair curling all up like she hated, her breath from her nose little white puffs. Her cheeks had two pink spots.

"Just shut up," she said.

"I didn't say anything," I said.

"Just shut up," she said.

I sat down on the top step. The roof of the porch dripped rain on my knees.

"Fucking Margo," Lalena said.

"I think it's a beautiful name," I said. "My name means something about somebody's mother. And their wife."

"Just shut up," she said.

"Well," I said. "What do you want to do now?"

Lalena didn't say anything. She stared out, puffing out of her nose.

Lady Jane came walking up the sidewalk under a blue umbrella. She got to the steps and looked up.

"Hi," she said.

Her Dutch-girl shoes kept her feet up out of the water.

I said, "Those are good rain shoes."

She came up the steps, folding the umbrella into itself, and she sang part of a rain song about the rain in summer.

I said, "Do you know the Lalena song?"

Lady Jane said, "Ah. Beautiful. Margo loved that song."

She started to sing, and Lalena said, "Shut up."

Lady Jane shut up.

I said, "It's a song about a whore."

Lady Jane sat down next to me. The rain dripped on the patches of her blue-jean knees, green velvet patches stitched around with gold thread.

She said, "A beautiful song. A love song."

Lalena didn't look at me, and she didn't look at Lady Jane. She hunched over herself and looked out at the rain.

"Then again," Lady Jane said. "A name is a very personal thing. It's your own personal symbol that you present to the world. You can always change it if it doesn't match."

I said, "Match what?"

"Match who you are," Lady Jane said.

I said, "You mean like if Lalena's not a whore?"

Lalena punched my arm hard enough to hurt.

"Hey," I said. "Not a whore. I said not."

"You said if," Lalena said.

"Huh?" I said.

"Just shut up," Lalena said.

"Violence is not the answer," Lady Jane said. "Love is the answer."

Lalena said, "You shut up too. Both of you just shut up."

After sitting there and just getting dripped on for a while Lady Jane said, "You can come visit if you want. I'll make tea."

She leaned over me, looking at Lalena.

She said, "I can help you find a new name."

Lalena said, "I don't need a new name."

Lady Jane went inside.

I sat there and picked at the knees of my blue jeans, looking for loose threads where it was starting to look like maybe a patch.

Feet down the steps behind us, and Lalena's daddy came out. He stood there, behind us, over us. I worked a thread loose, poking my finger into a hole in the seam by my knee.

He said, "Fuckin' rain."

He said, "Tell Sasha I'll be late."

He left.

Lalena said, "L."

I said, "What?"

She said, "L. Just call me L now."

"I don't know," I said. "L is pretty short."

Lalena said, "Just L."

"Okay," I said. "Okay, L. Hey, OK-L, get it? All letters?"

"Will you just shut up," Lalena said.

"You better quit telling me to just shut up, or I'll just leave," I said. "Maybe I'll just go to Constanzia's."

"No," Lalena said. "Let's go up to my room. It's too rainy."

"Well, I said. "Okay. Okay, L."

Lady Jane's yellow door was open, and the record player was on.

I said, "L."

Lady Jane turned the music down and said, "What?"

"Just L is her new name," I said.

"L is pretty short," Lady Jane said.

Lalena said, "L."

"You could spell it out," Lady Jane said. "You could spell it E-l-l-e. That's the same as L, but spelled out it's French."

"A French name?" I said.

Lalena said, "What does it mean in French?"

"Girl," Lady Jane said. "It means girl."

"Well," I said, looking at Lalena. "You're a girl."

"I know that, Sarajean," she said.

"I mean instead of a whore," I said.

WE STAYED in her room, and I practiced saying "Elle."

I said, "Elle, can I try on this top?"

I said, "Elle, go get us some crackers."

When Sasha and Dylan Marie came home I said, "Elle, I have to go home now."

Elle said, "No, stay over."

She went and asked Sasha could I stay over, and Sasha said, "I don't care."

"Well," I said. "Okay."

We stayed up late, Lalena being Elle, and me doing her homework. We took a bath with patchouli bubbles in the pink light, and I brushed my hair with Sasha's sparkly plastic hairbrush.

Elle said, "I'm not telling her my new name."

"Who?" I said, "Sasha?"

"Sasha," Elle said. "I'm not telling her. I'm just telling my daddy."

"Well, he'll tell her," I said.

"Not if I tell him not to," she said.

"Why not?" I said.

"Because he likes me better than her," she said.

"No," I said. "I mean why not tell her? What if she has to say something to you?"

"I'm just not telling her," Elle said.

Late at night, Lalena wasn't there. I got out of her bed in the dark, and I tiptoed through the dark of the other bedroom, past the big bed, past Dylan Marie's little bed, through the front room. The pink light of the bathroom lit out into the kitchen. I stopped halfway across the cold tiles, by the kitchen table.

Lalena's daddy sat on the edge of the bathtub, and Lalena stood between his legs, facing away. His legs were holding her, and his hands were in her hair, pulling back, his fingers all in her hair. His eyes were closed, and her eyes were closed, and he was breathing like running, breathing like crying, breathing like he couldn't breathe.

EARLY, BARELY light, barefoot down the stairs, holding onto my sneakers, down to the door, down to Seventeenth Avenue. I sit on the top step outside. The sidewalk shiny wet. Nobody walking.

At Colfax Street the light is green for no cars one way and red for no cars the other way. When it changes for no cars, I cross.

By Ogden Street the sky is lighter gray. I go in, to the locked door of the painted apartment, the key in my pocket, always in my pocket.

I take the candles out of the top drawer and line them up on the floor by the mattress. I get my shoe box of stuff. I wrap up in the green peacock cloth and sit on the mattress with my shoe box that I don't open, by the candles that I don't light. I listen for Jimmy Henry.

He used to wake up early every day, get out of bed early every day. Brush my hair in braids or barrettes. Whichever I wanted.

☮

LADY JANE came over to our house with daffodils. I was in my bedroom reading about Amelia Earhart, who flew away and never came back, or even said where she landed. Then Lady Jane's voice was in our front room. I went out there, and she had daffodils.

"Daffodils," I said.

"Spring," Lady Jane said. "Here. Put them in water."

There was yellow like the chalk at school. There was yellow like on the back cover of Nancy Drew books. Dandelion yellow. Sungold number seventeen. There was a girl in fifth grade whose name was Sunshine, and she always wore a yellow outfit of different yellows that didn't match right. Daffodil yellow came off on my finger when I touched the ruffly edge of the middle part, the daffodil part that stuck out and made it a daffodil instead of some other yellow flower.

The only thing that was the right size to hold the daffodils was the orange and brown glass mug from the root beer place on Colfax Street. Orange and brown and daffodil yellow wasn't very good. There were old jelly jars in the cabinet over the refrigerator. Old peanut butter jars. I climbed up on the counter. Behind the jars was the old teapot, the green apple with the smiley worm handle. The little lid with the leaves was gone, broken, too many little pieces even for glue.

The green apple teapot was perfect. The daffodil stems stuck straight up, the yellow all bunched together. I set the teapot with the daffodils in the very center of the blue kitchen table. Green yellow blue.

Then there was music. Jimmy Henry never played his records. It was Lady Jane, looking at all Jimmy Henry's records.

She said, "Wow."

She said, "Far out."

She said, "Little Miss Strange."

She looked at me, and then she looked at him.

He said, "Turn it down."

Lady Jane didn't turn the music down. She danced in front of the record player, danced in one spot mostly, looking at the records. Her long blond hair danced on her back down to the butt of her blue jeans, to the patches on her butt, blue-jean patches stitched around with purple thread. Lady Jane's hair was perfectly straight, all the way to her butt. Jimmy Henry sat on the couch, sitting still, his hair in a pony tail with a rubber band. Brown. Straight.

The daffodils stood up tall in the green apple on the kitchen table. Music in the front room. I got my book of *History of the United States* and sat at the kitchen table, setting my book perfectly in the middle between me and the daffodils. The daffodils were in the window reflection. I was in the window reflection. My hair was curly, always curly, even when I brushed it down flat and wet, it dried up curly. Dark brown. Amelia Earhart had blond curly hair in the picture.

The music stopped, and Lady Jane said, "Let's hear the flip side."

There was more music, more records, and after I went to bed I was awake for a long time, hearing music.

In the morning the light came into the kitchen window right on to the daffodils. Yellow green blue. The front room was dark, and the records were out, leaned up against the couch and some out flat on the applebox table. Jimmy Henry's door was shut, still asleep when I went to school.

AFTER SCHOOL Elle said, "Want to come over?"

"No," I said. "You can come over my house. There are daffodils."

We walked along Ogden Street. It was rainy. Not raining.

Elle said, "What did you get on the history quiz?"

"A," I said.

"Perfect A?" she said.

"Perfect A," I said. "None wrong."

Elle got a B.

"Pretty good," I said.

Elle said, "Great. B is great."

I said, "I think B is pretty good. A is great."

Elle said, "Shut up."

There was music coming down the stairs inside. The door at the top of the stairs was open, and there was drifty blue smoke in the air. Incense. Music and incense in my house. The records were all back on the shelf, and the daffodils in the green apple teapot were in the middle of the applebox table in front of the couch.

Elle said, "Those are daffodils huh?"

She dropped her coat on the couch. The couch pillows were all in a straight line, and Jimmy Henry's couch blanket was folded up. Lady Jane came through the kitchen doorway, wiping her hands on a towel.

She said, "Home so soon?"

"No," I said. "It's not soon. Now is when school always gets out. What are you doing?"

"I did a little tidying up," she said. "Are you hungry?"

I said, "No."

Elle said, "Yes."

Lady Jane said, "Want a grilled cheese sandwich?"

Elle said, "With mayonnaise?"

"Where's Jimmy Henry?" I said. "Why are you tidying up?"

Lady Jane went back into the kitchen. The front-room curtains were pulled back, and the front room was all afternoon light. The newspapers were stacked up by the door. The chair that was usually by the door was over by the applebox table, like someone could sit there and look at the daffodils.

Elle went in the kitchen and leaned on the counter, watching Lady Jane get out cheese and butter and bread. Big brown bread all still in a loaf, not cut. Not Safeway bread.

I said, "Where did that bread come from?"

Lady Jane said, "I did a little shopping."

She bent over, looking in the refrigerator.

"Mayonnaise," she said.

Purple-stitched blue-jean patches. She had on Jimmy Henry's tie-dye T-shirt.

I said, "Where's Jimmy Henry?"

Lady Jane said, "Aha."

She took out the mayonnaise jar. She had on big red winter socks.

I said, "Are those Jimmy Henry's socks?"

She put bread in the toaster.

Elle said, "Lady Jane, do you think getting a B on a history quiz is great?"

"Yeah," Lady Jane said. "B is great. Did you get a B?"

Elle said, "Yeah."

Elle looked at me and smiled.

Lady Jane looked in the mayonnaise jar and smelled it.

She said, "Do you want mayonnaise too, Sarajean?"

"No," I said. "I hate mayonnaise."

"You hate mayonnaise?" Lady Jane said. "Hate? That's a pretty strong passion. You shouldn't waste it on mayonnaise."

I said, "Waste what?"

"Your hate," Lady Jane said. "Your passion."

"Ooh," Elle said. "Passion."

The toasts popped up, and Lady Jane put in some more bread, put butter on the toasts.

I said, "When is Jimmy Henry coming back?"

She said, "I don't know."

She put buttered pieces of toast in the frying pan, butter side down. She laid cheese on the toasts and then smeared on mayonnaise. When the other pieces of toast popped up she buttered them and laid them in the pan on top of the other parts of the grilled cheese sandwiches.

"The secret of grilled cheese sandwiches," she said. "Toast."

She put a tin pie pan over the top of the frying pan like a lid. Our frying pan didn't have its own lid.

Jimmy Henry's bedroom door was open. The green blanket on the bed was all laid out straight. Incense smell, old laundry smell. The curtains were open, and outside the tree branches were blowing and wet, and there were wet shiny buds on the end of each branch. The moss on the roof of the front porch was bright wet green. There was one daffodil in a glass of water on the floor on the other side of the bed. The glass from the bathroom. Lady Jane and Jimmy Henry were doing it. They did it in here, last night, while I was in my bedroom asleep. Last night, while I was in my own room, it was passion in here.

The blanket was tucked in around the edges of the bed, the pillow exactly in the middle at the top. I pulled the blanket off and dropped it back in a pile. I took the daffodil out of the bathroom glass and shut the bedroom door behind me.

In the front room I put the daffodil back with the others. I moved the chair back over by the door. I picked up the green apple of daffodils and carried it into the kitchen. I put the daffodils on the kitchen table, right in the middle.

Elle said, "Nice daffodils."

Lady Jane smiled all big, looking at the green apple sitting there in the middle of the blue table. She got down a big red plate and set it in the middle of the table by the daffodils.

I said, "No."

Lady Jane said, "No what?"

"No," I said. "I hate red and yellow together."

Lady Jane said, "Hate?"

I said, "Hate."

She picked up the red plate and put it back in the cabinet. She got out a white plate and set it by the daffodils.

"Better?" she said.

I said, "And I hate mayonnaise."

LADY JANE had to go to work before Jimmy Henry came home.

"I'll walk you home, Elle," she said. "I have to take a bath before I go to the café."

She put on her coat over Jimmy Henry's tie-dye T-shirt. She took off his big red socks and rolled them up into a ball and set them on the couch, perfectly in the middle of the folded-up couch blanket.

"So," she said. "See you later."

She put on her own kneesocks, blue kneesocks, and her Dutch-girl shoes.

"Tell Jimmy Henry I said see you later," she said.

"Later?" I said. "Later when?"

She and Elle left. The record player was still playing a record. I turned it off and put the record back in its cardboard and put it back with the other records lined up across the shelf. I stacked my homework books on the kitchen table and sat there, looking at the daffodils. Jimmy Henry came home in a little while.

"Hi," he said from the front room door.

He came into the kitchen, looking around, looking at me and looking around.

"Lady Jane said see you later," I said. "She wore your tie-dye T-shirt."

"Well," Jimmy Henry said. "She'll bring it back."

"She put your socks on the couch," I said.

He went in the front room and came back, holding his rolled up red winter socks. He leaned against the doorway of the kitchen and looked at the socks. He looked at me, and he looked at the daffodils.

"Well," he said. "Nice daffodils, huh?"

THE NEXT day at school Elle said, "So."

"Just shut up," I said.

She said, "Jimmy Henry is balling Lady Jane."

I said, "You think you know everything."

"I asked her," Elle said. "I asked was Jimmy Henry and her boyfriend and girlfriend now."

"What did she say?" I said.

"She said friendship expresses itself in many ways," Elle said.

"Well," I said. "That doesn't mean anything you know."

"Yes, it does," she said. "It means they're doing it."

I said, "It doesn't mean that."

"Yes, it does," Elle said. "It means they're doing it."

The bell rang, so Elle went and sat at her desk. I sat down in my desk and got out my math book. I looked back at Elle, one row over, three desks back. She spread her knees apart and rubbed her hand between her legs and then sat up straight, trying not to laugh, looking at me from her eyes sideways, laughing. I turned around front, knocked my math book on the floor and picked it up quick. We were on page 194. I couldn't find page 194.

When I got home the stairway was dark, and I opened the door into the afternoon dark of our front room. The curtains were shut across the windows and Jimmy Henry was lying on the couch, the couch blanket all bunched up under his head like a pillow. He sat up when I came in.

"Hi," he said.

His bedroom door was open, into the dark of in there, the bedroom curtains shut. I put my books on the kitchen table by the daffodils, and got the potato chips out of the cabinet. I stood there, by the sink, eating potato chips, looking at Jimmy Henry's brown ponytail head over the back of the couch. The incense smell was still in the air.

I said, "Want a grilled cheese sandwich?"

Jimmy Henry said, "What?"

"Grilled cheese," I said. "You want a grilled cheese sandwich?"

"God," he said. "I hate grilled cheese sandwiches."

LATER, AFTER I was already in bed, the record player came on. I woke up enough to listen, and there was laughing, girl laughing, in between the sounds of music. Lady Jane out there with Jimmy Henry, laughing.

SOMETIMES WHITE daisies with dark yellow centers were in the green apple. Once there were pink carnations that smelled up the kitchen like clove gum, Lady Jane said their scent. A branch from an apple blossom tree. Beautiful round white tulips, white like candle wax, big and perfectly still, no scent. The kitchen was quiet in the mornings, like it was always quiet in the mornings, and Jimmy Henry's bedroom door was shut, like his bedroom door was always shut. If there were new flowers Lady Jane was in there, in Jimmy Henry's bedroom, in his bed, wearing one of his T-shirts.

There was music even when Lady Jane wasn't there. Jimmy Henry put on records, turned them over to the other side when they were done playing. He didn't look like he was listening. He didn't bounce his head or wiggle on his butt or snap his fingers. He didn't know the words.

It was always late, after I was in bed, when I heard Lady Jane.

RAIN BLEW sideways across the streets. It blew in ripples across the wide puddles in the parking lot of the Safeway store, and it dripped down between the houses, outside the tall window of the painted apartment.

All my best books were in the painted apartment, lined up on the purple shelf closest to the door, books that I had already read once and might want to read again. Not Nancy Drew. Nancy Drew was boring to read again after she solved the mystery. I traded my Nancy Drew books back in at Together Books, traded them in for more books. I kept *Peter Pan. Charlotte's Web. Grimm's.*

I was all wrapped up in the green peacock cloth, lying on the mattress by the window, the rainy afternoon dripping down. I always skipped school if it was rainy, and there wasn't a test. I was all wrapped up, reading *Little Women*, the part where Beth dies and the grass is green on her grave before Amy finds out, and I was crying and crying, like I always cry when Beth dies and Amy doesn't even know, and the rusty doorknob on the back door began to jiggle and click. I got up and the green peacock cloth was all tangled between my legs, and I got my sneakers in one hand and *Little Women* in my other hand and I was untangling my legs out of the green peacock cloth and the back door popped open. The wet rain smell blew in and the Cheshire Cat kid was there in the doorway, down on his knees.

"Hey," I said. "You can't come in here."

He dropped a long silver crochet hook on the floor and he grabbed it quick and he jumped up. His knees of his blue jeans were wet.

He said, "I didn't know no one was in here."

He put the crochet hook in his pocket of his jean jacket.

I said, "That door is supposed to stay locked."

He came in and shut the door.

"You scared the shit out of me," he said.

"Did you open that lock with that crochet hook?" I said.

He looked around. His hair was wet and stuck to his head.

He said, "I always wondered about this place."

I wiped my nose on my sleeve, wiped at my eyes.

"Yeah," I said. "Well, it's my place."

He said, "Yeah, right, you got your own place."

He went over to the shelf of books. I set my sneakers down on the floor, watching him. He looked at the shelf of books, and his hair dripped in wet curls against where his neck went thin and bones into his white T-shirt.

He said, "You read all these books?"

"Yes," I said. "They're my books."

"Got it," he said. "It's your place, they're your books."

He looked at me, looked at my face.

"What happened?" he said. "The old man throw you out?"

"Nothing happened," I said. "I was reading a book until you came in. Did you get that door open with that crochet hook?"

He said, "That makes you cry, reading a book?"

My cheeks got hot, and down my neck.

"I wasn't crying," I said. "It's a very sad book."

He sat down on the mattress, and he looked around some more, and I stood still and straight by the door and looked at him, a Mexican boy in the painted apartment, on the mattress by the tall window. He took the pack of Kools out of his jean jacket pocket, and the little box of matches.

I said, "Don't just be throwing matches around in here."

He lit his Kool and held the match for a second. Then he pinched the flame out with his thumb and pointer finger, and he put the match in his pocket, the same pocket.

"I might just be hanging around here," he said. "My old man threw me out."

"Here where?" I said. "Here here?"

He leaned back on one elbow on the mattress.

"Or here there," I said. "In that place next door?"

"That place is a dump," he said.

He blew a long puff of smoke into the air.

"Your old man threw you out?" I said.

"Asshole," he said. "He's an asshole."

I said, "So, did he pick you up and throw you? Or did he just say get out of here?"

I wrapped up closer in the peacock cloth. He tapped on his cigarette, tapping the ash into his hand. He rubbed his hand on his blue jeans and the ash disappeared.

"He says I got to go live with my grandma for next year," he said. "For junior high school. In fucking Tucson."

"You're in junior high next year?" I said.

"So what?" he said.

"Well, what's your name," I said. "I know it's not Cheshire Cat."

"Pete," he said.

"Pete?" I said. "That doesn't sound like a Mexican name."

He blew another puff of smoke.

"I know that book, with that Cheshire Cat," he said. "My sister has that book."

I said, "You read *Alice in Wonderland*?"

"Pedro Tomás Javier Jacinto," he said. "My name. Is that Mexican, you think?"

"Four names?" I said.

I sat down on the mattress on the other end from him. There was soap smell. Shampoo smell from his long wet hair.

He said, "You seen my brother around here?"

"That other boy that goes into that other apartment with you sometimes?" I said.

"Yeah," he said.

"Did your old man throw him out, too?" I said.

"No," he said. "He just comes and goes. He come around here much?"

"Sometimes," I said. "In that other place."

"He wants to get my ass," he said.

"Get your ass?" I said.

"He thinks I ripped him off," he said. "He thinks I ripped off his stash."

"He wants to beat you up?" I said. "Your big brother wants to beat you up, and your old man threw you out? What about your mom?"

"She has my new baby brother," he said. "My mom, her and my sisters, they don't know nothing going on."

He got up, standing up, still holding the cigarette that was all gone out, all rubbed into his blue jeans.

"So," he said. "I'll probably be back around later."

I said, "Are you going to get in with that crochet hook?"

I wiped my nose on the peacock cloth.

"Hey, man," he said. "You getting snot all over them nice birds."

I wiped at the cloth with my hand.

"Look," I said. "You can't just come in here all the time. And you can't let any other boys come in here. This place is secret."

Pete leaned over, looked at the green peacocks, his wet hair close, the shampoo smell close.

He said, "Those are peacocks."

There was a soft fuzz of maybe mustache on the skin under his nose.

"And you can't let Jimmy Henry know you're here," I said.

"No way, man," he said. "I can lay low."

I said, "Lay low?"

THE NEXT day I hurried to get home from school, but Pete wasn't there. There was an empty tuna fish can by the mattress, with cigarette butts soaking up the oil. The next day the tuna fish can was gone. A little Safeway bag stood up next to the mattress, with a red corn chip bag inside, and an empty pop can. The green peacock cloth was folded up like a pillow, smoothed down where Pete had his head on it. I put my face there. Shampoo.

Then the next day the back door was open wide and the rain was blowing in, all wet on the floor. The bottom drawer of the dresser was pulled out, and some of the pieces of bird cloth were on the floor. The baby blanket piece was all piled in the sink. At first it looked like there was black all over it, but then I saw red, dark red smeared on the light green. Red smeared all in the sink. Black red spots on the floor, black red blood spots.

I wiped the smeared blood up with the baby blanket, out of the sink, off the floor. I put the baby blanket into the trash, pushed it way down into one of the trash cans out by the garage.

After I cleaned all the blood spots, I went up in my bedroom, and listened. I listened for Pete to be in the painted apartment. For his brother to be in the other apartment. I listened for Jimmy Henry to come home. I listened for Lady Jane laughing. Mostly all I heard was rain, dripping down between the houses.

MY BIRTHDAY was in May, on a Sunday this year. When I woke up and went in the kitchen, the green apple was full of baby lavender rosebuds, in a square of sunlight. I sat into the bench of the table and touched one rosebud, as tiny as the tip of my finger. I pulled the green apple close and looked down into all the tight curls of lavender. Sniffed a tiny scent of rose. I touched my cheek to the rosebuds. I closed my eyes and opened my eyes, seeing the rosebuds again for the first time.

THE RAINY spring kept on being a rainy summer, or else cloudy and gray, different colors of gray clouds piled up on each other, or the sky would be all clouds in one part and blue in another part, or even raining and sun at the same time, and once a rainbow.

ERICO WAS digging in the flower box. Little plants sat in little square pots on the sidewalk, all lined up, and Erico dug deep with a little shovel, lifting out a shovelful of dirt and letting the dirt fall back into the flower box.

"Hey," I said. "New flowers."

"Hey, you," Erico said, standing up straight. "New flowers."

I dug my fingers into the loose black dirt, down to where the dirt was cold and damp. I scooped up a handful of dirt and let it fall back into the flower box through my fingers.

"Nice dirt, eh?" said Erico.

I said, "Nice dirt?"

"Here," he said, and he handed me the little shovel.

He said, "Work it with this. I'll go for the water."

I liked the way Erico said "water." "Wa-ter," in two parts.

The wooden handle of the shovel was warm from Erico's hand, smooth, warm, light-colored wood. I dug out little shovels of dirt and spilled the dirt off the shovel, onto my other hand, spilling the dirt through my fingers. Working it.

Erico came back out with a gray metal pail sloshing full of water.

"I'm working it," I said. "I like this little shovel."

"Trowel," Erico said. "That is a trowel."

He stood next to me, rolling up the sleeves of his shirt, long soft sleeves of faded blue plaid, old flannel. I dug with the trowel, deep into the soft dirt, and the damp dirt smell. I got down on my knees on the sidewalk, closer by the smell of the dirt.

"Okay," Erico said. "Now make eight little holes in a row."

He held up one of the little square pots.

"About this deep," he said.

I said, "All the way across?"

He said, "All the way across."

He set the little pots on top of the dirt in a row.

"There," he said. "Dig one hole for each pot."

"What kind of flowers are these?" I said.

"Petunias for the front row," he said. "Pink. Bright bright pink. Then marigolds for the back row. The marigolds are taller. Taller goes in the back."

"What color marigolds?" I said.

"Orange," he said. "Orange marigolds in the back, pink petunias in the front."

"Orange and pink?" I said. "Orange and pink? Do you think orange and pink go together?"

"They will be beautiful," Erico said. "Brighten the heart."

He poured water into each hole I made.

The petunia leaves were soft fuzzy leaves that curled in on themselves. Erico dug his fingers down into each pot, working a petunia out of each pot, setting a petunia in each hole.

"Carefully," he said. "Tender roots. If we are careful with the roots, we will have beautiful flowers soon. Just like with little girls."

"Little girls don't have roots," I said.

Erico said, "There are always roots. Roots are where you begin. Your mama plants you carefully, and there you are, growing."

He filled in the dirt into each hole, over the roots, the water and the dirt closing over his fingers with mud, until there was a long row of petunias.

I said, "My mama didn't plant me carefully."

I said. "She went away somewhere."

"But here you are growing," Erico said.

I said, "Her name was Christine Jeanette Blumenthal."

Right out loud.

Erico handed me the trowel.

"Here," he said. "Now another row for the marigolds."

The marigolds stood up skinny, and shiny dark leaves like fingers reaching out. I dug each hole, and Erico filled each hole with water, setting the roots into the mud, scooping the soft dirt around each marigold with his big hands, little skinny marigolds. When all the marigolds were in their row Erico poured the rest of the water into the flower box. Muddy water dripped out the bottom of the flower box onto the sidewalk, cold, wet, soaking through the knees of my blue jeans.

"How long until they grow?" I said.

"All the time," Erico said. "They are growing every minute. Even now, brand new, they are growing."

"I mean flowers," I said.

"That depends," Erico said. "On the sun. Maybe a month, maybe sooner."

My hands were covered with mud, all under my fingernails, and cold, cold from working the cold wet dirt, and the sleeves of my army coat were wet and muddy. Erico put the trowel in the empty pail, and he stacked up all the little pots, put them in the pail. He stood up, and his knees cracked, and he rubbed at his back. The sky had turned to dark gray clouds.

Constanzia didn't look up from her catnap when we went in.

Erico said, "Sh."

I followed him into the back, through the striped blanket that hung down across the doorway of their house part. He set the pail down in the corner.

It was only the kitchen in this part. The rest of their house was up the stairs. The kitchen was a big room around a table in the middle, and a black stove took up a whole corner. The shelf above the stove had jars, different shapes, red beans, purple beans, black beans. Jars of dried leaves. Jars of whole red tomatoes with long green beans and yellow seeds. Dried-out plants hung on strings from the ceiling, and long red peppers and shining white clumps of garlic. The tall window looked out back to the alley, the light mostly getting taken up by the vines and plants that grew in pots on the windowsill.

The sink was a square metal tub. Erico steered me over to it with his warm hand on my back between my shoulders. I pushed up the sleeves of my army coat. He turned on the water, hot, cold, a little more hot, a little less hot, the water pounding down into the deep sink. I let the warm water run over my cold fingers, up onto my wrists, the water running down muddy. Erico put his hands under the faucet. There was a bar of pink soap in a dish, and he made soap lather, and soap perfume filled the sink. Erico's hands under the faucet turned clean, brown hands, brown wrists with black hair, and soap lather. The very inside of his elbows was white, pale skin like my skinny white arms. I cupped my hands under the water and poured it onto Erico's wrists. He shook his hands into the sink and gave me a washcloth from a hook.

"Even the face," he said. "You even got mud on your face."

I wet the washcloth and twisted it out and wiped it warm and wet on my face, warm on my cold nose, cold cheeks. My eyes spilled over with tears under the warm washcloth, and I held the washcloth there, soaking up the tears, hearing Erico turn off the water, the soft sound of the towel.

He said, "Here you go."

I hung the washcloth over the edge of the sink and took the towel, a red-striped dishtowel, damp from Erico's hands, and he went back out to the shop. I wiped my face and hung the towel over the edge of the sink, next to the wet washcloth, soapy water sucking down the drain.

I went to the striped blanket and looked. They were standing by the front window, Erico tall, Constanzia small and soft shoulders. They looked out the front window, looked down at the flower box, talked in soft Mexican words I didn't know, couldn't hear. Tears rushed at my eyes again, and I held the tears back behind my eyelids until my eyes were okay, no tears, and my face was okay, no hurting behind it. I counted the stripes that went across the blanket in the order of the rainbow.

"Beautiful flowers, huh?" I said, stepping through the blanket.

Constanzia turned around from the window and clapped her hand in the air in front of her face, smiling at me. She came back over to the counter, and Erico went out the door. I was as tall as Constanzia now. I could see the top of her head, the gray hairs that popped up out of her braids.

She said, "Look here, Sarajean Henry."

She reached to a pile on the counter and picked up the green corduroy jacket. Dark green corduroy, a straight neat jacket like from a guy's suit, straight neat collar, dark green leather buttons.

"That army jacket you wear," she said. "That army jacket is rags now. Here, try this on."

The corduroy jacket was lined with soft shining cloth of dark maroon. It was too big.

"Perfect," I said. "It's beautiful."

"Grande," Constanzia said. She pinched at the shoulders, tugged at the sleeves.

"I love too big," I said. "Too big is perfect."

Constanzia folded up the sleeves at the wrists until my hands showed.

"We'll fix the sleeves up short enough," she said.

I took off the green corduroy jacket, and Constanzia sat down in her chair and spread the jacket across her lap. She reached through one sleeve, pulling the sleeve inside out on itself, and began to work at the stitching that held down the maroon lining.

"The horse patch," I said. "I can sew the horse patch onto the pocket."

Constanzia went "Mm," and worked, her hands fast, ripping the lining away from the inside of the sleeve.

"How much?" I said. "How much for that green corduroy jacket?"

"From me to you," she said. "Since you planted my flowers. Since you brighten my heart."

The ache rushed back into my face, and I whispered, "Thank you," quick, before the crying could get to my voice.

I whispered "Gracias," and I turned my face away, all the dark colors of the shop blurring.

THE GREEN jacket came down to the edge of my cutoffs, and my black hightops came up with only my bare legs in between. And the bright horse patch on my heart pocket.

And a book, from the box, in the inside pocket under the horse patch. Some of the books in Tina Blue's box were poem books, Japanese haiku poems that didn't have to rhyme, just tell little stories divided up into three lines. Elle liked Emily Dickinson poems better, since Emily Dickinson poems rhymed plus made sense.

"Haiku poems aren't really poems," Elle said. "Poems are supposed to rhyme at the end."

"Except haiku," I said. "Haiku poems don't have to rhyme."

All the books in Tina Blue's box had her name in the front. She like to make fancy swirly letters, especially her *B*s, big and round, with the last swoop going all the way through the bottom of the *B* to connect with the *L*.

I lined the poem books up on the shelf in the painted apartment with my other books. Early in the morning, when Jimmy Henry was still in his bedroom, maybe by himself, maybe with Lady Jane, I put on my favorite outfit and left. I walked over to Seventeenth Avenue. If it was raining, I ran over to Seventeenth Avenue.

The first thing to do on Seventeenth Avenue was check on the flower boxes. The marigolds grew faster than the petunias. If there was trash or cigarette butts in the flower box I cleaned it out. I sat on the edge of the flower box, watching the shine of the sun on the marigold leaves, waiting for Elle.

I didn't go to Elle's house. When she said, "Let's go to my house," I would say "No."

When she said, "Why not," I just said, "No."

I was sitting on the flower box waiting for Elle when I saw Pete. He came up the sidewalk with two other Mexican boys. His long black hair was all cut off.

"Hey," I said. "Hi."

Pete and the two boys stopped. They were taller.

I said, "You got a haircut."

One of the boys said, "Hey, Petey, who's your girlfriend?"

Pete shoved the big kid with his elbow.

I said, "I'm not anybody's girlfriend."

The other boys laughed, and one of them said, "Hey, Petey, you got a haircut," in a fakey girl voice.

Then the boy said, "Hey. Where did you get that patch man? That's a First Cav patch."

I said, "This horse patch? This horse patch used to be on my father's army coat."

Pete said, "That's Sergeant Henry's kid, man."

The other boys went, "Ooh."

The one boy said, "Sergeant Henry, man. That fucker's nuts."

I said, "Jimmy Henry's not nuts."

The boy said, "All them First Cav guys came back nuts, man. If they came back."

I said, "What's that, First Cav?"

"Vietnam, man," the boy said. "Flying them big-assed helicopters and shit. Killers. That's why bad-ass Henry's such a asshole. First Cav man, that's heavy."

"Jimmy Henry's not an asshole," I said. "And he's not nuts."

"He used to be nuts," the boy said. "Before you and your old lady showed up. He used to sit in there all fucked up, shooting off that gun sometimes. We was in that place downstairs just hanging out, and he shot that gun right through the floor, could of killed us."

The other boy was cracking up.

He said, "Yeah, remember that time he threw that other junkie down the stairs. I thought that guy was dead."

I said, "Hey, wait a minute."

I said, "You know who my mom was? You knew my mom?"

The boy said, "Nah. I just remember when you and her got there. Then Henry turned into a nice mellow junkie."

The other boy said, "That guy Sam? At the surplus store? He has one of them First Cav patches. Air Cavalry, man. He's nuts too."

Pete said, "Hey, man, I got to go."

Then the boy who said Jimmy Henry was an asshole, nuts, he said, "Yeah, Petey's got to go visit his PO."

He rubbed his hand over Pete's short hair.

He said, "Tell your girlfriend what happened to your all your pretty hair, Petey."

The other boy said, "Petey got busted, and they cut off all his pretty hair."

"Busted?" I said. "And they cut off your hair?"

Pete said, "Hey, man, fuck you," and he punched at the boy's arm.

"Yeah, a real criminal," the boy said. "Petey got busted ripping off a bird from the fucking pet store."

The boys were laughing and shoving at Pete. They were both a lot bigger than Pete.

Pete said, "Just fuck off, man."

"A little green parakeet bird, man," the one boy said. "The little birdie started squawking under Petey's jacket, and it blew the whistle on him. Now he's got to go see his PO and promise never to steal no more little birdies."

Pete said, "I got to go."

He walked away on the sidewalk, and the other boys went with him, laughing and hooting and all shoving each other.

First Cav.

Killers.

Nuts.

You and your old lady.

A nice mellow junkie.

A little green parakeet bird.

Elle came up the sidewalk and sat down next to me on the edge of the flower box.

She said, "What's up?"

I said, "Nothing."

She said, "What do you want to do?"

I said, "Nothing."

I LOOKED up "cavalry" in the *Webster's New Collegiate Dictionary*. "Cavalcade," "cavalier," "cavalla," "cavalry—horsemen," "an army component mounted on horseback."

"Jimmy Henry," I said. "Did you used to have a horse?"

"No," he said. "I never rode a horse in my life."

I said, "Did you ever kill anybody?"

He said, "Never ask anybody that question, Sarajean. Never."

He went in his room and shut the door.

1974

Margo came back home after fifth grade. Her hair was short, but not all the way short, and she was fatter. She had a new friend named Cassandra Wiggins, and they got an apartment upstairs from Together Books.

Elle and I sat in the empty front room, just a couch, and Margo's boxes.

Elle said, "I'm not living here with them."

"Why not?" I said.

"I already live with my daddy," she said.

The new apartment was big, a big main room that had wooden bookshelves in the wall, with jeweled glass doors that shut over the books. There was a window looking out over Seventeenth Avenue, across to the WHO'S NEXT USED RECORDS STORE sign. There were two bedrooms and a big bathroom with a bathtub standing on animal feet.

I said, "This place is better. This is a great apartment."

Elle said, "That Cassandra Wiggins gives me the creeps."

Cassandra Wiggins had short short black hair, and black lines painted around her eyes. Her pants were black and her T-shirt was black and she wore black cowboy boots with heels. That was her favorite outfit that she wore every day. Cassandra Wiggins was skinny, and she said her words funny. She was from New Jersey, and she stretched her mouth around the O sounds. She put Rs in where they didn't belong, and left them off from where they did.

Cassandra Wiggins was clunking around in the kitchen in her cowboy boots, and then she came clunking into the front room. I liked to look at Cassandra Wiggins, but I didn't like it when she looked at me.

Elle said, "Come on."

Cassandra Wiggins said, "Where are you guys going?"

Elle said, "We got stuff to do."

Elle headed out the door.

"'Bye," I said to Cassandra Wiggins.

We went down the stairs that came out in a door next to Together Books. Out on the sidewalk the wind was blowing cold, blowing trash around, blowing like about to rain.

I said, "She's your mother. Margo, I mean. She can make you live there right? Does she say you have to live there?"

"What do you know about mothers?" Elle said. "She can't make me do anything. Not if my daddy says I don't have to."

"What about your brothers?" I said. "Are they coming back?"

"Who cares?" Elle said. "They're not my brothers anyway. They're step-brothers."

"Are they staying at your grandma's?" I said.

"Just shut up," Elle said.

She smoothed her hair down. The wind was fuzzing it all up.

"Are you in a bad mood?" I said.

"No, I'm not in a bad mood," she said. "Just quit asking me stuff."

Lady Jane came walking up the sidewalk toward us, carrying a big grocery bag.

I said, "Uh-oh."

Lady Jane said, "Well, hi there. Hey, I hear Margo's out."

"Yeah," Elle said. "What of it?"

Lady Jane said, "Sarajean, guess what? I'm making spinach lasagna. For dinner. At your house, for you and me and Jimmy Henry. And you, Elle, if you want. It will be done around five."

She went on, up the street.

Elle said, "Spinach lasagna."

We went as far as Elle's house, where we sat on the steps. I took out my poem book from my inside pocket. Today it was a small square book, smaller than a regular book. The name was *Small Songs*, but it was just small poems. I liked to open it up to just any page and read the poem that was there.

I said, "Okay, listen to this.

> A reach of kelly
> Scattering golden crowns
> Elfin royalty."

I said, "That one's called 'Dandelions.' Get it? The kelly is the grass, like kelly green. Scattered golden crowns of elfin royalty means dandelions looking like elf crowns laying around in the grass. Get it?"

"Just a second," Elle said. "Stay here."

She went down the steps and back up the sidewalk, into Bill's store. She came back out in a little bit, unwrapping a chocolate candy bar with almonds.

She said, "Come on."

She went into the alley. Out of the wind. When we got back to the little metal steps Elle took a pack of cigarettes out of her back pocket.

"How did you do that?" I said. "Did you steal those cigarettes? How can you steal cigarettes from behind the counter?"

"Rip off," Elle said. "Don't say steal, say rip off."

She climbed onto the railing of the stairs.

"I just go in there and talk to that guy like I'm real cute," she said. "He likes me. He thinks I'm cute."

I said, "You're going to get caught doing that someday."

"Busted," Elle said. "Don't say get caught, say busted."

She lit one of the cigarettes. I lit one too. Elle tried to make smoke rings. I burned at the wrapper of the chocolate candy bar with the lit end of my cigarette.

Elle said, "Lookit."

Two Mexican boys were coming in the alley from the Logan Street end. I dropped my cigarette through the metal steps to the brick ground.

One of the boys said, "Hey, it's Petey's little girlfriend."

The other boy said, "Got another cigarette?"

Elle said, "Maybe."

The boy said, "What did you do, steal them from your mommy?"

"Why, is that what you do?" Elle said. "Who's Petey?"

"Nothing," I said. "I'll tell you later."

The two boys were dressed the same. Long black hair. White T-shirts. One boy's T-shirt said PROPERTY OF DENVER UNIVERSITY ATHLETIC DEPARTMENT on the front in old blue letters. No jackets.

Elle took one cigarette out of the pack and handed it to one of the boys, the one with the plain T-shirt. He took the cigarette and stuck it behind his ear.

The other boy said, "You're too young to smoke."

Elle said, "I'm twelve."

Elle wasn't twelve. She was eleven, same as me.

She said, "How old are you?"

The boy with the Denver University T-shirt said, "Guess."

Elle puffed on her cigarette, looking at him.

I said, "Where's Pete?"

Elle said, "Who's Pete?"

The boy said, "Pete's my little brother. The criminal."

Both boys cracked up laughing when the one boy said that.

"Come on, Elle," I said. "Let's go."

"So what's you guy's names?" she said. "I'm Elle. *E-l-l-e*. That's French for 'girl.'"

Pete's brother said, "Yeah, I seen you around."

Elle said, "You live around here?"

Pete's brother said, "Yeah. I used to live over by her house. Clarkson Street."

"Clarkson Street?" I said. "Clarkson Street is right behind my street. Where on Clarkson Street?"

Elle said, "So what's you guys' names and all?"

Pete's brother said, "What do you little girls do, just hang out in the alley and smoke your mommy's cigarettes?"

The other boy said, "Come on, Buddy, let's hit it."

Pete's brother said, "Yeah, man."

They kind of moved away, on down to the end of the alley. Elle watched them until they were gone around the corner.

I said, "Those are those guys that break into my house, you know, into that place downstairs."

"Those guys?" Elle said. "Those are them?"

"Yeah," I said. "That one guy, that one with the Denver University T-shirt? Buddy? He's Pete's brother. Pete's that other guy that gets in there, that one I talked to that time? The Cheshire Cat kid? I think that Buddy guy beat him up."

"Huh," Elle said. "Let's go."

"Here," I said, holding out the rest of the chocolate bar with almonds. She said, "I hate almonds."

She jumped off the metal stairs and headed down the alley. Same direction as the two boys.

I said, "Let's go the other way."

Elle kept going in her same direction. At the end of the alley she went back out on Seventeenth Avenue. Buddy and the other boy were gone. We walked along the sidewalk as far as Bead Here Now.

"Come on," I said. "Let's go in here."

Inside Bead Here Now was tall tables with boxes of beads all according to color. One table was all the reds, one table all the blues, each table all the different colors of each color, sorted out in boxes. I walked around each table. The green table was dark blue-green beads of glass, wooden greenish yellow beads, clay birds of perfect green. Eighteen cents each.

"Here," I said. "Elle, here. Kelly green. This is what kelly green is. It's like Irish you know?"

Elle was over by the wall, in front of a little round mirror on the wall, smoothing her hair down.

Next to the kelly green birds were African trade beads, Irish, then African. The African trade beads of the green table were green swirled in with purple. Twenty-two cents each.

I picked out two African trade beads and one kelly green bird. Then I went to the purple table. Plain round purple wooden beads. Bumpy purple clay beads, dark almost like black. Pinkish purple plastic beads like diamonds with glittery edges. One box had two beads left, long square beads. I held one up to the light. Purple glass. I took the last two purple glass beads. Fourteen cents each.

The walls were different kinds of string hanging in long loops, strings for beads, string for macramé.

The lady by the counter had a green paisley scarf all around her head, and she said, "Can I help you?"

I liked it when they said that in stores, "Can I help you."

"Yes, please," I said. "I need some purple string, please."

"What kind?" the lady said. "How much?"

There was light purple, dark purple, thick purple for plant hangers. There was shiny beautiful purple.

"There," I said. "That shiny purple. Will that purple go through these bead holes?"

The beads in my hand were sweaty. The lady picked each bead out of my hand, one bead at a time, and she held each bead up to the light and looked at the bead hole.

She said, "Yes."

"It's for a necklace," I said. "Enough string for a necklace, please."

She pulled a piece of the shiny purple string out of the loop and snipped it off with her scissors.

"One length," she said. "Of purple silk cord."

"One length?" I said. "That means like how long?"

"Two feet long," she said. "A two-foot length. There might be a little extra. You can tie your hair back with the extra."

She wound the length of purple silk cord around her fingers into a little loop.

A length of purple silk cord.

A reach of kelly.

Seventy-five cents for the length of purple silk cord. Ninety cents for five beads. Plus tax. The lady put the beads and the length of purple silk cord into a very small bag that said "Bead Here Now" on it in a circle.

She said, "There you go."

"Thank you," I said. "Do you know Fern?"

"Fern?" the lady said.

"That's her name," I said. "Fern. She used to make macramé on the sidewalk."

"No," the lady said.

"Oh," I said. "Okay."

Elle was way at the back of the store.

"Hey, Elle," I said. "Come on. I got some beads."

Outside I opened the bag to show Elle.

I said, "That's a length of purple silk cord."

"How much?" she said.

"Two feet," I said.

"No," she said. "How much did it cost?"

"Dollar seventy," I said.

"Ha," she said.

She opened her fist. Five little white beads like roses. She closed her fist over the beads and stuck her hand down into her pocket.

"Ivory," she said.

"That's not very nice," I said. "I like that bead lady. Ivory roses? Let me see those ivory roses."

She took out her hand and opened her fist to the ivory roses.

"That's not very nice," I said. "Stealing from a nice person."

"Yeah, yeah," Elle said. "Got any money left?"

I said, "Yeah. Some."

"Well," she said. "I got all my money left. Plus these beads."

We walked up the sidewalk, into the cold wind on my face and into my jacket.

"I bet that lady knew," I said. "It's different to steal stuff from Safeway than to steal from a little place where they're nice and say like, 'Can I help you.'"

"Rip off," Elle said. "Don't say steal. Say rip off. Let's go to my house. Get something to eat."

I said, "So why don't you just go rip off something to eat?"

"Oh, what's a matter?" she said. "Little Sarajean afraid she'll get in trouble? You never get in trouble."

"You're going to get in trouble," I said. "You're going to get caught."

"Busted," she said. "Don't say caught, say busted."

We stopped on the sidewalk at the steps of her house. The colored lights were on in Lady Jane's window.

Elle said, "I guess I'll go upstairs."

I said, "I guess I'll go home."

She said, "I'll probably come back out later."

I said, "I'll probably just be at home."

Elle went up her front stairs. I walked up the sidewalk, and then Elle went in her front door.

The sun was shining on the bench in front of Together Books. I set my Bead Here Now bag on the bench and sat down there. The wood of the bench was warm on the back of my legs. I closed my eyes to the sun, orange inside my eyelids.

"Hey there."

I opened my eyes to Cassandra Wiggins standing right by me.

I said, "Hi."

She sat down. I picked up my Bead Here Now bag from the bench in between us, and I put it in my inside jacket pocket, in next to *Small Songs*.

Cassandra Wiggins said, "What you got there?"

"Beads," I said. "For making a necklace."

"No," she said. "The book. What's the book?"

"It's poems," I said.

I took out *Small Songs* and showed it.

"It says *Small Songs*," I said. "But it's really poems. Small poems."

"You like poetry?" she said.

I said, "Yeah."

I flipped at the pages, looked down at *Small Songs*. Looked at the back cover. Flipped the pages backward.

Cassandra Wiggins said, "You ever write poetry?"

"No," I said. "I don't know how you write a poem."

"Bet you do," she said. "Here. Give me that bag."

Her fingers were long fingernails and two silver rings. Her big middle ring looked like it was braided silver around her finger. Her other ring was two little hands holding a little crown. She folded the Bead Here Now bag open flat onto the black of her pants, next to my bare leg.

She said, "Bead Here Now?"

"That's the name of the bead shop," I said. "Down there. See that round sign? Bead Here Now. Way down there."

"Right," she said.

She turned the bag over to the blank side.

"So," she said. "Tell me what's in this bag."

"Five beads," I said. "And a length of purple silk cord."

She sat back on the bench and looked at me.

"That's good," she said.

She took a short pencil out of the pocket of her black T-shirt.

"So," she said. "About these beads. Tell me about these beads."

"I paid for them," I said.

"No," she said. "What they look like."

"One is a bird," I said. "Green. Kelly green."

Cassandra Wiggins wrote "Kelly bird" on the bag in square printed letters.

"Green," I said. "It's kelly green."

She said, "If you leave out the word 'green' it makes it like a secret, right?"

"Well," I said. "I guess so."

"Secrets are the secrets of poems," she said. "So tell me about another one of the beads in this bag."

"African trading beads," I said. "Green and purple African trading beads."

"Now that is a great word," she said. "Africa is a great word. So you say this."

She wrote "Africa purple Africa Green" on the bag, under "Kelly bird."

I said, "Is this going to rhyme?"

"Don't know that yet," she said. "Any other beads in there?"

"Glass beads," I said. "Purple glass beads. Clear square purple glass beads. Two of them."

Cassandra Wiggins picked up the bag and looked in at the beads, shaking the bag and looking in.

"These are some nice beads," she said.

She put the bag down flat on her leg again and she wrote "Purple glass squares."

"And a length of purple silk cord," I said.

She wrote "Purple silk cord."

"It's one length," I said.

"So," she said, handing the bag back to me. "Look at those words. Which do you like best? Of all those lines, you know?"

Her thumbnail was short and jagged.

"Well," I said. "Purple silk cord, maybe. No, I guess kelly bird."

She said, "Kelly bird. Let's say it twice then, since we like it."

She wrote "Kelly bird kelly bird."

I said, "Yeah, kelly bird bead. I like kelly bird."

"Bead," Cassandra Wiggins said. "That's good, kelly bird bead. Hear that good b-d sound? Bird? Bead?"

She wrote "Kelly bird bead."

So now we can rhyme it," she said.

She wrote "Africa purple Africa Green."

"Green and bead?" I said. "That rhymes, green and bead?"

"Yeah," she said. "The *e* sound. It's a good rhyme. If it rhymes too exactly it gets boring."

She said, "Now what?"

"Well," I said. "There's the purple glass square ones."

"Okay," she said. "But let's say kelly bird again since we like it."

She wrote "Kelly bird kelly bird" again, just like at first. Then she wrote "Purple glass squares."

"Purple silk cord," I said.

"That's for stringing the beads on?" she said.

"Yeah," I said. "Plus there might be some extra. I can tie my hair back with the extra."

She wrote "Purple silk cord." Under that she wrote "Purple silk hair."

I said, "Purple silk hair?"

"Here," she said. "Read it. Read it out loud."

I read,

> "Kelly bird kelly bird
> Kelly bird bead
> Africa purple Africa Green
> Kelly bird kelly bird
> Purple glass squares
> Purple silk cord
> Purple silk hair."

Cassandra Wiggins said, "So, is that it? Is that the story of your trip to this bead place, what is it, Bead Here Now?"

I said, "Kind of."

"Except secet right?" she said. "Poems are secrets. Secrets for you, interesting words for other people that read them. Interesting words that make people think maybe they're in on the secret."

She said, "You like it?"

"Kind of," I said. "I don't know about the purple silk hair part."

"Here," she said.

She took the Bead Here Now bag and she pulled out the length of purple silk cord.

"Turn around," she said.

Her hands pulled my hair from behind, away from my face, twisting my hair together in a bunch, and then one end of the purple silk cord dangled over my shoulder. She tied it around the ponytail she was making back there, tied the purple silk cord into a bow. The long end tickled across my neck, and she pulled the bow tight.

"There," she said. "Purple silk hair."

The purple silk cord tangled into the curls of my hair. I couldn't tell from touching which was purple silk cord, which was hair.

Cassandra Wiggins said, "Got to go."

She stood up.

"Okay," I said.

I smoothed the Bead Here Now bag out flat on my leg.

"Thanks," I said.

"Welcome," she said. "Is it Sarajane or Sarajean?"

"Sarajean," I said. "Sarajean Henry."

"See you later, Sarajean Henry," she said.

She walked away on the sidewalk, clunking in her black cowboy boots.

THE KELLY bird hung exactly in the middle of the length of purple silk cord, and I tied a knot on each side to keep it there. Then the Africa trade beads, one on each side with some purple silk cord showing and then another knot. I tied one more knot after each purple glass square and I tied the ends together. No extra for my hair. The kelly bird went down to the middle of my T-shirt underneath. Secret. I put the Bead Here Now bag with the poem on there in my shoe box. Secret.

1975

E rico was planting new flowers in the flower box, marigold and
petunias, same as last year. He had a bucket of water, and the
trowel, and twelve little pots, six marigolds, six petunias.

Constanzia called, "Erico."

He went in and I lined up the pots, six and six, across the dirt.

Erico came back out and he said, "The toilet runs and runs. Now it doesn't
flush. I have to fix it, instead of plant these new flowers."

"Oh," I said. "Later? Can we plant them later?"

"You can plant them all by yourself if you want," he said.

"No," I said. "With you. I want to help you plant them."

"Tomorrow," he said, picking up the bucket of water, sloshing water over
the side. "Tomorrow morning."

I walked down Seventeenth Avenue.

The box with the *Rocky Mountain News* had all the newspapers sitting on
top of the box instead of inside. The *Rocky Mountain News* had a big picture
of a guy hanging off a rope from a helicopter that was flying away. The guy
was hanging in the air. The headline was all capital letters, SAIGON FALLS.
Nothing about that guy falling.

Together Books had their flag in their window the right way up.

Lady Jane was sitting on the front steps of their house.

I said, "Do you know is Elle home?"

"No," she said. "Nobody's home."

She had a *Rocky Mountain News*, and her nose was red and her eyes had tears.

"What's wrong?" I said.

"It's what's right," she said, holding up the *Rocky Mountain News*. "It's peace. Peace at last."

She stood up off the steps.

"Come on," she said. "Let's go to your house. Let's go find Jimmy Henry, is he home?"

"I don't know," I said, but Lady Jane took my hand and she started to run, sort of run, sort of skip, barefoot on the sidewalk. Kind of like a weirdo.

"What are you doing?" I said, trying to pull my hand back from her, trying not to run. "Isn't this kind of weird?"

She kept going. At Colfax Street we had to stop for the light, out of breath, and I got my hand back. We crossed and she didn't start running again, just walking fast.

The newspaper box on the Safeway corner had the *Denver Post*. Same picture of the guy hanging on the rope but the picture was bigger, and there were other people under the guy on the rope, people who were reaching up at him, like wanting to go, like getting left behind. The headlines were thick black letters, LAST TROOPS OUT OF SAIGON.

Lady Jane took money out of her pocket of her cutoffs and put some in the slot, enough for one *Denver Post*. She opened the door and took out the whole stack of newspapers and set the stack on top of the box.

"Free," she said.

At my house Sasha was sitting on the front steps, and Dylan Marie was standing by her. Dylan Marie had a stick that she was hitting on the railing. When we came up the sidewalk Dylan Marie stopped hitting the railing and dropped the stick and put her finger in her mouth.

"Go away," she said around her finger.

"What are you guys doing here?" I said.

Sasha and Lady Jane looked at each other.

I opened the front door, and glass crashed upstairs, breaking glass crash-ing, and I stopped.

"Get the fuck out of here."

It was a screechy yell from upstairs.

And then another voice, quieter, words I couldn't hear, another voice up there with the yelling.

"Fuck you and your Screaming Eagles, Hand, fuck you." The screechy yell again.

Lady Jane said, "Sarajean, come here, wait."

I went in, partway up the stairs, shaking in my legs, holding my breath. The door was open at the top of the stairs, and Elle's daddy was there, standing in the doorway, and Jimmy Henry sat in the corner of the couch. His face was red and he was choking hard with crying, and his hand hang-ing over the edge of the couch had a black gun.

Lady Jane yanked my arm from behind and pulled me back down the stairs. Out the door. She shut the door.

"What's wrong?" I said. "Why is Jimmy Henry crying? Why does he have a gun?"

Lady Jane said, "Sh."

More yelling.

Lady Jane said, "Shit."

A black and white police car drove up fast and stopped crooked at the curb and two policemen got out. They came up our sidewalk, all in blue, putting on their hats.

"We've had a report of a shooting," the first one said.

Dylan Marie said, "Go away."

More yelling upstairs. The two policemen looked at each other and the first one said, "Is that door open?"

They went in the door and shut the door behind them. The police car sat at the curb, the radio talking inside. Lady Jane watched the front door. Sasha pulled Dylan Marie into her arms and Dylan Marie looked at me. The whole day was quiet and sunny except for the police car radio, and my hands were sweaty inside my fists and I tried to breathe right and even.

They all came down the stairs and I stopped breathing, held my breath. Backed away from the door. The first policeman, holding the gun like it wasn't a gun, just holding it. His boots shook the porch boards. Jimmy Henry, the other policeman holding on to Jimmy Henry's arm from behind, his other hand on Jimmy Henry's shoulder. Elle's daddy. Jimmy Henry's hair was hanging down over his face. He didn't look up, didn't look at me. The policeman with the gun opened the back door of the police car, and the policeman holding Jimmy Henry made him get in. They shut the door on Jimmy Henry in the backseat, the sun shining in on him, and he didn't look out the window, and the policemen got in the front seat, and they drove away. Jimmy Henry's head in the back window.

Dylan Marie said, "Go away."

Elle's daddy sat down on the top step, and he put his face into his hands.

I said, "Is Jimmy Henry arrested? Did he shoot somebody?"

"Just the window," Elle's daddy said from inside his hands.

"The window?" I said. "He shot the window?"

My voice was too small.

"Why did he shoot the window?" I said, bigger.

Elle's daddy looked up out of his hands. His face was wet from crying, not crazy red and wet like Jimmy Henry's, just wet at his eyes. He looked at Lady Jane. He looked at me. Dylan Marie stuck her face into Sasha's hair.

I said, "Why is he crying like that?"

"The war," Elle's daddy said.

His voice was low and clogged with crying, and he kept talking, about the names of Jimmy Henry's friends, saying Sergeant Henry, in a voice like someone else, not Elle's daddy, a voice that ended up back in his hands.

I said, "Was he crazy there?"

"We were all crazy there," Elle's daddy said.

THE TOP half of the front-room window was gone, broken out in big smashed pieces down on the skinny sidewalk, and glittery slivers on the floor along the wall.

A jagged piece fell, all by itself, out of the window, slowly at first, and then it crashed down onto the sidewalk.

Lady Jane got the broom and started to sweep the slivers into the dustpan. I stood by the door and watched her and didn't help, and both of us stayed quiet, not a word, until Lady Jane got a piece of glass in her foot and she said, "Shit."

She stopped sweeping and leaned against the wall by the window, looking at bright red drops drip on the floor.

I went downstairs into the painted apartment and shut the door. I sat on the mattress and took off my green corduroy jacket and started pulling at the threads around the horse patch, biting the threads and pulling them away, pulling the horse patch off my green corduroy jacket. The green was a darker shape under there. I put the horse patch inside the envelope with the letter from my mother and tucked the flap of the envelope back in, the horse patch inside there, with the folded-up letter that had all our names.

When I went back up the glass was cleaned up from the floor. Big pieces still stuck out from the sides of the window. Lady Jane was sitting on the couch. She had a piece of toilet paper stuck on her foot.

She said, "I can stay here. It will be alright. Elle's daddy will go get him."

She patted the couch next to her.

"Come here," she said.

I stood still and straight by the door.

"When?" I said.

"I don't know," she said. "I don't know."

"What about the window?" I said.

She said, "I don't know."

☮

ELLE'S DADDY came over in the morning. He broke out the rest of the glass in the broken window, and I laid in my bed and tried not to hear glass breaking on the sidewalk, smashing and breaking, and then I left.

I walked down to Saint Therese Carmelite. I tried to see in the windows to the basement, down the basement stairs with the door that was painted red, and I couldn't remember if it used to be painted red. I went around back of the church where the brick walls had ivy, and through the parking lot and up the dead end street that came back out on Ogden Street. I walked around for a while.

THERE WAS a board nailed up over the broken out window and Jimmy Henry was back. His bedroom door was shut, and Lady Jane said, "Sh."

SHE WAS around a lot after that. In the mornings she was in our kitchen making coffee, wearing one of Jimmy Henry's T-shirts. She put flowers in the green apple, and she made bean soup and muffins or potato soup and muffins. She pulled the curtain closed across the nailed-up board. Jimmy Henry's door stayed shut.

Jimmy Henry finally came out of his bedroom when the kitchen sink broke underneath and water ran out on the kitchen floor. He came out and turned off the black faucet under there, behind the wastebasket.

He said, "You'll have to use the bathroom faucet."

He went back in his room.

ELLE'S BEDROOM in the apartment upstairs from Together Books was the little bedroom, three walls that were light orange and one wall, the wall with the window, that was pink. The window looked a little way across to the red brick wall of the next door building.

"Fucking Dylan Marie," Elle said. "Has to have her own room. My room. Has to have my room."

Dylan Marie didn't sleep in her baby bed anymore, so she got Elle's room. Dylan Marie was skinny and blond-headed and she always had a

runny nose, but besides that she was cute, blond hair like blond dandelion
fuzz.

"She's cute," I said. "You're her big sister."

"Half sister," Elle said. "Doesn't count."

"Like stepsister?" I said.

"Same thing," Elle said.

The new apartment was long wood floors and nothing on the walls, no
posters or anything. The kitchen was in the back. It was big and white in
there, and a shining green floor that Margo put wax on. All Margo's stuff in
jars was lined up along the counter, jars of noodles and beans and different
colors of peas. Jars of jelly were on the windowsill and the sun from the
alley came through in different colors of red and purple. There was a round
wooden table in the middle, and five different chairs. My favorite chair was
painted blue, with a flat velvety green cushion.

"Which is your favorite chair?" I said.

"All those chairs are ugly," Elle said. "Having a favorite chair is stupid."

The front room was just a long red couch of swirly scratchy stuff in the
middle of the wooden floor. The couch faced the window that looked out
to Seventeenth Avenue, and across at Who's Next Used Records. Who's
Next Used Records had a cartoon sign of two records with a boy face and a
girl face, and the record faces looked in the front-room window.

The only other thing in the front room besides the red couch was the
bookshelf with the beautiful glass doors. I opened one of the doors, unhooked the little gold latch.

Elle said, "You're not supposed to touch her stupid books."

Cassandra Wiggins's books.

I shut the glass door. Clicked the little gold latch.

"Cassandra Wiggins is pretty cool," I said.

"Yeah, groovy," Elle said.

I said, "Cassandra Wiggins is a poet, you know."

"How do you know so much about Cassandra Wiggins?" Elle said. "Wiggins. What a stupid name. Wasn't that some rabbit or something?"

"I like this place," I said. "This is a cool apartment."

"What's so cool about it?" Elle said.

"This front window is nice," I said. "It even opens up. At your other house it was too high up to even see the sidewalk."

Street sounds came up when I pushed the window open, and I leaned out and looked way down the street, and way up the street. I could see the flower box. Marigolds and petunias.

"Hey," I said. "Pink and orange. Marigolds and petunias."

Elle flopped down on the couch behind me.

I went in to Elle's new bedroom. Lighter pink. Lighter orange.

"Your new bedroom," I said. "Marigolds and petunias."

"Yeah, yeah," Elle said.

Margo's stuff was in boxes around the edges of the other bedroom, clothes folded into boxes and smaller boxes in boxes. One box next to the bed was turned upside down and an embroidered cloth, lavender cross-stitch on the hems, draped over like a tablecloth. There was a fat purple candle on a plate, and matches and an ashtray and a bottle of lotion. I rubbed some lotion on my arm. Strawberry. A dark red blanket covered the window.

The bathroom didn't have a window. A wooden box by the bathtub had all the bath stuff. A plastic fish. A glass bottle of peppermint stuff. Herbal shampoo. I rubbed some herbal shampoo on the other arm from the strawberry.

In the mirror cabinet over the sink there was toothpaste, aspirins, pink stomachache stuff. A blue and white Tampax box, half full of little white tubes in rustly paper. I took one of them out and put it in my pocket. There was a folded-up piece of paper in the Tampax box too. It said "How to Use Tampax Tampons for Complete Protection," and it unfolded to a cartoon drawing of the bottom half of a girl showing what was inside between her legs. I put the piece of paper in my pocket with the Tampax tampon.

"Let's go over to my house," Elle yelled from the living room, and I jumped, and shut the mirror door.

"No," I said.

"I have to go get some more of my stuff," she said.

I went in there, and she didn't get up off the couch.

"I left my lizard skin cowboy boots over there," she said.

"You said those boots are too small for you now," I said.

"So, what, I'm not just leaving them for Dylan Marie to wear someday," she said. "Sasha would probably throw them out."

"Why don't you sell them at Constanzia's?" I said.

"Yeah, yeah," Elle said.

She had her arm over her eyes.

WHEN I got home nobody was there. I looked in the refrigerator for a while. Then I went downstairs into the painted apartment. I sat on the mattress and took out the folded-up piece of paper from the Tampax tampons box. The drawing of the girl had names of her inside parts written around the outside, with arrows pointing in. "Ovaries." "Fallopian tubes." "Uterus." "Vagina." I flattened the piece of paper out on the mattress and took the Tampax tampon out of my pocket. The blue writing on it said "Open This End," and a blue arrow. I tore away the paper at the arrow, to the shiny white cardboard with the string hanging out one end.

There was a drawing of the girl's hand with a Tampax tampon in her fingers, and I held my hand just that way, the Tampax tampon in my fingers, my pinkie finger sticking out. The inside fell out of the cardboard tube, the string stuck to the end of it like it was a tail. It was the real Tampax tampon. I picked it up by the tail and laid it on the mattress next to the piece of paper. The girl in the picture had long pointed fingers and fingernails. My fingers were round finger ends and lumpy knuckle skin.

I got my shoe box out and put the Tampax tampon parts inside and the piece of paper inside. I took out Tina Blue's ring and put it on my finger, first on my ring finger, then on my middle finger. It fit, slipping around just a little bit, Tina Blue's silver ring shiny dark on my middle finger. I stuck my pinkie finger out, curving it out to the side. The ring was heavy and cold.

I took my poem book out of my jacket pocket, Rod McKuen, and folded my jacket into a pillow. Lying on the mattress, looking up at the purple ceiling, not opening to a poem. I twisted Tina Blue's ring around on my finger. I closed my eyes, and I unzipped my blue jeans and put my hand in, down into my underpants, in between my legs, the cold of Tina Blue's ring on my legs, on my skin down there. I held in one breath and pushed my finger up inside. I closed my legs together on my hand, and curled over on my side, moved my finger around in there. My heart was beating on my finger in there.

I woke up to the white of moonlight coming in the tall window on to the mattress. The moon took up the piece of sky between the houses, perfectly white, almost round. I got the peacock cloth out of the bottom drawer and pulled it over me. The white moon made the peacock cloth silver and darker silver, made Tina Blue's ring shine black on my middle finger.

When I woke up again, it was morning and bird sounds outside. Birds in the backyard. Bluejays out front, and rain dripping down between the houses. I got up, wrapped in the peacock cloth, warm in the peacock cloth, and my knees stiff. Out in the hall I listened up the stairs, listened to no sounds at all except bluejays. The peacock cloth trailed behind me up the stairs like a princess robe.

Jimmy Henry's door stayed shut. I went in the kitchen, sat on the bench, pulled the peacock robe around me. I laid my hand on the table and looked close into the flowers of Tina Blue's ring. The flowers had turned blackish all the time the ring had been in my shoe box and, up close, was a smell on my fingers.

Jimmy Henry's door opened, and I tucked my hand with the ring under the peacock cloth. He came into the kitchen doorway and leaned there. He didn't have his shirt on, just his blue jeans. His hair was tangled, hanging long over his bare arms. The dark hair on his chest swirled in a design over the bones of his ribs. His blue jeans hung down on more bones.

I said, "Hi."

He said, "You're up early."

"Yeah," I said. "You, too."

He rubbed his arms, rubbed his face, rubbed his eyes, and he came over and sat across from me, leaning on his elbows. He looked out the window. His long hair had thin gray in it.

I said, "You need to brush your hair."

He said, "I need to brush my life."

He looked back in from the window, looked at me, and there was a smile there for a second. The rain sound was light raindrops blowing onto the glass, and the heavy drops dripping down from the roof, onto the skinny sidewalk between the houses.

His bare arms had gray every once in a while in all the dark hair there. The insides of his arms were soft, white-looking, no hairs. No scabs. He leaned back in his chair and folded his arms across his chest.

"Is Lady Jane here?" I said.

"No," Jimmy Henry said. "I haven't seen her for a while. Have you?"

The green apple teapot was on the counter. Dried brown stems stuck up, and the counter was messy with dark curls of petals.

"No," I said. "I guess not."

He shrugged his shoulders.

"She'll be back around," he said.

Then it was back to just the rain blowing on the window, and the wet dripping down. I tucked my hands deeper into the warm of the peacock cloth, and Tina Blue's ring slipped around on my finger. I took the ring off my finger and put it into my jacket pocket. Then I pushed the peacock cloth away and got out of the bench. I got the hairbrush from the bathroom and handed it to Jimmy Henry, and he took it, and looked, running his thumb over the bristles. He raised his arms and closed his eyes, brushing his hair back from his face. The long muscles of his arm moved round and smooth and the ribs under the white skin of his side moved, and I looked away from the long dark hair under his arms.

I turned around to the stove and took out a wooden match from the box there, turned on the gas, swiped a match on the side of the box and I saw

down to my zipper, still unzipped, a zipper-shaped triangle of white underpants. The match didn't light and it broke in half and I dropped the box and
matches spilled down bouncing and clicking all across the floor. I turned
off the gas and got down to pick up the matches and pull my T-shirt down
over my zipper, the matches all over the floor under the table by Jimmy
Henry's bare feet, long bare toes. I came up and banged the top of my head
on the table.

"Jesus," Jimmy Henry said.

"Here," he said, handing the hairbrush to me. "I'll get the stove. You
should brush your hair."

I took the hairbrush and went in my room and dropped the hairbrush
on my bed. I zipped my zipper and buttoned the button and I picked up
the hairbrush and brushed at my hair, hard fast brushing, pulling out knots,
then slower and slower until my breath came back slower and even and
smooth in my chest.

When I went back out, Jimmy Henry was looking in the cabinet. He
took out a jar of instant coffee, and he looked at me.

"Yes, please," I said.

When the coffee was done, two cups steaming, smelling up the kitchen,
Jimmy Henry took his cup and headed out of the kitchen.

I said, "Are you going back in your room?"

He stopped, turned around, looked at me.

"I have to get dressed," he said. "I told Lady Jane I'd fix her door. It won't
shut right, she said."

"Oh," I said. "Good."

He looked at me for a second.

"Yeah?" he said. "Good."

THE REFRIGERATOR box was lying sideways against a garage door in the
alley behind my house. We stood the box up, taller than me, taller than
Elle, one end cut off, and the other end said "This End Up." The box tipped
back over sideways.

"Cool," I said. "Let's put it on the front porch."

"Why?" Elle said.

"Grab that end," I said.

We dragged the box around front, onto the porch, and laid it on its side along the porch railing. I crawled in.

Elle said, "What are you doing?"

I laid down on my stomach and looked out the end of the box, at Elle's bare bony ankles.

"You have freckles on your ankles," I said, touching her big ankle bone. Her foot jumped.

"That tickles," she said.

She bent down and looked in at me.

"Why are you in there?" she said.

"This is a very cool box," I said. "Come on in."

Elle got down and scooted feet first, on her butt, in beside me.

"I can't believe I'm doing this," she said, sitting next to me in the box, her head bent down.

She worked her fingers into her pocket and took out a roll of cherry candies. I turned over on my back and looked up at the piece of blue sky and clouds and red porch roof. The clouds piled into each other. The porch roof looked like it was falling in the sky.

I said, "See how the porch roof looks like it's falling?"

Elle laid down on her stomach next to me and looked out the end of the box.

"No," she said.

"It's not really falling," I said. "It's an optical delusion."

"Whatever you say," she said, laying her head down.

Her breath tickled the hair at my neck. Birds sounds and car sounds, far away, and up close, Elle, crunching on cherry candies, making the refrigerator box smell like cherry candies instead of cardboard box smell.

She said, "It's almost the end of summer vacation."

"I know," I said. "I'm glad."

"You are?" she said.

She leaned up on her elbow and looked down at my face.

"Why?" she said.

"'Cause we'll be sixth-graders," I said. "I don't know, I'm just glad."

Elle said, "I hope we get Mr. Rivera this year."

"I don't know," I said. "I don't know about having a man teacher."

"He's Mexican," Elle said. "You like those Mexican boys."

"I liked Pete," I said. "I don't like those other boys. I don't like that Buddy."

"Did you want to kiss Pete?" Elle said.

"No," I said. "I don't want to kiss anyone."

"You never kissed anyone," she said. "How do you know you don't want to?"

She said, "Want me to show you how to kiss a boy?"

I said, "What do you know about kissing?"

"I know about kissing," Elle said.

"Look," she said. "Like this."

She put her hand on the side of my face. Her fingers were cool, and she leaned her face over me.

"Close your eyes," she said. "You're supposed to close your eyes."

"Girls aren't supposed to kiss girls," I said.

"I know," she said. "Pretend."

I said, "Pretend what?"

She said, "Sh."

Her orange hair fell down into my face, and I closed my eyes. There was cherry sweet smell, then Elle's cherry mouth taste on my mouth and her fingers tickling on my face, on my neck. Tickling inside where I couldn't breathe, so I laughed, and opened my eyes up at her, her hair all around us, her eyes that color, her freckles on her lips that color, her mouth cherry candy pink. Petunias and marigolds.

"It's easy," she whispered. "Kissing is easy."

She kissed my mouth again, and again, little cherry tastes on my lips and cool fingers on my neck, and then cool fingers on the bare skin of my stomach under my shirt.

"Do you like it?" she whispered.

I said, "No," whispering back, and Elle's wet cherry tongue came into the "no" of my mouth, and a soft hurting sound from her mouth, and the pressing hurt of her fingers at my blue jeans, pressing there, and all of her, pressing down, onto me, and no breath, no breath in my whole self.

I pushed her away and laughed, catching at my breath and laughing.

"You're not supposed to laugh," Elle said.

"I'm sorry," I said.

Laughing.

I said, "Do it again."

MR. RIVERA had long sideburns, and he kept his pencil behind one ear. His black hair curled over his collar in the back, over the collar of his white shirt he wore the first day, a white shirt with blue stripes, tiny thin stripes, long sleeves, tiny buttons at the cuff. After lunch, Mr. Rivera rolled up his cuffs. He wore a gold watch, and a gold ring on his finger.

In Mr. Rivera's class, we got to decide where we wanted to sit.

"Unless," he said. "Your choice proves to be a problem."

I chose my desk perfectly in the middle, middle row, halfway back. John Fitzgerald Kennedy Karpinski sat in the very back row by the window. That proved to be a problem. He flipped his pencil right out the window, and Mr. Rivera said, "Mr. Karpinski, let's move you a little closer."

Right behind me.

John Fitzgerald Kennedy Karpinski whispered, "Hey, Sarajean."

"Just shut up," I whispered back.

ELLE GOT Mrs. Zimmerman. It was the first time ever we weren't in the same class. We met outside on the steps of school to walk home.

"Shit," Elle said. "Not fair. I wanted Mr. Rivera."

"At least John Fitzgerald Kennedy Karpinski isn't in your class," I said. "He got Mr. Rivera too."

"Mrs. Zimmerman," Elle said, and she kicked at a paper cup blowing on the sidewalk.

"Mrs. Zimmerman's nice," I said. "She's the music teacher sometimes." Elle said, "Mr. Rivera's cute."

"Well," I said. "Yeah."

OUR FIRST homework was a report. Mr. Rivera said there wouldn't be any other homework this week except this one report. We had until Friday to write it, written in ink, cursive. "What I Want to Be When I Grow Up."

FROM THE corner of Seventeenth Avenue I saw Erico at the top of a tall ladder, and I ran the whole block of the sidewalk and across Clarkson, but Erico was not painting a new sunface, he was fixing the sign. He scraped at the corner of where it said SOMEONE'S BELOVED THREADS, peeling curls of wood off the bottom edge so he could hammer there and the sign wouldn't bang in the wind anymore.

"Erico," I said.

"Yes," Erico said, not looking down.

"Erico," I said. "I thought you were painting a new sunface. When are you going to do that? It's almost gone off there."

A thin curl of sign wood caught on the leaf of a marigold tall in the back row.

"Erico," I said. "A marigold bracelet."

The marigold bracelet was perfectly curled, some color of white.

"Erico," I said. "What are you?"

He stopped scraping and looked down at me.

"What is that you say?" he said.

"You," I said. "What are you?"

I sat on the edge of the flower box.

"My father was from Oaxaca," he said. "So in Mexico City I was Oaxacan. Here in Denver, I am Mexican."

"No, like your job," I said. "You know, school teacher or mechanic. What's the name of your job."

Erico put his scraper in his back pocket of his tool belt and he took a folded-up square of sandpaper from his other pocket and he sanded at the bottom edge, making wood dust glitter in the air, and dust down on the marigolds and petunias.

"Hey," I said. "You're getting the marigolds and petunias all dirty."

He kept sanding.

"So," I said. "Are you a carpenter?"

"Yes," he said. "And as soon as I finish this being a carpenter I am going over to Mrs. Tilson's and become a plumber."

He hammered some more, and when he stopped hammering I said, "Erico, if you paint a new sunface you are a painter, too."

Erico started hammering again, and I ducked under the ladder and went into the shop.

Constanzia sat in her chair next to a tangled pile of blue jeans. She had her tape measure, and she measured how long one blue jeans leg was. Then she took her pen that hung around her neck on a chain and she wrote the number of inches on a little square of paper. She put the paper into the back pocket of the blue jeans and then folded the blue jeans over the arm of the chair.

She was humming a song. She looked up when I came in, humming a little louder to me, and then she looked back down to measuring blue jeans.

"Hi," I said. "First day of school. I got Mr. Rivera."

Constanzia looked up again and nodded her head. She stopped humming and she said, "This is your sixth-grade teacher, Mr. Rivera?"

"He's Mexican," I said.

Constanzia said, "You can practice your Spanish for him."

"No," I said. "He just speaks English, like American, no accent."

Constanzia said, "You let him know you know some of his language."

"But he isn't Mexican," I said. "Not like you. He just talks like he's from Denver."

Constanzia said, "We all came from somewhere else."

"What about me?" I said. "I'm not from anywhere. I'm from Denver."

Constanzia nodded her head.

"And your papa?" she said. "And your papa's people?"

"Well," I said. "He gave us this report, Mr. Rivera did. 'What I Want to Be When I Grow Up.' You're a shopkeeper?"

Constanzia started humming again, pulling a pair of blue jeans onto her lap.

"A tailor," I said.

She nodded her head.

I moved along the counter, putting my fingers into the shoe box lid filled with broken beaded necklaces and bits of gold chain and silver chain. Three boxes of sweaters were on the floor at the end of the counter, all different colors of sweaters folded up into each box, one box marked small, then medium, the large. On top of the large was a black stiff scratchy sweater.

"Mother," Constanzia said.

"Mother?" I said.

Constanzia said, "Shopkeeper. Tailor. Mother."

It was a pullover sweater. When I held the sweater up against me it went down to my knees.

"No," I said. "I think he means like your job."

The sleeves went down to my knees, too. The price of the sweater was two dollars. I put two dollars in the money drawer.

"It would be cool to be a teacher," I said. "Or an airplane pilot. I don't know too many things to be."

The sweater smelled old, like it had been somewhere else for a long time.

"Or a shopkeeper," I said. "Or waitress. Lady Jane is a waitress."

I folded up the black sweater.

"I guess I'll go," I said. "'Bye."

"Adios," Constanzia said. Goodbye.

THE NEXT day Mr. Rivera said, "Who has started on their report?"

Three girls raised their hands in the front row. I looked around at other kids looking around. John Fitzgerald Kennedy Karpinski said, "Hey, Sarajean, what are you going to be for your report?"

"I don't know," I said. "Sh."

"I'm going to be an astronaut," he said. "Or president. Ha ha."

"ELLE," I said. "What are you going to be when you grow up?"

Elle said, "Make clothes. I make great outfits."

"Tailor?" I said.

"Fashion designer," Elle said. "Say fashion designer."

"Do you have to go to college for that?" I said.

"Maybe," Elle said. "I might go to college. Margo went to college."

"Maybe I should go to college," I said. "I have to decide by Thursday night."

"I thought it wasn't due until Friday," Elle said. "Just say teacher."

I said, "I don't know about teacher."

"Just say teacher," Elle said. "He'll like that."

JIMMY HENRY was leaning on the kitchen table. He was drinking a beer, and he seemed like in a pretty good mood.

"Jimmy Henry?" I said, trying to make my voice like usual. "I have to ask you something."

"Oh," he said, looking at me, then looking out the kitchen window, his hair falling down into his eyes. He sat down at the table and he took out his cigarettes and he lit one.

"Okay," he said.

I said, "Did you go to college?"

Jimmy Henry said, "What?"

"College," I said. "I have to decide if I'm going to college. Did you?"

Jimmy Henry let out his breath in a long cloud of smoke.

"Yeah," he said. "I went to college."

"For what?" I said.

Jimmy Henry said, "For what?"

"Like teacher or what?" I said.

"Oh," he said. "For what. Not for anything. History, sort of, but I never finished. When I got out of the army I never finished."

"Finished?" I said.

"Degree," he said. "I never got a degree."

He said, "You like school. You should go to college."

"For what?" I said.

"Oh, that doesn't matter," he said. "You can pretty much decide when you get there."

I said, "I have to decide by Thursday night."

Jimmy Henry said, "Thursday night?"

"For my report," I said. "It's due Friday. Did you go to Denver University?"

"Iowa," Jimmy Henry said. "Simpson College. Indianola, Iowa.

"Oh," I said. "Okay."

Jimmy Henry got up, and before he could go away from the table I said quick, "Is that where your people are?"

I picked at the blue paint on the table where old wood showed through in the shape of a bird that was flying. I picked at the bird wing until it came apart into not a bird wing, and Jimmy Henry sat back down. He leaned on his elbow on the table and he picked at a long string coming out of the sleeve of his tie-dye T-shirt and he looked out the dirty kitchen window.

"No," he said. "They used to be. I don't think there's anyone there anymore."

"Where did they go?" I said. "Like your mom and dad?"

"My mom died," he said. "When I was a kid. My dad got married again. A couple times."

"Your mom died?" I said.

"Long time ago," he said.

He said, "I never lived in Indianola too much, just when I was little. When my mom got sick I lived for a long time with my aunt. Aunt Betsy. In Nebraska. And my grandma."

I said, "How old were you when your mom died?"

My voice was small, and Jimmy Henry was looking faraway out the window, to the wall of the house next door.

"Thirteen," he said.

"What was her name?" I said.

"Marie," he said. "Marie Anthony Henry."

I said, "What happened to your dad?"

"Nothing," he said. "They were divorced. I don't really remember him. I think he moved to Florida."

"Oh," I said.

It was quiet, and Jimmy Henry smoked, quiet.

"Indianola, Iowa?" I said.

"Yeah," he said. "It was a cool place to be a kid. Farms and all. Fields."

I said, "Did you live on a farm?"

"No," he said. "I think my dad sold insurance."

I said, "What about your grandma? And your Aunt Betsy?"

Jimmy Henry said, "They were old ladies when I was little. They died a long time ago. They're buried in Indianola. For some reason they all go back there to get buried. Rookery Bend."

I said, "Rookery Bend?"

"Rookery Bend Cemetery," he said.

He said, "Just some place on Earth they all go back to."

"Her, too?" I said. "Your mom?"

He said, "All the Henrys."

He sat there and looked out the dirty window. His hair was hanging down in his face.

☮

"ROOKERY: THE nests or breeding grounds of a colony of rooks"; "a crowded or dilapidated tenement or group of dwellings; a place teeming with like individuals."

"Rook: a common Old World bird"; "to defraud by cheating or swindling."

WE SAT on the metal steps in the alley. Elle had a cigarette. I had an apple. Elle hung her feet over the railing and bonged her cowboy boots on the metal steps.

"He didn't have a mom," I said. "His mom died when he was thirteen. Indianola, Iowa. It's all farms and fields."

"Jimmy Henry was a farmer?" Elle said.

"That's where they're are from," I said. "Constanzia said 'my people.' Well, she said 'your papa's people.' You know, like she says stuff."

"Jimmy Henry lived on a farm?" Elle said.

"No," I said. "His dad was an insurance guy. They don't live there anymore. But that's where they're all buried."

"All in the same place?" Elle said. "In like a big cemetery? Like with a big gravestone? Cool."

"Yeah," I said. "Rookery Bend Cemetery. It's a place on Earth they all go back to. That's like he said it, like that."

"Your mother's family too?" she said.

"No," I said. "I don't think so. He said like his grandma and his Aunt Betsy."

"Why don't you ask him," Elle said. "Say, 'Where is my mother's side of the family?' Just say it like that."

I said, "I don't think he knows."

"You're just afraid to ask him," she said. "I don't see why you're afraid to ask him."

"He doesn't like it when I ask him stuff," I said.

"So what?" she said.

I said, "So I don't want him to go back in his room all the time, that's so what."

My apple had a brown spot. I couldn't decide whether to eat around the brown spot or throw the apple across the alley.

I said, "What will you give me if I get this apple in that Dumpster from here?"

Elle looked at the Dumpster.

"Quarter," she said.

The apple splattered onto the brick wall above the open top of the dumpster.

"Part of it probably went in," I said.

"Doesn't count," Elle said.

"It should be worth at least a dime," I said.

"Doesn't count," she said.

COOKING SMELL filled up the stairway.

"Hey," I said.

Lady Jane was in the kitchen. Her hair was all under a paisley scarf that tied around to the back of her neck.

"Hey, yourself," she said.

I said, "What are you cooking?"

"Oatmeal cookies," she said.

"Oatmeal cookies?" I said. "Without raisins, I hope."

Lady Jane looked up from the mess she was stirring in a bowl.

She said, "You don't like raisins?"

"Yuk," I said.

"Well," she said. "The next batch can be without raisins. Do you like walnuts?"

"Yeah," I said. "I don't care about walnuts."

Jimmy Henry's bedroom door was open, and the curtains in there were pulled back, the sun coming in. The bed blankets were laid out neat, and Lady Jane's sweater hung from the doorknob. I took the sweater and laid it on the arm of the couch and shut the bedroom door.

Lady Jane hollered from the kitchen.

"Why don't you put on another album?" she said.

It was quiet, except for her banging around in there, yelling like I was all the way outside instead of right in the front room.

I said, "Where's Jimmy Henry?"

"Well," Lady Jane said. "I'm not sure. I think he went to see about a job. Maybe."

I said, "When will those cookies be ready?"

"Twelve minutes," she said, looking at the wrapper from the bag of walnuts.

The newspaper was folded up on the chair by the door. There was a stack of books on the applebox table. The top book said *Steppenwolf*. Inside the front cover it said "Tina Blue."

"Hey," I said. "This book is from the box."

Lady Jane came to the doorway

"I know," she said, wiping her hands on a towel. "We were looking for an address."

"Who?" I said. "You and Jimmy Henry?"

"Yeah," she said. "There wasn't any."

"Was Tina Blue your friend?" I said.

Lady Jane sat down on the arm of the couch, on her sweater.

"She wasn't anybody's friend really," she said. "Just Jimmy Henry's. She stayed by herself mostly. She used to take off for a while, just disappear, but she always came back after a while. A couple months. It just got longer and longer. She used to write every once in a while."

She slid down onto the couch, looking at nothing.

"That last time, she was going to stay, I know she was," she said. "She'd been gone, God, a year, maybe longer. She fixed that place all up downstairs."

She leaned her head back, her eyes all spaced out. Blue eyes, same blue like the paisley scarf.

"She was beautiful when she had it together," she said.

"Hey," I said. "Cookies."

Lady Jane said, "Shit," and jumped up off the couch.

The cookies were black around the edges.

"This oven cooks pretty hot," she said. "The next batch will be done pretty quick."

"I'll be out front," I said.

The burnt cookies smell came all the way out to the front porch. I picked at the peeling paint on the porch railing. It was gray under the red. Back when it was someone else's house, it was gray.

A black pickup truck with rusty red doors drove up and stopped at the curb, squeaking. Jimmy Henry got out of the driver side and slammed the door. He slammed it again.

"Hey," I said. "Where'd you get the truck?"

"Far out, huh?" he said, coming around the front end, up onto the sidewalk. He looked at the truck.

"Is it yours?" I said.

"Yep," he said. "Four hundred bucks."

"Wow," I said. "Why did you get a truck?"

"Work," Jimmy Henry said.

"Work?" I said. "You got a job?"

"Kind of," he said.

"Kind of a job?" I said. "What kind of a job? Driving this truck?"

"Kind of," he said. "Doing some work for some guys, working on some houses out in Aurora."

Lady Jane came out onto the front porch. Her hair was brushed down out of the paisley scarf and she had a white smear of flour on her face, and all over the front of her shirt.

"A truck," I said, and I opened the door at the curb to look in.

She said, "Did you get the job?"

"Yep," Jimmy Henry said.

She came down the sidewalk.

"Did they give you a truck?" she said, looking in the door at the curb, looking at the dusty brown seat of the truck.

"Nope," he said, "Bought it."

She said, "Far out."

I said, "Can we go for a ride?"

Lady Jane said, "I have cookies in the oven."

Jimmy Henry said, "You're making cookies?"

"No raisins," I said.

Jimmy Henry said, "Oh, well, that's a relief."

He kissed Lady Jane on her cheek, and got white flour on his nose. Lady Jane wiped the end of his nose with her finger, and then she kissed him on his mouth.

"Watch out," I said, and they had to get out of the way so I could slam the door, hard.

Lady Jane said, "I better check those cookies."

She ran into the house, and Jimmy Henry watched her. I looked over the side, into the back of the truck, leaves and dirt blown into the corners.

"Can I ride back here?" I said.

"Yeah," Jimmy Henry said, not looking. "Guess so."

"When?" I said. "Now?"

"Well," he said. "It's not quite legal yet. Tomorrow I'll get plates. What kind of cookies are they, besides not raisin?"

"Oatmeal," I said.

I NAMED the truck Blackbird, and the next Saturday Jimmy Henry and I went for a ride.

He said, "I have to take some cans of paint out to these guys."

He had a key on a twisted piece of wire, and he stuck it in and stomped on the pedals on the floor. Blackbird started up loud and filled with gas smell. We jerked forward, jerked again, and then we were driving on Ogden Street, making a lot of noise, Jimmy Henry stomping at the pedals and jerking on the handles and steering.

After a while he drove better, not so bumpy. We drove on Ogden Street to Colfax Street, and then we drove on Colfax Street with cars and buses and other trucks. Colfax Street went on until the stores and restaurants and little places were bigger places in the middle of parking lots. Colfax Street got wide and four lanes all the way across. Jimmy Henry steered with one hand on the steering wheel and his other arm stretched across the back of the seat, stretched across as far as me. He grabbed my hair and tugged. He did that a couple times, just driving Blackbird along Colfax Street out to Aurora.

Aurora was away from the Rocky Mountains, out where there was nothing past it, out where Colfax Street turned into being a highway. We turned off the highway, and Jimmy Henry shifted and stomped and slowed down to stopping to wait for our turn to get on another road. Quiet caught up to us. The dried yellow weeds clumped around the Stop sign and lacy black dead flowers blew from the wind.

"Dead flowers," I said.

Jimmy Henry leaned over and looked out my window.

"Yeah," he said. "Nice."

"No sidewalks," I said.

Jimmy Henry looked out my window again.

"Yeah," he said. "No sidewalks."

A sign said CHAPARRAL PRAIRIE ESTATES and we turned into an empty street there. It was a perfectly empty street. A brand new empty street that went straight out into a field of dirt, and made a corner there, and went on for a way through the dirt in another direction. Along one side of the street there were some neat stacks of wood lined up by square cement holes.

I said, "What's Chaparral?"

Jimmy Henry said, "I think it's some kind of weed that grows up in the mountains."

I said, "Are they going to fill this street up with houses?"

Jimmy Henry said, "I think that's the plan."

"Then what about the rest of this field?" I said.

"Probably," Jimmy Henry said. "Sooner or later."

He drove along the empty street partway down and then stopped. Blackbird jumped when we stopped.

"Wait here," he said, and he got out and slammed the door.

He took two big cans out of the back of the truck and carried them over to a stack of wood and some stuff piled up there. Two guys were sitting by the stack of wood. They were smoking cigarettes and one guy had a can of pop. Jimmy Henry set down the cans of paint and took out his cigarettes.

I laid down across the front seat and put my feet out the window, black hightops and blue sky with no clouds. There was the smell of gas and cigarettes and the dusty seat. Up in the sky, between my hightops, a bird floated in a wide circle.

I sat up and Jimmy Henry was still talking to the guys. He handed his cigarette to one of the guys, who smoked it and gave it to the other guy.

Out where the new empty street ended the brown field took off and went as far as the brown cloud that faded up into the sky, a brown cloud that went along the ground way out. Way out on the horizon. There was a single bird sound from far away.

Jimmy Henry came back across the dirt and got in.

I said, "There's a brown cloud on the horizon."

He said, "Huh?"

"Horizon," I said. "Brown cloud."

He looked out the window.

"Haze," he said. "It's dusty out here."

"Why are they going to build houses here?" I said. "There's nothing here."

"I guess that's why," Jimmy Henry said,

I said, "What's why?"

"I guess they're going to put stuff here," he said. "To go with the houses."

"Like stores and stuff?" I said.

He started up Blackbird's engine and we sat there bumping.

"Are those guys your friends?" I said.

"Just some guys," he said.

"Well," I said. "What are they going to paint?"

He said, "Huh?"

"There's nothing out here to paint," I said.

"Numbers," Jimmy Henry said. "On the curbs. Every hole gets a number."

I said, "Every hole gets a number?"

Jimmy Henry shrugged his shoulders.

We went back on the same highway, back toward where Denver was the tall buildings poking up out of the dark cloud.

"No mountains," I said.

"Haze," Jimmy Henry said.

I said, "Is it still a horizon if it's mountains?"

Jimmy Henry looked at me and he said, "I guess."

I said, "Let's just keep on driving and drive up there."

"Next weekend maybe," he said.

"Just us?" I said. "Or us and Lady Jane?"

"Maybe Lady Jane, too," he said.

"She probably has to work," I said.

LADY JANE didn't have to work. We all three got in Blackbird on Saturday morning.

I said, "I get to sit by the window."

Lady Jane sat in the middle, between me and Jimmy Henry, and the smell of her, her herbal musk oil from the little brown bottle, mixed in with the gas, the dust, the cigarette smell.

The mountains were flat against the sky. Jimmy Henry drove up the road that curved into the brown hills, toward blue pine trees filling up the hill-sides farther up. We drove slow, my ears popped, and the blue-gray mountaintops appeared and disappeared between the brown hills. Blackbird went slower and slower up the road, until Jimmy Henry turned into a gravel wide spot and stopped, and I got out.

The air was cold and the wind came from far away in the sky. The jagged blue mountaintops were still high and flat against the sky. From the fence at the edge of the gravel the hillside went down steep in a spilled mess of broken rock. Lady Jane came crunching across the gravel and leaned on the fence next to me, and she looked down at Denver, way down below. Denver spread away from downtown, out into the flat haze horizon.

I said, "It looks like a scab."

"It is a scab," she said. "A festering wound."

"Festering?" I said.

"Nasty," Lady Jane said. "Cities. Wouldn't you love to live up here?"

The hillside across the road was more steep fallen rock.

"There's nothing here," I said.

Lady Jane said, "It's so quiet."

"It's quiet 'cause there's nothing here to make any noise," I said.

She said, "I'd love to live out of the city. Maybe someday soon."

"Where?" I said. "Like here?"

"Some little town," she said, staring out, all spacey eyed. "In the mountains, or by the ocean. I'd have a dog and a fireplace."

"A dog?" I said. "What kind of dog?"

"An Irish setter," she said. "I'd name him Boo."

I said, "Boo?"

"Boo," she said. "Corn muffin?"

I said, "What?"

"Do you want a corn muffin?" she said. "I made some corn muffins."

We went back to Blackbird, and Lady Jane and Jimmy Henry sat inside and ate corn muffins, her scooted all the way over next to him, and I ate my crumbly pieces of corn muffin sitting on the side of the back, my legs hanging over.

Nothing but rocks.

When it was time to go, Jimmy Henry said we had to go back down.

"This old thing had to crawl to get this far," he said.

I stayed in the back riding back down the road. I tucked down in out of the wind, under the window. The wind blew at me anyway, blew dirt up into my face from the back of the truck, and in my mouth. Behind us, and above us, the mountains slid by in the sky.

THE OTHER sixth-grade girls sat at the other end of the bleachers. They practiced singing songs and putting on makeup.

"Weird," Elle said. "Singing songs."

"Why?" I said. "They know all the words."

"Those girls are weird," Elle said.

Mr. Rivera played basketball during lunch. He rolled up his cuffs of his shirt and he put on white sneakers and a whistle. Sometimes his shirt came untucked out of his pants, and sometimes he undid his tie at the top and dark curly hair showed. He waved his arms for signals, and his shirt was wet from sweat under his arms.

Back in class, Mr. Rivera would be changed back into his brown shoes and his tie back the right way, and his hair damp and curly around his face. He had a sweaty smell that mixed in with soap smell from his white shirt.

After school we went to my house first, to see if Blackbird was there, to sit in the back, parked at the curb. We sat up on the side of the back, hanging our feet over the edge, or we sat down in the back and had cigarettes, until it was too cold to stay outside.

We were sitting in the back when Lady Jane came walking on the sidewalk in her clogs, and we got down to where she couldn't see us. She went up to the front door and let herself in with her own key.

"Looks like dinner tonight," Elle said.

"I don't know," I said. "She didn't have a grocery sack."

Elle said, "Maybe she's just going to go get in bed with Jimmy Henry for a while."

I said, "Is that all you ever think about?"

"No," Elle said. "Do you ever hear them?"

"No," I said. "Shut up."

Elle scrunched over next to me, and the wind got at us, cold wind, cold metal smell.

"Snow," I said.

"What do you want to do?" Elle said.

"Homework," I said. "I have homework."

She said, "Come over my house to do your homework."

I said, "I'm not doing your book report for *Banks of Plum Creek*."

"Why not?" Elle said. "You read it already."

"I'll tell you what it was about," I said. "But I'm not writing your whole book report."

"Just write what it was about then," she said.

I said, "They got completely buried in the snow, even their house."

"Good," Elle said. "Write that."

"You write that," I said. "Didn't you read it at all?"

"I think I read part of it," she said.

I said, "When is it due?"

"Day after tomorrow," she said. "No, day after that."

"Well, just read it," I said. "I don't even know for sure if I read that same one. There's a whole bunch of those books. They just kept moving around and all, different houses."

"Come on," she said. "Just come over."

The sky was dark clouds down low, early night, and squares of yellow light coming on in houses. My house stayed dark. Jimmy Henry's windows, two windows across the front upstairs, stayed dark.

I said, "Just a second."

Around the side of the house, on the skinny sidewalk, I could see up to our front-room window, our kitchen window. Dark.

I went back out front. Elle was down in the corner, trying to light a cigarette, and the wind kept blowing out her matches.

I said, "Let's go over your house."

Nobody was home at Elle's new apartment, but lights were on.

"Cassandra Wiggins," Elle said. "She always leaves the lights on."

"When she goes to bed, she leaves the lights on?" I said.

"The little lights, like that one by the couch," Elle said.

In the kitchen, Elle opened the refrigerator and stood there, looking in. I sat on the green chair with the blue velvet cushion. Elle slammed the refrigerator door and opened a cabinet door.

"Do you have a jar of coffee?" I said. "We could make coffee."

"I hate coffee," she said.

She sat on the couch, next to the little lamp. The lamp had a little white lampshade.

"Hey," I said. "Go get a scarf. Do you have a paisley scarf?"

"Maybe," she said.

She went in her room, and when she came back she had a square of paisley scarf, big paisleys that looped in together with pink and gold and purple. I draped the paisley scarf over the white lampshade, and the pink and gold and purple paisleys lit up from inside, lit up the front room pink.

"Brilliant," Elle said.

I said, "The quality of the light is the quality of the dark."

"Is that a poem?" Elle said.

"I think so," I said. "Those are my favorite kind of paisleys."

Elle said, "What, purple and pink?"

"No," I said. "Those big swirly ones that go all together. I hate those little ones that are just all by themselves in rows."

The Who's Next faces looked into the front-room window, and the heater under the window clanked on and hissed. I pushed my sleeves of my black sweater up over my elbows.

Elle said, "That sweater stinks."

I said, "This sweater is wool."

She said, "Smells like cat if you ask me."

I said, "This is a very cool sweater."

Elle pulled off her cowboy boots and dropped them on the floor, one boot, then the other boot.

She said, "I'll show you what's cool."

She went in her room and turned on the light in there. The light from her bedroom doorway made the pink light in the front room plain and hard.

I said, "Turn off that light."

When Elle turned off the bedroom light and came back out, she had on a long silky robe with big sleeves, orange and red and Chinese letters, and a wide white sash.

"It's a kimono," she said. "It's silk."

She swirled around, and the bottom of the kimono swished on the bare wood floor. I touched one long sleeve, soft cold silk.

"Where did you get it?" I said.

"Sasha," Elle said.

"She gave it to you?" I said.

"No," Elle said. She danced in her bare feet, danced into the middle of the floor and bowed to me. The colors of the kimono changed in the pink paisley light.

"Silk," I said. Saying it was like breathing.

Elle said, "Come here."

I followed her into the other bedroom, the big bedroom, and she turned on the light at the switch and went to one of Margo's boxes. She pulled out a thin white dress. The dress had little ribbon straps, and a long ribbon on the front, between gathers of silk.

"It's a nightgown," Elle said. "Put it on."

She danced away, out into the front room.

I took off my black sweater, my hair snapping up from static, took off my hightops and my socks and my blue jeans and stood on the bare floor. I put the white silk over my head, and it dropped cold onto my bare skin. I touched the front of me, down the silk, the front of my legs, and goose-bumps rushed all over me from cold and silk.

Elle was still dancing around in the front room, and when I went out there she said, "I can see your underpants."

And she said, "Dance."

I made a little circle, holding the lacy bottom edge out, lace tickling my ankles. Elle danced in a circle around me, the kimono sleeves flying out like angel wings.

"Sing," she said.

"Sing what?" I said.

"Don't you know a dancing song?" she said. "Dance like a ballerina. And sing."

I dropped the lacy edge to the floor and raised my arms and I sang,

> "Lavender blue, dilly dilly,
> Lavender green,
> When I am king, dilly dilly,
> You shall be queen.
> Who told you so, dilly dilly,
> Who told you so?
> 'Twas my own heart, dilly dilly,
> That told me so."

I sang the words over again, trying not to laugh, laughing anyway, and we danced around the front room, around the couch and out into the middle of the floor, bowing and sweeping long silk, dancing up on bare pointed toes, around the paisley lamp and under the glass doors of the bookshelves that flashed pink lamplight from their jeweled edges.

When I stopped singing the song, Elle fell onto the couch, and I jumped up onto the couch next to her and sat down slow, white silk spreading out around me like a flower turned over. My toes under the flower were warm on my bare legs, and the red couch stuff was scratchy.

"What a weird song," Elle said. "Where'd you get that song?"

"It's an English folk song," I said. "Mr. Rivera taught it to us."

"He sang it to you?" she said, sitting up and pulling her hair back off her neck, away from her face. Her neck was bare, and pink from the pink light, and her face was pink.

"He likes to sing," I said, "He sings, like, that song, and songs from history."

"I saw Mr. Rivera in his car at the Safeway," Elle said. "He was with his wife."

"When?" I said. "What does his wife look like?"

"She had long black hair that was curly, and a red ruffly shirt," Elle said. "She has big boobs."

"You're lying," I said. "You didn't see them."

Elle wiggled down into the cushions next to me.

She said, "They were kissing, and he put his hand inside her shirt."

I said, "You liar."

"Really," she said. "Here. He did just like this."

She pushed me back against the scratchy back of the couch and she kissed me on my mouth, laughing, then not laughing, and she touched her hand on my chest. Her fingers touched through the gathers of silk, touching me, touching me on my nipple, like touching inside my stomach, and I pushed her away.

"Liar," I said, and I laughed, trying not to laugh.

"You always laugh," Elle said. "Quit laughing."

She put her hand on my face and kissed again on my mouth and she whispered, "Close your eyes and don't laugh."

She kissed me on my neck, and on my shoulder, and when she kissed me soft at the bottom of my throat I couldn't help it, couldn't help laughing.

The door at the bottom of the stairway opened, and we both jumped up. Elle ran across the bare floor to her bedroom, and I grabbed the pink paisley scarf off the lamp and ran after her, into the bedroom, and she shut the bedroom door. She turned on the bedroom light switch.

Margo said, "Lalena? Are you home?"

"We're in here," Elle said loud through the door. "We're in here doing homework.

She was trying not to laugh.

"And besides it's Elle, damn it," she said. "My name is Elle."

"My clothes," I whispered. "My clothes are in her room."

We stood still and listened at the door, Elle listening to Margo, no cowboy boots, no Cassandra Wiggins, just Margo. I listened to Elle, to her breathing. Wispy orange curls behind her ears and damp on her neck. Margo went into the kitchen, and Elle opened the door a crack and then went through the crack. I draped the pink paisley scarf over the doorknob. Elle came back holding my blue jeans and my black sweater, my hightops and my socks.

I pulled the ribbon straps off, and the silk nightgown dropped to the floor around me. I stepped out of the circle of silk and picked the nightgown up and laid it on the mattress.

Elle said, "You're going to need a bra before me."

I held my hands up over my chest, one warm hand flat over each cold nipple bump.

"No, I'm not," I said. "They haven't even started yet."

Elle said, "Mine are."

She pulled at the top of the kimono and looked down in at herself.

"You can barely tell," I said. "Maybe a little."

I pulled my sweater on over my head, and I sat down on the mattress and pulled on my blue jeans. I didn't want to put my clothes back on. I wanted to dance around in the silk nightgown. I wanted to wear the silk nightgown with the kimono over it. I wanted to eat a candy bar and be by myself in Elle's new apartment with the pink paisley lights and look at Cassandra Wiggins's books. I wanted it to start snowing so much there would be no school tomorrow. I wanted a red ruffly shirt.

Margo said, "Do you guys want some rice and tomatoes?"

"No," Elle said through the door. "Sarajean's doing my book report for me."

"I am not," I whispered.

Margo said, "That's very giving of Sarajean, but you should do your own homework, Lalena."

"It's Elle, damn it," Elle said. "My name is Elle."

1976

The first day of junior high was assembly, and all the kids sat in the bleachers to hear Mr. Withers give a speech. Mr. Withers was the principal of Mountain View Junior High School.

"Americans," Mr. Withers said. "You are here to become strong Americans, to guide us through our next two hundred years."

"Yeah, yeah," Elle whispered. "He looks about two hundred years old."

I said, "Sh."

Mr. Withers told us who other people were, Mr. Sherett, who was the dean of the boys, and Miss Purcell, who was the dean of the girls. When he said their names, Mr. Sherett and Miss Purcell stood up from their seats on the bottom bleacher so we could see who they were. Miss Purcell was an old lady, with hair curled up tight, and red lips.

Elle whispered, "Those are the biggest boobs I ever saw."

I said, "Sh."

They took up the whole front of Miss Purcell's blouse.

Elle and I had the same homeroom, Hand, Henry, alphabetical, but we didn't get to be locker partners. My locker partner was a girl named Marcia Henson. Marcia Henson wore a light blue skirt and light blue sweater on the first day of school, and she said, "You better not keep any of your drugs in this locker."

I said, "Drugs?"

Marcia Henson said, "I plan on joining Young Americans for Freedom, and we don't believe in drugs and peace and all that hippie stuff."

Marcia Henson's little square-toed shoes were blue too.

The cafeteria was different stuff everyday for sixty-five cents, out of big square pans, goulash or shepherd's pie or macaroni and cheese, and big soggy biscuits soaked yellow in margarine. The Mexican cafeteria ladies scooped stuff out onto a plate and handed the plate across the counter. They wore hairnets and just talked to each other.

The door of the gym was right across from the cafeteria, and there would be Mexican boys standing around there. I saw Pete there. His hair was long again, and he wasn't any bigger, he was smallest of all the Mexican boys standing around there. His face was bigger maybe, maybe just his nose was bigger.

There were lots of Mexican kids in junior high. The Mexican boys stood around together, and there were Afro kids who stood around together. The white kids were just kind of everywhere else. The Mexican girls liked to hang out in the second-floor bathroom during lunch, right by my home room. They smoked cigarettes in there, and sprayed hair spray.

The Mexican girls had long black beautiful hair. Some of the Mexican girls wore corduroy pants, tight, different colors, and some had short tight skirts and nylons.

One Mexican girl in the bathroom had a run in her nylon, and she put nail polish on there. She put a dot of pink nail polish at the top of the run, bending backward, dotting the nail polish on the curve of her leg below her knee. A tiny dot. She straightened up and she put the tall gold cap back on the bottle of nail polish, and she said to me, "What are you looking at?"

"Nothing," I said.

ELLE LOOKED close into the mirror in her bathroom and painted a long swoopy line of black across each of her eyelids.

"I don't know," I said. "It looks kind of weird."

Blondish reddish eyelashes stuck out from under each black swoop.

"You're right," she said. "I need black mascara."

I TOOK Tina Blue's silver ring to school every day, taking the ring out of my inside jacket pocket on my way down the stairs, wearing it on my middle finger on the way to school, putting it back in my pocket before I got there, before I saw Elle. I wore my blue jeans and a different colored T-shirt and my green corduroy jacket, and black hightops, and no bra. I didn't have a bra. I didn't want a bra.

There were special blue and white sweatshirts that said HORNETS on the front. The Hornets were the football team. The sweatshirt had a cartoon drawing of a mean-faced hornet wearing a football helmet. Everyone who wore a Hornets sweatshirt to school on Thursdays got off fifth-hour study hall to go to the gym, and yell rhyming cheers with the cheerleaders, who wore blue pleated skirts with white in the pleats. Blue and white were the school colors. I didn't have a Hornets sweatshirt. I didn't want a Hornet sweatshirt. I liked fifth-hour study hall.

The only other class I liked was English, Mrs. MacVey, third floor, third hour. Mrs. MacVey dressed weird, not straight, not like a teacher, not like anybody I ever saw before. She wore full skirts, not A-line, not pleated, and bowling shirts with different names embroidered over the pocket. The first time Mrs. MacVey wore a bowling shirt, it was a yellow bowling shirt that said JOSIE over the pocket. The next time she wore a bowling shirt, it was a blue bowling shirt that said FRANCIE.

Mrs. MacVey said, "I don't like bowling, but I love bowling shirts."

She hung her little sweaters on her shoulders, and the ninth-grade kids called her Mac.

I always sat toward the back of Mrs. MacVey's class. When Mrs. MacVey looked around for someone to call on, I hid behind the head of whatever kid was sitting in front of me.

Mrs. MacVey said things like "allegory," "satire," "the richness of the imagination."

She assigned us *The Hobbit* to read, so I went to Together Books after school. I bought a used copy, with a bent cover and "Bobby" written inside, in square printed letters, and a pencil drawing of a curvy knife with a fancy decorated handle. I didn't know who any Bobby was, but he was good at drawing, and he didn't wreck his book very much, except for bending the cover, and not even very much. It cost twenty-five cents.

I took *The Hobbit* home in my inside jacket pocket. Blackbird wasn't there. I went into the painted apartment and folded up my jacket for a pillow on the mattress. I was up to page 81 when the back door rattled and clicked, and then it opened and there was Pete.

"Hey," I said, and then I didn't know what to say.

"Hi," I said.

Pete leaned in the doorway, and I sat up, and started to stand up, but then I just sat on the edge of the mattress.

"I saw you at school," I said. "You go to Mountain View Junior High."

Pete said, "You in seventh?"

"Yeah," I said. "Seventh grade."

He came in and leaned against the wall by the little dresser.

"I have to read this book for English," I said. "Mrs. MacVey."

I said, "You in ninth?"

"Yeah," he said. "Again. Half a year. I got to make up some stuff. I missed a bunch of school in Tucson."

His voice was scratchy.

He said, "Anybody home upstairs?"

I said, "No."

Pete came over and sat on the mattress. He took out a pack of Kools and he shook out a yellow cigarette that was a joint, twisted in yellow joint paper.

I said, "Is that a joint?"

"Yeah," Pete said. "Want to get high?"

"No," I said. "I don't know."

He held the joint in his teeth, holding it, lighting it, touching it just to his lips and sucking in the smoke. He held the smoke in and didn't breathe out, and he handed the joint to me.

He said, " 'Ere."

I took the joint between my fingers and looked at it, and then I touched the pinched end to my lips and puffed a tiny puff. The joint tasted like incense.

"I don't think you got any," Pete said. "Take a bigger hit."

"A bigger hit?" I said.

"And hold it in," he said.

I took a bigger hit.

The joint smoke exploded in my throat, and I coughed and coughed and coughed, and Pete watched me coughing. When I finally stopped coughing, he said, "I think you got some that time."

He smoked the joint, taking hits, looking at me, my face all tears from coughing. When he handed the joint back to me, I shook my head no. Pete took one more hit, and then he pinched the lit end of the joint with his fingers. He put the joint back in his Kool pack, and the Kool pack back in his pocket.

"Get off?" he said.

"Off?" I said.

"It's good grass," he said. "From Panama."

The back door was still open, and the afternoon sun was in the backyard, shining orange on the sumac leaves. There was dust in the air that glittered. I went out to the back porch, where the sun on the porch boards was warm, and I sat down on the porch boards. Warm under my butt. The fall grass in the backyard was tall and yellow and words whispered in it.

"Hey," Pete said.

I jumped.

He said, "See you around."

I said, "Where are you going?"

My mouth was dry and echoey.

I said, "Where are you going," listening to it again.

Pete was gone.

I shut the door and went around front, along the skinny sidewalk, up the front stairs.

When Lady Jane woke me up it was almost dark. She stood in my bedroom doorway, with the light on in the kitchen behind her.

"Are you sleeping?" she said. "The front door was wide open. Is this your book? *The Hobbit*?"

My eyes hurt from the light behind her.

She said, "It was on the front porch, on the top step."

I said, "Are you going to make dinner?"

ELLE HAD Mr. Massey for English. Mr. Massey's class had to read *The Pearl*. He gave them a take-home assignment.

Elle said, "What would it take for you to write my take-home assignment for me?"

"I can't write your take-home assignment," I said. "I never even read that book."

"Look," Elle said, holding up a copy of *The Pearl*.

"It's really thin," she said. "You could read it in one day, I bet."

I took *The Pearl* and looked at the pages. One hundred forty-two pages.

I said, "I'll write your take-home assignment in trade for your truckers."

"Those overalls?" she said. "Pick something else."

I said, "The truckers."

Elle said, "How about my lacy shirt with the big sleeves?"

I said, "The truckers."

She said, "How about that paisley vest with the shiny stuff?"

"The truckers," I said.

She got the truckers out of one of her drawers and dropped them in a heap on her bed. I sat down and folded them up, tucked the buckles and straps in and folded the truckers up to take home.

"You never even wear these truckers," I said.

"Why do you call then truckers anyway?" she said.

"I don't know," I said. "That's just what they're called."

"They're called overalls," she said, and she tossed *The Pearl* on top of the folded-up truckers.

I read *The Pearl* that night and the next night. I wrote about it in fifth-hour study hall, wrote long answers to all the questions on the take-home assignment. I gave the answers to Elle after school so she could write them over in her own handwriting. She got an A.

"Next time you better not write such long answers," she said. "B would be better. Now you better tell me what that stupid book is about."

I said, "It was all in the take-home assignment."

"Well, I didn't read it," she said. "I just copied it over."

"Well, read it," I said.

"What?" she said. "Read that whole book?"

"No," I said. "Read the take-home assignment."

FOREST GREEN number fourteen. I started with leaves going up one strap, and came down the other strap with more leaves. I sewed a patch over one knee, even though there was no hole there, a patch of green velvet sewed on with royal purple number eight. Then purple flowers around the patch, and more leaves going out from that.

The first day I wore my truckers to school, I wore them with my black T-shirt and the kelly bird beads.

Marcia Henson looked at my truckers, and she looked at my embroidery, and she said, "Are those marijuana leaves?"

I said, "I don't smoke marijuana."

"You can go to jail," she said. "Or worse. You can become a heroin addict."

"I don't smoke marijuana," I said. "These are asters, and these leaves are aster leaves."

I said, "You have a run in your nylons."

I walked away down the hall. I looked back once, looked back at Marcia Henson, who was sticking her leg out, looking for a run in her nylons.

One thing about Marcia Henson, though. There was a little pink box in the back of her shelf in the locker. It said "Miss Deb," and it was Kotexes.

THE ALLEY was out of the wind, and Elle and I walked along, sliding across ice puddles. I had a pack of Kools.

"I can't believe you bought Kools," she said.

"I like Kools," I said. "Kools are cool."

Elle said, "Say 'out of sight.' Don't say 'cool.'"

"That's really stupid," I said. "I hate 'out of sight.'"

We were behind Someone's Beloved Threads when three boys turned into the alley ahead of us.

"Uh-oh," I said. "Let's go in here."

I went to bang on the back door of Someone's Beloved Threads, but Elle said, "Hey."

She said, "That's your boyfriend, Pete."

She said, "He hasn't been around here for a long time."

"He goes to Mountain View," I said. "He's not my boyfriend."

It was Pete and Buddy and some other kid who wasn't a Mexican kid.

I said, "Hi, Pete."

Elle said, "Hi, you guys."

The other kid who wasn't Mexican said, "I know you. You got Massy for English."

Elle said, "Yeah, I seen you in there."

Nobody said anything else, just looking around the alley and down at the bricks, and then Pete said, "Know anyplace to hang out? Maybe smoke a little get-high?"

He said it to me.

I said, "No."

"Get high? Grass?" Elle said. "We can go over your house."

She said it to me.

I said, "No."

Elle said, "Downstairs at your house."

I looked at Elle and tried to make my face say 'shut up,' but Elle said, "Come on Sarajean. Let's go over your house. We can go in downstairs."

I said, "I don't have the key."

"Well, that other place," she said.

Buddy said, "Is your old man home?"

"Yeah," I said. "I think so."

"Forget it, man," he said. "I ain't going near that fucker. Come on you guys, let's go see is Rita at home."

Pete said, "See you later."

He said it to me.

The three of them walked past us, down to the end of the alley.

"God damn it, Sarajean Henry," she said. "Shit."

"What?" I said.

"I want to smoke some grass," she said. "Don't you want to try it?"

"Maybe," I said. "Can't you get some of Margo's?"

"I can never find where she hides it," she said. "Shit."

I said, "I don't like Buddy."

Elle said, "I wonder who Rita is."

She looked after the three of them. They turned the corner, out to Seventeenth Avenue.

"Come on," Elle said, and she headed down that way.

"Oh, man," I said. "I don't want to follow them. Come on, let's go into Constanzia's."

Pete and Buddy and the other kid were out on the corner.

"Hey, you guys," Elle said. "You can come over my house. I live upstairs from Together Books. My mother's not at home."

Pete looked at me.

Buddy said, "Far out."

Elle said, "Well, okay, come on."

She went first, back up the sidewalk, and then Buddy and the other kid and then Pete and then me went after her. She opened the sidewalk door with her key.

"Up here," she said, and she went in. Buddy next, and then the other kid. Pete went in, and I went last, up the stairs.

"Nice place," Buddy said when we were all inside. "You live here with your mom?"

"Yeah," Elle said. "My name is Elle. *E-l-l-e.* In French that means girl." She said, "So you got some grass?"

Buddy laughed, and Elle laughed. Nobody else laughed. I stood by the kitchen door, and Elle opened the front window and looked out.

Buddy took a joint out of the pocket of his shirt, and he lit the joint with a silver lighter. He took a hit and handed the joint to Elle. Elle smoked the joint just like Buddy, holding it between her thumb and pointer finger. She gave the joint back to Buddy, and he held it out to Pete, and Elle started coughing loud. The air filled up with the sweet burny smell. Pete came over to where I was standing by the kitchen door and gave me the joint. I took a tiny hit and held the smoke in and didn't cough, and I thought maybe Pete smiled when I gave it back to him. After the second time Pete brought the joint over to me, a warm buzzy blanket wrapped up around my chest. I slid my back down along the doorway and sat on the floor between the kitchen and the front room, Elle laughing, and then Pete left and I got up and went in the kitchen, and rubbed my hand on the green velvety chair cushion, and the colored light came in through the jars on the window sill. When I went back out in the front room, everyone was gone, until I looked over the back of the couch and saw Buddy, and Elle was lying under Buddy, little bird sounds coming from Elle, Buddy lying on top of her, his blue-jean butt bumping, and Elle's skinny freckly arms around him, grabbing at his butt.

I went back in the kitchen, and I didn't hear the little bird sounds in there. What I heard was my own heart inside me.

I went back in the front room, and didn't look at the couch, out the door and down the stairs.

Icy bits of snow coming sideways through the air, and the sky high and white. My chapped lips burned, and I pulled my hands up into my sleeves. I couldn't remember what summer felt like, couldn't remember my lips not chapped and my fingers anything else but cold. I folded my arms across my chest tight, tight over the sore bumps that were going to be breasts, Elle's breasts already bigger, not just hard little nipples but real breasts under the nipples, and maybe Buddy's hands on Elle's chest where she had breasts.

Breasts. Boobs. Titties. Stupid words, no good words. Big soft breasts like Margo, hanging down under her soft blouses, soft, swinging moving breasts. Cassandra Wiggins's breasts, high hard bumps under her black T-shirt that disappeared to nothing when she wore her black sweatshirt. Sasha's breasts getting her shirt wet when Dylan Marie cried. Elle's daddy.

I crashed right into John Fitzgerald Kennedy Karpinski, knocked him into the side of a building.

I said, "What are you doing here?"

He said, "Jeez, Sarajean, it's a sidewalk."

"Well," I said. "Sorry."

John Fitzgerald Kennedy Karpinski said, "What's the matter with you?"

I started to say "Nothing." I meant to say "Nothing."

I said, "Marijuana."

"You look it," he said. "You should see your eyes."

"What's wrong with my eyes?" I said.

I looked at my face in the window of a building, and couldn't see anything except the outline of me and John Fitzgerald Kennedy Karpinski standing on the sidewalk, and then, in the next window, me and John Fitzgerald Kennedy Karpinski again, walking on the sidewalk.

He said, "Got any more?"

"No," I said.

"That's okay," he said. "That's far out. I didn't know you get high."

"I don't," I said. "I mean, I just did. Once. It was the second time."

He said, "I thought you just read books and got all As and shit."

"As and Bs," I said.

He said, "Where are you going?"

"Nowhere," I said.

John Fitzgerald Kennedy Karpinski turned off Seventeenth Avenue onto

Clarkson Street, away from my house. I turned with him, looking at his feet, my feet and his feet, just the same, same steps, same shoes.

"Hey," I said. "Black hightops."

Another block, walking into the wind and icy snow bits on my face, the only warm part of me my arms wrapped around me.

"I got to go in here," John Fitzgerald Kennedy Karpinski said.

It was a restaurant, a big window fogged over from inside, people sitting along the window in booths. All across the top, over the window, was a beautiful sign with swirling letters made of leaves and flowers, all different colors. I tried to read the words in all the leaves and flowers up there, and I leaned back and back, stepping back and back, and my one foot went down off the curb and I sat down hard on my butt in the street. John Fitzgerald Kennedy Karpinski cracked up. From sitting in the street I could read the words—CELESTIAL TEA PALACE.

Lady Jane came out of the door that was at one side of the big window. "Sarajean?" she said. "Sarajean. Are you alright?"

She came over to the curb.

"Get up out of the street," she said.

Another lady came out of the door.

"JFK, baby," the new lady said. "Where have you been? It's freezing out. You kids come in here and get warm."

Lady Jane held the door open, and I followed John Fitzgerald Kennedy Karpinski and the other lady inside, him still laughing. I started to laugh, because of him laughing, the laughs coming up out of me like hiccups, surprising me, like I didn't know I had to laugh.

John Fitzgerald Kennedy Karpinski said, "Okay, now try and maintain."

I quit laughing long enough to say, "Okay, JFK Baby."

Then the laughing was all over me again, and JFK Baby pushed me into a booth and slid into the booth next to me. Lady Jane and the other lady stood at the end of the booth, looking at us, their arms folded across their chests exactly the same, each with a pencil sticking out from behind one ear, looking at us in the booth.

JFK Baby said, "Frostbite of the brain."

Lady Jane said, "Do you want some lentil soup? We have lentil soup."

"I guess so," I said, trying to hold my voice in a line.

Lady Jane and the other lady went away. I shoved John Fitzgerald Kennedy Karpinski with my shoulder.

"Sit over there," I said.

He got up and sat in the seat across from me. He pulled his arms out of his coat and took the blue stocking cap off his head, and his stringy blond hair crackled with static electricity.

I said, "So, JFK Baby," and I started to laugh again.

"Just JFK," he said. Serious.

"Okay," I said, trying to be serious back at him. "Okay, JFK."

I said, "Is that your mom?"

"Yeah," he said.

He pushed a basket of crackers at me, little packs of two crackers each, and I tore at a pack and put both crackers in my mouth at once, and took another pack. John Fitzgerald Kennedy Karpinski watched me eat crackers until the basket was empty, and then he said, "Try and maintain."

There were some guys sitting at the counter by us, but they were turned around eating, not looking at us. A lady in the booth past us sat with her head right behind John Fitzgerald Kennedy Karpinski.

I leaned across the table and whispered, "What were we just talking about?"

"Nothing," he whispered back. "But if you don't stop now, you're going to accidentally eat that cracker basket."

I swallowed hard to hold any laughing in, starting to laugh again, and Lady Jane came back with two bowls of soup and a basket of more crackers. She set the bowls of soup down, one in front of me, one in front of John Fitzgerald Kennedy Karpinski, and then she sat down next to me.

She said, "It's almost dark. Pretty late for you to be wandering around in this neighborhood alone, isn't it?"

"I wasn't alone," I said. "I mean, I was, but that was before I was in this neighborhood. Before that, when I was alone, was when I crashed into JFK here."

I said, "JFK Baby."

The laughing got me again, and Lady Jane looked at me. JFK ate calm, even spoonfuls of soup.

A guy behind the counter, in a little window there, yelled out "Order up," and Lady Jane jumped up and went back there.

JFK said, "I'd shut up if I was you. That would keep you safe."

"Safe from what?" I said, looking behind me. I couldn't exactly tell, but the guy was maybe leaning his head by me, like listening.

JFK kept eating soup, shaking his head.

It was warm enough in the café that I took off my jacket. My hands were stinging from finally being warm, and my nose was starting to run, thawing out a little.

JFK's mom went by with a plate full of a big sandwich. She wore a name badge that said Lulu.

I said, "Your mom's name is Lulu Karpinski?"

"No," he said. "Bell. Nancy Bell. She just made up Lulu to go with Bell for her name badge."

I said, "Your dad is named Karpinski?"

"He was," he said. "He's not around anymore. So, is Lady Jane your dad's old lady now?"

"Well," I said. "She doesn't live there, if that's what you mean."

He said, "Your mom never came back, huh?"

"No," I said. "I don't even remember her."

"I remember when she left," he said. "I remember my mom saying when she left."

I crunched the empty cellophane plastic wrappers in my fist, and when I let go, they popped apart like I had never crunched them.

"Your mom knew my mom?" I said.

"My dad never came back," JFK said. "He was around sort of after he got out of the army, and then he just quit coming over to our house, and then someone told my mom he went back east for a job."

He broke crackers into his bowl.

"I never liked him much," he said. "Lalena's mom came back."

"Elle," I said. "You're supposed to say Elle. Besides, Margo didn't leave, Margo got busted."

Lady Jane came back over to the booth.

She said, "I have one more table to finish, and then I can leave. If you want to wait, I can walk with you."

"Walk where?" I said.

"Home," Lady Jane said. "I'll walk you home."

"Okay," I said. "Can I get some more soup?"

"And crackers," JFK said. "She needs some more crackers."

MOUNTAIN VIEW Junior High School was down Ogden Street away from Colfax Street past Saint Therese Carmelite to Sixth Avenue. After Saint Therese Carmelite, Ogden Street wasn't houses anymore. It was little apartment buildings with little sidewalks and names, like Mark Twain. The Mark Twain had a curvy sidewalk going to the front door and a black metal gate across the front door and perfectly round bushes on both sides. It said MARK TWAIN over the front door in thin silver letters, and it was the last place on Ogden Street before I had to turn onto Sixth Avenue.

Sixth Avenue was no houses, and no apartment buildings, just all stores and bars and stuff. Poretti's Pizza, Kwik Shop, Carl's Cash and Loan, the Texaco station, and cars parked all along the side of the street, except at the bus stops, up Sixth Avenue, away from the mountains, away from downtown, toward Cheeseman Park, to Mountain View Junior High, which sat in its own parking lot, behind a fence.

I waited for Elle at the gate of the fence. The first bell rang, and then the second bell rang, so I went in, across the parking lot, through the big doors, into all the crowds of kids, to my locker.

Marcia Henson said, "Your boyfriend was here looking for you."

I said, "What boyfriend?"

She said, "How many do you have?"

"None," I said. "I don't have a boyfriend. Was it a Mexican kid?"

Marcia Henson flipped her perfect straight hair back and looked at me, looked at my outfit like she didn't like it much, looked at my hair like it was a mess.

She said, "You go out with Mexicans?"

"Well," she said. "He wasn't Mexican. He was a hippie, with blond hair. Long blond hair."

The third bell rang, which meant hurry up and get to first hour or else go to Miss Purcell's office and explain why not and get a late excuse. Marcia Henson clicked away down the hall in her little shoes that were red suede shoes today, and red knee socks. The reds didn't match very well.

I went to first hour, Spanish. Señora Caswell spoke only in Spanish after the last bell, and we were only allowed to speak Spanish too. Señora Caswell wasn't Mexican. She was kind of fat and had light brown hair and light blue eyes. She pronounced the words as beautiful as when Constanzia and Erico talked together, but slower. The Mexican kids weren't allowed to take Spanish. They had to take French or German.

Señora Caswell stood up in the front of the room and spoke in Spanish, and we had to answer in Spanish when she called on us. When Señora Caswell stood up there speaking in Spanish, her mouth fluttering the *R*s, it was like listening to music that didn't have words. When Señora Caswell called on me, it was like I hadn't been listening at all.

If I didn't have Spanish first hour, I would skip more often, but I never wanted to miss Spanish class.

At lunch I went to my locker and waited there for Elle. I saw her, finally. I saw her way down the hall, tugging down at her blue suede miniskirt, looking around at all the kids.

"I waited for you this morning. You were late," I said. "God. What is that? Is that a hickey?"

Elle put her hand there, touching her neck. She smoothed the wide collar of her lacy white shirt with the big sleeves. Smoothed the wide collar open.

"That's gross," I said. "Did Buddy do that?"

She said, "He's really far out. He's a junior. He goes to Silver State High."

"A junior?" I said. "That's like sixteen or seventeen."

"Seventeen," Elle said.

"You're only twelve," I said.

"Almost thirteen," she said.

I kept looking away from the hickey, looking at it and looking away.

She said, "Let's go find Pete."

"No," I said, "He hangs out with the ninth-grade boys by the gym."

"Come on," she said.

"No," I said.

"Why not?" she said. "I thought you liked him."

"Not like that," I said. "Why don't you button your collar or something?"

John Fitzgerald Kennedy Karpinski came up to us then, sliding on his black hightops so that they squeaked, slid up to me and Elle and he said,

"Hi. Hi, Lalena."

He looked at her neck.

"Elle," she said. "My name is Elle."

She pulled her wide lace collar up.

"Oh, right, Elle," he said. "Hi, Elle."

Elle said, "I'm going to go find Pete. I got to ask him something."

"Ask him what?" I said.

Elle turned away and walked down the hall. Her lacy shirt was see-through, her bra straps showing through the lace. And her blue suede miniskirt, and her black tights, and her cowboy boots. Elle walking, down the hall by herself, lacy shirt, bra straps, and I didn't want to be in school anymore today.

I said, "Want to skip this afternoon?"

"Who, me?" said John Fitzgerald Kennedy Karpinski.

"Yeah," I said. "Yeah, you. JFK."

"And do what?" he said.

He looked around, at the kids around us, kids at their lockers, walking by.

He said, "Want to go get high?"

"I don't have anything to get high on," I said.

JFK leaned close to me and whispered.

He said, "I do. I pinched some from Lulu Bell's stash."

I watched Elle all the way down the hallway. She never turned around, kept walking, around the corner toward the stairs down to the gym.

"Okay," I said. "Let's go. We have to go out the door by the science lab, where the back driveway is."

"I'll meet you there," JFK said. "I just have to go by my locker."

We walked back to Seventh Avenue, and then up toward Cheeseman Park. Bright sun, cold wind, black crusty snow along the edges of the street. My fingers ached. My face ached. My insides ached.

JFK said, "So, how do you get an absence excuse?"

"Just write one," I said. "And sign your mom's name."

"Can't they tell?" he said.

"You have to disguise your handwriting," I said. "And then, if you ever really do get sick, and she writes you a note, just redo the note yourself so the handwriting matches. That's all."

"Far out," he said. "So, can you roll a joint?"

"No," I said. "I never tried."

"I've tried," he said, "Can't. We need a pipe."

"Let's go over to Colfax," I said. "Mystic Trends Smoke Shop and Incense Emporium."

"Oh, yeah?" he said. "You mean buy one?"

"How do you usually do it?" I said.

"Toilet paper roll," he said. "You know, the cardboard? And tin foil."

Well," I said. "It would be a lot easier to go buy a pipe than to go buy toilet paper and unroll it all."

We turned back toward Colfax.

JFK said, "Do you skip a lot?"

"No," I said. "Not too much."

"What do you usually do?" he said.

"Nothing," I said. "I usually just do nothing."

"Just walk around?" he said, bouncing along next to me.

"Yeah," I said. "Just walk around. And not talk."

"Oh," he said.

Bells jingled on the door of Mystic Trends Smoke Shop and Incense Emporium, rows of brass bells on a curly wire hanger. JFK pushed the door shut behind us and stood there, looking at the gold bells, running his hand over them, jingling them.

"India temple bells," the guy behind the counter said.

He had long blond hair and a long blond mustache and a blond beard. He looked like the picture of Nathaniel Hawthorne.

"What's happening?" he said.

"A pipe," JFK said.

"For a present," I said. "For my father. It's his birthday."

"In the glass case here," the guy said, looking down at the counter he was leaning on.

The glass case was three shelves of all pipes sitting on red velvet cloth. The pipes were lined up by size, and by what kind of pipe, and the light in the case made the pipes glitter.

"Bongs and water pipes back here," the guy said. The shelf behind the counter was all the tall pipes.

JFK whispered to me.

He said, "How much money do you have?"

"Four dollars," I said. "And about eighty cents."

"I have a ten-dollar bill," he said.

The cheapest pipes were little metal pipes, made of pipe parts from under the sink. Pipe pipes. Two dollars ninety-five cents. Then there were little wooden pipes, smooth and polished, small enough to go in a pocket.

One of the wooden pipes had a tiny lid that went over the hole. Four dollars fifty cents. The pipes on the second shelf were fancier, wooden, carved with flowers and leaves. One had a face, and a big open mouth where the marijuana went in. One was a laughing elephant. Eight dollars for the elephant. The bottom shelf had the most beautiful pipes. They were white like china, with India designs painted on in thin lines of color. Twelve dollars.

"The little one with the lid," I said.

The guy took the little wooden pipe with the lid out of the case and handed it to me. It was smooth red wood, and a tiny gold screw held the lid in place. I pushed the lid aside with my finger, pushed it back over the little hole.

"I think he'd like this one," I said, loud to JFK, nodding my head. I set the pipe on the counter.

"Yes," JFK said in a loud fakey voice, worst liar I ever heard. "I think your dad would like this one."

"And a screen?" the guy said.

"A screen?" I said.

"Yes, please," JFK said.

The guy put a tiny round gold screen on the counter next to the pipe.

"One free screen with each purchase," the guy said.

JFK said, "Why, thank you, sir."

Outside, JFK said, "Where should we go?"

"Cheeseman Park?" I said.

"Where?" he said. "Where in Cheeseman Park?"

"The pavilion?" I said. "We can get down out of the wind."

I put the little bag with the pipe and the screen into my inside jacket pocket and we walked up Colfax to the first corner.

"Let's get off Colfax," JFK said. "What if my mom goes by? What if your dad goes by? Busted."

We walked toward Cheeseman Park, walking on Fourteenth Avenue, Thirteenth Avenue, over to Twelfth. The houses by Cheeseman Park were mansions, and I walked slow, looking through the trees and bushes, looking in to tall windows with big curtains and gates inside gates and long driveways. There were no cars parked along the street and no people walking on the sidewalk.

We crossed the park, walking on frozen brown grass, to the white pavilion on the far side. There was no one near the pavilion, no one playing Frisbee on the grass, no dogs running around. Not one cloud in the blue sky, and the wind made all my skin hurt. JFK's long hair blew around, and he took a stocking cap out of his coat pocket and pulled it down over his ears. The stocking cap was blue and red stripes. It looked dumb. It looked warm.

The pavilion was a big slab of concrete with square pillars at the corners. In the summer there was music there sometimes, and people sat around on the grass. Now, it was just a big cold slab of concrete with peely white paint. We went to the far corner and sat down out of the wind. I took the bag out of my pocket and took out the pipe and the little gold screen.

"What's the screen for?" I said.

"So the marijuana doesn't get in your mouth," he said. "Look."

He worked the gold screen down into the hole of the pipe. Then he took a piece of toilet paper out of his coat pocket, and unwrapped a tiny clump of marijuana.

"A bud," he said. "Acapulco gold."

"Acapulco gold?" I said.

"Finest marijuana in Mexico," he said.

He slid the little lid across the hole.

"Great pipe," he said.

He shook the pipe upside down with the lid closed.

There was enough of the bud for each of us to get hits three times, then it was gone. JFK shook the black clump of ash out and closed the pipe's little lid. He put the pipe in his coat pocket.

The warm buzz settled in my chest, and I leaned back against the cold cement side of the pavilion. The cold sun turned warm on my face, and I closed my eyes for a long, long time.

"Hey," JFK's voice came from far away.

"Hey," he said again.

I opened my eyes, and he was right next to me.

"What do you like to say?" he said. "Pot? Or grass? Or reefer? My mom says reefer."

"Marijuana," I said. "Marijuana."

"That's Spanish," he said. "Mary Jane. It means Mary Jane. Some people even say that, Mary Jane."

"Maria," I said. "Mary is Maria."

JFK said, "Maria Juana."

He said, "Does Lalena get high?"

"Just shut up about Lalena," I said.

JFK said, "Sorry."

"Elle," I said. "You're supposed to say Elle."

I closed my eyes again. A dog barked far away. Elle was probably in fourth hour now. Elle had English class fourth hour. Mr. Massey. That other kid was in her English class, that other kid who was with Pete and Buddy. Yesterday. My mouth was so dry I couldn't swallow.

"Let's go somewhere," I said, getting up.

JFK said, "Where?"

"I don't care," I said. "Anywhere. But when we get there, you have to take off that hat."

"You don't like my hat?" he said, looking up at me.

JFK was skinny and pale skinned, and there were freckles on his nose, and his nose was runny. His eyes were light blue, and he squinted up at me.

"Just kidding," I said.

He said, "My grandma made this hat for me. I got it for my birthday last year."

We walked back across the crunching frozen grass. The mountains were gray and white, flat against the sky, past the downtown buildings poking up, past the gold dome of the capitol building.

"I like watching my grandma knit," JFK said. "I like her hands. They're like crepe paper. Crinkly, like crepe paper."

I said, "Do you know Constanzia? At Someone's Beloved Threads?"

"That old Mexican lady?" he said.

I said, "Why is my mouth so dry?"

"Cotton mouth," he said. "It means you got high."

"Cotton mouth?" I said. "Cotton mouth is a snake."

JFK said, "Don't say snake."

"Why not?" I said. "You said snake first. Cotton mouth."

"No no no," he said, running ahead of me on the grass. "Don't talk about snakes please please please."

"Okay," I yelled. "I won't. Wait up."

I ran to catch up to him, and he kept running, and we both ran all the way back across Cheeseman Park, the cold wind behind us, pushing behind us. We stopped running when we got back to the sidewalk, back to the mansions.

"What you want to do now?" JFK said. "Where do you live?"

"Ogden Street, by the Safeway store," I said. "Where do you live?"

"Clarkson Street," he said. "I wish I lived here."

"This house?" I said, looking at the big white house, a big white house with black shutters, and a wide yard, and trees.

"Yeah," he said. "Or that house. Any of these houses. I wish we were rich."

I said, "What would you do if you were rich?"

"Go to college," he said. "I want to go to college to be a scientist."

"You said you wanted to be an astronaut," I said. "You can still go to college if you're not rich. You can get a scholarship if you're smart."

"I'm smart," he said.

We got to Corona Street.

"That's where Elle used to live," I said, pointing.

JFK said, "You said shut up about Elle."

"Well, yeah," I said. "Shut up about Elle."

"Why?" he said.

"'Cause she's my best friend," I said. "What kind of a scientist?"

"Huh?" he said.

"What kind of a scientist?' I said.

"Biology, I guess," he said. "Did you guys have a fight?"

"Do you have Mr. Mitchell for biology?" I said.

"Yeah," he said. "Fourth hour. Probably right now."

"Me too," I said. "Second hour. We're going to dissect worms, you know."

I said, "Worms are like snakes you know."

JFK took off running down the sidewalk.

"No no no," he yelled.

"Snakes," I yelled. "How can you be a biologist and not like snakes?"

We got to the Safeway store, and JFK quit running. I caught up with him, breathing hard, big puffs of white breath.

"Which house?" he said.

I said, "The red one."

Blackbird was parked out front.

"Jimmy Henry's home," I said.

"How come you say Jimmy Henry" he said. "How come you don't just say Dad? Or just Jimmy?"

"I don't know," I said. "He's just Jimmy Henry. Do you always call your mom Mom?"

"No," he said. "Sometimes I say Lulu Bell. It cracks her up."

I sat down on the curb at the edge of the parking lot and looked at our house. Bluejays in the holly bushes. I looked down the street as far as Saint Therese Carmelite. My stomach felt empty.

I said, "Remember when you used to pick your nose?"

JFK said, "I never picked my nose."

"At Free School," I said. "So no one would hold your hand."

"No, I didn't," he said.

"Yes, you did," I said.

"No, I didn't," he said again. His voice was smaller.

He said, "I don't remember that."

He took his hat off and stuffed it into his pocket.

He said, "Do you think it's after two o'clock? My mom goes to work at two. We could go over my house."

"Well," I said. "Okay."

JFK lived in a square brick apartment building on Clarkson Street, just past the dead end of Tenth Avenue, past the parking lot of Saint Therese Carmelite. It wasn't a very big building, two floors. The hallways had long orange and brown rugs. It smelled like tuna fish. JFK and his mom lived on the second floor, in the back. Their front room was full of sun, and warm. JFK pulled his hat out of his pocket and dropped his coat on the couch.

The walls of the front room were covered with posters. A girl with no clothes, just her necklaces covering her up. A fairy ship in black light colors. There was a KEEP OFF THE GRASS sign over a doorway. I went and looked in the door.

"That's my mom's room," JFK said.

It was dark in his mom's room. I turned on the light. A mattress on the floor piled high with blankets. A dresser with a mirror. There were photographs stuck into the edges of the mirror, and I went up to the mirror and looked close.

"That's me," JFK said.

Pictures of JFK when he was a baby, his mom holding him up for the camera, his mom kissing him on his head, him sitting in his mom's lap. JFK when he was older, standing next to an old lady in blue jeans and a straw hat. JFK with his face painted with blue stars. JFK smiling with no front teeth.

"She's my biggest fan," JFK said. "That's what she say, she says, 'I'm your biggest fan.'"

My own face was there in all the middle of all the curling edges of the photographs, my own face looking out from the mirror. Brown hair in a mess. Red nose. Chapped lips. I had never seen me in a baby picture.

"Uh-oh," JFK said. "Stuck in the mirror. Be careful."

"What do you mean?" I said, watching my mouth move around the words.

"Get high, get stuck in the mirror," he said.

"I forgot we were high," I said. "Do you think we're still high?"

"I don't know," he said. "Do you want to smoke some more?"

"No," I said. "I got to go."

"Hey," he said. "Are you bummed out?"

"I got to go," I said. "'Bye."

I went out the door, down the long hallway, orange rugs, outside. I walked on the sidewalk, watching my shoes on the sidewalk, walked back to Ogden Street. Blackbird was still there. I stood on the sidewalk in front of my house, peeling red paint, curtains closed across the upstairs windows. Downstairs window all boarded up.

I went in, finally, and Jimmy Henry was sitting at the kitchen table, the *Rocky Mountain News* all spread out in front of him.

"Home so soon?" he said.

I said, "Yeah."

I got out a box of crackers and sat across from him.

"Do you have any baby pictures?" I said.

I stuffed my mouth with crackers, three crackers, four.

"Of you?" he said.

I nodded.

He said, "No."

"How come?" I said, cracker crumbs spilled out of my mouth.

He took a big breath and rubbed his face with his hands. When he breathed out, he blew the cracker crumbs off the table into my lap. I started to laugh, a little laugh, and kept laughing. I took the cracker box into my room and shut the door, sat on my bed, and when I wasn't laughing anymore I was crying, quiet crying, hugging the cracker box close and crying.

THE SNOW piled in a smooth mound in the flower box. There were no footprints in the snow outside the door, and the sign said CLOSED, even though it was Saturday morning. I tried to open the door. I banged on the window, looking in. No lights. I banged again. Then I went around to the alley, stepping high in snow that came up to my knees. I banged on the back door of Someone's Beloved Threads. No one came.

I went down Seventeenth Avenue. Together Books was open, and the light inside there was warm and yellow. I went into Together Books instead of upstairs to Elle's.

There was the lady sitting at the desk, and the certain smell in there, old paper smell.

I said, "Hi."

She looked up from the book she was reading.

"Hello there," she said.

I went to the shelf of poetry books. They were all leaning against each other, skinny odd sizes, different shapes. There were pictures on the wall there, Walt Whitman in his hat, and a picture of Emily Dickinson. I wandered along the back wall, past the gardening books, all green. Cookbooks. Spirituality. Literature, five shelves. Philosophy. I wandered all around until I was back to the front door.

"Looking for anything special?" the lady said.

"No," I said. "I guess not."

I went back outside.

The snow came down in thick flakes that fell straight, no wind. It didn't even seem cold. I kicked the snow off the bench outside the window and sat down. There were no cars, and some people walked by quiet across the street.

Cassandra Wiggins came out of the doorway and turned up the other way, walking fast up Seventeenth Avenue. Disappearing in the snow. Then Margo came out.

"Sarajean," she said.

"Hi," I said.

She said, "Where's Elle?"

"I don't know," I said.

She said, "Isn't she with you?"

"Well," I said. "She was. I don't know where she is now."

I said, "Maybe over at her dad's."

Margo looked at me, looked at my face. I looked at the snow.

"Lots of snow," I said. "Over a foot."

"Yeah," Margo said. "Well, I have to go to work. There's soup up there for later, just heat it up. Don't you want to wait upstairs?"

"That's okay," I said. " 'Bye."

Margo walked up the block. I watched her as far as the food co-op.

After a while I went back to Someone's Beloved Threads. I banged on the door, looking in through the window and banging, and Erico came through the striped blanket. He came and opened the door.

"Not open today," he said. "Mama's sick."

"Sick?" I said.

"A cold," Erico said. "In bed."

"Oh," I said. "Okay. 'Bye."

Erico shut the door and I watched him go back into the kitchen, back through the striped blanket.

I banged on the door again. Erico came back out, and opened the door.

"Can I come in?" I said. "I can work in the shop today while Constanzia's in bed. I can work for you today."

Erico looked at me, and he looked past me out at the snow.

"I can be the shopkeeper," I said.

"Why not?" he said.

He held the door open for me, and I stamped the snow off my sneakers and went in. The bottoms of my blue jeans were frozen and stiff with crusted frozen snow. Erico turned the sign around so it said OPEN, and then he went back behind the counter and he turned on the lamp on the table. I went around to the lightbulbs, pulling the strings, lighting up the shop.

"So," he said. "You want to be the shopkeeper. How much do you want to charge for this day's labor?"

"No," I said. "I'll just be here to work, in case anybody comes in."

Erico smiled at me, and my face got warm.

"I'll make you some hot chocolate," he said. "With cinnamon."

He went back through the striped blanket. Behind the counter, I sat in Constanzia's chair and took off my sneakers. They were wet and the laces were packed with snow. My socks were wet too, and I took them off and got some other socks out of the sock box. The sock box was all odd socks that had lost their mates, ten cents each. I picked out a purple wool sock and a green wool sock. When Erico came back out and I said, "I have to borrow some socks until mine are dry."

He set a cup of hot chocolate down on the table next to Constanzia's chair. Cinnamon smell steamed up out of the cup.

"Thanks," I said.

"I'll be upstairs," he said. "I can hear you if you holler."

"Okay," I said.

I took the hot chocolate and went to the front window, and looked out through the hanging clothes. The quiet snow fell. My toes burned and tingled, turning warm in the green and purple socks.

There was a new box of stuff behind the counter, by Constanzia's work table. I poked through the clothes in there, and then I set my hot chocolate down on the table and sat down on the floor next to the box. I pulled out the blue jeans, three pairs, and set the blue jeans aside, by Constanzia's chair, so she could measure them. I took out a shirt and put it on a hanger, and put the hanger on a special nail in the counter. Two shirts. Three shirts. I folded up a red sweater and put it on the work table. In the bottom of the box was a blue-jean jacket.

I pulled out my box of embroidery stuff from under the counter and pulled the embroidery hoops loose from all the thread. Fit the hoops onto the wide plain back of the blue-jean jacket. The colors of embroidery thread were all tangled together in the box, beautiful silky colors shining in the dark light of the little lamp. Violet number twenty-five. I started making a row of French knots straight across the back of the blue-jean jacket, violet

French knots shining in a row. When I went all the way across, I started a second row of French knots. Turquoise number fourteen. Nobody came in all morning.

Around noon Erico came back down.

"I'll be right back," he said.

When he came back, he said, "I called the doctor. When he comes, send him back through here."

He wiped his hand through his hair, through the snowflakes all in his black hair.

"Why?" I said. "Is Constanzia sicker? You said just a cold."

"A fever now," he said. "Just to be safe, we call Doctor Michaelson."

He went back upstairs.

I went to the window and watched for Doctor Michaelson. A man went by, but he kept walking, past the door. A man and a lady came in.

I said, "Are you Doctor Michaelson?"

The man said, "No."

The lady said, "No."

They didn't look like a doctor. They both looked around the shop for a while, and the lady tried on sweaters from the box. I went and sat behind the counter and didn't make any more French knots.

A fat man with a beard came in and he wore a big coat.

He said, "I'm Doctor Michaelson."

"Here," I said.

I went to the striped blanket and pulled it to the side. I pointed to the stairs.

"Up there," I said.

The lady bought a white mohair sweater for four dollars, and then she and the man left. I started another row of French knots, pale pink number ten. I listened for sounds from upstairs. When Doctor Michaelson came back down the stairs, out through the blanket, I got up from Constanzia's chair.

"Is she okay?" I said.

Doctor Michaelson looked at me over the tops of his glasses.

"Who are you?" he said.

"Sarajean," I said. "Sarajean Henry."

"Well, Sarajean Henry," he said. "I think she'll be fine."

He left.

Erico came back down the stairs, putting on his jacket as he came through the blanket.

"A prescription," he said. "I'll be right back."

He hurried out the door, and I went to the window and watched Erico's back, watched Erico hurrying and slipping through the snow.

I sat back down in Constanzia's chair and worked on the row of pale pink knots. The shop breathed when the heater came on, and the warm air blew on my feet in the green and purple socks. I looked at the ceiling. I had never been upstairs.

I started a row of spring green number twenty-one, and Erico came back when I was halfway across. He went through the shop and up the stairs without saying anything.

Then Elle came in, snow all in her hair, snow on her shoulders, stamping her cowboy boots, slamming the door behind her.

"Sh," I said. "Constanzia is sick."

"I thought I'd find you here," Elle said. "I went to your house."

"Margo asked me where were you," I said.

"Shit," Elle said. "What did you say?"

She looked in the little mirror on the counter and smoothed her hair behind her ears.

"Did you tell her you were at my house?" I said.

"Well," Elle said. "Not really. I just kind of let her think that."

"Where were you?" I said.

Elle said, "Guess."

I started another French knot.

"No," I said. "I don't want to guess."

"I kind of went to a party," she said.

"All night?" I said.

Elle picked at the corner of her eye where the eyeliner was smeared.

I said, "Did you tell Margo you were going to my house, and then stay out all night?"

"I got drunk," she said. "I threw up in the toilet at these guys' house."

"What guys?" I said. "Were you there with Buddy?"

"And some other guys," she said. "Pete was there. It was far out. Until I threw up. There was a guy there with a guitar. I drank peach wine."

I said, "Did you stay all night there?"

"Yeah," she said.

She tried to see the top of her head in the mirror.

"Is my part straight?" she said.

"You slept at their house?" I said.

"Well, kind of," she said. "On the couch. These guys have this apartment right on Colfax. Up by Colorado Boulevard."

"You slept on the couch?" I said. "Where did Buddy sleep?"

"He left," Elle said. "But I met this other guy. I can't remember his name. So what did you tell Margo?"

"Nothing," I said.

"What are you doing?" she said, looking at the rows of French knots.

"I'm working," I said. "Constanzia is sick. I'm staying here to keep the shop open."

Elle went to the front of the shop and looked out the window.

"It's snowing like a mother," she said. "We're going to get maybe another foot."

She came back to the counter, leaned on her elbows, watched me make a French knot.

"That's beautiful," she said. "Is it yours?"

"No," I said. "It was in this box of stuff."

Elle said, "Want to go back over those guys' apartment with me tonight?"

"No," I said.

She came back behind the counter and sat on the floor, her back against the counter, across from me. She leaned her head back and closed her eyes.

"I don't feel very good," she said.

"Want some aspirins?" I said. "Is it a hangover?"

"I don't think so," she said. "I don't think you get a hangover if you throw up."

She said, "Why don't you want to go over there with me? It's just a little way up Colfax."

"I don't like Buddy," I said. "Those guys are too old to hang out with."

"I don't have any fun when you're not there," she said.

I stopped in the middle of a spring green French knot. She still had her eyes closed, her head leaned back against the counter. There was a new hickey down low on her neck, a little purple half-moon shape, down low where her freckles started up again. Above that her neck was white and thin, up to her pointed chin. I set the blue-jean jacket on the arm of the chair and went over next to her. I bent down, and my knee cracked. She didn't open her eyes. I touched the hickey. It was smooth. Nothing at all, just color.

"Don't let them do that to you," I said. Whispering. "It's ugly."

A tear wet the corner of her eye and ran down the side of her cheek. I wiped at the tear with my finger. Her eyes still closed.

She said, "What do you know."

"Nothing," I said. "I don't know anything."

Elle opened her eyes and looked at me. Her beautiful cinnamon-colored eyes, all red now, her pale eyelashes wet, her pointed freckled nose with a tiny clear drop hanging off the end.

The door of the shop opened. Elle wiped her nose on her sleeve, and I stood up. Two ladies came in, laughing, stamping snow off their feet, snow in their long hair.

"Hello," I said.

"Where's Constanzia?" one lady said.

"She has a cold," I said. "In bed."

The lady said, "Oh."

The other lady said, "Is Erico here?"

"Upstairs," I said. "Should I holler?"

The two ladies looked at each other and started laughing.

"That's okay," she said, the lady who asked was Erico here.

They went to the back of the shop by the big pieces of material hanging up. Talking. Their shoulders touching. From behind they looked the same, long brown hair, blue jeans, hiking boots. One taller. Laughing.

Elle stood up next to me.

"I guess I'll go home," she said. "How long are you going to be here?"

"I don't know," I said. "Until six I guess. Want to come over tonight?"

"I don't know," she said. "Maybe. Maybe I'll come back later."

"Okay," I said. "There's soup. Margo said there's soup."

She left, and when she went out the door, another lady came in.

"Hello," I said.

The new lady said, "Hi," and she looked around.

It snowed all afternoon, and I made five more rows of French knots. Midnight blue number twenty-four. True red number six. Light orange number fifteen. Dove gray number eighteen. Pale yellow number twenty-one. Erico didn't come back down until it was almost time to close. I heard him in the kitchen, and I went back and looked through the striped blanket. He was standing by the sink.

"Hi," I said.

He looked up from running water into the kettle.

"Why don't you take this tea up to Mama?" he said.

I stepped into the kitchen. Erico put the kettle on the stove, and he took down a red and yellow box of teabags from the shelf. He put a teabag in a white mug, hanging the tag carefully over the side.

"Is she better?" I said.

"She slept all afternoon," he said.

I leaned on the kitchen table and watched the kettle. Erico watched the kettle. When it started to whistle he turned off the gas and poured the hot water into the mug, filling the mug, setting the kettle back on the stove, picking up the mug, dangling the teabag in the mug. Swishing it around.

"There you go," he said, taking the teabag out, dripping.

I took the mug, and I went up the narrow wooden stairs by the striped blanket.

At the top of the stairs was Constanzia's and Erico's apartment. The front room was small, a couch covered with another striped blanket, and two big soft chairs facing each other. A table with a radio and a television with a coathanger attached to the top. The walls were dark old paint, and pictures in frames. A picture of Jesus with his heart all lit up. A picture of Virgin Mary standing on the world, stars all around her head. I went down the little hall, and the first door was Constanzia's bedroom.

She was in her bed, a big bed, in a tiny room. There was one lamp, a little glass lamp, on the table next to her, not very bright. She was awake, sitting up against a pile of pillows, in all the blankets. She said something in Spanish, looking at me.

"Hi," I said, whispering.

"So," she said, in a voice like a cold. "You are our shopkeeper today, sí?"

I set the mug down on the table, next to a pile of beads, by the lamp.

"Are you better?" I said.

She took the mug, wrapped her hands around the mug and held it, not sipping, holding it. She leaned back into the piled-up pillow and closed her eyes.

Her long hair was loose around her shoulders, tangled in a knitted dark shawl. Her nightgown was white colored, tiny buttons at the front, gathers at the cuffs, a thin edge of lace. There was the flowery smell of powder, there was the smell of the tea.

The only other furniture in the room was a big dresser of dark wood, next to the window. A lace scarf was laid across the dresser top, and a statue of Virgin Mary stood in the center. There were small photographs standing in little frames, and a silver-handled hairbrush. I pushed open the curtain. The snow fell through the light of the streetlight.

"It's still snowing," I said.

Constanzia sat up and sipped at the tea. She pushed her hair back over her shoulder.

"Do you want your hairbrush?" I said.

I picked up the silver hairbrush. The handle was cold and smooth, and the silver was designed across the wide back of the brush in swirls. I took the hairbrush over and sat on the edge of the bed.

"Shall I brush your hair for you?" I said.

Constanzia's face wrinkled up into a smile, and she sat up a little more.

I took up the long hair on her shoulder, heavy black and long white mixed in, and I brushed the tangles out smooth. Constanzia closed her eyes, she sipped, and I brushed her hair over my hand. In the dark light of the glass lamp, the deep wrinkles of her face were soft, crepe-papery.

After a little bit Constanzia reached over and set the mug on the table and picked up the beads, shiny wooden beads with silver beads here and there, and a dark silver cross. She wrapped the loop of the beads around her hands and leaned back into the pillow. I brushed her hair out onto the pillow, and she closed her eyes again, clicking the beads in her fingers, her lips moving. When her lips stopped moving, when the beads rested, still tangled around her fingers, I got up off the bed and put the silver hairbrush back in its place on the dresser.

The photographs in the little frames were two little Mexican kids, laughing, in the sun, a young smiling Mexican lady with a lace scarf on her head, a man with dark hair and a mustache, wearing a white suit. Not smiling. Serious.

I left the bedroom, looking back once at Constanzia, her hair all around her face. Sleeping.

Erico was in the kitchen. He sat by the table, his legs stretched out in front of him, stirring a cup of coffee with a spoon.

"Sleeping," I said. "Can I come back tomorrow and work again?"

He looked at me. Serious.

"If you want to," he said. "I go to mass at eight. We open at twelve o'clock on Sunday."

"I know," I said. "I'll be here at twelve."

"'Bye," I said.

Erico said, "Thank you. You are a good girl."

"'Bye," I said.

I went out, through the shop. At the door, I turned the sign around, CLOSED, and shut the door tight behind me.

It was still snowing. Erico had shoveled the sidewalk in front of the shop, and the snowplow had left a high pile of snow along the curb up and down Seventeenth Avenue. I climbed to the top of the pile of snow and walked along the top, up the street. At Together Books I looked up at Elle's window. The lights were on up there, so I went in, up the stairs. The stairway smelled like dinner. At the top of the stairs I knocked and opened the door.

"Hello," I said.

Margo and Cassandra Wiggins were on the couch, sitting close to each other, and Margo jumped up.

"Sarajean," she said.

She pulled her shirt together over her breasts.

My face got hot and I stepped back into the doorway.

"I was looking for Elle," I said.

"She's over at your house," Margo said. "She said she's spending the night with you."

"Oh, yeah," I said. "Well, I was at Constanzia's. I wasn't home yet."

Margo buttoned her shirt up, getting the buttons wrong, walking over to the doorway.

"Constanzia's sick," I said, backing down the stairs. "I was working at the shop."

"I guess I'll go over my house." I said, not looking at Margo, at the bumps of her nipples in her shirt.

"Okay," she said. "She just left a little while ago."

She stood at the top of the stairs, and I went back down, fast, back out into the snow.

I walked fast up Seventeenth Avenue, my breath making clouds in my face. My face was hot, hot that went all the way down my middle. All the way home.

Jimmy Henry was lying on the couch, the record player had a record on, Lady Jane was standing by the stove in a cloud of steam from a pot.

"Is Elle here?" I said.

Jimmy Henry said, "No."

"We're making spaghetti," Lady Jane said. "Where have you been all day? Out playing in the snow? Do you ever make snow angels, we used to make snow angels."

"No," I said. "At Someone's Beloved Threads. Was Elle here?"

"No," Lady Jane said. "Here. Want to stir these noodles while I make salad?"

I dropped my jacket on the chair by the door.

"Okay," I said.

I went into the kitchen and took the big spoon, stood there in the bubbling steam. I stirred.

MARGO'S BREASTS, dark round nipples hanging down, disappearing under her shirt.

SUNDAY MORNING the sun came up on the new snow. It was late in the morning, bright sun, when I got up. Lady Jane was making French toast, and Jimmy Henry was gone. He came back with the *Denver Post*. He offered me the funnies.

"So," he said. "What's up with you today?"

I looked at the French toast, and my stomach twisted with a cramp. I pictured piling the French toast in on top of last night's spaghetti.

"Someone's Beloved Threads," I said. "I'm going to work there today. Constanzia is sick in bed. A cold."

"Noon," I said. "After mass."

"No, thank you," I said to Lady Jane, the French toast bright eggy yellow on the red plate.

I put on my purple T-shirt and my blue jeans and tied my hair back with my red paisley scarf. Then I changed into my truckers, which felt better.

The cold bright sun made my eyes water, and I got an ice cream head-ache in my forehead. I walked along the sidewalk in little shoveled paths beside the snow mountains the snowplows had left along the curbs.

Erico was out in front of the shop, shoveling. When I got up to him he stopped, leaning on the snow shovel, squinting in the brightness.

"She still has the fever," he said. "She feels better, I think."

I said, "Is it time to open?"

"Not quite," he said.

He laughed.

He said, "But go ahead."

I went in and turned the sign around to OPEN. I turned on the lights, and the light behind the counter. I went to the front window and pushed away the clothes hanging across. The sunlight came in, lighting up the dust in the air.

The blue-jean jacket was folded up on the work table, the rows of French knots perfect straight rows. I ran my hand flat over them, rows of bumps. Rows of tiny colored nipples.

Erico came in and leaned the snow shovel against the door.

"I'll make us some hot chocolate, sí?" he said.

"Sí," I said. "Por favor."

I wandered around the shop. Tucked the hangers of shirts back straight into the rack. I took the button box from the counter, sliding my hands through the buttons, looking out the window into the brightness.

Erico brought the hot chocolate with cinnamon, in a white mug, and he said,

"I'll be upstairs."

Lots of people walked by the window, and people were in and out the door. I stood by the window and watched, and Seventeenth Avenue was full of people. Cassandra Wiggins went by, and I went back behind the counter.

Margo came in.

"How's Constanzia?" she said.

I looked out the window.

"She still has the fever," I said.

I looked at the sweater boxes, at the blue sweater sleeve dangling over the side of the Large box.

"I don't know what you girls find to do all night," she said. "Staying up so late. Elle's been dead asleep ever since she got home this morning."

I poked my fingers into bits of beads and necklaces in the box on the counter.

"Well," Margo said. "Come by later if you want to. You know you can come over anytime."

She left. I went and folded the blue sweater.

It was almost four o'clock when Elle came in. She wore a red turtleneck shirt, and she had mascara and black eyeliner on her eyes.

I said, "I don't even want to hear about it."

"I just ended up staying home last night," she said. "I was really tired, you know? I just stayed home. So, are you still working?"

The red turtleneck made her face look greenish. Her eyes were bloodshot under all the black.

"I got to go to the store," she said. "Margo's making cookies. She said come on over, so maybe see you later?"

She said, "'Bye," and the door slammed shut.

I said, "'Bye."

My stomach was hurting.

When it got dark Erico came downstairs. I was standing at the counter, stringing beads onto a long nylon thread. He came and sat in Constanzia's chair, rubbing his face in his hands. I showed him the money box from the drawer.

"Look," I said. "Busy day."

He looked up, smiled, and he slapped his hands on his legs.

"Yes," he said. "Busy day. Thank you, you are a good girl."

He took the money box, and he took out a ten-dollar bill.

"Here," he said. "A good day's work. You want to come tomorrow, after school?"

"Thanks," I said, taking the ten-dollar bill, looking at the president there. "Thanks. Yes, I'd love it, to work tomorrow."

"Okay," Erico said. "Thank you, Sarajean. And Mama too, Mama says, 'Thank you, Sarajean.'"

"Okay," I said. "See you tomorrow. Tomorrow I'll measure the new blue jeans in the box, okay? Tell her that."

I walked home in the early frozen dark, my hand in my trucker pocket, my ten-dollar bill in my hand in my trucker pocket. No one was there when I got home. The lights were on, and there was leftover spaghetti in a pan on the stove, but no one was there.

I didn't eat any spaghetti. My stomachache was back, a stomachache that came and went away, and then it would hurt again. I got on my bed with my book for English, *Huckleberry Finn*, and laid it open on my stomach.

I felt wet between my legs, and I reached my hand down into my truckers. My underpants were wet. My hand came up red. My stomach jumped at the red blood, and I got up and ran in the bathroom, shutting the door, pulling the trucker straps down off my shoulders. My underpants were red. I got my periods.

My hands were shaky, and I folded up a piece of toilet paper and folded it over the red spot in my underpants. I pulled my truckers back up, and I got my jacket, and I went out the door, to Safeway, walking careful with the toilet paper folded in between my legs. I got the small size box of Tampax tampons and took it to the cashier. I took it to the lady cashier.

She said, "One ninety-four."

I gave her my new ten-dollar bill.

I wanted to say, "It's my first period."

I wanted to say, "It's my first box of Tampax tampons."

I said, "Thank you."

I TOOK money from people, or I pointed to stuff. Blue jeans over there. Extra Large sweaters in the same box as Large. Baby clothes on the other side of the door. I worked on the blue jean jacket, starting a row of French knots, canary yellow number twelve, down the front, next to the buttons.

I worked in the shop all week, after school, and every night Erico gave me a five-dollar bill.

Constanzia stayed in her bed.

"Better," Erico said. "She sleeps."

"Better," Doctor Michaelson said. "She is doing very well, considering."

"What does that mean, considering?" I said.

Doctor Michaelson said, "She is very lucky to have such a helper."

ON SATURDAY morning Constanzia came down to the shop for the morning. She sat into her chair.

"Look," I said. "I arranged the shirts by color."

"And see?" I said. "I found new buttons for this pink blouse."

"And look at this beautiful blue-jean jacket," I said. "How much do you think we should charge for it now, all decorated with French knots?"

"Constanzia," I said, whispering to her close. "I got my periods. My first period."

Constanzia took my hand and squeezed. She got up out of her chair, and she went up the stairs. She came back down, and she stood close to me, and she handed me a small white box, old white, yellowish white.

"A young woman," she said.

Inside was a flat blue charm on a thin silver chain, lying on a piece of cotton. Bright blue, turquoise blue, sky blue. In the blue was a Virgin Mary, in her long robe, standing on the world. All blue.

"I have saved it for my granddaughter," Constanzia said. "But there is no granddaughter. It is a Miraculous Medal."

"But I'm not Catholic," I said.

"The Holy Mother watches over all God's children," Constanzia said. "It is right for you."

The back of the medal was silver, with an M, and a cross, and stars.

"Is it alright if I wear it?" I said.

Constanzia took the box out of my hand, and she took the medal by the silver chain and stepped around behind me. She fastened the medal around my neck, the tiny chain tickling there, the blue medal laying on the chest, just where I could barely see it.

"It's beautiful," I said.

I tucked the medal its silver chain, inside my T-shirt, and I kissed Constanzia on her cheek, my lips on her smile wrinkles.

"A young woman," she said.

She sat down in her chair. She went to sleep. A catnap.

I got a shirt out of a pile of shirts, and looked through the button box for matching buttons to sew on where they were missing. Constanzia coughed in her sleep, and I sewed buttons on the shirt.

THE SUN stayed bright and the air was cold, and the deep snow didn't melt away. The snow stayed in drifts at the curbs, getting blacker each day from cars, and stained yellow spots from dogs. The temperature never got above ten degrees for two weeks. Erico came back at night when it was time to close the shop, came back from fixing people's heaters and frozen pipes.

ELLE SAID, "All you do is sit in that shop."

She kicked the toe of her cowboy boot at my locker door.

"I have fifty dollars saved up," I said. "I get paid five dollars every day."

The second bell rang.

"Next week," I said. "Constanzia is gong to teach me how to use her sewing machine."

"What are you going to do with all that money?" Elle said.

"I don't know," I said. "Save it."

She said, "Want to buy a lid?"

I said, "A lid?"

"Grass," Elle said. "A lid is a little baggie of grass."

"For how much?" I said.

"Ten dollars," she said. "One baggie costs ten dollars. We can split it."

"Okay," I said.

I gave her one of my five-dollar bills.

"Come over when you get off work," she said.

"No," I said. "Meet me at the shop at six, okay?"

"Okay," she said.

At six o'clock I waited outside Someone's Beloved Threads. It was dark and the sky was beautiful with stars. I waited until the clock on the wall inside the shop said six twenty, and then I walked down Seventeenth Avenue. I stopped outside of Together Books and looked up at Elle's window. The lights were on up there. I sat on the bench, kicking the snow under the bench into a pile until I was frozen, and then I went up the stairs and knocked on the door at the top of the stairs. Cassandra Wiggins opened the door.

I said, "Hi."

Cassandra Wiggins opened the door a little more.

"Come on in," she said.

"Is Elle here?" I said.

"No," she said. "Nobody's at home. I just got here."

"Well," I said. "I better go. Elle might be over at my house."

I stepped back away from the doorway.

"Wait," Cassandra Wiggins said.

She said, "Why don't you come in? I haven't seen you for a while."

She opened the door wide. The lights were on, the little light by the couch, the lights in the kitchen.

"I better not," I said. "I better go see if Elle is at my house. You know, waiting for me there, maybe."

I turned to go back down the stairs, and my hightops squeaked on the floor, wet, snow melting, and Cassandra Wiggins said, "Wait."

She stepped back from the doorway, back into all the light.

"Just for a little bit," she said. "I want to talk to you."

She walked over by the couch, looking back at me, and she sat on the arm of the couch. I came in, and I shut the door behind me, and stood right there, still and straight by the door. Cassandra Wiggins crossed one leg over her other leg, her long black jeans, her pointy-toed cowboy boots. She folded her arms over her chest.

"Sarajean," she said.

I leaned back against the door. Folded my arms over my chest.

"So," Cassandra Wiggins said. "How you doing?"

"Okay," I said.

"Everything's okay?" she said.

"Yeah," I said.

The Who's Next face looked in the window behind her.

"Well," she said. "I wanted to talk about something important."

I put my fists into my jacket pockets, wrapping my cold fingers inside each other.

She said, "You know what I think is the most important thing there is?"

She looked at me.

"Yeah?" I said. "No."

"People loving each other," she said.

The glass doors of the bookshelf were open.

She said, "Sometimes people don't understand about that."

One jeweled edge caught the light from somewhere, caught the light and threw it back pink.

"There are different ways of loving," she said. "Like, Margo is my best friend. But she's my special best friend."

Her cowboy boot up on one knee jiggled.

"Sometimes women love each other," she said.

I waited.

She said, "Do you know what I mean?"

"No," I said. "Well, kind of."

"What do you think I mean?" she said.

My nose was starting to drip. Thawing out.

"It's like this," she said. "Sometimes two women love each other."

She said, "It's a secret, that's all. But you can be in on the secret."

My toes were going from frozen to wet.

"Yeah," I said. "Well."

I said, "Okay. But I have to go. I have to go find Elle. I told her six."

Cassandra Wiggins stood up. She shut one of the glass doors. She shut the other one, and the little latch clicked. She put her hands in her back pockets.

She said, "So, we're okay, right? With this secret?"

"Yeah," I said.

"I got to go," I said.

"'Bye," I said.

Walking fast.

Some girls in the bathroom were talking about some other girl who was lesbian. They said that. They said she would never have a baby, because lesbians didn't get periods. But Margo had Elle. And John and Robbie. And there were Tampax tampons in the cabinet over the bathroom sink. Maybe it was just Cassandra Wiggins who was lesbian. Lesbians kissed each other. Instead of ever kissing guys, they just kissed each other. Touched each other's breasts.

LADY JANE sang songs in the mornings at our house, little bits of songs from the radio, or songs from the records she played, Jimmy Henry's records. She never knew all the words, just little bits of words that she sang over and over. Sometimes when I came home at night, Lady Jane was there, singing the same song she had been singing in the morning.

Her blue sweater with the leather on the elbows was hanging on the back of the chair by the door one morning. The blue sweater never moved after that, or maybe she put it on sometimes and then put it back on the chair. Scarves started to hang from doorknobs. One night there were wet blue kneesocks hanging by the towel in the bathroom. Brown sandalwood soap was in the soapdish by the bathtub. There were long blond hairs mixed in with the brown ones in the hairbrush, long blond hairs, long straight brown hairs, and my long dark curling hairs, all in our hairbrush.

I kept my Tampax tampons in my dresser drawer, in with my underpants and socks. I kept my money from Someone's Beloved Threads in there, in with the Tampax tampons.

I didn't tell Elle that I started my periods. I didn't tell Elle that Lady Jane was moving into our house, one piece of stuff at a time. When I saw Elle at school, I didn't tell her anything. I looked at her without looking at her eyes, at her face, at her neck.

At lunchtime Elle hung out by the gym door sometimes with the Mexican guys, sometimes Pete, sometimes out in the hall with the other guys who weren't Mexican, where the eighth-grade girls were sometimes hanging out too. She would lean against the wall and laugh. I saw her from the doorway of the cafeteria when I stood in line there. I heard her laughing when I got my tray and went inside.

WHEN I got home our house was dark. No Blackbird. I went to the front door, and into the hallway, and there was laughing. From inside the painted apartment, laughing and someone talking. I went to the door and listened. I got down and looked under the door.

The light of the candle lit up the floor, the mattress. Elle was sitting on the mattress.

She said, "Don't."

She said, "Come on."

She said, "Listen to this."

She held up a book. My book. My book *Peter Pan*, from the shelf in there. She started to read out loud.

"Fairy dust," she read.

Then she started laughing, stopped reading and started laughing.

Black hightops walked past the candlelight, and a hand reached down and took my book away from Elle and dropped my book on the mattress, and Pete sat down next to her. Pete took Elle's hair in his hand and he put his face into it, covering his face with Elle's hair. He wrapped her hair around his hand and pulled, pulling more of her hair, pulling her face to his face.

Elle said, "Don't."

Pete said, "Don't what?"

Elle said, "Don't do that."

Pete took Elle's hair in both of his hands, and he pulled hard, pulled Elle's head back, and he put his mouth on her neck.

Elle whispered, "Don't."

I got up. I couldn't get the key out of my pocket, couldn't unbutton my jacket, my fingers wouldn't work like fingers, and I heard my own breathing. That was all I heard, my own breathing, no laughing, no talking inside, no Elle saying, "Don't."

I went back out on the front porch, slamming the front door behind me, and I ran out to the sidewalk, ran across Eleventh Avenue, across the Safeway parking lot. When I got to Colfax Street I stopped running, and walked down the street through the people there, walked looking at my feet, looking at the sidewalk going by, hearing Elle saying "Don't," hearing my own breathing. Hearing my own name.

Blackbird was at the curb, at a bus stop, and Jimmy Henry leaned across the seat, rolling down the window.

"Sarajean," he said. "Sarajean."

I stopped and looked at him through the clouds of my own breath.

"Sarajean," he said. "Where are you going? Didn't you hear me?"

He said, "Hop in."

I opened the rusted red door and got in. The heater was on, and I shut the door, shut myself into the warm dark inside of Blackbird.

"Where are you going so fast?" he said.

He said, "I'm going over to the Celestial. Want to go?"

Celestial Tea Palace was noisy and steamy and yellow bright and full of people. Jimmy Henry went to a seat at the counter, and I walked right behind him, sat down next to him. Lulu Bell went by us with four mugs of coffee and she said,

"Hey. Late rush."

She set one of the coffees down in front of Jimmy Henry and she hurried away with the other three. Jimmy Henry looked at me, and then pushed the coffee to in front of me. I poured in milk from the pitcher, poured in sugar from the sugar shaker, stirred the coffee, stirred and stirred, the coffee swirling around in the mug, the spoon clinking in there.

Lady Jane came up to the counter in front of us.

"Hi," she said. "I'll be here for a while yet."

She leaned across the counter and kissed Jimmy Henry on his nose. She put a coffee mug in front of him, and she poured it full.

Jimmy Henry said, "Are you hungry?"

"No," I said.

He said, "Want anything?"

"No," I said.

He said, "How's Constanzia?"

"She's all better, pretty much," I said. "She takes catnaps."

Lulu Bell went by again, carrying three plates of sandwiches in one hand, alfalfa sprouts popping out of the sandwiches like little hairs all over the plates, on the floor, and a pot of coffee in her other hand.

She said, "Hey. Why don't you guys come over later? We'll be out of here about eight. We could get a pizza and watch TV."

Jimmy Henry said, "You have a TV?"

"JFK talked me into it," Lulu Bell said. "He can talk me into anything."

His biggest fan.

She went off with the three plates and the pot of coffee, and Jimmy Henry said, "Want to go? Watch TV and eat pizza?"

"I don't know," I said. "So, how come you never took any baby pictures?"

Jimmy Henry leaned his elbows on the counter, one elbow on each side of his mug, and he rubbed his face.

"I was in Vietnam when you were a baby," he said.

Lady Jane came up to the counter in front of us.

"So," she said. "Want to go watch TV with Nancy and JFK?"

"You mean Lulu?" I said.

"Well, yeah, Lulu," Lady Jane said. "That isn't really her name you know. It's just kind of a joke. Want to go?"

Jimmy Henry didn't look up.

I said, "Okay."

We all got in Blackbird, Jimmy Henry driving, and Lady Jane and Lulu. I rode in back. I sat under the window, under their three heads. We went past Colfax Street and down to Sixth Avenue and stopped at Poretti's Pizza, and Jimmy Henry went in. I looked at Lady Jane and Lulu through the window. Lady Jane's long blond hair tied back with a bandanna. Lulu had short curly hair that went into little curls on the back of her neck. She wore gold hoops in her ears.

When Jimmy Henry came back out with the pizza he handed it to me.

"Here," he said. "This will keep you warm back there. Don't eat it all before we get there."

JFK SAT on the couch in their front room, and the TV was on. He wore cutoffs, and no shirt, and no shoes or socks, and the heater hissed steam in the corner.

"Hey," Lulu said. "Lord it's hot in here."

"Pizza," JFK said. "I'm pretending it's summer."

JFK's ribs poked out, and his hair hung down over his skinny shoulders like it tickled. He climbed over the back of the couch toward the pizza box.

"Far out," Lady Jane said. She took off her coat, and she stepped out of her clogs and took off her socks, wiggling her bare toes.

"What's on TV?" Lulu said.

"The *Million-Dollar Movie*," JFK said. "It starts right after this stupid *Fairy Tale Theater*."

"What's on *Fairy Tale Theater*?" Lulu said.

"It's 'Rapunzel,'" JFK said. "It's like halfway over."

I got a piece of pizza, and I sat on the floor in front of the TV. The prince was climbing up Rapunzel's hair, which was already cut off by the witch. The long braid hanging out the window of Rapunzel's tower showed kind of purple on the little TV set. I took off my jacket, and I took off my sweater.

"Hot, huh?" said Lulu, running her fingers through her short hair. "Maybe we should turn the heat down a little?"

"Just take off your shoes and socks," JFK said. "Put on your cutoffs."

I lifted my hair off my neck.

"Lulu," I said. "Want to cut my hair?"

"Sure," Lulu said. "You need your ends trimmed?"

"No," I said. "I want it short. Like yours."

"Oh, no, honey," she said. "You have such pretty hair."

"Yes," I said. "I want it short. Like your hair."

Lady Jane said, "That's a big decision. Why don't you think about it?"

Jimmy Henry was looking at me.

"What do you think, Jimmy?" Lady Jane said.

"He doesn't care," I said. "It's my hair."

Jimmy Henry said, "She's never had short hair. It's always been long."

"Well," Lulu said. "I can do it. Are you sure you want it this short?"

"Cool," JFK said. "Guys with long hair. Girls with short hair. Cool."

Lulu and I went into the kitchen and she set a chair in the middle of the floor.

"Stick your head under the faucet," she said. "Your hair has to be wet."

She handed me a towel, and when my hair was soaking wet, I sat in the chair, and she wrapped another towel around my neck. She took a beaded leather pouch out of the drawer.

"My scissors," she said.

The scissors made long smooth sounds, and slick wet clumps of my hair fell on the kitchen floor. Lulu's hands tickled my head, and she cut, and cut, and cut, and cut my hair all off.

Finally she stepped back and looked.

"There's a mirror in the bedroom," she said.

I went through the front room.

"Wow," Lady Jane said. "Far out. Short."

Jimmy Henry looked.

The face that looked back from the mirror, looked back out of JFK's baby pictures, only kind of looked like my face.

ELLE CAME up to me at my locker.

"Wow," she said. "You cut your hair."

She said, "Who cut it for you?"

I said, "You were at my house last night."

"It looks pretty cool," she said. "Kind of a shag."

I jammed my afternoon books onto the top shelf.

"We were waiting for you," Elle said. "Pete opened the door to that cool apartment."

I took out my morning books.

"What?" she said. "What's wrong?"

"So is Pete your new boyfriend?" I said.

I balanced my books between the side of the locker and my leg, looking up on the shelf for my English folder.

"What were you doing?" Elle said. "Spying on us?"

I looked at her and she didn't look at me. No new hickeys. Her orange hair all around her head. Long orange hair. I slammed my locker door shut, without my English folder.

"I got to go," I said, and I walked away, and Elle said, "You said he wasn't your boyfriend."

I forgot to ask her about the baggie of marijuana.

I saw Pete at lunchtime, by the gym door. I looked at him until he looked at me. I kept looking at him, and he came over to where I was, across the hall. He walked slow, and some of the other Mexican boys watched him walking. They were all bigger than Pete. His hair was the longest of all the Mexican boys.

He said, "I didn't know that was you at first. You got your hair cut."

Smiling.

I said, "If you ever come to my house again, I'll tell Jimmy Henry you're there."

His smile kind of stopped right on his face.

I walked away, into the cafeteria, the back of my neck naked.

ELLE WAITED for me after school, next to my locker, leaning there.

I said, "Hi," and went past her to my locker, opened the lock.

She said, "Want to do something?"

"Like what?" I said.

I stacked up my English book, my biology book, my folders for homework.

"I don't care," she said.

"Right now?" I said. "I'm going over to Someone's Beloved Threads."

She said, "I'll walk with you."

We went down the long hallway, all the kids hurrying to get out, and me not hurrying, not saying anything to Elle, and my face all stiff with just looking at the door, looking outside, not looking at Elle.

At the Sixth Avenue gate, kids crowded out in different directions, up Sixth Avenue, down Sixth Avenue, across the street in crowds. Not waiting for the light.

Elle said, "Are you mad at me?"

I said, "I just hate it."

"What?" she said.

"I don't know," I said. "I hate those guys, and I hate those hickeys, and I hate those black lines you put on your eyes."

"You don't like my eyeliner?" Elle said. "Why not? And besides, I don't have any hickeys. See?"

She pulled down at the neck of her shirt, and I didn't look.

She said, "That was just kind of an accident."

I said, "Getting hickies is an accident?"

She said, "Who cut your hair?"

"JFK's mom," I said. "We were eating pizza."

Elle said, "JFK?"

"John Fitzgerald Kennedy Karpinski," I said.

"You call him JFK?" she said.

"His mom works at that place with Lady Jane is all," I said. "She cut my hair over at their house."

"Who all was there?" Elle said.

"Me and him and Lady Jane," I said. "And Lulu, or Nancy, or whatever his mom's name is. And Jimmy Henry."

"Does Jimmy Henry like it?" Elle said.

The slushy snow along Colfax Street was melting into black puddles in the street and trash floating, cigarette butts and French fries.

"So," Elle said. "Is Lady Jane going to move into your house you think?"

A page of newspaper. A tiny mitten with red snowflakes.

Elle said, "So what if she moves in and everybody's all happy and your real mom shows up?"

The light changed, and Elle jumped across the puddle. I walked around the puddle, out into the intersection, and a car beeped at me, like about to run me over. I jumped back onto the curb, and the papers in my English folder scattered out, my new homework, my old homework, all in with the wet trash.

"Shit," I said, and I tried to get the wet papers out of the puddle and my biology book dropped right in. Elle grabbed at the papers that were blowing down the street, and I picked up my biology book that looked wrecked. Looked wet in all its pages.

Elle said, "Here."

"Give me that," I said, grabbing the handful of papers.

"Well, don't cry," she said.

"Just shut up," I said, down on the sidewalk, my wet stuff, and the cold wind up Colfax Street blowing more of my stuff away.

I stacked my English book and my folders on the sidewalk, and jammed the wet papers into a folder, in with the dry papers that didn't get blown away, and I picked them all up in one arm, and my wet biology book.

"Why do you carry all that shit around anyway?" Elle said, handing me more wet papers. "Why are you crying? Quit crying."

"It's my homework," I said. "Just shut up."

"Okay, okay," she said. "Just come on."

She pulled my arm, pulling me across the street.

"Come on," she said.

"Leave me alone," I said.

"What, leave you alone?" she said. "You're a mess. Wipe your nose on your sleeve or something."

"Just shut up," I said.

I wiped my nose on my sleeve.

When we got to Someone's Beloved Threads, Elle came in with me. Constanzia smiled and nodded and didn't say anything, or get up from her chair. She was sewing a shirt sleeve. I put my books on the counter, and opened up the wet pages of my biology book. The pages were just wet at the edges, but the cover was soaked.

"I dropped my book in a puddle," I said to Constanzia.

"Put it there, by the heater," she said.

I laid my book open on the floor, and the warm air blowing from the heater vent blew at the pages, lifting each page a little. I spread my homework papers across the counter, the wet ones and the dry ones, trying to put them in order, trying to see which ones were gone up Colfax Street.

"See, it's okay," Elle said, leaning on the counter, poking in the box of broken necklaces. "You get all freaked out about nothing."

"It isn't about nothing," I said. "It's about getting As."

"Bs are just as goods as As," Elle said.

"How would you know," I said. "You don't even get Bs. You get Cs."

"Cs and Bs," Elle said.

Constanzia laid the shirt aside and got up slow out of her chair.

"I'll be back after a little nap," she said. "Erico is out in the alley, out back. Hammering at something."

She went through the striped blanket, and her slow steps went up the stairs.

"I really like your hair," Elle said.

"Just shut up about my hair," I said.

"Why are you mad at me?" Elle said. "Did I knock your books into a puddle? No. I'm trying to be nice."

"Why?" I said. "Why aren't you with your boyfriend?"

"Look," she said. "I don't even like Pete. I don't want to be his girlfriend. Buddy either. I think I like that guy Neal."

"You going to let him pull your hair and give you hickies on your neck?" I said.

Elle let the broken necklaces pieces drop back into the box. My biology book pages blew in a papery drying sound. Erico hammering out back. I ran my fingers in little circles on the counter, leaving little circles on the glass. The door opened, and shut, and Elle was gone.

AT LUNCHTIME Elle was by our lockers, and she was talking to a girl named Talia. Talia was an eighth-grader. Talia wore a leather coat, not a jacket, a coat. Talia wore her leather coat all the time, like an outfit, and blue suede boots.

Talia smiled and said hi to me.

"Sarajean," Elle said. "Are you working today?"

I said, "Yeah."

She said, "Want to go over my house with Talia and me first?"

She leaned close to me when I unlocked my locker.

"She has a joint," Elle whispered.

"Hey," I said, whispering back. "What about that lid you were going to get? With my five dollars?"

"I'll have to owe it to you," she said.

I sorted out my books, my morning books on the shelf, taking down my afternoon class books. Talia leaned against the lockers. Talia had smears of white under each eyebrow, and she had glittery lavender eye shadow on her eyelids.

Talia whispered to Elle. Then Elle whispered to me.

"Unless you want to go now," she said.

Math was going to be a workbook day, just working at our desks. Biology was going to be handing back yesterday's test and going over everybody's wrong answers. Then study hall.

I said, "I'll meet you out back by the driveway."

THEY WALKED together, talking, walking next to each other on the sidewalk.

"Baby powder," Talia said. "You put baby powder on your eyelashes first, and then mascara, and it makes your eyelashes really thick."

Elle said, "Do you take your mascara off with Vaseline or something before you go to bed?"

"No," Talia said. "Just leave it on. It builds up after a while. I think your eyelashes just get thicker and thicker."

"Doesn't it sting?" I said. "Baby powder? In your eyes?"

Talia looked kind of sad.

"A little," she said.

It was cold in Elle's apartment, and no one was there. Elle turned on a radio that sat on the windowsill. Commercials came on, a guy jabbering fast.

"New radio," I said.

Elle sat down on one end of the couch, and Talia sat on the other end. A big space between them. I leaned on the windowsill, by the new radio, the cold air from the crack under the window's bottom edge coming up through my jacket.

Talia opened her purse, a brown leather shoulder strap purse, and she reached around in it. She took out a big joint. Bright pink. She smoked some, and Elle smoked on it.

Strawberry. The wet end of the joint tasted like strawberry.

"Strawberry," I said.

Talia blew out a long cloud of smoke.

"Strawberry Easy Widers," she said.

I took a big hit and held it in until I started to cough.

"Easy Widers?" I said between coughing and coughing.

"Easy Wider rolling papers," Talia said. "They come in strawberry and spearmint. But the spearmint makes your mouth green."

She took the pink joint and smoked, not coughing, and handed it to Elle. Elle didn't cough either. I didn't stop coughing, and after Elle and Talia handed the joint back and forth a few times, Talia pinched the lit end out and put the joint back somewhere in her purse.

She said to Elle, "Did you get high?"

"Yeah," Elle said. "What you want to do now?"

"Let's go downtown," Talia said. "May Company. Try on makeup?"

Elle went out the door, and Talia followed right behind her. I turned off the radio dial, and went out, shut the door and went down after them, hurrying down the stairs to one step behind Talia, to the leather smell of Talia's black coat. We got outside, to the sunny sidewalk, and the cold wind.

Elle turned around to me and she said, "How about you Sarajean? Want to go downtown?"

I said, "I don't know."

The sun lit up Elle's hair, red, orange, blond, dark, bright, gold, and the wind blew it all into kinks and curls, like Elle hated. Talia's hair was long and straight, light brown, hanging straight and shiny brown down the black leather. The wind shining in her hair. Talia taller than Elle, Elle small-looking. Their feet matched in steps, Elle's cowboy boots, Talia's blue suede boots, and I took one black hightop step for every two steps they took, then one step for every three steps they took, and when they crossed Logan Street, I turned, and disappeared out of the noisy wind, away from behind them.

I went down Logan Street to the alley, and then into the alley, behind

Bill's Market, empty boxes all smashed and stacked up flat, behind Elle's old house. Under the third-floor bathroom window, used to be a sunporch.

At the Grant Street end of the alley I went back out to Seventeenth Avenue. Elle and Talia were down past Bead Here Now. They went down the hill, to Lincoln Street, and turned the corner on Lincoln. Disappeared.

The round Bead Here Now sign was squeaking, blowing in the wind. It was warm in there, out of the wind. Dark in there, out of the sun.

The lady said, "Hi, there."

She was watering the plants in the big macramé hanging in the window.

I said, "Hi, there."

I went in slow circles around the tables of colors, and then I went in smaller circles between the tables of colors. I bumped into a lady between the green table and the purple table.

"Sorry," I said.

"Sarajean?" the lady said. "Sarajean, is that you?"

"I don't know," I said. "Yes, it's me."

The lady was all dressed in blue, a blue skirt and a blue sweater, and she had a small blue scarf sitting on her head.

"Fern," the lady said. "Remember me?"

"Fern," I said.

"From Saint Therese Carmelite?" the lady said. "Free School?"

Then her face looked right.

"Yeah, Fern, I remember," I said.

"Except I'm not Fern anymore," she said. "I'm Sister Ann Josephus."

"Sister what?" I said.

"Sister Ann is fine," she said. "Fern was kind of a name I chose for a while."

She had a white shirt that buttoned at the neck, and a silver cross necklace.

"Oh," I said, "Are you a nun?"

"Almost," she said. "Look at you."

She put her hands on my shoulders. I was almost as tall as her.

"Short hair," she said. "But besides that, you look just the same."

"The same as in Free School?" I said.

She laughed, and laughing made her Fern the rest of the way, Fern from Free School.

"Look at that pretty short hair," she said. "What is happening in your life? You still live in Denver?"

"Well, yeah," I said. "Same place as ever. I go to Mountain View Junior High."

She dropped her hands from my shoulders, and her face got serious, and I remembered how Fern's face got serious so fast like that.

"Same house?" she said. "On Ogden Street?"

"Yeah," I said. "Me and Jimmy Henry."

"What about Tina Blue?" she said.

"No," I said. "She never came back. That apartment is still empty."

I said, "Lady Jane tried to find her. Remember Lady Jane?"

"Lord, yes," she said. "Ruby Tuesday? Lucy in the Sky?"

"So what's your name?" I said. "I mean, what's your name to call you?"

"Oh, Sister Ann," she said. "I haven't taken my final vows yet, but I'm Sister Ann. Ann was the mother of Mary."

I said, "Mary, like Jesus's mother?"

"Yes," she said. "That Mary."

"I have a Mary," I said.

I pulled the silver chain out from under my shirt and showed the bright blue medal.

"Ah," she said, "Beautiful."

She took the Mary medal in her fingers and looked close, her face by my face. Grayish blue eyes. Pale eyelashes. No smell. Her long bony fingers.

"Constanzia gave it to me," I said. "I'm not Catholic."

She stepped back and looked at my face.

"Beautiful," she said. "So grown-up."

My cheeks got warm and stiff into a smile.

"And John Fitzgerald Kennedy Karpinski?" I said. "He's kind of a friend of mine."

She said, "The last time I heard from Tina Blue she was back in Omaha."

I said, "Are you still a teacher? A nun teacher?"

"No," she said. "I work at a place called Saint Mary's of the Valley. Out by Ogallala?"

"Oh, yeah," I said. "I know about that place. It's for girls that get pregnant when they're still in high school,"

She smiled.

"Kind of famous, huh?" she said.

"Do you still do macramé?" I said.

"I teach some of the girls to do it," she said. "I'm just here to go to a meeting. Kind of a meeting. At the Cathedral of the Holy Mother?"

"The white church," I said. "Margo likes that church."

"Margo," she said. "And Lalena. Lovely Lalena."

"Elle," I said. "We have to say Elle now. Because of Lalena being a whore in a song. Oh. Sorry."

"That's okay," she said.

She said, "I have to go."

She leaned forward and kissed me on my forehead.

"Be good, Sarajean," she said. "I'm glad I saw you."

She turned around and started away, out from the tables.

"Wait," I said.

She turned around.

"That scarf," I said. "How does that scarf stay on your head?"

"Bobby pins," she said.

"Oh," I said.

"Well," I said. "'Bye."

"'Bye, Sarajean," she said, smiling, and I could feel the place on my forehead where her lips touched.

When I left I went as far as Bill's Market. I bought the biggest bag of potato chips they had in there, and out on the sidewalk I filled my mouth up with as many potato chips as I could fit in there before I even started chewing seriously.

At Someone's Beloved Threads Constanzia was talking to two girls at the counter, and all three of them looked through a big box of stuff. She looked at me, smiled at me, smiled at the two girls, kept talking. I stood by the window, looking out the window, eating the potato chips. All of them.

When the two girls left I went back behind the counter. I threw the empty potato chip bag in the trash back there. I sucked the potato chip grease off my fingers. Constanzia was sorting out the clothes.

"Guess what?" I said. "I know a nun."

Constanzia stopped sorting out the clothes and looked at me.

"Sister Ann something," I said. "She used to be Fern. Now she's a nun."

Constanzia nodded her head and started sorting out the clothes again.

She said, "My sister became a nun. She became Sister Ursula when she took the veil."

"Bobby pins," I said. "They keep those veils on with bobby pins."

WHEN I got home Lady Jane was there, but not Jimmy Henry.

"Hey," I said. "Remember Fern?"

"Fern?" she said. "Oh yeah, how could I forget, the Jesus freak."

"She was a Jesus freak?" I said.

"She totally weirded me out," Lady Jane said. "She was always asking the weirdest questions."

"Well," I said. "She isn't a Jesus freak anymore. She's a nun."

"You're kidding," she said.

"I saw her today," I said. "Sister Ann something."

"Perfect," Lady Jane said. "A fucking nun."

"Boy," I said. "I bet it's a triple sin or something, to say that."

"Yeah, that's what she always was talking about," Lady Jane said.

THE NEXT morning Elle was in the second-floor bathroom before first hour. She was smearing copper glitter on her eyelid from a little square plastic box that looked like blue pearl.

"Wow," I said. "Cool."

"Where did you go yesterday?" she said.

She closed one eyelid and looked at the coppery stuff on there.

"I guess I got lost," I said. "Do you remember Fern, from Free School?"

"Fern?" Elle said. "No, I don't remember Fern."

She started copper on the other eyelid.

"That color is beautiful," I said. "Copper. It all goes. You're a cinnamon girl."

"Is that a poem?" Elle said.

"No," I said. "I think it's an old song."

Elle clicked the blue pearl box shut and she put it into a brown leather shoulder strap purse.

"Hey," I said. "You got a purse. Is that real leather?"

"Yes," she said. "Real leather."

"Did it cost a lot?" I said.

"Nope," she said.

She blinked her copper eyelids at me.

AT THE end of the day, I got to my locker just when Talia and Elle were walking away, up the hall, walking together, not looking back. Talia taller than Elle. Elle small.

IN THE morning, Lady Jane made oatmeal. She stood at the stove, stirring the oatmeal in the pot, wearing a long blue plaid shirt. Jimmy Henry's plaid shirt. I sat at the table, looked out the window. Looked at the funnies that were still there from Sunday. Lady Jane put a bowl of oatmeal in front of me, and she sat down across from me with another bowl of oatmeal for her.

"Where's Jimmy Henry?" I said.

"Still asleep," she said. "Want some honey?"

I scooped a glob of honey out of the sticky jar and stirred it around in my bowl of oatmeal.

"Milk?" she said.

I poured in some milk and stirred it around.

"You're going to be late," she said.

I stirred the oatmeal in my bowl.

"Are you okay?" she said.

"Yeah," I said. "But I don't think I'll go to school today."

"Are you sick?" she said.

"No," I said. "I just don't think I'll go to school today."

"Why not?" she said.

I scooped out another glob of honey and ate it off the spoon.

"Is the coffee water hot?" I said.

Lady Jane said, "Is something bothering you?"

I got up and opened the cabinet, a mug, the jar of instant coffee. I lit the fire under the kettle.

"Is something wrong?" Lady Jane said.

I said, "I'm just letting my oatmeal cool down."

Jimmy Henry's bedroom door opened, and he came into the kitchen. He had on his blue jeans and no shirt, no socks. Long, tangled hair.

"Sarajean's not going to school today," Lady Jane said.

Jimmy Henry got down a mug and looked at the jar of instant coffee.

"Want to make some of that for me?" he said.

I put a spoon full of instant coffee into his mug, and he sat down at the table.

"Oatmeal?" he said, looking at the bowls. "So, how come you're not going to school today?"

"Because I'm a little truant," I said.

Jimmy Henry picked up my oatmeal spoon and dug into the jar of honey. He scooped out a glob and ate it off the spoon.

"Well," he said. "As long as you have a reason."

The kettle started to jiggle, and I turned off the fire and poured hot water into my mug, into Jimmy Henry's mug.

"Let's go for a ride," he said.

"Ride where?" Lady Jane said. "I have to go to work."

Jimmy Henry said, "We'll drop you off."

After Celestial Tea Palace Jimmy Henry turned around and drove Blackbird out Colfax Street, away from the mountains, past the parking lots and past some rows of little houses, past a trailer court, and then another, past the other highways turning away into the wide, flat places where there wasn't anything. He drove with one hand and smoked a cigarette with his other hand.

I said, "Who lives out here?"

"Ranchers," Jimmy Henry said. "I guess."

Riding along, Blackbird bumping smooth and fast, quiet under the noise of driving, warm dusty smell of gas and Blackbird's heater. It felt like smoking marijuana.

Jimmy Henry turned off the highway at the next road that came up, and we drove over that road, looking at the sun. Same as the other road, except there was the sun.

A sign said DEER TRAIL—POPULATION 865.

"Deer Trail?" I said.

Little places started to come up out of the empty flat, trailers parked way off the road, houses with sheds and cars, a leaning barn right next to the road, and then a gas station, and signs. SAM'S HARDWARE. JB CAFE. FIRST PRESBYTERIAN CHURCH—ALL WELCOME. The houses got closer and closer to each other. Jimmy Henry slowed way down and we passed a sign that said DEER TRAIL ELKS CLUB WELCOMES YOU.

I said, "Deer Trail Elks?"

Jimmy Henry turned into the parking lot of the JB Cafe.

We went in through the screen door, inside to cigarettes and coffee smell and fried smell. The waitress came over with the coffee pot in one hand and two mugs in her other hand, clinking.

She said, "Morning."

"Morning," Jimmy Henry said.

The waitress set the mugs down.

She said, "Coffee."

Jimmy Henry said, "Please."

I said, "Please."

She filled each mug with a dump of coffee perfectly to the top, and she said,

"Breakfast?"

Jimmy Henry looked at me. I looked at him, looked at the waitress, stiff hair twisted up on top of her head, pencil sticking out, glasses, skinny, yellow blouse. White apron with a pink stain. Behind her, on the counter, there was a glass case with donuts and pieces of pie on plates.

"Can I have a donut?" I said.

She said, "Donut?"

"Please," I said.

"Sugar or glazed?" she said.

I said, "Sugar?"

Jimmy Henry said, "Two of them."

The waitress went back behind the counter, set the coffee pot back on its place, slid the back of the case open, one long smooth move. She took two sugar donuts out, two plates, one hand, slid the back of the case shut, back out from behind the counter, brought us the donuts.

Jimmy Henry said, "Thanks."

I said, "Thanks."

She took the pencil from behind her ear with one hand, took a little pad of paper from her apron pocket with her other hand, scribbled there, tore off the page and put it on the table. She stuck the pencil back behind her ear.

She said, "Welcome."

She went back and sat at the counter. There was a newspaper open at the crossword puzzle.

Jimmy Henry sat facing the window, and he stared past me, staring out, squares of windowlight in his eyes. I turned around and looked out where he was looking, an empty lot across the street, some wood buildings out past the empty lot. A pickup truck went by. I turned back around, and Jimmy Henry was looking at me, my eyes and his eyes, and his eyes crinkled into a smile for a second.

"Welcome to Deer Trail, Colorado," he said.

"Why did we come here?" I said.

He said, "Sugar donuts, I guess."

There was glitter of sugar in his beard, and gray in with the long light brown and darker brown.

"You've got gray," I said. "In your beard."

"Gray?" he said.

"Well," I said. "Gray and sugar."

The smile came back into his eyes, and was gone again, and he smoothed his hand down his beard.

He said, "Who'd of thunk."

I said, "What?"

He said, "Who ever would of thunk that I'd live long enough to get gray."

"How old are you?" I said.

"Thirty-three," he said. "End of the line for some guys."

"Some guys?" I said. "Huh?"

"Jesus," he said. "I guess that's how old Jesus was."

"Jesus?" I said. "Were you Catholic?"

"No," he said. "Lady Jane was going on about some Jesus freak she used to know. I don't usually think too much about Jesus. I remember he was thirty-three when he got crucified."

I said, "Do you remember Fern? From Free School? Lady Jane said she was a Jesus freak."

"No," he said. "I kind of avoid Jesus freaks."

When we were done with coffee and sugar donuts we went back outside, out to Deer Trail. Past the JB Cafe there were some more buildings, and another road. Jimmy Henry and I walked along the broken sidewalk, dead grass edging into the cracks. Just walking. Past Sam's Hardware. Past the Conoco station. There was a little store of junk, no sign with a name, but a sign that said OPEN.

"Let's go in here," I said.

I pushed open the door. It was cold inside, and it smelled like oil, like gas.

A table right by the door was full of dishes, different plates, a leaning stack of bowls. Jelly jars. A row of Yogi Bear glasses, Yogi Bear running around each glass with a picnic basket, and his hat flying off his head. A counter, and a long shelf went back from the counter, a shelf with tools lined up. Jimmy Henry walked along the shelf of tools, his hands in his back pockets. Looking.

A guy came out from somewhere behind everything, kind of an old guy. Wearing truckers.

He said, "Morning."

Jimmy Henry said, "Morning."

I said, "Morning."

The clothes were over in a corner, old suit jackets, weird old dresses, all on hangers on a round rack. On top of the rack, sitting in the middle by itself, there was a brown hat. It was an old guy hat, kind of wide. It was a Walt Whitman hat. I tried the hat on, and it was too big, came down warm and soft over my ears, all around my head.

"Mirror up here," the guy said.

I went up and looked into the little square of mirror hanging on the wall. A perfect Walt Whitman hat.

"How much for this hat?" I said.

The guy said, "How much you think?"

I took the hat off and looked at it, at the curled edges of the wide brim, the soft brown wool, the leather band around the inside.

I said, "Four dollars?"

"Sounds fair," the guy said.

I put the hat back on my head and I gave the guy four dollar bills. Then I looked back in the mirror.

"Buy a new hat?" Jimmy Henry said.

"Yeah," I said, looking at the side of my head as far as I could see in the mirror.

"It's just like Walt Whitman's hat," I said.

Jimmy Henry said, "I guess I didn't know Walt Whitman had a hat."

NO ONE was allowed to wear a hat in school, which was a school rule. No hats between the third bell in the morning and the last bell of the afternoon. I kept my Walt Whitman hat in my locker, on top of my stack of books.

Marcia Henson said, "What is that?"

"It's a hat," I said.

Marcia Henson said, "Tss."

Marcia Henson liked to say words that were really just sounds.

Sometimes she said, "Ka."

Sometimes she said, "Ffuh."

When Marcia Henson said sounds, the sounds always meant the same thing.

I said, "This is a hat just like Walt Whitman wore."

Marcia Henson said, "Puh," shaking her head, walking away.

Talia came up to my locker. She kind of leaned on the open door and she said,

"Where's Elle?"

"I don't know," I said. "Late, I guess."

"Nice hat," she said.

I said, "It's a Walt Whitman hat."

Talia said, "Who?"

"Walt Whitman," I said. *Leaves of Grass.*

Talia leaned close to me.

She said, "Want to buy a lid?"

I leaned close by Talia and I said, "Not that kind of grass. He was a poet."

"Who?" she said.

"Walt Whitman," I said.

She said, "Well, if you do, let me know."

I said, "Do what?"

"Want a lid," she said.

"Oh," I said. "Okay."

"Okay what?" she said. "Okay you want one?"

"Well, okay," I said.

"I'll see you after school?" she said.

"Okay," I said.

After the last bell, at my locker, Talia was there, and Elle was there.

Elle said, "Let's go over your house."

"My house?" I said.

"Get high," she said.

"I don't know," I said. "There might be somebody there."

I stacked up my books, took out my English book, my math book. I put on my Walt Whitman hat.

"I have to go to Someone's Beloved Threads," I said.

"You never want to do anything anymore," Elle said. "And that is really a weird hat."

Talia said, "I kind of like that hat."

Elle said, "You do?"

I shut my locker door.

I said, "This is a very cool hat."

We went outside the school, and when we got out to the sidewalk, Talia said, "So, you want one of these lids?"

I said, "Okay."

She walked next to me on the sidewalk, close, and then she put her hand into the outside pocket of my jacket, and then she stepped away, leaving the soft whispery plastic baggie in there.

"Ten bucks," she said.

I got two of my five-dollar bills out of my inside jacket pocket and gave them to her, folded, secret, into her hand.

"Cool," she said.

Elle said, "So, are we going to go get high or what?"

"I can't," I said. "I have math homework. I can't be high for math homework."

Elle lit a cigarette, and she walked on the sidewalk in her cowboy boots, and I walked behind her. Talia walked next to me.

Talia said, "Where did you get that hat?"

"At the Deer Trail store," I said.

She said, "Deer Trail?"

"Deer Trail," I said. "It's some little town."

She said, "Can I try it on?"

Elle flipped her cigarette out into the street and jammed her hands into the pockets of her jean jacket.

"Maybe some other time," I said. "You need a mirror to try on a hat anyway." When we got to Colfax Street Elle said,

"Let's go try on some lip gloss."

I said, "Lip gloss?"

"Lip gloss," Elle said.

She said, "See you later."

Talia said, "See you later, Sarajean."

They turned up Colfax Street together, away from Someone's Beloved Threads, Elle right next to Talia on the sidewalk, talking to her.

JFK CAME into Someone's Beloved Threads, and I said, "What are you doing here?"

He said, "Jeez, Sarajean, I came to see you."

Constanzia catnapped.

My math homework was spread out all over the counter, and JFK leaned across my papers.

"I still got that pipe," he whispered.

"Well, we can't do it in here," I said.

"Maybe after," he said.

"Okay," I said. "Hey, get your elbows off there, I have to hand that in."

"What time?" he said.

He picked up the paper and smoothed out where he had wrinkled it up.

"Six," I said.

He giggled. He gave me the peace sign, and he kind of scooted out the door.

"What a weirdo," I said, and Constanzia nodded in her catnap.

He came back at six, and I met him outside after I turned the sign around.

"So, you work there all the time now, huh?" he said.

"Where should we go?" I said.

"My house?" he said.

"No," I said.

I didn't say stinky orange rugs. I didn't say baby pictures.

"It's not too cold out," I said, "It's getting kind of like spring. Let's go in the alley."

We got into a corner of a dumpster and the brick back of a building, and I pinched some of my new marijuana into the little pipe.

He watched me.

He said, "Got a lid, huh?"

JFK faced the corner, out of the wind, and he lit the pipe. He held his breath and handed the pipe to me. It took four matches before I got the hot marijuana taste going down my throat.

I said, "So, how about if I keep this pipe for a while?"

"Sure," he said. "Want to smoke some more first? Or, maybe want to give me a little bud or two to take home with me?"

We walked up into the next alley, by the back doors of buildings, three dumpsters, a stack of wet magazines all tipped over.

"Wow," JFK said. "Look at that."

One of the wet magazines was lying open, out in the middle of the alley, and the picture was open to the streetlight shining on there. It was a picture of two naked women, and one of the women was lying on her back with her legs wide apart. She had her hands on her own breasts, long red fingernails. The other woman was kneeling next to her, putting her one hand's fingers in there, in between the other woman's spread-apart legs, and her other hand on her own butt. Long red fingernails.

JFK said, "God damn."

He said, "They're doing it to each other."

"Lesbian," I said.

My voice was a shaky whisper, and I cleared my throat and I said it again. "Lesbian."

I said, "Come on, quit staring like that."

I started walking down the alley, and JFK caught up.

He said, "Wow."

"Quit saying wow," I said.

We crossed Thompson Street.

He said, "So that's how lesbians do it, huh?"

"How should I know?" I said. "I don't care."

Long red fingernails. Up in there.

"Come on," I said.

It came out in a whisper.

"Come on," I said, louder, not a whisper. "This pipe won't stay lit."

We walked back out on Seventeenth Avenue.

"So how come you work at that place all the time?" JFK said, looking backward toward the alley still.

"I'm saving my money," I said. "I might save it for a sewing machine."

"Are you going to work there this summer, like all summer?" he said.

"I don't know," I said. "Look, where are we going?"

"I go visit my grandma in the summer," he said. "She lives up in the mountains. I go there for the whole summer."

"What about your mom?" I said.

"No," he said. "She has to work. She comes up when she gets two days in a row off. Estes Park."

"Why do you go there?" I said. "What do you do all day?"

"Go fishing and stuff," he said. "Hang out. I go up there on the bus."

"There's nothing to do up there," I said. "There's nothing but rocks. I'm going to work all summer."

"And hang out and wear makeup?" JFK said in a singy voice.

"I don't wear makeup," I said.

"Lalena does," he said. "You can see where it stops on her chin, where it's a different color from her neck."

"Elle," I said. "You're supposed to say Elle."

"And Talia," he said. "Talia puts on lips like a movie star. Big shiny pink movie star lips."

He smooched out his lips, and I tried not to laugh, and I had to start laughing anyway.

"Shut up," I said.

"Is Lalena your best friend?" he said.

"Shut up," I said.

At Lady Jane's house, Lady Jane was out on her front steps, standing there by a big box. There was another box, a smaller one, already taking up the second step.

JFK and I both said "hi" at the same time.

Lady Jane stood up straight, and she rubbed at her back.

"Hi, you guys," she said.

"What's that?" I said.

"Well," she said.

She said, "It's some dishes."

She sat down on the top step.

"I'm going to rent Tina Blue's apartment," she said.

"The painted apartment," I said.

"Well," Lady Jane said. "Yeah."

She tugged up the leg of her blue jeans and pulled her kneesock back up to her knee.

"The landlady told Jimmy Henry to see if he can rent it," she said.

Red kneesocks with yellow stars on the side.

"He's going to get the electric turned on tomorrow," she said. "He couldn't find the key. I haven't been in there yet."

She pulled the blue-jeans leg back down over her kneesock.

She said, "It's been like eight years."

"Better me than some stranger," she said.

"Sarajean?" she said. "Don't you think?"

JFK said, "Want me to help you carry some stuff?"

He picked up a box from the second step.

"Careful," Lady Jane said. "The elephant teapot."

"I have to go," I said. "I forgot my math homework at Constanzia's. I have to go get it."

"Here," JFK said. "Here, I'll carry that other box instead."

"That's okay," she said. "Jimmy Henry's coming over with his truck."

I turned and ran up the sidewalk.

I ran on the sidewalks until my breath cut into the inside of my chest. I slowed down to walking fast, crossed Colfax Street against the light, and a car beeped at me.

I said, "Fuck you," and never stopped.

My apartment. The painted apartment.

I stacked my books from the shelf in a tall stack and carried them up the stairs.

All the birdcloth.

My shoe box, and the candles, and the old ends of candles that rolled around in the top drawer, dark green, red. The purple one.

I took it all into my bedroom, and I sat down on the bed and pressed my fingers flat over my eyes and sat, still, and the light of my eyelids flashed like my heart beating, slower and slower.

1977

The front door was open, and the apartment door was open. I saw all the way through to the alley, the back door wide open too. Laughing came through the doors, and paint smell, and I went to the doorway at the back of the hall. Lady Jane stood on a ladder in the middle of the floor, and she was painting with a paint roller, painting wide streaks of white across the purple ceiling, half of the ceiling white already.

JFK was painting into a corner. He had speckles of white in his hair, paint on his face, paint on his skinny arms.

He said, "It's going to take two coats."

A half white room, patches of white, purple showing through.

Lady Jane climbed down the steps of the ladder, and came over to me in the doorway, and turned to look at the half white, half purple.

"We got yellow for the shelves," she said. "For over the green. Yellow trim."

A white lightbulb shone down from the middle of the ceiling. The mattress was gone. The little dresser was out on the back porch.

She had Jimmy Henry put the door back on the closet, and then she painted the door yellow. She put a piece of yellow and orange tie-dye across the tall window, and then she put her table there. The piece of yellow and orange tie-dye had straps hanging from the ends.

"It was a dress," she said. "A bridesmaid dress. We all had a different color. I'll just cut those straps off. Now I won't have to just stare out at the wall of the house next door."

She painted the little dresser shiny white, and then she decided she didn't like it. When I came home from school, the little dresser was out back by the trash cans.

She wound her Christmas tree lights around the railing of the stairs.

"It was so dark in that hallway," she said.

THE FIRST day of summer vacation Elle came over early. I was sitting on the top step of the front porch, and she came walking along the sidewalk, walking slow. She had a bandanna tied around her chest like a halter top, a triangle of red bandanna, and her cutoffs hung low, under her bellybutton, her bare stomach curving in, curving out.

She sat down next to me on the top step.

"What's the matter?" I said.

She said, "Why are you wearing that hat?"

I said, "You look like you've been crying."

"Talia split," she said.

"Split?" I said.

"Los Angeles," she said. "She has to go stay with her dad and her step-mother in the summer. She got on a bus. She has to go there every summer."

"Wow," I said. "Bummer."

She picked at the pink nail polish on her toenails.

I said, "What's she going to do in Los Angeles?"

"I don't know," Elle said. "How should I know?"

We sat there on the top step, Elle sniffing, me being quiet, Talia riding away on a bus. Elle's hair was piled up on top of her head, her shoulders bare, freckles, bony.

"Want to get high?" I said.

"Okay," she said.

I said, "Come on up."

We went up the stairs, and Elle said, "How come there's Christmas lights?"

"Don't ask me," I said.

I got the wooden pipe out of my top drawer and put a little clump of marijuana in it, took it out to the front room where Elle was flopped on the couch.

"Cute pipe," she said.

"It's half mine," I said. "Half mine, half JFK's."

She held the pipe out, looking at it.

"You mean John Fitzgerald Kennedy Karpinski has had his lips on this pipe?" she said. "That creepy little weasel."

"Here's some matches," I said.

She lit the pipe, and I got a stick of incense, took the matches back, lit the incense. The blue smoke of incense curled into the cloud of marijuana smoke, sandalwood smell, marijuana smell.

"I can't believe you hang out with him," she said.

She handed me the pipe.

"I don't really hang out with him," I said. "He's gone for the summer anyway. At his grandma's in the mountains."

I said, "I never got high first thing in the morning before."

"The only difference is you forget you're high," Elle said.

"I always forget I'm high," I said. "Until I like walk into the middle of the street, or start cracking up, and then Jimmy Henry just stares at me, and then I remember I got high."

"You think he knows you get high?" she said.

"No," I said. "Does Margo know you get high?"

"My daddy knows," Elle said. "He doesn't care. Margo doesn't know anything."

I said, "Does she know you smoke cigarettes?"

"No," she said. "Probably. I don't know. What do you think Jimmy Henry would do if he walked in right now and we're getting high?"

"I don't know," I said. "Nothing probably. Go in his room and shut the door."

I got up and opened the window.

The air of summer touched my arms, and I leaned out, looking down at the skinny sidewalk. I picked at the dark peeling paint, dropping the bits down. The window below me opened, and Lady Jane's head poked out. Her part in her hair was crooked. I flicked a little piece of paint down, a tiny bit that landed on her head. I picked off another piece and dropped it, and she jerked her head back when it fell past her face. I turned back into the room.

Elle was picking at her toenails.

"Got any pop?" she said.

Music came up from downstairs, and Elle looked up from her toes.

"What's that?" she said.

"I don't know," I said.

"I mean where's it coming from," she said.

"Lady Jane is up," I said. "Want some coffee?"

Elle said, "I hate coffee."

She came to the window and leaned out next to me.

"That must be weird," she said. "Her living there."

"I don't care," I said.

She said, "So, does she come up here all the time?"

Elle's hair tied up in a rubber band wisped out around her ears.

"Sometimes," I said.

"Or does he go down there?" she said.

She had freckles on her ears.

"I don't know," I said. "She just lives there now is all. Who cares."

Elle said, "Do you hear them?"

"God, Elle," I said, and shoved her with my shoulder.

I went and picked up the pipe from the applebox table. It was all smoked up. I put it in my pocket.

"Come on," I said. "Let's go to the store and get a pop."

We started down the stairs, and when we got to the bottom, Lady Jane opened her door.

"Hi, you guys," she said. "Where you going?"

"Nowhere," I said.

She said, "Want some French toast?"

I said, "No."

Elle said, "Yeah."

Elle went back to Lady Jane's open door, and I stood at the front door, looking out at the empty street.

"Come on, Sarajean," Lady Jane said.

I shut the front door and went back there.

Elle went in, to the middle of the room.

"Wow," she said. "Sure looks different."

I stared at her and she shut up.

Lady Jane said, "We can eat outside if you want. I got a table for the back porch."

She went over in the corner and opened the yellow-painted cabinet over the stove. The dishes in the cabinet were stacked up, big plates, little plates, coffee mugs all lined up, all different colors.

"Here," she said, handing plates to Elle. "Take these out back."

The table on the back porch was a round wooden table, with a book under one leg, and a lacy tablecloth, the lace torn into holes along the edges. Elle set the plates down, one by each chair, three chairs.

"Far out," she said. "Food."

There were shelves made of cement blocks and boards, and little house-plants in pots were lined up across the shelves. There were bigger pots, red geraniums, yellow marigolds, around the bottom of the sumac tree.

"Hey," I said. "What happened to the ivy tub?"

Lady Jane came out with two glasses of milk.

"I got rid of it," she said. "It was all falling apart, and the ivy was all weedy. It's spread all back to the garage. You want milk, don't you?"

She set the glasses of milk on the table and went back inside.

Elle said, "Milk?"

I picked up one of the glasses of milk and took it with me, to the edge of the porch. I sat down there, looking at the sumac tree, looking at the marigolds, at the geraniums. I poured the milk into the dirt. Elle came and sat next to me with the other glass of milk, and she poured it into the dirt. The milk puddled there, and then slowly soaked in.

"This place looks pretty nice now," Elle said. "It used to be all dark in there. You think she'll stay living here?"

Lady Jane came out with forks and knives and laid them on the table. "Almost ready," she said, and went back in.

"Is she always like that?" Elle said.

"Like what?" I said.

"I don't know," Elle said. "Like giving you a glass of milk and shit?"

Lady Jane came back out with the frying pan.

"Here we go," she said, singing out the words.

"Like that," Elle whispered.

I sat in the chair with my back to the open door of the yellow and white apartment. A crow landed in the sumac tree, the twisty branch bending down. The crow landed there, stretched its shining black wings out wide, and it screeched. Lady Jane jumped up.

"Shoo," she yelled. "Git."

"God damn it," she said.

"Why don't you like crows?" I said.

"He gets in the trash," she said. "Plus, there are baby sparrows in the eaves, and I'm afraid he'll get them."

"Do crows do that?" I said.

"I don't know," she said, looking at the crow.

He looked back at her with one black eye.

"He goes kind of nice with those yellow and red flowers," I said.

"Crows can be powerful allies," Lady Jane said. "But, I guess the deal is, you never know whose allies they are."

Elle looked me, rolled her eyes around.

I said, "Is that in your Audubon book?"

"No," Lady Jane said. "It's a Yaqui way of knowledge, or something."

"Yaqui?" I said.

"It's a Mexican thing," Lady Jane said.

Lady Jane went to the edge of the porch, and she stamped her bare foot. The crows spread his wings wide and screeched again, lifting out of the sumac tree, to the roof of the garage, and then away over the alley, shining black like white in the sun.

LATE AT night, I could hear them, when I was lying on the couch in the front room, reading, or just lying there, summer bugs ticking at the light in the ceiling. The sounds that came up from the tall narrow window were Lady Jane laughing ha haha, Jimmy Henry's quiet voice, not talking, his quiet voice down there in the dark. And then, after a while, nothing.

THE FLOWER box was white petunias in the front, and tall red zinnias behind, red zinnias so tall I could see them at the bottom of the window from inside, red along there.

I went to the shop every day, down the alley to the kitchen door. Erico was there sometimes, and he would say, "Ten o'clock."

And I would say, "Ten o'clock."

I went through the striped blanket, through to the front door. I turned the sign around from CLOSED to OPEN, and I opened the front door. The morning air came in the shop, morning air smell, and old clothes smell, coffee from the kitchen, sometimes coffee in a cup that Erico brought out to me.

Constanzia came down after I got there. She sat into her chair, her breathing careful. Sometimes she went quietly back asleep and sometimes I looked at her sleeping face, her sleeping hands in her lap.

One day Erico leaned a big ladder against the front of the shop outside, and he went up. I went out the door, and he was scraping the peeling old sunface away, messy bits dropping onto the red zinnias, on to the white petunias.

"Erico," I said. "Is it time to paint a new sunface? Finally?"

He kept scraping, and the old design of sun and leaves fell to the sidewalk in bits, and down on my face in bits. I moved out to the edge of the sidewalk.

"Erico?" I said.

He stopped scraping and looked down at me.

"Let's paint crows on there," I said.

"Maybe Friday we can draw a new design," he said. "First we have to scrape. Then sand. Then prepare a new surface."

"Why all that?" I said.

"Patience," he said. "For the sake of patience."

He scraped all that afternoon, across the top of the door, and down the sides, getting down off the ladder, moving the ladder to a new spot. I watched him from inside, his feet in brown boots on the ladder, and people walking around the ladder, people looking up at him.

The next day Erico sanded the wood around the door with his electric sander, the thick orange cord running through the shop to the big plug in the kitchen. Buzzing sharp and loud. There was dust, glittery in the air by the door, white on the windowsill, white on the red zinnias. Gray on the white petunias.

Then Erico had to go work somewhere else, and for two days the doorway of the shop was bare new-looking wood. On Friday there were cans of paint stacked by the door, and Erico painted the wood light gray.

"That's not a very pretty color," I said.

"Primer," Erico said. "It is the color of patience."

"LADY JANE," I said. "I need to look in your bird book."

She got *Birds of the World* down from the yellow shelf, and she set it on the table by the tall window. She pulled the orange and yellow tie-dye to the side so there would be light.

"Crows," I said. "I need to look at crows."

She sat down in the other chair at the table.

"Crows?" she said. "Why?"

"Just because," I said.

The crow picture was a crow looking straight up off the page, up at me.

"This isn't a very good picture to try and copy," I said. "I need a sideways crow."

"Try raven," Lady Jane said.

The raven was perfect. He was bigger, and he faced sideways in the picture. His beak was bigger, and bigger wings.

"What's the difference between a raven and a crow?" I said.

"Different birds," Lady Jane said.

She said, "Ravens are better."

"Why?" I said.

"Smarter," she said. "Tricksters."

"Yaqui?" I said.

"I guess," she said.

I DREW the raven over, onto a big piece of paper, and I showed it to Erico.

"A raven," I said. "One at each corner."

I said, "Tricksters."

He looked up at the doorway, bare, painted gray.

"I don't know," he said.

"Pretend it's just a crow," I said.

"Well then," Erico said. "If we are going to try and trick a trickster, we better paint the doorway blue first."

I said, "Blue?"

"On the background," he said. "All around the door."

"Why does it have to be blue?" I said.

"A blue doorway," he said. "Welcomes friendly spirits. Keeps out the evil ones."

"Oh," I said. "Do you believe in evil spirits?"

"Only when they try to come into my house," he said.

He painted blue all around the door, a middle kind of blue, not light blue, not dark blue.

"Like sky," I said. "How about branches? There were branches there before."

Constanzia came out and looked at the blue.

"He says evil spirits will stay away now," I said. "Because of the blue."

Constanzia looked up at the blue, and she looked up at Erico on the ladder, and she looked up at the sky. Then she went back in the shop.

"Erico," I said. "Doesn't she like it?"

Erico came down the ladder, and he stood on the sidewalk. His hands were covered with blue paint, and he wiped at them with an old white towel that was covered with blue paint. He looked up at the doorway, and he looked into the dark of the shop, wiping at his hands. He turned and he looked at me. I was almost as tall as Erico's shoulder. His black hair curled down around his ears.

"Old people," he said, "see more. Perhaps it is foolish, this talk of tricking spirits."

"What do you mean?" I said. "Like she doesn't believe in spirits? Is it something about being Catholic?"

"Perhaps they sit at her feet," Erico said. "Perhaps they sit at her feet and wait. In the long silences."

"Wait for what?" I said. "You mean when she's sleeping in her chair? Is it like guardian angels?"

Erico looked at my face, and I looked at his face, at his eyes. I looked, and I couldn't see his eyes, and I wanted to look more.

I said, "Are your eyes black or brown?"

He crinkled into a smile, and something was different in a moment, something that became new blue paint, and a day of summer, and Erico, tall, and he turned and climbed back up the ladder.

I went inside.

"Constanzia?" I said. "Constanzia, do you want some coffee? And then can we work on the sewing machine? The zipper foot maybe?"

Constanzia was sleepy, and maybe her eyes closed.

"Constanzia?" I said. "Can we do the zipper foot today? And then maybe tomorrow the buttonhole maker?"

"Sí," she said. "Some coffee, sí."

I went back in the kitchen, and poured warm coffee from the pot on the stove. I stirred in brown sugar from the jar, three spoons. When I took the coffee out to her, her head was dropped down, and her breathing was soft sleeping breathing.

"Constanzia," I said, and I set the coffee down on the table.

"Mm," she said, waking up a little, and then back into her catnap in her white wicker catnap chair, the old wicker color showing through.

I went outside.

"Erico," I said. "Will there be leftover blue?"

"Yes," he said from up on the ladder.

"Tomorrow," I said. "Let's paint Constanzia's chair with the leftover blue."

Erico looked down at me.

"I will," he said. "I will do that."

I went back into the shop, and I sipped at Constanzia's dark, bitter coffee.

When I took my bath that night, I unhooked the silver chain of the Mary medal. I only ever took it off for my bath. The medal was bright blue, magic blue, safe blue.

THE WEEKENDS were crazy busy on Seventeenth Avenue, people walking up and down the street, sometimes the same people, walking up and down the street. Sasha came in, with Dylan Marie right behind her close. Sasha carried a big box, and Dylan Marie hid her face behind Sasha's butt.

"Does she like clothes?" I said.

"Hats," Sasha said. "She likes hats."

My Walt Whitman hat was behind the counter. I put it on. Dylan Marie watched.

Sasha started laying things out on the counter for Constanzia to look at. I went to the shelf under the window, where the hats were piled up.

"Dylan Marie," I whispered.

Dylan Marie looked around at me, and I held up a wide straw hat. She kept watching me, and I put the straw hat back on the shelf and held up a purple baseball hat. Dylan Marie smiled and turned her face back into Sasha.

"Here," I said.

She wouldn't look at me again. I went back behind the counter, and as I went by Sasha and Dylan Marie I put the purple baseball hat on the floor there, by their feet. I watched through the glass counter. Dylan Marie picked up the purple baseball hat, and she held it to her chest and she put her face back into Sasha's leg. When they left, Dylan Marie was still hanging onto the purple baseball hat, hanging on to it and chewing it.

"I guess I gave away that purple baseball hat," I said.

"Such a little blond one," Constanzia said. "So much alike, those two, mother and daughter. Daughter?"

"Yes," I said. "Dylan Marie."

The purple baseball hat cost one dollar. I put one dollar in the money box.

After Constanzia went upstairs for an afternoon nap, Elle came in.

"Look," she said. "I got a postcard. Look."

She handed it to me out of her shoulder strap purse. The picture was of city lights, and then the ocean, and the sky dark orange and streaks of purple, and the water of the ocean looked pure gold.

> Dear El— It really looks like this because of smog.
> I have a boyfriend named Dirk. What a weird name?
> I am a waitress. XOXO—T

"She has a job already," Elle said. "And a boyfriend."

"X-O-X-O-T," I said.

Elle took the postcard back and looked at the front of it, and she looked at the back of it. She put the postcard back into her purse, and she took out a silver lighter. She snapped it open and lit it, snapped it shut.

"You got a lighter," I said. "Let me see that."

I lit the lighter and then snapped the top down, opened the top and lit the lighter again. One hand.

"Far out," I said.

"Quit wasting lighter fluid," she said. "Give me that."

She took the lighter back and she put it into her purse.

"What else do you keep in there?" I said.

"Just stuff that I need," Elle said.

She walked to the front window, swinging her butt, bouncing her purse on its long shoulder strap, from her bare shoulder, all freckles.

"That purse is longer than those cutoffs," I said.

Elle's cutoffs were cut off short, and torn up the seam at each side.

"I can see your underpants when you walk like that," I said.

Elle looked down at herself. She looked at her own butt.

"Red underpants?" I said.

"Foxy, huh?" Elle said.

"I don't know," I said.

"You wouldn't know," Elle said. "Look at you."

My blue jeans were cut off long, down by my knees, and baggy, and my long T-shirt hanging out.

"You could fit two people in those cutoffs," Elle said.

"Well," I said. "I have to keep stuff in my pockets."

"You should get a purse," she said.

She said, "You've been wearing those same sneakers since third grade."

"Not the same ones," I said,

"They look like the same ones," she said. "I can see your toe."

She wandered back and leaned on the counter, kicking at it in a slow rhythm.

"Don't do that," I said.

She ran her fingernail along the crack between the glass countertop and the wood, her pink polished fingernail running through the gritty dust trapped there, crunching like sugar.

"Don't do that," I said.

Elle said, "Are you going to work all day again?"

"Yes," I said. "Zigzag. Today we're going to do zigzag, after Constanzia's nap."

The shop was cool and outside was hot. People walked by the window in a slow easy way, bare arms, guys with no shirts, girls with long hair pulled up off their necks. Talking came in the door and then faded away, sandals slapping away up the hot, bright sidewalk. A little fan hummed back and forth behind the counter, cool air across the back of my neck.

Elle said, "There's nothing to do."

"Zigzag," I said. "When Constanzia comes back down, zigzag."

"You just like saying zigzag," Elle said.

There was a pile of stuff at the end of the counter, and I sorted through it. Blue corduroy pants. A pink sweater.

"Look," I said.

Pale gauzy cloth was twisted around the arm of the pink sweater, a white, long-sleeved shirt.

"You should buy this," I said. "It's a good sunburn shirt."

Elle got sunburned again and again. She wore little halter tops sometimes, and her bare shoulders burned over and over, and her back. Once her shoulders were so sunburned there were watery blisters that peeled away and left white shadows in with the freckles.

The white shirt was see-through, long and loose. Elle put it on over her strappy little top. The shirttails went down past her cutoffs.

"Too big," she said.

"Perfect," I said. "Too big is cool."

Elle said, "What do you know about cool."

She let the shirt slip off her bare pink freckled shoulders, let it drop to the floor.

"Hey," I said. "Pick that up."

She picked up the shirt and dropped it on the counter. I picked the shirt up and looked at it. Tiny buttons of dark shell went down the front, and one on each sleeve, There was no collar, just a button there. The color of the cloth was dark white. The color of the cloth was ivory. Ivory number nine.

Elle said, "Now what?"

She said, "Why don't you come over to my house tonight?"

"I don't know," I said.

"Nobody will be home," she said.

I said, "You always say that."

I spread the shirt flat on the counter, and I drew on there with a pencil. A leaf, like a hand, with long curling fingers. Short, light pencil lines, next to the top button.

Elle said, "I can get a bottle of peach wine. Or cherry."

"You threw up last time you got that stuff," I said.

"Yeah," she said. "But then you don't get a hangover."

"If you don't get drunk you don't get one either," I said. "Smoking marijuana is better."

"Do you have some?" Elle said.

"No," I said.

"Me either," she said. "But I know who does."

I fit the embroidery hoops over the thin cloth.

"Should I try to get some?" Elle said.

"Oh sure, just like last time," I said.

"Got any money?" she said.

"Yeah," I said.

I pulled a long thread separate from the skein of ivory number nine, bit it off, licked my finger, twisted a knot.

"Well, give me ten bucks," she said.

"Ten bucks?" I said. "What about you, don't you have any money?"

"Not with me," Elle said. "I'll pay you back."

"You still owe me three dollars from when you bought that white eye-shadow," I said.

"Highlighter," Elle said. "It's highlighter."

The needles in the card were set in there in an even row from small to big. I took out the smallest. The material of the shirt was so thin. And one single strand of ivory number nine.

"How about it?" Elle said.

I closed one eye, aimed the thread perfectly through the eye of the smallest needle.

"First try," I said.

I set the threaded needle down on the glass of the counter. I gave Elle my five-dollar bill from my back pocket.

"This is all I have," I said.

"I need ten," she said, picking up my five-dollar bill.

"That's all I have on me," I said, watching my five-dollar bill go into Elle's shoulder strap purse.

"Can't you get more?" she said.

"That's all I have on me," I said.

"Well, borrow some out of the drawer," she said. "They wouldn't care."

"They wouldn't care if it was, like, for something else," I said. "But not for buying marijuana."

"They wouldn't even know," Elle said.

The corners of the shop had dark shadows in the boxes of old curtains and big pieces of cloth. Shirts hanging across the rack by the door moved when the air of the fan touched there. The red of the zinnias at the bottom edge of the window was hard hot red, baked bright by the sun out there, and there were gray dust bunnies at the bottom corner of the door, tangled though with tiny colors of thread. Sandals slapping by on the sidewalk. Perfect.

I said, "No."

"Well," Elle said. "I'll see what I can do."

She raised her arms, tucking in the loose strands of her hair, tied up on her head. The pale hollow of her armpit was a bumpy rash from shaving off the fuzzy red hair in there.

"See you later," she said.

She went out the door, stepping onto the bright sidewalk, her hair a hot light, an impossible color, and then she went away, up Seventeenth Avenue.

The second leaf was almost done when Constanzia came down to the shop. Her arms were wrinkled and bare and silver bands clinking like tiny music at her wrists. She went to the doorway and looked out at Seventeenth Avenue, stepping out into the sun, and she looked at the zinnias and the petunias and she came back in, smiling, nodding her head.

"Mm," she said, sitting down into her chair. Her new blue chair.

She took a piece of work from her sewing basket, and she let it lay there in her lap, under her hands, under the quiet of the silver bracelets.

"Perfect, sí?" I said.

"And look," I said. "Ivory leaves. I'm making ivory leaves."

"Ivory leaves," she said, "Mm."

She said, "Maybe the zigzag tomorrow."

"Tomorrow would be okay," I said. "Tomorrow would be perfect."

BY THE time the shirt was finished, ivory leaves on each side of the dark shell button at the neck, it was mine, and I took it home with me that night.

There was no Blackbird at the curb. Our apartment was still and hot. I turned on water in the bathtub, cool water, and I poured in perfumey pink bubble bath. When the water and the bubbles were up to the faucet, I got in, the cool water rushing over me in goosebumps. The bathroom was dark, the bathroom door open just a crack. Bird sounds came in, a siren far away, the singy hum and clank of the refrigerator. The water dripped, and the foam of the bubble bath made its own small noise. I closed my eyes, lying back into the cold curve of the bathtub, breathing in the chills.

The door out in the front room opened.

Jimmy Henry said, "Are you home?"

"I'm in the bathtub," I said.

His footsteps went into his bedroom, and then they came into the kitchen. He opened the refrigerator door, and there was the metal opener on the bottle cap, and the bottle cap bouncing on the floor and the refrigerator door shut again.

"You in there in the dark?" he said.

I said, "Yeah."

He went away then, away from the kitchen, out to the front room, down the stairs. I slid under the water, bubbles tickling around my head, cold water filling up my ears, and the squeaking of my butt on the bottom of the bathtub. Then I got out, splashing, the air warm on my skin.

The ivory leaves shirt was soft as pajamas, tickled my legs. I put on a pair of old men's shorts of some dark maroon silky stuff. My skin was cool and tight, touched by my clothes. Shadows touched into the corners of the kitchen.

I made a peanut butter sandwich and sat in the bench of the kitchen table. Music came up through the kitchen window.

"Turn it down," I said.

The door in the front room opened, and Lady Jane came in.

"Hi," she said. "Are you hungry?"

She turned on the front room light, the bright yellow of it filling the kitchen with hard dark.

"Are you sitting there in the dark?" she said.

I said, "Turn it off."

She turned the light off and the evening shadows came back in.

She came into the kitchen.

"Are you hungry?" she said. "We're having gazpacho. It's Margo's recipe."

"I'm having peanut butter," I said.

"Well, bring your sandwich and come on down with us," she said. "It's so nice. Out there. Out back on the porch."

"It's nice here," I said. "Up here. At the kitchen table."

Lady Jane said, "It's a shame to be inside on such a beautiful evening."

"It's right here," I said. "The evening. It's right here."

The air of the window smelled of cooling cement and the dust of the thin curtain. Orange was starting to color the sky over the roof of the house next door, and there was the night sound of a cat.

"Okay," Lady Jane said. "But come down if you want. It's so nice there."

She left, leaving the door open. I got up, and the bare backs of my legs were sticky damp on the bench. I shut the door.

"It's nice here," I said.

"Ivory leaves," I said.

I got a book of poems that had no rhymes and sat back at the kitchen table. I read out loud, reading the lines like sentences, stopping at periods, or maybe at the end of an idea that seemed like a sentence. Listening to the sound of me.

Feet came up the stairs, and I stopped reading, and waited for Lady Jane to open the door.

It was Elle.

"Hi," she said. "Can we come in?"

"Who?" I said.

"Me," she said.

She came in, and two boys came in behind her, and I held my poem book up in front of me, in front of the thin cloth of the ivory leaves shirt, and nothing on under there.

"Hey," I said.

Elle turned on the light in the front room.

"Turn that off," I said.

"What are you doing?" she said, coming into the kitchen.

The two boys stood by the door in the front room, blue jeans, T-shirts, two boys I didn't know.

"Turn that light off," I said.

"That's Mike and Billy," Elle said. "Are you home by yourself?"

One of the boys turned off the light switch by the door. They both stayed right there, by the door.

"Elle," I said.

She sat down by me, and she smiled close at my face, all sweet wine smell.

"Got a lid," she said.

"Well," I said. "You can stay but they can't."

Elle took a plastic baggie out of her purse and held it up.

"Want to smoke some?" she said.

"No," I said, and I lowered my voice to her.

"Who are those guys?" I said. "I don't want any guys in here."

"Want to go hang out?" she said.

"No," I said.

"Look, you guys," I said to the two boys in the front room. "You got to go." They both turned to the door.

"Just a second," Elle said. "I'll come out in a second. Go wait out front." They left.

"Who are those guys?" I said.

"My friends," Elle said.

She dumped marijuana out onto the table, and the little seeds scattered.

"God damn it," I said, putting down my book and elbowing her out of the bench.

"What a weirdo," she said, picking up my book. "Sitting here in the dark, reading poems. And you're wearing that shirt. You know I can see your boobs."

I got a baggie from the second drawer, and I pinched up some of the marijuana into it. I took the emptied-out baggie from Elle and brushed the rest of the marijuana off the table into it. She leaned against the refrigerator and watched me.

"Here," I said. "Your half."

There was a black shadow of eye makeup under her one eye, and the pink on her cheeks was two dark smears.

"You don't have to go," I said. "Who are those guys?"

"Mike and Bobby," she said.

"Billy," I said. "You said Billy before."

"Something," she said. "Billy maybe."

She put the marijuana into her purse.

"That one guy has a car," she said. "One of them. Want to go riding around?"

"No," I said. "Don't go riding around with them. Are you drunk?"

"I got to go," Elle said, heading out through the front room. She went around the far side of the couch, going toward the door, then toward the wall, and when she got to the door she grabbed at the doorknob. She left the door open behind her and went down the stairs, stopping twice, and then going on, out the front door.

I said, "Elle."
I said, "Lalena."

IN THE morning she was in front of the shop, sitting on the edge of the
flower box, the early sun shining on her hair, and on the red zinnias. She sat
still, looking down at the sidewalk, her hair hanging down around her face,
her arms bare and pink and skinny, leaning with her elbows on her knees.
She looked small, and she didn't look up when I got close.

I said, "Hi."

She jumped.

"God," she said. "Hi."

She squinted up at me. There were two pimples, one right next to the
other, on her chin.

"I don't feel very good," she said.

I said, "Do you have a hangover?"

"No," she said. "Maybe."

I pinched a brown shriveled flower off a petunia, poked it into the dirt.
Sat down next to her.

"Did you take some aspirin?" I said.

"I tried but it made me puke," she said.

"I thought you said that cured a hangover," I said. "You said you don't get
a hangover if you throw up. Puke. 'Puke' is a stupid word."

Elle burped and she went, "Oh."

Seventeenth Avenue was quiet and empty. The air smelled cool, like it
was going to be hot again later.

I said, "Were you hanging out with those guys all night?"

Elle went, "Huh?"

"Them," I said.

The two boys walked slow on the other side of the street. They crossed
a block down, and up the sidewalk toward us.

Elle said, "Shit."

"What?" I said.

"Just maintain," she said.

The boys came closer, walking easy, opening a pack of cigarettes, knocking into each other, laughing.

"They don't look like they feel as bad as you do," I said.

Elle pushed her hair back from her face, sat up straight, smoothed her hands down the front of her shirt. There was a hickey down low on the side of her neck.

"God," I said. "A hickey. Did one of those guys give you a hickey?"

"Sh," she said.

"Why do you do that?" I said.

"I told you," she said. "It's just kind of an accident. Shut up."

The two boys got to us.

"Hi," said one of them, the one with darker hair, longer.

The other boy had light hair, almost blond, pulled back in a little ponytail. He smiled, looking away and then back, standing on one foot. Then standing on the other foot.

Elle said, "Hi."

"I got to go in and open the shop," I said.

Elle grabbed at my arm when I stood up, her fingers pinching at my elbow skin.

She said, "So what are you guys doing today?"

She didn't let go of my arm.

She said, "Did you find a place to crash?"

"In the alley," the dark-haired boy said, putting his hands in his pockets, bouncing. "Just up there, around the corner."

"I got to go in," I said.

"Sarajean works here," Elle said.

I jerked my arm out of Elle's fingers, and she gave me a look.

"'Bye," I said to those guys.

"Come by later," I said to Elle.

I walked to the end of the block to go around to the back door of the shop, and all their eyes behind me.

The sun hadn't reached into the alley yet. Erico sat on a box by the back door, leaning against the brick of the wall, looking up, into a leafy vine covered with red flowers. He held his coffee cup in his hands, and the sleeves of his light blue shirt were folded back, his dark arms resting. His eyes moved to me and smiled, and he stood up and went in, and he came back with another cup of coffee, for me, and he sat back down on the box. Bees buzzed around the flowers of the vine in heavy swoops, and thin bits of clouds crisscrossed the long blue sky above the alley.

When I went in, through the striped blanket, turned the sign around, Elle and the two boys were gone. Cigarette butts were stuck in the dirt under the zinnias, and I picked them out. I filled the bucket from the kitchen with water and took it back out, and soaked the dirt under the flowers.

Elle came back late in the afternoon. She had a smear of skin-colored makeup, somebody else's skin color, pale whitish cream, covering the pimples on her chin.

"Are you better?" I said.

"Oh, yeah," she said. "I took a painkiller. Billy had some codeine painkillers."

"You hanging out with those guys?" I said.

"They're from Kansas," she said. "They're just passing through. Except they might hang around since their car is a kind of piece of junk. It might not make it up over the pass."

"How old are they?" I said.

She said, "There's a concert tonight, at Cheeseman Park. Want to go? It starts at seven."

"What concert?" I said.

"Outside, on the grass," Elle said. "At the pavilion. Come on, it won't be so hot out then."

I said, "Are those guys going?"

"I don't know," Elle said. "They took off. I don't know where they went."

"Maybe," I said. "Come by at six, when I'm done."

"We can go by your house on the way," Elle said. "You can change your clothes."

"Change my clothes?" I said. "To go to the park?"

"Well," Elle said. "I just thought you might want to."

ELLE CAME at ten minutes after six. She had on a black halter top with little stars, tied with strings. Her eyes were painted with dark lines and bright copper, beautiful witch eyes.

"Let's go get high at your house," she said.

Lady Jane's door was closed, no music, and my house was empty and quiet.

"I don't know," I said. "Want to just hang out here?"

"No," Elle said. "We're going to a rock concert."

She sat down at the kitchen table and put a little bit of marijuana into a flat Zig Zag paper. She picked the paper up carefully and twisted the ends together in a joint that looked like a piece of candy. She lit the joint with her silver lighter. Seeds popped, and joint sparks landed on the table.

"It's going to be cold out, on the grass, when the sun is gone," I said. "Want to take a shirt?"

"No," Elle said. "I won't be cold."

I smoked, and handed the joint back to her. The joint was burning at the side, instead of at the end, falling apart. Elle licked her finger and wet the side of the joint.

My truckers hung on the back of my bedroom door. I put them on over my T-shirt, and then I looked at the ivory leaves shirt, hanging from the closet doorknob. I slipped the straps down and changed my T-shirt for the ivory leaves shirt, tucked the long shirt tails down into the loose trucker legs. Did up the straps, and the front of the truckers covered up the front of me.

"Good outfit," Elle said. "Now let's put some eye makeup on your eyes."

"No," I said.

"Just some eyeliner maybe," I said.

"No," I said.

We walked outside, up to the corner, and up Eleventh Avenue. When we got to the corner of Eleventh Avenue and Corona Street, I looked back. The mountains were dusty blue outlines, the sun low over them, a smear of orange across their tops.

"Mountains," I said. "Look at them."

Elle said, "I wonder if there'll be lots of people there."

"No," I said. "Listen. If you look at the mountains, your eyes will remember how to see far away. It's practice for your eyes."

"You're high," Elle said. "Come on."

"There's your old house," I said.

"Which one is it?" Elle said. "They painted it and now I can never tell which one it was."

"The second one," I said. "The blue one."

We went on up Eleventh Avenue. The big houses set back in gardens. At the last corner before the park, a dark, dented station wagon stopped at the curb.

"Hey, Elle."

"God damn it," I said.

"Hi, you guys," Elle said. "Are you going to the concert?"

They turned off the engine, and got out. The light-haired boy was driving, and he got out, and came around, and the other boy got out and leaned there, on the car.

"We might head out tonight," the light-haired boy said. "South, so we don't have to go over the pass."

The other boy said, "What's this concert?"

"In the park," Elle said. "Want to go? Want to get high?"

"Sure," he said. "Hop in."

"No," I said.

Elle looked at me right in the face. Witch eyes.

"Come on," she said. "Let's go. Come on."

I said, "I don't want to."

"Why not?" Elle said.

Her face in the dark light was so beautiful, her witch eyes dark and beautiful. I tucked my arms inside my truckers.

"I think I'll just go home," I said. "I don't feel like it."

"Well," she said. "Maybe I'll come by later. Maybe tomorrow."

"Yeah," I said.

They all got in the car. Elle in the middle. I stood on the corner, and the car drove up to the next corner, and turned away gone.

I went back. Toward Ogden Street, down the hill of the sidewalk, through cool air under bushes. The sky over the outline of the mountains was spread with orange light. At Corona Street I turned up to Elle's old house. It was blue now, light blue, and white on the windows and doors, and white porch steps. Elle's old bedroom window was a bright gold square of sunset. The front door opened and three people came out, talking, hurrying, down the steps, and I went past the house up the sidewalk.

Colfax Street was busy with people, their talking going past me and around me, and me just walking under the lit-up signs. The sky was orange all the way down Colfax Street to the black outline of the capitol dome. At Ogden Street I turned toward my house. The Safeway store lit up the corner, and my house, dark red, like black, behind the holly bushes.

The porch was dark around me. The sky was dark when Blackbird drove up to the curb. Jimmy Henry got out and slammed the door shut, came around the front of the truck, up the walk, his shirt hooked on his finger over his shoulder. He sat down next to me, laying his shirt across his knees, finding the pocket, getting out cigarettes, matches. He flipped the match, still lit, out to the sidewalk, and it went out and disappeared in the dark. We sat there, Jimmy Henry smoking. Me just sitting there.

IT WAS two days before Margo came into Someone's Beloved Threads.

"Sarajean," she said. "Is Lalena staying with you?"

"Elle," I said.

"No," I said.

Heading out. South. Not over the pass.

CASSANDRA WIGGINS said, "Have you heard from her?"

"No," I said.

She said, "Did you two have a falling out?"

"No," I said.

She said, "I thought you were best friends."

"We were," I said. "We are. Best friends."

JIMMY HENRY said, "Do you know where she went?"

"Maybe California," I said. "Her friend Talia went to California."

He said, "Why?"

"Why did Talia go to California?" I said.

He said, "Why would Lalena go there?"

"Elle," I said. "You're supposed to say Elle."

ELLE'S DADDY said, "Was that girl in trouble?"

"In trouble?" I said.

"You know," he said. "In trouble."

"No," I said.

My cheeks went all hot.

"Who did she go with?" he said.

"I don't know," I said. "Maybe some boys from Kansas."

THERE WAS another red-haired girl on Seventeenth Avenue. I saw her through the window of the shop, across the street, and I went to the door, ran to the door. It wasn't Elle. The next time I saw the other red-haired girl, same thing. I ran to the door, and it wasn't Elle.

LADY JANE and Nancy were out on the back porch. Lady Jane's long hair was wet and combed down straight, and she was sitting up cross-legged on the table. Nancy sat in the chair behind her, trimming the long ends of Lady Jane's hair.

"Just maybe a quarter of an inch or like that," Lady Jane said.

The air was cooling into dusty, weedy backyard evening, marigolds, shampoo, marijuana. I watched from the end of the skinny sidewalk, Lady Jane sitting perfectly still, her eyes closed, and every time Nancy's scissors went snip, Lady Jane's nose wrinkled. The shoulders of her T-shirt were wet from her wet hair, and wet down the front, her breasts showing through her wet white T-shirt.

Nancy sat back in her chair.

"Okay," she said. "Enough torture."

I stepped back, went to the front porch, top step. The laughing came out to me, and then quiet, only the traffic sounds, and bits of voices without words. Doors closing, and then the front door opened behind me.

"Hey," Lady Jane said.

Nancy said, "Sarajean, want to go with us? Downtown to the Greyhound station? To meet JFK?"

"Yeah, walk downtown with us," Lady Jane said.

She had on a different T-shirt, dark blue, with old white letters that said FAMILY ZOO."

"Why is JFK coming home?" I said.

"Just for the weekend," Nancy said. "Hold on a second. My scissors."

She went back inside, and Lady Jane sat down next to me on the top step.

"Nancy's a little freaked out," she said, low voiced. "About Lalena taking off."

Nancy came back out, her haircutting scissors in her hand, and she put them in her leather pouch that dangled from her belt loop.

"Okay," I said.

They walked together on the sidewalk, me behind. Lady Jane's hair was drying, the thick, even, new cut ends of it down to where her back pockets curved across her butt.

Nancy was shorter, and her shape was no shape next to Lady Jane.

Nancy's cutoffs hung straight off her hips, and the only part of her that looked like a girl was her dangly earrings, long loops of blue and purple beads. Her neck was thin and white up to her short hair, and the curved pink edge of her ears poked out of dark curls.

She stepped away from Lady Jane and turned around to me.

"Come on," she said. "Don't walk behind."

She took my wrist and pulled me into the space between them.

THE GREYHOUND station was one whole block, and the lit-up greyhound dog turned in a slow circle over the wide glass doors that cut across the very corner of the building. Down the corner one way there was no sidewalk, just driveways, all oil spotted, and huge doorways, and the running rumble of buses in there.

Inside, Nancy went up to a high wooden counter and looked behind it, at a signboard on the wall under a big clock. A long list of city names, and numbers, under ARRIVING FROM and DEPARTING TO. The sign didn't say Estes Park.

"Boulder," Nancy said. "The bus goes through Boulder and then comes here."

The fuzzy voice from the loudspeaker said, "Now boarding for Glenwood Springs, Grand Junction, and points west."

The bus wasn't supposed to arrive from Boulder for fifteen minutes. Nancy went over to the guy behind the counter.

She said, "Is the bus from Boulder going to be on time?"

The guy looked around at all his papers, and he looked at his watch, and he looked at the signboard. He looked at the big clock on the wall.

"About fifteen minutes late probably," he said.

Lady Jane said, "Let's go eat French fries."

She got in line at a counter in front of a glass case. There were sandwiches wrapped in plastic, and pieces of pie wrapped in plastic, the plastic pulled tight, squishing out the red cherries of the cherry pie, the apples of the apple pie.

". . . Sterling, North Platte, Omaha, and points east."

Nancy and Lady Jane ate all the French fries, even the crispy nubs soaking in ketchup and oil and salt at the bottom of the little cardboard dish.

Finally Nancy said, "Come on."

We went back out to the main part, by the long rows of chairs, and people sitting with backpacks and suitcases and boxes, and other people standing around, watching the people coming into the bus station through the big doors from the buses.

JFK was tan, and his hair was lighter. Bigger than Nancy. Taller. Just as skinny as her. We went outside and JFK kept looking around, looking at the people, looking at the buildings. Nancy laughed.

She said, "Did you sleep on the bus?"

"Yeah," he said. "I guess so."

She said, "Did you eat?" Laughing.

"Yeah," he said. "But let's eat again."

Nancy kept laughing, no matter what he said.

LADY JANE lit candles on her back porch, and she and Nancy started spaghetti, talking noisy in the kitchen corner of the apartment, and laughing. The backyard was dark, and JFK sat on the edge of the porch looking up at the sky.

"No stars," he said.

He said, "So, how come Lalena ran away?"

"I don't know," I said.

He said, "You think she'll come back? For school, maybe?"

"I don't know," I said.

He said, "Where do you think she went?"

"I don't know," I said. "California, maybe. Maybe points south."

He said, "She didn't hitchhike did she?"

"I think she went with some guys in a car," I said.

He leaned close to me.

"Got any marijuana?" he said.

"Yeah," I said.

"Well," he said. "Let's smoke some."

"I'll load up the pipe," I said. "I'll bring it down here. We can smoke out there, by the garage."

Upstairs was quiet and dark, and the sounds of Lady Jane and Nancy came up between the houses. I put some marijuana in the pipe, smoked some.

Points south. New Mexico. Arizona.

Los Angeles. The ocean.

She would get sunburned all the time.

I put on the ivory leaves shirt, over my T-shirt, and took the pipe back downstairs.

IT WAS a picture of a tall pink building on a sunny day, and it said, "I Miss You—XOXO Elle." I leaned the postcard on my dresser against the wall where I could see it from my bed.

X-O-L.

JIMMY HENRY and Lady Jane talked about Elle, just to each other. Not to me, not when I could hear, just sometimes "Elle" in the air, when they were in the kitchen and I was in the front room, or "Elle" in the space between the houses, above the skinny sidewalk.

"Elle may be doing okay," Lady Jane said. "If she was in trouble, they would have heard."

Jimmy Henry said, "I was pretty much on my own when I was thirteen."

"Not me," Lady Jane said. "Dad never let me out of his sight."

She said, "I was his favorite."

I STAYED in bed in the mornings until the downstairs doors all quit slamming, open and shut, and the morning took over. Then I made my coffee and took the cup into Jimmy Henry's bedroom. The air in there was quiet and cool, and he never slept there anymore. The bed was always neat, and there was no smell of warm sleeping. I opened the curtains across and sat in the middle of the neat bed. The birds in the trees right outside the window fussed and chirped, and I drank my coffee.

In Jimmy Henry's bedroom, in the summer morning, I didn't remember school, I didn't remember anything. I sat in the middle of his bed with my coffee in the cup and the birds outside, not doing anything, like I was never going to do anything again.

I said, "Elle."

I said, "Jimmy Henry."

I said, "Dad."

Saying words out loud into the empty quiet of Jimmy Henry's bedroom made the words come back to me all odd, like they were brand-new words I had never heard before, made-up words.

I said, "Christine Jeanette Blumenthal."

Sometimes, instead of saying words out loud, I just tried to breathe.

ON THE Fourth of July it was ninety degrees and all the stores were closed. Lady Jane wanted to go for a ride to the mountains. Jimmy Henry sat at the back porch table, drinking a beer, ten o'clock in the morning, his hair tied back from his face into a ponytail, no shirt.

"Morrison," Lady Jane said.

She brushed her hair.

"Let's go to that little town called Morrison," she said. "It's not very far. There's a hotel there, with a funky old bar. We could have gin and tonics."

Jimmy Henry said, "It's too hot to move."

Lady Jane bent over and hung her hair down, brushing it upside down. Jimmy Henry watched her.

"We could take Margo," she said from upside down under her hair. "It would cheer her up."

Jimmy Henry said, "She has the dragon lady to cheer her up."

Lady Jane stood up straight and flipped her hair back, and looked at me.

I sat on the edge of the porch eating my toast like all I was interested in was eating my toast.

She said, "Be nice."

He said, "I'm not nice?"

The butter dripped through the big holes in the toast, Lady Jane's home-made bread. Butter dripped into the powdery dust along the edge of the porch, making little beads of butter mud. Behind me, Jimmy Henry and Lady Jane moved together, and there was the soft sound of clothes touching, skin touching, a kiss. I stood up, and when I turned they were moved apart, looking at each other. Jimmy Henry leaned back in his chair. He picked up his beer can and tossed it into the bag standing next to the table.

"How about it?" he said. "Want to go for a ride?"

"No," I said. "I think I'll go read."

I went upstairs, and I slammed the door. It made me jump, slamming the door like that.

I looked in my closet. I opened my top drawer. My middle drawer. Nothing. I felt like doing nothing, and I listened for sounds from downstairs. I went in the bathroom, and I looked at the face around my eyes in the mirror, the only light coming in from the kitchen window.

My mother's face.

Somewhere it is Fourth of July, and there is this woman getting ready to have a picnic, or go see fireworks or something, and she looks like me. Brown eyes. Skinny nose with a bump. Pointy chin. Elle said heart-shaped. She said I have a heart-shaped face, and that her face is oval-shaped, and oval-shaped is the best.

Maybe her name isn't even Blumenthal anymore. Maybe she married some guy and changed her name. But maybe she's still Christine.

Jimmy Henry came upstairs, and I went out in the kitchen. He picked up the keys to Blackbird off the applebox table.

"Sure you don't want to go for a ride?" he said.

He tossed the keys from one hand to the other hand.

I said, "When are you coming back?"

He shrugged.

I said, "I'll just hang around here."

"Okay," he said. "See you later."

He left. He never looked right at me, and then he left. I stood in the kitchen staring at the door until I had to blink, and the whole house was quiet, and Blackbird starting up, driving away.

Sun came in all our windows, and it was as quiet as night.

I went down the stairs. The Christmas lights were plugged in, shining single dots of color. I opened the front door, and the bright colors of the lights washed out pale. I shut the door, back to colored lights and dark, and I went back to Lady Jane's door. Pushed it open. Shut it behind me.

It was all messy and yellow and white. A pink blanket was piled up on the bed, and sheets with cartoon animals all over them. Blue-striped pillow. One pillow.

I sat at the table by the tall window and pushed open the yellow and orange tie-dye bridesmaid dress and I looked down to the skinny sidewalk. A dark green leather-covered book was on the windowsill, under the yellow and orange tie-dye bridesmaid dress.

Lady Jane's handwriting was round and neat, no slant, and it filled up most of the green book, running straight and neat across pages with no lines.

> He is my soul mate.
> I want to have his child.
> A man needs to have his own child.

I turned to another page.

> His lips on my breasts makes me cry.
> Lips to breast.
> Lips to belly.
> Lips to pussy.

I shut the book and laid it carefully back in the corner of the windowsill. He kisses her down there.

I got up from the table and stood in the middle of the room, looking back there where I couldn't see the green book.

Pussy. Elle says "cunt." She says the Mexican boys say "cunt."

The yellow-painted shelves were full of stuff, a lot of books, *Birds of the World*, the white elephant teapot. The white elephant teapot sat up in its same place as when Tina Blue lived here. Tina Blue's white elephant. The handle was broken off now, the elephant had no tail. It was in its same place, up high on the shelf. I reached up to the high shelf and took the teapot down, and the teapot rattled. Inside were the two broken pieces of the elephant's tail, and some loose beads, dark red beads.

I took down *Birds of the World* and set it on the table. I opened to pileated woodpecker, and turned pages, the light shining on the glossy pictures, not really looking at them. There was an envelope in western meadowlark. The stamp was a beautiful yellow bird that looked like the western meadowlark picture. I couldn't read the bird name on the stamp. The post office mark covered up the writing on the stamp. The return address said "Omaha, Nebraska." There was a little blue heart, drawn kind of crooked, with "Blue" written inside the heart. The envelope was empty. I folded it up and put it in my pocket.

Her bathroom smelled of sandalwood soap and strawberry shampoo. I opened the mirror cabinet over the sink. Musk oil in a tiny brown bottle. A flat blue plastic case that snapped open. Birth control pills, yellow pills in three rows, orange pills in the last row. Sasha had birth control pills. Elle said the orange pills were fake, the yellow ones the important pills.

His own child.

What would she do, just give him a baby? Like my mother gave him me?

I went back up to my room and got Tina Blue's ring out of the pocket of my jacket, and put it on my finger. I put the string of kelly bird beads around my neck, and the purple silk cord tangled in with the Mary medal.

I changed from my T-shirt into a pajama top, shiny light blue with lacy ribbon straps and long ribbons down the front. The warm Fourth of July air felt all over my skin, and where the silver touched me was cool.

Jimmy Henry's bedroom was the coolest quietest place, just the birds and sometimes a car. I lay down there, in the middle of Jimmy Henry's bed, the green blanket scratchy against my back through the pajama top. The beads and the Mary medal slid across my neck, tickling there, and I lay my hands on my chest and closed my eyes and moved my hands down, inside my cutoffs, cool silver on the warm skin of my stomach. My finger found the tiniest wettest fold of skin and touched there, touching and touching until I couldn't breathe, and then touching until breathing came easy again, after the little noise, that broke loose, from my own throat.

BANGING ON the door downstairs woke me up quick, and I got up quick off the bed and went down to the front door. Margo and Cassandra Wiggins.

Dragon lady.

"Los Angeles," Margo said. "Is Jimmy here? We have to go to Los Angeles, to get Lalena."

"They went for a ride in the mountains," I said.

"She got busted," Margo said. "For shoplifting. The police called, they're holding her in a juvenile facility until I can go get her. She's okay. They found her."

Cassandra Wiggins leaned against the railing, her face not saying anything. Margo looked hot and pink and her hair curled around her forehead all sweaty.

"I guess they'll be back in a while," I said. "You mean go there? Drive to Los Angeles?"

"Yeah," Margo said. "We have to go get her. The police can only release her into my custody."

She turned to Cassandra Wiggins.

"Let's just wait here okay?" she said, and Cassandra Wiggins shrugged her shoulders, stood up straight, and they both came in, past me, up the stairs. I shut the door and followed them up. The Christmas lights sparkled on Tina Blue's silver ring, and I took it off and put it in the pocket of my cutoffs.

Margo sat down heavy on the couch, leaned her elbows on her knees, pink, round knees. Cassandra Wiggins looked around the front room, looked at the top half of the window all boarded up. Looked at me.

"Hey," she said.

She reached out at me, touched the string of kelly bird beads, her cool fingers touching the skin of my neck.

"I remember these," she said.

I stepped back.

"Yeah," I said.

I tucked the beads inside the pajama top and crossed my arms over my chest, warm skin creeping up my neck, to the one spot where her fingers touched.

Margo said, "If we leave right now we can get there by tomorrow afternoon, maybe tomorrow night."

"Is she in trouble?" I said. "For shoplifting?"

"They'll just let me take her," Margo said. "I can just bring her home with me."

"Did you talk to her?" I said.

"No, I talked to some lady cop at the juvenile facility," Margo said.

"Does she want to come home?" I said.

They both looked at me.

"She's my little girl," Margo said. "She has to come home. Little girls belong with their mothers."

"Or their fathers," I said.

"No," Cassandra Wiggins said. "No."

Cassandra Wiggins and Margo looked at each other until Margo looked down at her knees. Cassandra Wiggins sat down across from her on the applebox table.

She said, "Margo."

I stood still and straight by the door, and Margo and Cassandra Wiggins were just there, without me, two other people in my house. I went around the couch, into the kitchen, into my bedroom. I changed the pajama top back into my T-shirt. I put Tina Blue's silver ring into the inside pocket of my jacket. There was the quiet sound of them talking, no words coming back to me.

JIMMY HENRY let Cassandra Wiggins and Margo drive Blackbird to Los Angeles.

"Drive the desert at night," he said. "Don't let it overheat."

Lady Jane said, "Call the café if there's a problem."

I said, "Can I go?"

Everybody said, "No."

Blackbird drove away, and Lady Jane and Jimmy Henry stood on the top step of the porch, watching Blackbird go up Ogden Street, Cassandra Wiggins driving.

Dragon lady.

Jimmy Henry's hand touched up and down Lady Jane's back, his fingers not quite just barely touching through her skinny summer shirt.

I GOT home from the shop and Blackbird was back. I ran up the stairs. It was just Lady Jane and Jimmy Henry sitting at the kitchen table, and they stopped talking and looked at me.

"Is Elle back?" I said.

Jimmy Henry didn't say anything, and Lady Jane said,

"Yeah. She's back."

I said, "I'm going over there."

I turned around to go back out and Jimmy Henry said, "Wait."

I turned back around, and he didn't say anything.

"What?" I said.

"Maybe you should wait," he said.

"For what?" I said.

Jimmy Henry looked at the table, and Lady Jane looked at Jimmy Henry.
"What?" I said. "What's going on?"

Jimmy Henry said, "Did you know those guys Lalena went to LA with?"
"No," I said. "Just some boys. From Kansas maybe."

"You should have told us what you knew," he said. "You should have told us that she wrote to you."

The postcard from Elle was lying on the kitchen table, the picture of the tall pink building.

"That's mine," I said. "That was in my room."

My bedroom door was open.

"You went in my room," I said.

"I did it," Lady Jane said. "I'm sorry. I saw it on your dresser and I looked at it."

"You went in my room," I said.

"Sarajean," Jimmy Henry said. "This was serious. Lalena could have been in trouble."

His voice was trying to be different.

"I don't care what you say," I said, my voice shouting. I didn't know what to say, and I looked in at my dresser. The top drawer was open, and my stuff in there, my mother's letter, the horse patch, all my stuff.

"Sarajean," Lady Jane said. "I'm sorry. I just looked at this because it was on top."

Jimmy Henry said, "Sarajean, we have to talk. About things."

"No," I said, my thoughts going away like crazy, and Tina Blue's ring was in my jacket pocket, my jacket hanging there on the doorknob of my room.

"I don't want you ever in here," I said, not shouting, stepping into the doorway of my room.

Jimmy Henry pushed his hair away from his face and he reached his hand out at me.

"Baby," he said. "Come here. Sit down and listen."

"No," I said. "I'm going over Elle's. I don't want to talk to you."

His hand dropped to the table, his hand a fist, closed.

"Sarajean, don't get in trouble," he said. "You don't understand, I can't help you if you get in trouble."

In trouble. My face got hot.

"I'm not going to get in trouble," I said.

My voice was shaky down in my chest.

I took my jacket off the doorknob. The end of my arm, my hand holding the jacket and Tina Blue's ring in the pocket, like someone else's hand attached to me, and I looked at Jimmy Henry so he wouldn't look at my jacket, his hair hanging down into his face. I backed out of the kitchen and I went out the door, and down the stairs, and when I got to the sidewalk I walked slow and started to breathe right again.

The door at the top of the stairs was open, and I looked in.

I said, "Hello?"

Elle was lying on the couch. She sat up when I said that, sat up and looked over the back of the couch. She was sunburned.

"Hi," I said.

She lay back down on the couch.

"You're home," I said.

"No shit," she said.

"I got your postcard you sent," I said.

"I wasn't sure what the address was," she said.

"Yeah, well, I got it," I said. "When did you guys get back?"

"This afternoon," she said.

She stared at the ceiling.

"You're all sunburned," I said. "Did you get sunburned at the beach?"

"No," she said.

She closed her eyes and turned over on her stomach. Her back was sunburned too, white lines in the hot pink where another halter top had been tied across.

"We never went to the beach," she said. "It was too far away."

"I thought Los Angeles was at the beach," I said.

"Los Angeles is really big," she said.

"So, what's it like?" I said.

"Big," she said.

She sat up and rubbed her face.

"Fuck," she said. "I'm really burnt out. Of course Cassandra Wiggins Hardass had to drive all the way, no stopping."

Dragon lady.

"They were pretty freaked out," I said. "Even Jimmy Henry got all weird."

"My mother cried all the way home," Elle said, and she laughed. "I couldn't believe it."

"Yeah, well," I said. "If I'd a known you were going there I would have said look in the phone book."

"For what?" she said.

"Blumenthal," I said. "Christine Jeanette Blumenthal. Maybe she lives in Los Angeles."

She sat up and stretched her arms, and then she sat back down and started poking around in her leather shoulder strap purse that was on the floor by the couch. She closed her eyes, reaching around in there with her eyes closed, instead of just looking.

"So, where were you?" I said. "Were you staying at Talia's house?"

"Couple days," she said. "And at her boyfriend's apartment."

"He has his own apartment?" I said. "How old is he?"

"Him and some other guys," she said. "This one guy, Bart, liked me."

"Bart?" I said.

Elle said, "And . . ."

She looked at me.

I said, "And what?"

"God," she said. "You are so dense."

"What?" I said. "He's like your boyfriend now?"

She leaned back, her eyes closed, smiling, her eyes closed.

"We did it," she said.

I almost said did what, and then I knew, and my neck got hot and my face got all stiff.

Did it hurt, did it bleed, what if you got pregnant.

"Aren't you going to say anything?" she said.

She was looking at me. Smiling.

"I don't know," I said. "Did you like it?"

"Of course," she said. "God. Did I like it."

"I mean him," I said, all nervous. "Do you like him? Is he going to write, or something, you know, like is he your boyfriend now? Bart? His name is Bart?"

"I'm going back," she said. "As soon as I can figure it out."

I said, "Back to Los Angeles?"

"Back to Los Angeles," she said

She lay back down on the couch, on her sunburned back.

She said, "Got any grass?"

"At home," I said. "Oh, shit."

My marijuana. The little pipe. In my top drawer.

"What?" Elle said. "Oh shit, what?"

"My marijuana," I said. "It's in my drawer. Lady Jane went snooping around in there. I wonder if she got it. Shit."

"You just left it lying around?" Elle said.

"No," I said. "It was in my dresser drawer."

"Like that's going to keep them out, a drawer," Elle said.

"I have to go home," I said.

"Come back if you still have any grass," Elle said.

JIMMY HENRY sat at the kitchen table. The apartment was almost dark, just him, in the last light from the kitchen window. He looked at me and I got mad, looking back at him, sitting there like he was all sad. When I got to the doorway of the kitchen I saw my mother's letter, on the kitchen table, and the inside of me jumped a sharp jump.

He said, "I have to ask you, Sarajean."

Then he didn't say anything, and I held my breath, standing still and straight by the door.

He said, "Do you remember coming here? Do you remember her? Do you remember me?"

I said, "Remember you?"

"The first time," he said. "The first time. The first time you came here?"

I said, "Came here from where?"

"You were only about three," he said. "I don't know from where. She said you were with her friends, and that she was going to go get you, and then she brought you here."

"Was I born here?" I said. "In Denver? I thought I was from Denver?"

"No," he said, "Council Bluffs. Your birth certificate said Council Bluffs."

"My birth certificate?" I said. "I didn't know I had a birth certificate."

"I don't know where it is," he said. "I think she took it last time she left. And she left this."

His fingers touched in an arch on the envelope on the table. The name side up. His name.

He said, "I was in Vietnam."

He said, "I didn't meet your mother until you were about three, and she brought you here."

And then it was perfectly quiet, and perfectly still, and in the perfect quiet and stillness what he was saying wrapped around me until the understanding got to my chest with a big slow opening. When it got to my throat I said, "You're not my father."

"Yeah," he whispered. "I'm not."

"Who is?" I said.

"I don't know," he said.

I turned away, went to the couch. I sat down on the arm of the couch. When I looked back in the kitchen, at him sitting there in all shadow now, at the table, he didn't look any different. He didn't look at me. He looked at his hand. At the letter on the table.

Music came up from downstairs. Too loud. The walls hummed.

"Does she know?" I said.

Jimmy Henry said, "Who?"

"Lady Jane," I said.

"Know what?" he said.

"I don't care," I said. "Anything. Does she know about you? Does she know my mother?"

"Yeah," he said. "She tried to help find her. We just never knew where to look."

"I wish she wouldn't play her records so loud," I said. "How come you never told me? Seems like you should have told me."

Jimmy Henry rubbed his eyes. He straightened the letter on the table so it was perfectly square in the middle of the table in front of him.

"It was kind of to keep you safe," he said.

"Safe?" I said.

"Well, so nobody would make you go to a foster home or something," he said. "I don't know."

I said, "What's my name?"

Little Miss Strange.

"Blumenthal," he said.

Jimmy Henry saying that word, that name, in a small voice looking down, his hair hanging down, made everything different, finally, him, me, our house, all of it floating, and mostly me.

Sarajean Blumenthal.

I went downstairs.

I sat on the front step.

You're not my father, you're not my father, beating like the guitar sounds, beating like a heart might beat, over and over, and then just father father father and then father a strange sound that wasn't a word. Strange. Strange.

He came down and, out the door. He leaned on the railing at the other end of the top step.

I said, "Is that why I always said Jimmy Henry?"

"I guess," he said. "It was just a cute thing you did at first. You liked to say that, Jimmy Henry, like it was all one word. It made me laugh."

Then he said, "I'm sorry."

He was barefoot, white toes that curled in under his long white bare feet.

"I didn't laugh for a long time before that," he said. "Before she brought you here."

I stood up.

"I got to go walk around," I said.

At the corner I turned and looked back at our house and Jimmy Henry was gone. The front porch was empty.

ELLE WAS still lying on the couch, like she hadn't moved.

I said, "I'm back."

"You get your grass?" she said, not opening her eyes.

"I forgot," I said.

"Shit," she said. "Why don't you go back and get it."

"Because," I said. "Because Jimmy Henry's not my real father."

"What's that supposed to mean," Elle said, her face in her arm, her voice sleepy.

"He told me," I said.

"Well, that's weird," she said.

She sat up.

"He never even knew my mother until I was already three years old," I said. "That's what he told me. Just now."

"So your mother just stuck you with some guy who wasn't even your father?" Elle said.

"I guess," I said. "I guess they were going together."

"So who's your real father?" she said.

"He said he doesn't know," I said.

"Yeah, right," she said. "Just like he didn't know your mother's name, and then he had that letter."

"My real name is Sarajean Blumenthal," I said.

She said, "Sarajean Blumenthal?"

Weird, her saying that.

She stood up and stretched her arms up.

"Well," she said. "What do you want to do?"

She went to the window and looked out, up and down Seventeenth Avenue.

She said, "Let's go buy some cigarettes. Got any money?"

"Yeah," I said.

I went behind her down the stairs, and we walked down to Bill's Pepsi Store. Everything looked the same, Seventeenth Avenue, the Lair Lounge.

"Palm trees," Elle said. "They're so weird. They're really ugly, palm trees are, big hunks of dead bark hanging off."

We waited at the counter to buy cigarettes. Elle pointed at small yellow boxes under the counter back there. The boxes said "Trojan" in red letters.

"Those are rubbers," she whispered. "Bart had some of those."

I said, "You're not a virgin anymore."

"He showed me the box," she said. "He didn't open it."

"What if you got pregnant?" I said. "You know that place, Saint Mary's?"

"I didn't," she said.

We went back in the alley, back to the stairs, same stairs. The alley was dark, and window light, and cars going by at the Logan Street end.

"I came from Council Bluffs," I said. "I'm not even from Denver."

"Bart Allen," Elle said. "He has long straight blond hair and blue eyes. He said he's the bad man. That's a song."

"So, how old is he?" I said.

"I think sixteen," she said.

"I have to keep saying my name is Sarajean Henry so they won't put me in a foster home," I said.

"Or Juvie," Elle said. "I had to sleep in a bunk bed. The girl under me kept crying. And it stinks."

She said, "Sarajean Henry sounds better than Sarajean Blumenthal anyway. Blumenthal is kind of weird."

"It's not my name," I said. "Henry isn't my name."

"Why are you crying?" she said. "Quit crying."

"I don't know why," I said.

Elle sat next to me, and the heat from her sunburn reached across the space between us, and we smoked cigarettes.

After a while she said, "Want to back to Los Angeles with me?"

"No," I said. "When?"

"I don't know," she said. "I got to figure it out."

We stayed there late, smoking the cigarettes, and Elle talking mostly about Bart Allen, and I didn't do anything, not even cry after a while.

THE KETTLE whistling woke me up. The cabinet door opened and shut. Jimmy Henry getting up from the bench. He got up and made coffee and sat back down out there. Finally I had to get up and get dressed. I had to pee.

There were two mugs on the table, one waiting.

He said, "I'm glad you know. It was always a drag."

"What was a drag?" I said, passing in front of him to the bathroom door.

"You not knowing," he said, and I stopped and didn't turn, stopped there, looking into the bathroom, looking at the toilet.

He said, "I knew I had to tell you. If she never came back. I guess I always thought she would. Come back."

I squeezed my legs together for a second.

"So, she was from Council Bluffs?" I said.

"I don't think so," he said. "That's where she was when you were born."

When you were born.

He blew at the coffee in his mug.

"Why did she leave me with you?" I said. "If you weren't even my real father?"

He said, "She would take off, and leave you with one of her girlfriends for a while, different girlfriends. I'd go get you, and then you would be here when she came back. She usually came back here first, when she came back. To this red house, she liked it that this house was red, she said she could always find it."

"What girlfriends?" I said.

"Katie," he said. "Lady Jane. Except she was Ruby then. Other girls I didn't know. She had other friends, other boyfriends too, I guess."

"You weren't even her main boyfriend?" I said.

He laughed. One short laugh. He pushed my coffee across the table and I took it and leaned on the counter, leaning with my legs pressed tight I had to pee so bad.

"I was kind of fucked-up a lot," he said. "Except when you were here. Then I kind of kept it together."

"What about her mom and dad?" I said.

"She never told them about you," he said. "I don't think she ever told them anything after she left home. You know, like she just took off. That was what she always did."

I sat down, in the chair, and tucked my hands into my lap. I pressed my fist in between my legs.

"Why?" I said. "Why did she always do that?"

Jimmy Henry breathed in, held the breath for a moment, breathed out.

"I have to pee," I said.

I got up and went in the bathroom.

Jimmy Henry said, "I don't know, it wasn't that kind of thing where we talked to each other about things."

My peeing was too loud to hear what he said next.

I flushed, even louder, and then I said, "What?"

I opened the door.

He said, "She was a junkie."

The toilet water ran loud, like the handle needed to be jiggled.

"So were you," I said.

"I know," he said. "I'm not anymore."

"I know," I said.

I reached back in and jiggled the handle.

"I have to go open the shop," I said.

"MAMA HAS a cold," Erico said.

He unlocked the door, turned the sign around to OPEN.

"I'll be back in a little while," he said. "She's sleeping. It is okay, you can be here by yourself, okay?"

"Yeah," I said. "By myself is okay."

I leaned on the counter. Seventeenth Avenue was quiet like Sunday, and I tried to think of what day it was. Not Sunday. Some Lady Jane song about Sunday morning got stuck in my head, but I didn't know any of the other words, just "Sunday morning."

Erico came back, and he went upstairs.

Margo went by, past the red zinnias.

Elle came in about noon.

"Did you say anything to Margo?" I said.

"What?" she said. "About Bart? Shit, no."

"No," I said. "About me and Jimmy Henry."

"No," Elle said. "I'm not talking to her. She's driving me nuts, wanting to know all the time where I am and when I'm coming back and all."

"She knew my mother," I said.

"Ask her," Elle said. "Did they take your grass?"

"No," I said.

"I don't suppose you have it with you," she said.

"No," I said.

PEOPLE WANDERED in and out of the shop, and Constanzia stayed in bed. Erico came back in around four.

He said, "Why don't we close early? Mama isn't feeling too good."

"I can stay," I said. "I don't mind."

"It's okay?" he said.

"Yeah," I said. "By myself is okay."

THE DAYS just kept being like Sunday somehow.

☮

LADY JANE said, "She was pretty fucked-up. Jimmy was too, but he could take care of you."

MARGO SAID, "I didn't hang out with those guys. She used to drop you off sometimes, and then take off with Lalena's daddy. They were into downs."

NANCY SAID, "It will all make sense someday."

ELLE SAID, "Fuck it. Let's go to Los Angeles. You have some money don't you?"

JIMMY HENRY said, "Want some coffee?"
He said, "Are you going to the shop today?"
He said, "I'll be down at Lady Jane's."

THE PURPLE plastic peace symbol keychain. A pink silk scarf with long fringe. A little square copy of *The Prophet* that I never read. Jimmy Henry's war medal. The horse patch. A tiny bell in the shape of an owl. The Kelly Bird poem. I laid the pink scarf out flat, and set *The Prophet* there, and I put all the other things on top of *The Prophet* and I tied the corners of the scarf into one knot, so it made a little bundle, with the flat book at the bottom. I put the pink bundle away, in the corner of my closet, behind the box of bird cloth.

CONSTANZIA STAYED in bed for the whole week. Doctor Michaelson came over three times. After Doctor Michaelson left on Friday afternoon, Erico came downstairs and he leaned in the doorway, in the rainbow stripes of the blanket, and he said, "We have to close the shop for the weekend."
"Why?" I said. "I can be here by myself. I can work."
"I think Mama will go in the hospital," he said. "The doctor said pneumonia."

"Oh, no," I said. "Pneumonia? They can cure pneumonia. Lots of people get that."

I said, "Right now?"

He sat on the edge of the table, next to Constanzia's sewing machine, his face even with my face, dark eyes. I could never tell the color of Erico's eyes.

"She's sick," he said. "My sister is coming from Las Vegas."

"Your sister?" I said.

Erico nodded yes.

His sister.

"She is driving from Las Vegas," he said. "Maybe she'll be here tomorrow."

"I didn't know you had a sister," I said.

"Emilia was a dancer," he said. "In Las Vegas. After she came to this country and got a divorce."

His voice was so quiet that I wanted to whisper, and I thought about kissing Erico on the mouth, his eyes closed, and his arms around me like in a kiss. He stood up, and went and turned the sign around to CLOSED.

"Come over like regular on Monday," he said. "We'll see how things are."

EMILIA. ALL weekend, in my room, or on the couch reading, Lady Jane's music and Jimmy Henry being quiet, and him hanging around at our apartment instead of Lady Jane's, I thought about Emilia.

I didn't think about Constanzia, in a white hospital bed, coughing and nurses.

Elle came over and she cried because Bart Allen promised he would send her a letter and he didn't. When Elle kept talking about Bart Allen I didn't think about Emilia, and after Elle went home, I thought about Erico, Erico's mouth, and closing my eyes and pretending about Erico, and wishing Jimmy Henry would go hang around at Lady Jane's.

MONDAY MORNING, the back door of the shop was open, and Erico sat at the table in the kitchen.

He said, "Emilia hasn't come yet."

"Is Constanzia home now?" I said.

"No," he said.

The brick edges of the doorway cut into my hands, old bricks, broken. The day behind me in the alley was sunny and morning, and the kitchen was dark and quiet and Erico's chair squeaked. He got up and leaned on the table, folding his arms, facing me. He closed his eyes and opened them.

"I will be at the hospital today," he said. "We won't open the shop."

"What about Emilia?" I said, tears pouring over, and me and Erico both pretending I wasn't crying, and then tears on Erico's face.

"I don't know," he said. "She may come today."

He started to the stairway.

"Erico," I said, like a scream in a whisper. "Wait."

And he came back, and pulled me to him, his arms around me somehow and my face in his shirt, and he said it.

He said, "Mama is not better."

He said, "She might not get better."

"Please let me stay," I said, trying to breathe. "I can keep the shop open all day, please."

His arms fell away, and his pale plaid shirt stepped away, and I wiped my nose on the sleeve of my T-shirt.

"Okay," he said.

ELLE CAME in.

"Constanzia is sick," I said.

She said, "Oh, no. Sick sick? Really sick?"

"In the hospital," I said, and then I was afraid to say anything else.

Elle said, "Want me to hang out with you?"

I didn't say yes and I didn't say no.

MARGO CAME in, and Elle said, "I'm hanging out here, in case that's what you want to know. Constanzia is sick."

Margo said, "Sick?"
"In the hospital," I said. "Pneumonia."

SASHA CAME in, looking for Erico.
"My window fan is broken," she said. "Last time he fixed it for me."
"At the hospital," Elle said. "Constanzia."
"In the hospital," I said. "Pneumonia."

ELLE WENT home after noon.

AT SIX o'clock I turned the sign around CLOSED.
Behind the counter, on the floor, my back leaned against the side of Constanzia's blue-painted chair, I pulled out the box of embroidery thread. I sorted my fingers around in the tangled skeins, worked my fingers into the whole tangle and picked it up, threads and knots and a gold paper band dropping back into the box, onto the floor.
The big pieces of cloth, curtains, tablecloths, the dark hanging colors along the back wall, and the boxes, stacked square. I got under there, got down on the floor like it pulled me, lying down in the dark under the dusty old smell, and I slept there all night.
Early in the morning, quiet people in the kitchen.
Erico and Emilia sat at the table. She was old, with black hair and red fingernails, and bare feet in copper sandals. They both looked up at me with surprised eyes in the doorway.
"I fell asleep," I said.
They looked at me.
"Are you Emilia?" I said.
She looked at Erico, and back at me, and she nodded her head yes.
"Well," I said. "I'm Sarajean. Sarajean Henry."
"Hello, Sarajean," Emilia said in a scratchy deep voice.
Erico said, "You slept out there all night?"
"Under the curtains," I said.

He said, "Please, go ahead, get some coffee."

I poured a cup of coffee and stood by the stove. The coffee warm in my hands.

"Emilia arrived late," Erico said. "Late last night. We're going to the hospital now."

"Should we open the shop today?" I said.

"Maybe late," Erico said. "Maybe at noon."

"Okay," I said.

Emilia said, "You say a prayer, okay?"

"Well," I said. "I'm not a Catholic."

"What is this?" she said, reaching, pointing with her red fingernail to my beads, and the blue Mary medal on the silver chain.

"Constanzia gave this to me," I said. "Even though I'm not a Catholic."

Emilia got up and leaned close, looking close, and her light blouse fell open at the collar, and she had a blue lace bra. She touched the Mary medal, looked at the back of it, and she laughed.

"Ha," she said, low and funny. "That used to be mine. She took it back when I got divorced."

Emilia and Erico looked at each other, and Erico shook his head. They didn't look like brother and sister. They just looked like two Mexican people.

"Well," I said, closing my fingers over the Mary medal.

"Oh, no," Emilia said. "Don't worry. It belongs to you now. It was a gift."

Emilia's car was parked on Seventeenth Avenue, right in front of the shop, a black car covered in thick dust. Nevada license plates covered in thick dust. She and Erico got in, Emilia driving, driving away to the hospital.

I walked way up the alley, then on Colfax Street to Corona Street, and past Elle's old house. At the corner of Corona Street and Eleventh Avenue I looked for the mountains, but the blue haze hid them. Cheeseman Park was empty except for one guy in a suit going across the grass and dandelions.

I sat at the edge of the grass, under a new tree, and I picked dandelions and made a dandelion rope, until all the dandelions around me were strung together, and then I moved to another spot.

ERICO SAID, "She has passed on," and I heard the words in my head the very moment before he said them.

He touched my shoulder.

"She was easy in her going," he said.

THEN CAME the rest of that day, and the next day.

LADY JANE made a wreath of white flowers and ivy. She hung it on the door of the shop.

Erico wore a white shirt buttoned up to his neck, and he and Emilia talked in low voices and short words to the people who came into Someone's Beloved Threads.

Cassandra Wiggins brought a bottle of whiskey, and Emilia added some to the coffee she poured.

Elle sat out on the flower box, and I went out and sat next to her. The street had waves of heat in it, and Elle gathered her hair up on her head, twisting it until it stayed up in a knot, and red curls floated around her ears. Her ears had silver hoops pierced through.

"Hot," she said.

I said, "You got your ears pierced."

"Yeah," she said. "Margo did it."

"When?" I said. "Did it hurt?"

"Well, yeah, some," she said. She touched one silver hoop with her fingertip. "I had to hold ice on there until my ear froze, and that hurt, plus it kept dripping down my neck."

Where the little silver hoop poked through Elle's ear looked swollen and there was a dot of blood right there.

"Does it hurt now?" I said.

"It was a bitch sleeping," she said. "About every ten minutes I had to wake up because my ear hurt because I was laying on it."

The guy from Uncle Sam's Attic came up to us, up the sidewalk. He had sunflowers tied together with a green string.

"Hi," he said.

He looked into the door of the shop.

"A few folks in there, huh?" he said.

His beard was all gray, pale and dark and white in it, and he was bald on top. He had a little square cross for an earring.

"Think there's a jar for these?" he said, holding out the sunflowers. Huge, and velvety black centers.

I said, "The blue *olla*. On the shelf over the stove."

"Oh," he said. "Okay."

He went in.

"*Olla* means jar," I said.

"Yeah," Elle said. "That's what I thought."

I said, "I hate this sun."

It glared off the sidewalk and it shimmered off the black street, and when I looked up it was squinting into the light at Jimmy Henry. He stopped at the door.

Elle said, "Hi."

"Hi," he said.

He looked at me, and I looked back at him. I didn't want to say hi. Hi. It was a silly word. He went in and I watched in the door. He went to Erico and took Erico's hand, to shake hands with him, and they held their hands together and I saw that they were friends. They stood close, front to front.

Elle stood up.

"It's too fucking hot," she said. "Let's go over my house."

Erico pulled Jimmy Henry over to Emilia, and they were all three talking. They looked at me, and I hated Jimmy Henry for that.

Elle said, "Come on over. You can get me high."

"Okay," I said.

It was cool and empty in the apartment upstairs from Together Books. I gave Elle my little pipe and took off my hightops. I wiggled my toes.

"You smoke," I said. "I don't want any."

She took the pipe and went into the bathroom. She turned the water on in the bathtub and came back out, puffing clouds of marijuana smoke around. I lit a stick of incense and stuck it in the Buddha on the kitchen table.

"Are you taking a bath?" I said.

"Just a bird bath," Elle said.

She unbuttoned her shirt and handed me the pipe.

"I said I didn't want any," I said.

"Oh," she said, and she puffed some more. She dropped her shirt on the bathroom floor. She had a pink bra.

"A bird bath?" I said.

"Cool," she said. "Cool water."

She went in the bathroom, and I went as far as the bathroom door. Elle pushed off her tight cutoffs and got in the bathtub, just partly full, with bubbles foaming up. She took the pan that was for rinsing hair and splashed water over her shoulders, on her chest where her breasts were. She splashed a pan full of water in between her legs, wetting the dark red curls. Then she stood up, got out. She got a towel.

"Go ahead," she said. "You'll feel better."

I unbuttoned my shirt and hung it on the doorknob. Elle went past me, out the doorway. I took off my cutoffs and my underpants and I got in the tub, cool water trickling in from the faucet. I got down, goosebumps all over, and splashed the cool water all over, my face, my chest, down my back. In between my legs. Then I got up, and out.

"Hey," I said. "You want me to turn this water off and let it out now?"

"I don't care," she said.

I turned off the water and left the plug in. It smelled damp and flowery in there. I put my shirt back on, long soft blue cottony stuff, and I picked up my cutoffs and my underpants. I went to the doorway of her bedroom.

Elle was flopped down on the bed, a big white shirt wrapped around her, one button buttoned.

"Where's that pipe?" I said.

She held her hand up.

I took the pipe and put it in the pocket of my cutoffs. Then I laid down on the other side of Elle's bed. My skin was cool and tired. I closed my eyes, but when I closed my eyes tears rushed at them from behind, and I opened them, staring at the pink ceiling.

Petunias and marigolds.

I woke up once, Elle breathing, sleeping, curled next to me. Snoring a little snore. Me on my back, and Elle's hand was resting on my chest, palm down, fingers spread, curled, resting. Freckles on her fingers. I turned my face to her face, lying by me so close. A spot of dark blood on her ear.

JIMMY HENRY brought the sewing machine to our house. He set the sewing machine on the kitchen table, closed in its suitcase box, and the box of extra bobbins and sewing machine needles and the zipper foot.

He said, "We'll get a special table for it. In your room? Or in the front room?"

"In here I guess," I said, sitting on the edge of my bed, the sewing machine taking up all I could see of the kitchen table.

I STAYED in my room most mornings, lying in my bed. The music would come on downstairs, and then Jimmy Henry would come up from Lady Jane's, quiet, bare feet into his room, into the bathroom, and into the kitchen. He made coffee in the coffee pot. He made toast. Sometimes he would leave after that, and Blackbird would drive away.

Sometimes he would knock one small knock on my door.

Who's in there sleeping.

"There's coffee," he would say.

"See you tonight," he would say.

After he drove away I got up, went downstairs, locked the lock on the front door.

One morning Lady Jane came out into the hallway. She wore Jimmy Henry's tie-dye T-shirt and just underpants.

"Hey there," she said.

"Hello," I said, not stopping, going up the stairs.

She said, "Wait."

"What?" I said, waiting.

"I don't know," she said, coming to the bottom of the stairs. "Want to have some tea?"

"No," I said. "No thanks."

"Well, listen," she said. "Let's go out for breakfast together. Want to? To the café? I have to work lunch, so I could just go in early and have breakfast. Want to?"

She stood there, untangling one of the Christmas lights from its cord.

"I'm not too hungry," I said.

"Well, I wanted to talk to you," she said.

"About what?" I said.

"See how you're doing," she said.

"I'm doing fine," I said.

She tangled the Christmas light back into its cord again.

"Lalena came over a couple times," she said. "I guess you weren't home."

"Elle," I said. "You're supposed to say Elle."

"Elle," she said.

Lady Jane came around the railing and up the stairs to where I was. She sat down, and she patted the step next to her.

"Just sit down for a minute," she said.

I sat down next to her on the step.

"Have you been over to the shop?" she said.

"It's closed," I said.

"Yeah," she said. "I know."

"Elle told me," I said.

Lady Jane's feet were tanned from sandals, white marks across the top of each foot from her sandal strap.

"Why don't you go over there?" she said. "Say hi to Erico?"

My feet were bare white toes, white up my ankles to where it turned tan from wearing hightops.

"Sarajean?" she said, and I quit looking at my feet, and looked at the Christmas lights.

"I think he'd like that," she said. "I think the spirit of Constanzia touched you and it would make Erico less lonely to see you. You know?"

Her voice was kind of shaky. She put one arm around my shoulder and hugged a quick squeezy hug, and she smelled like Jimmy Henry in his T-shirt. I stood up.

"Maybe," I said.

I went up the stairs. I heard her stand up behind me. I went in, and I shut the door quietly. I shut the door of Jimmy Henry's bedroom. I went in my room, and I shut the door, and I got back on my bed with my book.

That night, late, dark, when everything was quiet, I got up. Jimmy Henry's bedroom door was still shut. I went out the front door and out into the night lit by streetlights and the red Safeway sign.

Colfax Street was still busy, cars and doors open into bars with music. I crossed and went as far as Ogden Street and Seventeenth Avenue. People were hanging out on the steps way down in front of the Lair Lounge. The yellow sign of Bill's Pepsi Store.

I crossed to the other corner.

Lights were on in the window above Together Books.

The windows above Someone's Beloved Threads were only dark.

Two guys walked by me, slowing down.

"Hey, baby," one of the guys said.

I said, "Fuck you."

That made them laugh.

They kept walking, down the sidewalk, down Seventeenth Avenue.

☮

JIMMY HENRY was sitting on the front step. He was smoking a cigarette, an orange dot on the front porch. No shirt, no shoes. Just in his cutoffs, his skin all white.

"Kind of late for you to be wandering around, isn't it?" he said.

Fuck you.

Who do you think you are, my father?

That made me laugh, and I just kept walking, into my house and up the stairs.

End of Summer, 1977

Elle left again right before school started.

Jimmy Henry came home in the middle of the day, came to my open bedroom door.

"Lalena took off again," he said.

"Elle," I said. "How come nobody calls her Elle? She changed to Elle years ago, you know."

"Sarajean," he said.

He came in, leaned on the doorway.

"Do you know where she went?" he said.

"Los Angeles," I said. "She said she was going back there."

"Who did she know there besides that girl Talia?" he said.

"She had a boyfriend," I said.

"She took her daddy's money," he said. "He owed that money to some other people. It was a lot of money."

"Dealing, huh?" I said.

"What did she say to you?" he said. "Did she say anything? Listen, this is important."

"I haven't talked to her in a while," I said. "I haven't even seen her."

He rubbed his face in his hands.

"What a fucking mess," he said.

"Why is it a fucking mess?" I said.

Jimmy Henry's hair had long streaks of gray at the front.

"It just is," he said.

"Was it your money, too?" I said.

"What was this boyfriend's name?" he said.

"I don't know," I said. "Bart something."

"I can't remember," I said.

Bart Allen.

"Please, if you remember, tell me," he said. "Okay? Please, promise? And if she gets in touch with you?"

"Yeah, okay," I said.

JFK CAME over, and Nancy, downstairs at Lady Jane's. Jimmy Henry was down there, and JFK came up and opened the door into the front room.

"Don't you believe in knocking?" I said.

"Knock knock," he said. "Hi."

"You home now?" I said, sitting up, putting my book face down on the applebox table.

"Yeah," he said. "I got home Monday."

He was tanned dark. His long hair was blond almost to white, and so were his eyebrows.

"So, some excitement," he said.

"You mean Elle?" I said.

"Yeah," he said. "I think she really fucked up this time."

"How do you know?" I said. "What do you mean?"

"Hanging out at the café," he said. "You can learn a lot if you hang out and just act like a goofy kid who isn't listening."

"Like a creepy little weasel?" I said.

"Exactly," he said.

He sat down on the applebox table and started to pick carefully at a scab on his knee.

"That's gross," I said. "Go do that somewhere else. What did you hear them say?"

"Well, there's lots of people looking for her this time," he said. "Her dad was dealing, and I don't think it was marijuana either. 'Cause there's guys in suits involved."

"What's that mean, 'guys in suits'?" I said.

"Well, actually that's just a saying, 'guys in suits,'" he said. "The one guy was wearing a pretty nice suede jacket, though."

"So what's that supposed to mean," I said.

"It means coke," he said.

"Why does it mean coke?" I said.

"It means a lot of dollars," he said.

"A fucking mess," I said.

"Exactly," he said. "Got any marijuana?"

"No," I said.

"Well," he said. "Ta-dum."

He held up a wrapped up piece of tinfoil.

"What did you do?" I said. "Rip off your mom?"

He looked like I hurt his feelings.

"I don't rip off my mom," he said. "I just borrow it. I always put some back in her stash when I get some of my own."

"Yeah, sure," I said.

"In fact," he said. "Sometimes, when she doesn't have any, I plant some in her stash spots where she'll find it and think she forgot about it."

"You're kidding," I said.

"Nope, not kidding," I said. "She has stashes all over the place, so I know she can't remember them all. Plus people that smoke marijuana forget things a lot."

"I don't believe it," I said.

"Hey, I'm a nice guy," he said.

"Yeah," I said. "For a creepy little weasel."

Nancy called up the stairs that they were going to Celestial Tea Palace.

"I'll meet you there in a while," JFK yelled back.

The doors downstairs opened and shut and opened and shut and then everybody was gone and the house was quiet, just me and JFK. He unwrapped the tinfoil and he pinched some marijuana into the pipe. I took it and went over by the window, and sat on the open windowsill under the boarded-up top half. A light was on in Lady Jane's, a square of light on the skinny sidewalk.

JFK said, "So, you want to walk over to the café with me?"

"No," I said, handing the pipe out to him.

"Come on," he said. "I don't want to walk over there by myself."

"Why not?" I said. "Scared?"

"High," he said.

He smoked on the pipe and blew the smoke out the window.

"Yeah, well, me too," I said. "And I like being home by myself when I'm high."

"Walk over there with me and I'll give you some of this bud to keep for when you get back," he said.

"Oh, man," I said. "I don't feel like it."

"Come on," he said. "Wear that goofy hat."

GARAGE DOORS next to the sidewalk, and big places with big closed-up doors. Boarded-up walls with spray paint FUCK YOU and KILL FOR JESUS and FOR SALE/FOR LEASE. A weedy empty place behind a tall wire fence, all grown high with Queen Anne's lace, and we walked fast, not talking, crunching on broken-out streetlight glass. It was apartments again after Nineteenth Avenue, small buildings, front doors open to hallways and some lightbulbs in there. There were some streetlights. Then Celestial Tea Palace, all colors from the painted sign and lights inside and people in the windows and we walked faster to the open door.

"Powwow," JFK said.

I said, "Huh?"

"Over in the corner," he said. "Be mellow."

"Huh?" I said.

"Don't stare," he said.

Jimmy Henry leaned against the wall by the round corner table. His arms were crossed over his front, and he stared down at his feet. Margo and Cassandra Wiggins were in the chairs there, along the wall, and Elle's daddy sat back in a chair, tipping it back on its two back legs.

Nancy came up from behind us. She kissed JFK on his cheek. He was taller then Nancy. I was taller than Nancy.

"Can I have a chocolate shake?" he said.

"Yeah," she said. "You want it with chocolate ice cream?"

"Yes, please," he said. "Sarajean wants one too."

"No, I don't," I said.

"Yes, you do," he said, looking at me for a quick look.

"Yes, she does," he said back to Nancy.

Nancy went back behind the counter.

"Why do I want a chocolate shake?" I said.

JFK moved down the row of seats along the counter.

"The shake machine is down here," he said.

Toward the round table in the corner.

He said, "The chocolate ice cream is just past the shake machine."

He went to an empty seat, three empty seats in a row, toward the end of the counter, not all the way to the end. There were empty seats at the very end.

"What about those seats?" I said, talking into the back of his shoulder, talking down low.

"Not cool," he said. "Too obvious. You would not make a successful espionage agent."

Nancy was at the shake machine.

"I'm making these kids some shakes," she said to the lady working back there, the other waitress. She got busy, scooping out chocolate ice cream from the freezer. JFK put his finger to his lips and tipped his head toward the round table.

"That truck won't make it across the desert again," Jimmy Henry was saying.

Margo was sniffing and all teary.

Cassandra Wiggins said, "What about Sasha's car? Will that make it?"

"Probably have to," Elle's daddy said. "Might have to borrow the keys though. She says her and the kid are leaving for Ohio next week."

Cassandra Wiggins said, "She wouldn't call the pigs about her car getting ripped off, would she?"

"I doubt it," he said.

The shake machine turned on a high buzzy whine.

"Last time Elle took off," I said, leaning closer to JFK, talking from under my hat. "They drove Blackbird to go get her. She got busted shoplifting, and Margo and Cassandra Wiggins had to go get her out of Juvie."

The shake machine whined on and on, high and low and whining. I sneaked a look back to the round table. Cassandra Wiggins was talking. She tapped her pointer finger on the table, talking to Elle's daddy. Margo sat all soft and slumped looking into her tea.

Then Lady Jane got there. She had Queen Anne's lace in a glass of water. She set the glass on the table in front of Margo, and Margo looked up, pink face all teary. Cassandra Wiggins got up, standing up straight, tall, and she hugged Lady Jane, taller and straighter than Lady Jane, short dark hair, long blond soft hair, for a second. Then Cassandra Wiggins went back to the phone hanging on the wall by the end of the counter.

The shake machine went quiet. Nancy took the metal cup of chocolate shake and she poured the shake into two glasses.

"Want anything else?" she said.

"No, thank you," I said.

"Cinnamon toast," JFK said.

He kicked my leg under the counter.

"No, thank you," I said.

I kicked him back.

"Okay," Nancy said.

She went back through the doors into the kitchen.

"Cinnamon toast?" I said.

"It's not on the menu," JFK said. "She has to go make the cinnamon sugar stuff, and then come out and make the toast. It takes her forever."

Cassandra Wiggins hung up the phone. She took a paper napkin out of the holder on the counter, and she took a short pencil from her T-shirt pocket, and she wrote down the number from the phone. Then she went back to the round table, and she stood there, her cowboy boot feet wide apart, her hands in her back pockets.

"Don't look," JFK whispered. "Just listen."

I couldn't hear Cassandra Wiggins talking. I heard her leave. Cowboy boots going behind us, and Margo with her, Margo not making any noise at all.

"Cassandra Wiggins hates Lalena's dad," JFK said. "And he says she needs, well. He hates her too. I think."

Elle's daddy. Dragon lady.

"I hope they never find her," I said.

DARK LOW sky and wet fog made everything dark wet and quiet. Jimmy Henry's alarm clock rang in his room, and then his belt buckle hit the floor. His bare feet slapped into the kitchen. He knocked on my door.

Who's in there sleeping.

Little Miss Strange.

"First day of school," he said.

The white fog, lying down still and heavy below my bedroom window, the pink glow of it in the parking lot of the Safeway store getting lighter and thinner since earlier, six o'clock maybe, since I had been leaning at the bedroom window.

I opened the door.

"You're up," he said. "All dressed."

"So are you," I said.

He said, "Want some toast?"

"No," I said. "No thanks."

"Foggy," he said.

"Yeah," I said.

He filled the coffee pot up with water and set it on the stove. I went back to the window of my room and pulled the window shut, the sounds of coffee behind me in the kitchen. The fog clouded the inside of the window, and I drew a ticktacktoe game, XOXOX, and I lost. I wiped the ticktacktoe game away and the fog slowly clouded the window again. The warm smell of toast.

Jimmy Henry was buttering two pieces of toast when I went back out there.

"Real butter," he said, "Not margarine."

The stick of butter was cold, on a cold blue plate right out of the refrigerator. Jimmy Henry tore holes in the toast trying to spread the hard cold butter.

"Look," I said.

I took another knife out of the drawer, and I scraped along the top of the stick of butter. Thin yellow curls peeled up.

"Like that," I said, dropping the curls of butter onto the toast.

"Pretty smart," he said.

"Yeah," I said. "That's me, pretty smart."

"Here, take this one," he said.

He gave me the piece of toast that didn't have butter holes. I leaned against the table, eating, looking at my toast between bites. Jimmy Henry put two more pieces of bread in the toaster, humming a little bit of a song, and wrapping the bread wrapper back up with a little twist of his fingers.

"So," he said. "What classes do you have?"

His voice was pretty awake. The coffee wasn't even perked.

I said, "Spanish. English. Algebra. Civics, which is the eighth-grade name for social studies."

"Algebra, huh?" he said.

"Yeah," I said. "And something else. That's only four."

He said, "Your hair looks nice. Pretty short huh?"

I had trimmed it myself, snipping away at the ends. I closed my eyes to cut the back. Elle closing her eyes to reach around in her shoulder strap purse. It was a short choppy shag haircut, uneven didn't matter.

The other toasts popped up, and Jimmy Henry tried to butter them. He didn't tear holes in the toast. He pretty much dented up the butter. I took the other piece of toast when he handed it to me and I went back in my room. Jimmy Henry messed around with the coffee pot, and the coffee pot gurgled and perked, taking up the quiet space made by me leaving the kitchen.

Jimmy Henry was singing the song now. He knew all the words.

It was too early to leave for school, but when Jimmy Henry went into the bathroom, I went out the front door, and when I got outside to the sidewalk I walked away fast, into the thin white fog, down Ogden Street toward Sixth Avenue. I was the only person out there, the only person out in the fog. Fog in Denver was weird, and I walked along the sidewalk like a secret.

Sixth Avenue was busy, the little grocery store was lit up. A sign on the door said OPEN. A sign in the window said COFFEE TO GO. The cement floor was sticky, and there were flies stuck to a paper strip hanging from the ceiling over the counter. The old lady behind the counter had an apron that was so clean it looked silly, pulled white and tight across her big stomach. She had little glasses on a big nose.

When she gave me my coffee, she said, "There ya go, kid. Quarter."

"Got any milk?" I said. "Got any sugar?"

She wagged her hand at a corner of the counter, and there were some napkins piled up, and a box of sugar, and a thing of powder creamer. I made the coffee thick and sweet and white.

I said, "Thanks."

She said, "Yeah."

She sat back down on a chair back there, groaning, sitting hard, and she opened up a *Rocky Mountain News*.

"Can I get a pack of Kools?" I said.

"Nope," she said. "Ya not old enough."

"Oh," I said. "Okay. 'Bye."

The coffee tasted mostly like the cup. The gray of day was brighter, and the fog was fading away. Fog hung at the corner, and when I got to the corner, the fog had moved back to the door of the grocery store, and up to the other corner. Fading away.

The tall windows of Mountain View Junior High were lit up, square and yellow, and the building sat in the middle of an empty parking lot. Some cars were parked in the teachers' lot.

My ring. In my inside jacket pocket. I set my coffee on a newspaper box, and I put the ring on my finger, cold and silver, and I folded the sleeves of my green corduroy jacket up to the elbows. The cuffs were getting short and ragged. The maroon lining was shredded inside the sleeves. My green corduroy jacket. Tears stung at my eyes, stinging there, and then fading back into my brain, wherever tears went.

FIRST ASSEMBLY was in the gym. Mr. Withers made his same speech about becoming good Americans, and having goals and dreams, and being equal, and not doing drugs or else you get kicked out for good. He introduced Miss Purcell and Mr. Sherett again.

Seventh-grade kids watched. The eighth-grade kids and the ninth-grade kids didn't watch so much. I sat near a bunch of eighth-grade girls who kept squirting perfume on each other. They wore skirts and blouses and nylons, all of them.

I looked for red hair. I looked for JFK.

The marching band came in behind Mr. Withers and marched around the gym behind him, all in blue and white marching band uniforms, playing marching band music so loud that the seats of the bleachers shook. Kids started stomping and yelling, except the Mexican kids, and then the football team, every boy wearing a white shirt and a tie, went out there by Mr. Withers, and the cheerleaders in their pleated cheerleader skirts and blue underpants.

The bleachers shook. I burped powder creamer up into the back of my throat. I held onto the wooden edge of the bleacher and looked down through all the kids in front of me, rows of kids between me and the hallway door to the hallway where the bathroom was. My throat filled up, and I covered my mouth with my sleeve and tried to swallow back down and my eyes got all watery.

Then I shivered, from my butt all the way to the back of my head, and then I was okay. There was a nasty burning at the back of my throat and in my nose. I wiped my mouth with my sleeve. The kids around me were standing and clapping and cheering and squirting perfume, and the football players were running in a wide circle around Mr. Withers. He stood there at the microphone with both his arms raised for victory, and the cheerleaders bounced onto each other's shoulders until they made a triangle of blue and white little skirts right behind him.

When the football team stopped running and Mr. Withers put his arms back down, the gym got quiet right away, and the triangle of cheerleaders stayed balanced up three cheerleaders high. Mr. Withers talked some more. Little gobs of puke smeared the inside of my sleeve, and I folded my arms across my chest, across the sharp pukey smell all mixed in with the taste of perfume.

Mr. Withers said, "Go forth and learn."

THE SECOND morning of school was already warm and blue when I left. Jimmy Henry's door stayed shut. I didn't wear my jacket, and partway to Sixth Avenue I remembered my ring, wishing for it, and wishing for wet white fog.

My new English teacher was Mrs. Shore. She was a short old lady with thick tie-up shoes. She assigned us to read *Heart of Darkness*, writing *Heart of Darkness* on the chalkboard with short quick letters, turning around and slapping chalk off her hands and staring at us in our seats.

By the end of the day I still didn't know who my locker partner was. Maybe I would get a locker to myself. Or Elle would come back and she could be my locker partner. Hand, Henry, alphabetical.

I got home and the front door was open wide, the door at the top of the stairs wide open too. I went up the stairs, tired, homework books, and Lady Jane was sitting on the arm of the couch, her face all in her hands.

I said, "What the fuck."

Lady Jane jumped up.

"Oh, God," she said.

The records from the shelf were all over the floor, and the pillows from the couch were on the floor, and the applebox table was on its side, everything was on the floor. The kitchen drawers were pulled out and stuff was on the floor in there, spoons and forks, the dishtowels from the second drawer, the stuff from the third drawer. Jimmy Henry's bedroom door was open and the drawers were pulled out of his dresser, his clothes were pulled out of his dresser, his green army bag lying in the middle of his bed zipped open.

Lady Jane said, "Oh, God."

"What happened?" I said. "Where is he?"

"They took him away," she said, choking with crying. "Busted."

"Busted?" I said. "For what?"

"I don't know," she said. "It was undercover cops."

She wiped her face with the edge of her long skirt.

"God, I'm glad you're here," she said. "Come on, we have to get you out of here."

I went to my room. All messed up, my dresser drawers dumped out, all my clothes on the floor. My Tampax tampons box. I picked up the box and looked, my money still safe inside. I put the money into my blue-jeans pocket, my fingers shaking, my knees shaking.

I said, "What did they dump out my stuff for?"

My voice shaking.

Lady Jane came as far as the doorway.

"Looking for dope?" she said. "I don't know. I was downstairs, I heard all the noise. I know they saw that letter from Tina Blue."

"What letter from Tina Blue?" I said.

"Come on," she said. "We have to get you out of here. They probably went to look for you at school. They'll probably be back with someone from some juvenile department."

Lady Jane's eyes were red and snot dripped down from her nose to her lip. She looked crazy. She sounded crazy.

"Are you crazy?" I said. "Tina Blue?"

I pushed my folded-up blue jeans and cutoffs off the bed. I kicked at the pile of underpants on the floor, and the socks, and I picked up my underpants. Stuff all over the floor. The letter from Christine Jeanette Blumenthal was on the top of my dresser and I picked it up.

Tina Blue.

Lady Jane said, "They'll take you away. They'll put you in a foster home or something while they look for her. Come on, just leave this stuff. We'll go over to Nancy's."

She pulled my arm, and I let go of the underpants, dropped them back on the floor. I held on to the letter, and Lady Jane pulled me by my arm, across forks and spoons and slipping on album covers and over the newspapers and out the door. Down the stairs.

"Come on," she said. "Come on."

"Lady Jane, wait," I said. "What about Jimmy Henry? Doesn't he get bail or something?"

"He's been busted before," she said. "A gun charge. I don't know. There might have been a second offense that time. I don't even know what he was dealing. Maybe he wasn't dealing. I don't know."

Running and walking and running, holding on to my arm by the wrist, pulling me along the sidewalk, down Ogden Street, past Saint Therese Carmelite, around the corner onto Ninth Avenue and down Ninth Avenue toward JFK's apartment building on Clarkson Street.

"Tina Blue?" I said.

"If we couldn't find her before I don't know how we're going to find her now," Lady Jane said, looking back behind us.

Tina Blue. Christine Jeanette Blumenthal. Thin loopy Bs.

We went into JFK's building, up the stairs, down the long striped hallway. Lady Jane knocked on the door, tried at the doorknob, knocked again. JFK opened the door.

"Hi, you guys," he said.

Lady Jane pulled me inside and shut the door and turned the lock.

JFK said, "What? What's going on?"

"Tina Blue," I said. Maybe not really saying it.

"Jimmy Henry got busted," Lady Jane said.

"Shit," JFK said. "Wow. When?"

Lady Jane sat down in the middle of the couch.

"Okay, now," she said. "I have to think."

Her face kept talking, her mouth moving, a clear drip of snot hanging at the end of her nose caught the sunlight that came through the bamboo shade and sparkled like a tiny star.

My heart belongs to purple.

Lady Jane said, "When is Nancy getting back?"

"Don't know," JFK said.

Lady Jane said, "Where is she?"

"Just out messing around, I guess," he said. "She doesn't have to work tonight."

"Oh, God, work," Lady Jane said. "I have to go call in."

She stood up.

"I'm going to go call work," she said. "And then I have to go find Lalena's daddy."

JFK sat down on one end of the couch, and he looked at me.

"Elle," he said. "You're supposed to say Elle."

"He might know what's going on," Lady Jane said. "You guys stay here. If Nancy comes home, tell her I'll be back as soon as I can. Tell her I might need her to work for me tonight. Don't let anybody in."

She left, and I turned the lock behind her.

"Now what?" JFK said.

I sat on the other end of the couch from him.

"I don't know," I said.

"Are you scared?" he said.

"I don't know," I said, my whole self zinging from him saying that.

He said, "He was dealing coke?"

I said, "Do you remember my mother?"

"Huh?" he said.

"Yeah," he said. "She came over to our house sometimes, when we lived on Lincoln Street."

"Tina Blue," I said.

I call myself Tina Blue.

JFK sat there, the space of Lady Jane in between us on the couch, a quiet around us, inside, outside the window, everything quiet and quieter.

I CALL myself Tina Blue.

I have fled the dark heart of America.

And I am hiding.

AND INTO the quiet I said, "I know."

JFK said, "You know what?"

"I know where she's hiding."

"Hiding?" he said. "Who's hiding?"

"Tina Blue. Christine Jeanette Blumenthal."

He said, "Where?"

I said, "Omaha, Nebraska."

He said, "Omaha, Nebraska?"

I said, "Do you remember what she looks like?"

"Well, yeah, kind of," he said. "Don't you?"

"If you asked me this morning did I remember Tina Blue I probably would of said yes. Long hair. I remember her eyes closed. But now I don't know. I can't think of her face. There was a little dot on her neck. She had a flower-painted teapot. And pink joints, she kept pink joints in one of those carved wooden boxes with the ivory flowers on the lid."

"God," I said. "My ring."

JFK just looked at me, watching me.

"You have to go over my house," I said.

"Why?" he said. "We're supposed to wait here."

"In my bedroom, on the doorknob," I said. "I need my green jacket."

"Your green jacket?" he said.

"Yeah, get it," I said, picking up his hand with my hand, putting my key into his hand, into his thin fingers.

"I don't want to go over there," he said. "What if the cops are there?"

"Please."

I looked at him, at his face, brown smooth cheeks, light gray-colored eyes that looked right back at me and didn't want to go over there.

"Please," I said.

"Okay," he said, looking down, his long, light-colored hair falling over his eyes, and I touched his hair, soft hair, touched his shoulder, the bones of his shoulder through his T-shirt, sorry for saying please like that, sorry for saying please and making him look away.

"Hurry up, okay?" I said.

WAITING AT JFK's, waiting for him to come back, I looked at my face in the mirror, with JFK's baby pictures all around. I looked in the mirror for Tina Blue's face, the face I couldn't remember now. The only face I saw was the same face I always saw, my face that never changed, and baby pictures, all around my face in the mirror.

JFK opened the door, and he held my green jacket. I took it and closed my hand around the ring in the pocket. The same ring that had never changed, the cold circle of it the same as the day under Tina Blue's window, and I took the ring out of the pocket, Tina Blue's silver flowered spoon ring, Christine Jeanette Blumenthal's silver flowered spoon ring, my mother's silver flowered spoon ring.

"That's her ring?" JFK said.

"Well, yeah," I said. "I got it when she lived there."

I put it on my finger. JFK stood still and straight by the door, and when I looked at him he looked away.

"Thanks," I said.

"So what are you going to do?" he said. "How do you know she's in Omaha?"

"I'm going to go there."

"Where?" he said. "Omaha? Nebraska?"

"I have the address. I have the envelope. I've been using it for a bookmark."

"A bookmark? What envelope?" he said. "How are you going to get to Omaha, Nebraska?"

"I don't know yet."

IT WAS getting dark, and Lady Jane wasn't back.

"How are you going to find her?" JFK said. "Maybe you could just live with me and my mom. What about school? You know, Jimmy Henry might get off with just probation, or parole or like that. Why don't you just write to her? You don't even know how long ago she sent that letter to Lady Jane."

He stopped.

"Are you worried about him?" he said.

My stomach jumped. Jimmy Henry.

"I guess it depends on a lot of stuff," JFK said. "Now, don't get mad, but was he doing junk? I remember when he used to do that, but I thought he didn't do it anymore because my mom says junkies are the scourge of the earth, junkies and Jesus freaks, and now she hangs out with him and Lady Jane, so I didn't think he was into that anymore."

"JFK," I said. "You've got to shut up. I don't know what to do, and you've got to shut up."

Then I was crying and JFK shut up.

FINALLY THE thing to do was just leave.

"Leave?" JFK said, and his voice squeaked. "What do you mean, leave? Don't leave. Wait here for my mom. You can stay here tonight."

"I'm going to Omaha tonight," I said.

"You mean leave for Omaha?" he said. "How can you leave for Omaha?"

"What am I supposed to do, wait to get put in a foster home? Or Juvie? Look, I know her address. I can just go find her. Just don't tell anyone. If I can't find her, I'll just come back."

"I can't," he said. "I can't not tell anyone. I'm a bad liar. My mom always knows."

"Well, just say I left," I said. "But don't say where."

JFK got up off the couch and leaned against the kitchen doorway, and he crossed both arms over his chest.

"Oh, man," he said. "I think this is a bad idea. How can you get to Omaha? What are you going to do, just walk up to some house and knock on the door and say 'Hi, you're my mother'?"

He frowned. He played with his lip with his finger.

"Okay," I said carefully. "I won't do it. But I have to go get some things at my house. Homework stuff."

"Really?" he said.

"I'll be right back," I said.

He stood up straight.

"Okay," he said. "We can make hamburgers and wait for my mom and Lady Jane. My mom will know what to do, don't worry. Lady Jane gets kind of nuts sometimes, you know?"

"Macaroni and cheese," I said. "Let's make macaroni and cheese."

"Okay," he said. "I think we got some macaroni, and I know there's cheese."

"Okay," I said, leaving, walking down the striped carpet, down the hall. Not looking back at him. My stomach jumping.

"Put the macaroni water on," I said.

THE LIGHT of the sky was gone, and the light up there was the light of streetlights, and the pink Safeway light, hard against the sky, city night sky. "In the city night sky," Erico said, "it is never dark. The light cannot escape. The sky of night here is never black."

HI, YOU'RE my mother.

THERE WERE no lights on at our house. From under the corner tree of the Safeway parking lot, the dark red of our house disappeared, just a dark place across the street. Blackbird was parked out front. I went back down the block, into the alley. Into my backyard.

Black sweater. Truckers. Ivory leaves shirt.

Marigolds at the edge of Lady Jane's porch were yellow like white in the dark, and the marigold smell, and the stink of the garbage cans. The window of the empty apartment covered thick and hidden with black grime, and I wanted to be in there. I went to the skinny sidewalk and never made a sound.

The click of the key was loud, the latch click of the front door shutting behind me loud too, and I stood still in the dark at the bottom of the stairway, trying to listen past the doors, into Lady Jane's, upstairs, no sound, my heart pounding in my head. Not breathing.

The pounding stopped when I started breathing again.

I went up the stairs one slow step at a time.

Record covers on the floor in the front room. I stepped wide across the forks and stuff on the kitchen floor. I closed the door in my room, closed the door and closed all the pink Safeway light in with me.

I stepped on my Walt Whitman hat, and I picked it up and put it on. I picked up the horse patch.

The book on the floor by my bed had the envelope with the yellow bird, and the blue heart, and Tina Blue's address. Fourteen twenty Belmont Street. Omaha, Nebraska. I stared hard at the address, in the dark light, and then folded the envelope and put it my my inside jacket pocket.

The box of birdcloth was dumped out in the closet, and the smell was the dusty smell of the back corners of Someone's Beloved Threads. I put the cloth close to my face, wanting that smell, wanting that smell down inside me where the crying was, wanting to sit in the dark closet and cry into the smell of the birdcloth.

I untied the pink scarf knot around *The Prophet*, the bell owl, Jimmy Henry's Purple Heart. I hooked my front door key to the purple plastic peace symbol key chain. I put the horse patch inside *The Prophet* with the Kelly Bird poem. I tied the scarf corners together again.

Leaving.

KNOCKING ON the door. Hello? Are you Tina Blue?

Do you know who I am?

THE CRYING stopped, thinking so hard on what I would say. A car door slammed out on the street. Nothing. Some other car, not somebody coming in here to get me, to take me to some juvenile place.

FUCKING JIMMY Henry.

HIS ROOM was black, light from the streetlights shining onto the ceiling over the top of the curtains. I pulled one curtain open enough to let some streetlight in. The dresser drawers were pulled out, and his socks and stuff dumped on the floor, his T-shirts dumped on the floor in their folded stack. His tie-dye T-shirt on the top of the stack. It smelled like laundry soap, smelled like Jimmy Henry. I wiped my nose with it. I wanted him to be walking in right now, in a skinny T-shirt that smelled like soap, wanted him to say, "It's alright. We'll go together, in Blackbird, we'll drive to Omaha and find her together. It's alright, baby."

HE DOESN'T want to find her. Fucking Lady Jane.

☮

I SHUT myself in the bathroom and turned on the bright light, not looking in the mirror. My toothbrush, the toothpaste, a comb, the hairbrush. Jimmy Henry's long hair was tangled all through the bristles. Lady Jane's sandalwood soap was in the soapdish with Jimmy Henry's white soap from Safeway. I took Jimmy Henry's soap. I folded the bathroom things into a towel.

The green canvas bag wasn't very full.

I STILL have all your books.

THE WEBSTER'S *Collegiate Dictionary* was open on my dresser top, and I turned the pages to the *S* page, with the papery blue flower, black-looking in the dark of my room. The star on the page of "Sarah," black-looking in the dark of my room. I untied the pink square bundle and laid the flower into a page of *The Prophet*. I tore the Sarah page out of the dictionary, the tearing of it loud, the last noise I made in my room. I put it in my heart pocket.

And then I left.

From the front porch Ogden Street was empty, nobody out. The street was empty up past the Safeway store, and empty down the sidewalk under the trees as far as Saint Therese Carmelite. The night had turned windy, a piece of trash blowing in the street, and the papery blowing of leaves in the trees, a sound that seemed loud, and wasn't.

Eleventh Avenue went down the hill toward downtown, and all the lights of Denver spread out wide. Crossing Clarkson Street, I picked out the one light in the front of JFK's apartment building, him waiting, making macaroni and cheese, and me out here leaving.

"I'll call you," I said. "I'll call you at the café."

"Sorry," I said, not sorry, walking down the hill of Eleventh Avenue.

At Lincoln Street I turned toward Colfax Street, past Colfax Street, going down the sidewalk, holding on to my hat in the wind. At Seventeenth Avenue I stopped, even though the light was green, I stopped. Seventeenth

Avenue went back up the hill from Lincoln Street and I could only see the dark hanging shape of the sign at Bead Here Now.

Closer to the Greyhound station places were open and there were people hanging out on the sidewalks. A guy sat on the sidewalk at the corner, drunk looking, all sloppy and sleepy.

"Nice hat," he said.

I said, "Thanks," and I walked past him, crossed the street, even though the light was red.

"I'll give you a buck for that hat," he yelled after me.

I kept walking.

"A buck," I said. "I paid four bucks for this hat."

A man leaning by the telephone pole at the other corner looked at me, me talking to myself.

He said, "Hey, little guy."

He thinks I'm a boy.

I kept walking.

THE GREYHOUND Bus greyhound hummed around in its big circle, and I pushed through the doors not looking up, walked right up to the end of a line of people at the counter. There were eight people waiting in the line. Eight people and then I had to know what to say.

Omaha.

Points east.

Omaha, Nebraska, please.

"One ticket to Omaha," I said to the guy behind the counter.

He didn't look up from all the papers on the counter.

He said, "One way or round trip?"

"One way, please," I said.

I said, "How long is round trip good for?"

"Ninety days," he said.

He looked at me.

"One way," I said.

"Twenty-two fifty," he said.

He wrote on the ticket, tore along the dotted part, tucked part of the ticket inside another part and put the whole thing into its own folder. I put a twenty-dollar bill and a five-dollar bill on the counter. He already had two dollars and fifty cents there.

"Thanks," I said.

"Nice trip," he said, not looking at me again.

The sign on the wall behind the counter didn't say Omaha anywhere on it, except for LINCOLN-OMAHA, DEPARTING AT 10:35 P.M. It was eight-fifteen. Two hours and twenty minutes. I pulled down on my hat and went around the rows of orange seats to the back wall, by the garage doors, a row of empty seats in the corner. A lady across from the empty seats was looking at a magazine, and she didn't looked up when I sat down. I slid the green bag off my shoulder. I pushed the bag under the seat.

The loudspeaker said, "Now boarding for Colorado Springs, Pueblo, Trinidad, and points south."

Loud and echoey, bus engines loud in the garage, and people lining up to go out there, to points south.

Eight seventeen.

I put my ticket in my inside pocket of my jacket, and I took out the envelope. Fourteen twenty Belmont Street, my stomach jumping. Hurting.

WHY DIDN'T you ever come back?

Did you mean to never come back?

"NOW BOARDING for Greely, Cheyenne, Scott's Bluff, points north."

I didn't look up from under my hat. I didn't know what I would say. I didn't know what she would look like. Fourteen twenty Belmont Street.

MY HEAD dropped and I woke up scared. The clock only said nine-ten. I stretched my arms out in front of me straight until my shoulders made little popping sounds.

A cigarette machine was next to the doorway of the bus station restaurant. I dragged my green bag out from under the seat and pulled the strap onto my shoulder, and walked over to the cigarette machine, right up to the cigarette machine with the big yellow and red sticker that said "Minors by Law Forbidden to Operate This Machine," and under that a row of lit up pictures of the different brands. I counted out coins, dropped them clanking loud into the slot, not looking around, and I pulled out the knob under the Marlboros picture. I put the Marlboros in my pocket, and I turned and walked back to my same seat not looking around and not looking at anybody.

The air of the bus station was cloudy with smoke. Ashtrays were at the end of each row of orange chairs, most of the ashtrays full of paper cups. I didn't have matches. I put my hand in my pocket, the pack of Marlboros feeling nice and smooth and square.

Nine-fifteen. Every time I looked at the clock my heart thumped.

Nine-sixteen. Thump.

"Now boarding for Los Angeles."

The lady across the seats from me slapped her magazine shut and stood up. She patted her curled hair, stuffing the magazine into her big purse. She picked up a little flowered suitcase out of the seat next to her and smiled at me without looking at me and went and got in line at the garage door.

I pulled my bag out again and went over to a stand of magazines and cough drops and stuff. I picked a tube of chapstick out of a holder on the counter.

"Forty-nine cents," a girl behind there said.

I put two quarters on the counter, and I said, "Got any matches?"

She put one penny and one pack of matches on the counter, not looking up, looking at a magazine. I put the penny and the matches in my pocket, not saying thanks, and I went back toward my same seat going the other way around all the chairs, along the wall with the row of pay telephones. One telephone had a telephone book hanging on a wire cord.

Celestial Tea Palace. I wrote the number on the envelope, under "1420 Belmont Street."

"Now boarding for Sterling, North Platte, Lincoln-Omaha, and points east."

My heart went bang.

I SLID into two empty bus seats and pushed my bag underneath. The tall cushions hid me into the little space of seats, I couldn't see in front of my seat, or to the seat behind me. Tall people moved down the aisle, past me and my two seats, and there were the easy sounds of people settling into seats around me. The garage outside the bus windows was busy and noisy, and inside was dark and quiet. Then the bus driver got on, and he shut the door, shutting the quiet dark in, and he drove out the wide doors, and I left.

I left Denver.

The bus turned away from downtown, in a direction I had never been, out Nineteenth Avenue, over to Twenty-fifth Avenue and then farther, block after block to Seventy-second Avenue, shacky little houses in rows, and gas stations and little grocery stores on every corner.

At Seventy-second Avenue the bus made one last wide turn onto a highway, the streets of little houses scattering out, Denver scattering out into smaller and smaller lights and houses, away from the side of the highway. Denver disappearing behind me. The bus going faster and faster, in with the lanes of traffic. My heart going slower and slower. Even, and not beating hard.

THE BUS seat is so big that I am weightless, curled under my jacket, no backbone pressing, no body, no earth under me, just the hum of highway. The bus window is the window of night, tiny lights way out at the edge of darkness. Quiet talking here and there around me, a crunch of plastic bag, potato chips in little yellow bags on a rack in the bus station. I am hungry for an instant, and then I want a cigarette, just for a second, and then nothing. I want to think about Tina Blue. I try to force my thoughts to be about

Tina Blue, but it's not Tina Blue, it's Jimmy Henry. His thin arms, the smooth inside muscle of his arm under the short sleeve of his T-shirt, the clean inside of his elbow after he quit doing junk and the tracks healed and went away, only a smooth white lump over the blue vein. Brushing my hair. Putting the brush down on the bed and taking me by my shoulders and turning me around to his tired face, his soft beard, kissing me on my mouth, soft, kissing long on my mouth, wet and soft.

My heart beats all over my body.

My stomach is sick.

He is not my father.

And it never happened, never was like that.

It is an argument between my brain and the sick in my stomach, and I lose, I lose Jimmy Henry's soft wet mouth on my mouth, his arms pulling me against his chest, his hands in my hair. I lose him, and I ride in the dark tall bus seat, my heart beating all over, in between my legs, deep, up, in there, pussy cunt fuck, and my wet fingers in there, pussy cunt fuck, dirty words making my fingers work. Curled under my jacket in the dark of the bus.

I WOKE up when a lady sat in the seat next to me.

"Oh, hello there," she said, loud but in a whisper.

An old lady, with gray hair, and a big square purse that she tucked down into the side of the seat in between us.

Outside was a dark street, the corner of two dark streets, a stoplight hanging over the middle of the corner, shining steady red, bouncing in the wind. Through the windows on the other side of the bus was a little restaurant, lit up.

"Well," the old lady said. "A bit late as usual, but we should still get to Omaha by tomorrow night, not too late tomorrow night. Are you going all the way to Omaha?"

She buttoned her sweater buttons, and unbuttoned the bottom one. She smoothed her hands down her front, patted her lap, looked up and down the bus aisle.

"It's a windy one out there," she said, turning back straight in her seat, poking her hair behind her ears, patting her purse. "First of the fall rains no doubt. It's going to be a hard winter this year. The bluejays are fighting with the crows just to beat the band, that's always a sign, you know."

The bus pulled away, out into streets, and down dark streets in a dark town. Dark stores, and houses, and then the street turned back into being a highway.

"Funny time of night to be leaving," the lady said. "But I can't get to Omaha too early or my son-in-law can't pick me up, and my girl is home with the new baby, I have a new granddaughter, you see. I was there right after she was born, three months it's been, but they change so fast, three months is a long time, especially for a summer baby. They named her Melissa. There never has been a Melissa in our family. I guess it's kind of French."

I slipped my arms back into the sleeves of my jacket, and found my Walt Whitman hat, fallen down in between the seat and the window, and I put it on.

"Now do you need to use the little boys' room before I settle in here?" the lady said.

I said, "What?"

"If you need to climb over me you better do it now," she said. "I always get snoozy on late-night bus rides, so here, you just hop out now."

She tucked her knees to the side so I could get out past her, so I did. My knees were shaky, my feet not feeling completely on the floor of the bus. The bus going one way, me going the other way.

The bathroom light turned on when I opened the door. The bathroom was like a tin can, tin can door, tin can sink, tin can toilet, and the loud bus engine coming up. The stink was like pee and pine cleaner. The mirror was a tin can mirror, not glass, and my face in the mirror was wavy and scratchy. I backed against the wall, trying to see did I look like a boy standing there. All I could tell was it was someone wearing a green jacket and a hat.

The tin can toilet seat was cold, and my stomach hurt when I peed. I leaned my elbows on my knees, closed my eyes, rubbed my face, sitting there, the highway going by under my bare butt on the toilet. I held my hands in front of my face and looked at my ring. I touched the silver flowers on my lips, and I smelled my fingers. I looked at my fingers, and my underpants, leaned down to smell my underpants, my same own smell. I didn't wash my hands.

"THERE YOU are," the old lady said, pulling her knees to the side again. "Climb back in here. You can go back to sleep, don't mind me, I'll be snoozing away here in a little bit, by the time we get to Ogallala I'll just bet."

"This bus goes to Ogallala?"

"Oh yes," she said, "Right by Ogallala. Oh golly golly we used to call it. Oh golly golly. That always got the children laughing, I'd say, here we are, oh golly golly. Someday I'll be saying, here we are Melissa, oh golly golly. Of course, they might just call her Missy, that's a good nickname for Melissa."

The old lady hummed a little bit, and she tugged at the cuffs of her sweater and all. I leaned back into my seat and looked out the black window. Headlights coming the other way lit up the side of the road, weeds and yellowy bushes for a second. Somebody toward the back laughed every once in a while, a short ha-ha little laugh, like telling a long story with funny parts. One voice talking and then laughing.

The old lady started to snore a quiet buzzy snore, and then a clack clack clack started from the front of the bus. I stood up partway. Windshield wipers clack clack clack in the dim light of the front of the bus.

OGALLALA WAS a big highway crossing, and the town lights were off a ways. The bus drove into a gas station, past semi trucks all pulled in under orange lights, to a restaurant attached to the gas station, and a little store, all one big place set in the middle of cement.

The bus driver stood up and stretched his arms out to the sides and then he said, "Fifteen minutes, folks."

The old lady didn't wake up. People from other seats did, got up and went up the aisle. I stood up and looked down at her. Her knees were smooth bumps covered in big flowers on her dress. I stepped high over her knees, stepping sideways, and she didn't wake up.

The air smelled wet. Rainy. Not raining. The cement was shiny with water and orange lights, and oil colors, and the oil smell was in the wet air.

I went as far as the row of candy and pop machines, and I bought a can of pop, warm quarters from my pocket dropping loud into the slot. My hands were warm. I took the pop back to the bus. Some other people from the bus were coming away, or getting back on already. The bus engine hummed gas smell into my face, and I went around past, to the other side. The yellow lines on the cement led out to the dark open edges of the lights, led out to nothing out there. I set the can of pop down on the cement and I took out the pack of Marlboros, tore open the top, let the wind blow the clear wrappings out of my fingers.

A gust of wind across the cement had a gust of raindrops in it. I breathed in the wet smell. The cigarette made me high, then sick, then okay, and I dropped the last part of it on the wet cement. The lit end sogged out.

I went back around to the door of the bus, and the old lady was there, right in the door, sticking her face out, sniffing the air. She stepped back into the bus to let another guy get back on, and then I got on, and she was standing in the aisle by our seats.

"Hello, there," she said. "Here we are."

I waited for the oh golly golly part, but the old lady yawned and rubbed her eyes. I got back into my seat and she sat back into her seat and tugged at her sweater, She rubbed her hands together, held them with her fingertips tucked in, and she rested them together like that in her lap. My hands were cold, cold can of pop, and wet.

"That's bad for you teeth," the lady said. "That soda pop, I don't know how you kids drink so much and have any teeth left in your head."

The bus drove out of the place and left all the lights behind us. I pulled my green bag out far enough to unzip the zipper, enough to pull out my black sweater. I made a pillow against the window, so I could just open my eyes and see out to the blackness, the wool scratchy and then warm on my face and on my neck.

I OPENED my eyes to gray. Too gray, bright in my eyes like grit, and I closed my eyes until my heart started to beat like a fast drum, waking up on this bus.

The gray was thick fog laying out along wet weedy fields. Nothing else was out there, just the side of the road going by, and I closed my eyes again, pulled my hands under my shirt, skin and skin, back to sleep.

The old lady's chirpy talking came into my sleep, and I kept my eyes closed.

"Way too soon, oh, way too soon," she said.

"It is for my delphiniums, I know that," another voice said. "I was hoping for another bloom."

I looked out at storming-down rain.

"Well, look who's awake under that hat," the old lady said. "Not that you've missed much Nebraska countryside in this rain. Do you have to go to the bathroom?"

She tucked her legs to the side.

"No," I said. "That's okay."

She straightened back up and talked to the other lady across the aisle, talking about green tomatoes. Talking about the rain. Talking about the road.

"It used to be this bus went through Saint Francis and Bird City and then headed north a little ways on, around McCook," she said.

"Well, it took three days to get to Omaha that way," the other lady said. "This way we'll get there by ten."

Ten o'clock. Ten o'clock tonight. I couldn't think of what day today was.

"I have people in Bird City," the old lady said. "Can't even get there on a bus anymore, can't get there unless my girl and her husband come and drive me, and you know, he's got his business, busyness I call it, busy all the time."

People in Bird City.

She smelled like licorice drops.

I got *The Prophet* out of the partly open zipper, pretending to read, the rain not stopping. My eyes felt burning and wanting to close.

JFK WOULD have for sure told by now.

Maybe not.

Jimmy Henry might be out on bail. Elle's daddy might have got him out. Elle.

Lalena. Lalena was a better name. I'll tell her. Lalena is prettier than just plain Elle. Margo loved that damn song.

Sarajean.

I OPENED the folded page from the dictionary. Sarah with a tiny blue star. Spelled with an *H*. Wife of Abraham. Mother of Isaac.

"Oh, now what's this?" the old lady said. "Tearing pages out of a book?"

I folded the page back into *The Prophet*.

"I found it," I said.

"Defacing books," the old lady said. "If I caught one of the children doing any such thing as might damage a book, they got their library cards taken away."

"I found it like this," I said. "I didn't do it."

"Well, I hope not," she said.

She looked at my face, at my jacket. White hairs stuck out of her nose. She looked at my shoes. My purple socks showed through the holes. She looked back at my face.

"I'm Mrs. Smit," she said. "Not Smith, Smit. It's German, a good German name. It used to be Schmidt. It was changed when my people came here, Ellis Island you know."

"Oh," I said.

People in Bird City.

"And your name?" she said.

"Me?" I said, looking quick out the window, faking a cough.

"Bird," I said.

"Bird?" she said.

"Bird," I said. "Bird Isaac."

"Bird Isaac?" she said. "Bird Isaac?"

"Well," I said. "Yeah. Bird Isaac."

She said, "Bird Isaac, is Bird some family name?"

"Kind of," I said.

"Well, you can't tell if it's a girl's name or a boy's name," she said. "And you don't look very much like a little girl. Last night in the dark I thought you were a boy. How old are you?"

"Sixteen?" I said.

"Seems to me you'd want to dress up a little bit to go traveling," she said. "Why do you cut your hair so short?"

"I don't know," I said.

"Well, that's a very pretty ring you have, anyway," she said.

I covered my ring with my other hand.

"Thank you," I said.

"Bird Isaac," she said. "So they call you Bird? Just Bird?"

"Yeah," I said.

I opened *The Prophet.*

"Sounds like some hippie name," she said. "I know of one girl, her mama used to do my hair, named her baby boy Freedom. She was divorced, the gal that did my hair. Her girl moved to Denver right after high school, never did come back. Freedom. We never got a wedding announcement. Are you Catholic? That's a Virgin Mary medal right?"

I tucked my beads, my Mary medal, back into my T-shirt.

"I know quite a few Catholics," she said. "We're First Protestant Church but we always got on well with the Catholics. I had a young girl babysit for me, she was Catholic. She had one of those blue medals. Very pretty. Seems like you might want to take those hippie beads off, they're getting tangled up in the chain."

The window was fogged over on the inside, and I wiped at the glass. Rain and fields and the wet black edges of the road. I closed my eyes, wanting to have tears, warm wet tears, and afraid of Mrs. Smit, that she would see me cry, that she wouldn't shut up.

"So, won't this rain just ruin the rest of your dahlias?" she said.

I leaned my forehead on the cool wet glass, warm tears easy in my eyes.

BIRD ISAAC.
Elle.
Lady Jane.
Tina Blue.
Freedom.
Little Miss Strange.

THE WIND blew at the sides of the bus, and the bus slowed down, and the windshield wipers clacked faster. The road curved one way and then the other way along the edges of muddy fields.

"This storm is really slowing us down," Mrs. Smit said.

MIDNIGHT LATE, and the downtown bus station was busy with people hurrying around outside the bus. Mrs. Smit was standing up before the bus engine was even turned off.

"Well, goodbye, Bird," she said. "Goodbye, Bird, doesn't that sound odd? Doesn't sound Catholic."

She stepped out into the bus aisle, people leaving the bus, out into the garage. Gone. When the bus was empty I pulled my green bag onto my shoulder and went bumping along the empty aisle, off the bus. The bus driver was outside, smoking a cigarette, watching a guy take suitcases and boxes out of the baggage place under the bus. I went behind the bus driver, into the door of the bus station.

Echoey loud, shiny big floor, rows of blue seats.

Midnight.

Omaha.

I dropped my bag onto a blue seat and rubbed at my shoulder. I stretched my arms out front, closed my eyes, and the noise around me got louder, and there was ammonia smell. I dropped my head down until my neck made a popping sound and my face went warm.

When I opened my eyes, the light was brighter.

"Omaha," I said.

My voice didn't make any sound at all, like the word just dropped onto the floor.

A sign at a hallway said LA IES LOUNGE. I pulled the strap of my bag back onto my shoulder and went through the rows of blue seats, past a row of telephones. Phone books hanging on cords. An old lady was poking into the trash can at the end of the row of telephones.

"Bathroom on the right," the old lady said, talking down into the trash can.

The gray door under the LA IES LOUNGE sign had no doorknob, just a square of clear plastic showing where to push. The part of the door around the square of plastic was gummy black. I shoved the door open with my butt.

The ammonia cleaner smell was pissy. A row of sinks went along one wall, under a cloudy mirror, under a buzzy flourescent light.

I set my bag on the floor under a sink and got out the tied up towel, and balanced it on the edge of the sink. I set my comb on the back of the sink, in between the faucets, and I stared at my face in the mirror, my fingers looking for my toothbrush, toothpaste. There was splashing and flushing behind me in one of the toilets, and the hallway door opening let in noise from out there, and then shut out the noise again.

"Bathroom on the right."

The old lady was looking in the trash can inside the bathroom door. I turned away from her, felt around in the folded towel for my toothbrush, my eyes closed, and I heard the old lady scuffing across the floor behind me, and I jumped when she reached in front of me and grabbed my comb off the sink. The folded-up towel hit the floor and my stuff scattered, and the old lady said, "It's mine."

She looked into the mirror and combed my comb through her snarly hair, not looking at me, both of us in the mirror, her face frowning and combing and talking without words, my heart beating as far down as my elbows, as far down as my knees.

"It's mine," she said again, and she turned away and started to the door, combing at her hair with my comb. Her legs were thick and bare, old men's shoes scuffing on the floor, out the door.

My toothbrush was lying on the floor, lying on its side on the wet floor.

I said, "Fuck."

I kicked the toothbrush and it went spinning across the bathroom floor, spinning to the feet of a girl coming out of one of the toilets. She looked at me.

"This toothbrush," she said. "It has offended you?"

She leaned on the doorway of the toilet, leaned in a long black coat, white face and red lips with lipstick, black hair.

I said, "What?"

Her lips were so red I couldn't tell if she was smiling or trying to be funny or what.

"Yes," I said. "That toothbrush has offended me."

My face started to go easy into the funniness of saying that, and the girl took her hand out of a long black fold of her coat. White hand, silver rings, black gun. Little black gun.

She said, "Shall I shoot this toothbrush?"

The buzzing light buzzed louder and the light got brighter for an instant and the black and the red of the girl got blacker and redder where I was afraid to look at her hand, at the gun.

"No," I said. "Don't shoot the toothbrush."

The bathroom settled back around me. The girl held the gun up, not pointing at the toothbrush, looking at the gun.

"It's not loaded," she said. "I don't know how to get bullets."

Her hand with the gun went back into some deep pocket somewhere in the long black coat, and she left, black boots, out the door, and I was alone in the bathroom.

"Fuck," I said.

My head went dizzy when I bent to pick up all my stuff on the floor. I dragged my bag back onto my shoulder and went out the door, past my toothbrush lying on the floor.

The old lady was farther up the hall, messing around in another trash can. I went to the row of telephones and opened one of the phone books.

Five Blumenthals. No Christine. No C. J.

No Tina Blue.

The glass doors of the bus station opened out to the sidewalk and the foggy night smell, gas smell, the same wet smell as Ogallala. I walked up the sidewalk a little way, away from the doors, away from the gas smell. Halfway up the block I stopped and leaned against the side of the bus station building, slick pale colored bricks. The street was a little bit of a hill, and up and down the block ended in fog lit up by streetlights. I lit a cigarette and leaned there, looking around.

Omaha.

Up the street one way a sign said INTERNATIONAL HOUSE OF PANCAKES. The sign turned around above the fog, OPEN 24 HOURS WELCOME. I smoked three cigarettes in a row, lighting one cigarette off the other, the sign turning around, the other buildings on the street dark and empty, broken looking, with boards nailed up, and black windows.

Three people came walking down the sidewalk, boots on cement. The girl from the bathroom and two other kids, blond hair, one for sure a girl and one I couldn't tell. They walked past me, and the girl from the bathroom looked toward me but not at me, her long black coat wrapped around her like a tall black crow. The three of them walked down to the other corner and stopped there. I looked up the street the other way, and when I looked back, they were gone.

☮

FOURTEEN TWENTY Belmont Street.

Tina Blue.

Are you Little Miss Strange?

"SO, ARE you just hanging out or what?"

I jumped up straight from leaning on the building. The girl from the bathroom was right next to me. I looked for her hands.

She said, "You coming or going?"

"I don't know," I said. "I just got here."

She said, "Got another cigarette?"

I took out the pack of Marlboros and handed the pack to her. She took one hand out of her coat, no gun, and took a cigarette and stuck it behind her ear. She handed the pack back to me. She had silver rings on all her fingers.

"So where did you just get here from?" she said.

"Denver," I said.

"Well, Denver," she said. "Want to meet my friends?"

She didn't look at me. She looked around the street. Her two friends were gone. Not anywhere in the fog.

"Where are they?" I said.

She jerked her thumb toward the International House of Pancakes sign. There was a ring on her thumb.

"You might as well," she said. "The rent-a-cop will chase you off unless you have a bus ticket. You have a bus ticket?"

"One-way," I said.

"One-way ticket to Omaha?" she said.

"Well," I said. "Yeah. I'm kind of looking for someone."

"Someone hanging out at the bus station in the middle of the night?" the girl said.

"No," I said. "I don't think so."

"Well," she said. "You want to meet my friends?"

She kept looking away. In the streetlight light her lips looked black.

I said, "Okay. I guess."

I pulled my bag onto my shoulder and stood there for a second. The girl didn't move, leaned there, looking at the sign turning around above the fog. Then she straightened up, and we started walking up the street, together, away from the bus station lights, the fog closing in around us, the girl's boots loud on the sidewalk and echoing and sounding like Cassandra Wiggins.

At the door of the International House of Pancakes the girl stopped and took the cigarette out from behind her ear. She lit the cigarette with a colored plastic lighter, her rings on her fingers clinking. Then she pushed through the door ahead of me, the cigarette dangling from her red mouth.

She went to a booth by the back. The two blond kids sat there next to each other. One was a girl and one was a boy. The girl from the bathroom sat down across from them. I dropped my bag off my shoulder onto the floor and stood there for a second. The two blond kids looked at the girl.

"This is Denver," she said. "She has a one-way ticket to Omaha."

She patted the empty seat next to her, looking across at the two blond kids.

I shoved my bag under the table and sat down on the edge of the booth seat. The two kids looked at me. They looked exactly alike, long blond hair. The girl had silver dangling earrings. The boy had a T-shirt that said NIXON FOR PRESIDENT.

A waitress in a pink waitress uniform came to the table with four cups hanging off the fingers of one hand and a coffee pot in her other hand. She set the coffee pot down and then the four cups. She dumped a splash of coffee into each cup, filling the cups, slopping coffee over onto the table. She pulled a fistful of creamer packets out of her pocket and dropped the packets onto the table. Then she left.

"So, Denver," the boy said.

He took out a cigarette and lit it with a match, and he handed the cigarette to the blond girl without looking at her, and she took it, without looking at him. She looked at me. He lit another cigarette and offered it to me.

"No, thanks," I said.

Their eyes were pale pale blue.

"You just get here?" he said.

He had a nice voice, smooth and deep.

"Yeah," I said. "I'm kind of looking for someone."

"Well," he said. "I'm Marcus. And this is Marcy."

The blond girl looked away, looking around the restaurant, smoking her cigarette.

"Are you guys twins?" I said.

"Yeah," he said. "That's what they tell us."

The girl next to me laughed when he said that.

"And you've already met Jade," he said.

"Jade?" I said. "Your name is Jade?"

"Jade," she said.

"Well," I said. "Hi."

Nobody said anything. I reached for the sugar shaker, couldn't reach far enough, and Jade slid it at me. I grabbed the shaker right before it went off the edge of the table.

"Got any place to go?" Marcus said.

"Tomorrow," I said. "In the morning. Fourteen twenty Belmont Street. You know where that is?"

Marcy looked at me.

"What are you looking for on Belmont Street?" Marcus said.

"I don't know," I said. "My mother."

"Your mother a biker?" he said. "Belmont Street. Shit."

"What do you mean?" I said.

Marcy stood up and got out of the booth. She didn't say anything, just went to the very back of the restaurant, around a corner back there.

Jade said, "Denver here doesn't know if she's coming or going."

The coffee was only warm, and sweet from sugar, no coffee taste.

I said, "Is it very far, Belmont Street?"

"Far enough for me," Jade said.

Marcus didn't say anything, just sort of looked at Jade.

A guy came up to the table. He was skinny and had short hair and a mustache. Marcus and Jade just looked at each other.

The guy said, "Where's your sister?"

Marcus kept looking at Jade and he said, "Guess she's not here."

"I'm looking for her," the guy said.

Marcus finally looked up at the guy and he said, "Maybe you ought to send her a Valentine's Day card."

"Tell her I'm looking for her," the guy said.

He left, and Marcus and Jade went back to looking at each other.

The counter that went by the booths was full of people. A fat guy sat closest to us, his back to our table. His jacket rode up on his back and his butt crack showed, and pimply hairy skin. He got up off the stool just when the waitress came by with the coffee pot. She had to stop short, and coffee sloshed onto the floor.

"Watch it," she said.

She filled our cups back up with coffee, my cup, Jade's cup, Marcus's cup.

"That's your free refill," she said.

Marcus said, "Why, thank you, you are too kind."

"I know it," the waitress said.

Jade said, "Our other friend here will be right back."

The waitress looked at Marcy's cup. She slapped a piece of paper onto the edge of the table and left.

"So, Denver," Marcus said. "Want to get high?"

Pretty light blue eyes.

"I don't know," I said.

The windows were steamed up, and it looked black and drippy outside, and I wanted to go back to the bus station and wait. For morning.

"At our place," Marcus said.

"Your place?" I said.

"Yeah," he said. "It's just up the street. The service isn't as gracious as it is here, but the ambience is comparable."

"Well," I said. "Okay."

 High in Omaha.

Marcus stood up, and Jade tossed her cigarette into the ashtray, not putting it out, just tossing it there, smoking, in with the pile of butts.

"What about your sister?" I said.

"She had somewhere to go," Marcus said.

He bent down and pulled out my bag.

"Thanks," I said, reaching for it.

"Allow me," he said.

He carried my bag, and I walked behind him, and Jade behind me. The skinny guy with the mustache sat, watching us, at the end of the counter by the door. At the cash register Jade put the bill for the coffee on the counter and reached into her pocket. She took out two dollar bills.

"Here," I said, digging a quarter out from all my change.

"I'll buy," Jade said.

"No, here," I said, putting my quarter on the counter.

"In that case you're two cents short," she said. "Tax."

It was raining outside, light rain coming down through the fog. I stood in the doorway of the International House of Pancakes for a second, wanting my bag back, looking back down the block through the rain at the bus station.

Marcus turned around and said, "Come on, Denver."

I followed him and Jade up the hill of the sidewalk, the rain coming down harder.

STEPS WENT down into a little room with windows looking up at the sidewalk, the light from the streetlights coming in. Marcus switched on a lamp, and he dropped my bag onto a couch. Stacks of records and magazines were around on the floor, dark shaggy carpeting, tapes scattered across the seat of a chair. The place smelled like cat, and it was cold. I sat down on the edge of the couch, next to my bag. I leaned my elbows on my knees and rubbed my eyes hard, and when I opened my eyes again a cat sat in front of me, staring up at me. I kissed at it. The cat stared. Flat gold eyes.

"Tangent," Jade said.

She scooped the cat up and tossed it across the room, the cat's four legs clawing the air as it flew and landed in the chair. Tapes clacked to the floor as the cat hit and took off, around a corner, gone.

I said, "Tangent?"

"Always off on a tangent, that cat," Marcus said.

"Too much acid, that cat," Jade said.

Marcus turned the dial on a heater that ran along one wall. The heater clicked and ticked and started to glow orange on one end. He went over to the kitchen part of the room and he opened the oven door wide and turned the oven on. Then he came over and sat next to me on the couch. I scooted over until the wet from my bag came through my blue jeans. Marcus took out a cigarette pack, and he shook a yellow joint out of it. He lit the joint with a match and took a big hit, and handed the joint to me. He had long thin fingers. I took the joint, and my fingers were shaking. I took a small hit, a small careful hit, and handed the joint back to him. The taste was sweet and strong, and after the third time he handed the joint to me, my fingers stopped shaking, and my breath eased in my chest, and when he handed me the joint again I shook my head no.

"Sure?" he said.

"I don't want any more," I said.

Jade sat across the room in the chair. She still wore her long black coat, the coat with the gun in the pocket, and she took the gun out and looked at it up close.

I said, "How come you have a gun?"

Jade didn't look up at me, looking at the gun, holding it in the light of the lamp. The gun was kind of blue.

"I think it's kind of pretty," she said.

Marcus got up and took off his jacket, an old suit jacket. His arms were skinny and pale, pale like his hair, pale like his face. The apartment was warmer.

I said, "Where's the bathroom?"

"Back that way," Marcus said. "You can't miss it."

I stood up and slid my jacket off my arms and laid it carefully on top of my bag. I went back toward where the cat had disappeared.

There were two doors. The first one I pushed open was the bathroom. Tangent sat in a corner on a pile of towels and clothes. A litter box was under the sink, and the stink of it made me want to cry. I held my breath, peeing as fast as I could. The toilet wouldn't flush. It hadn't been flushed in a while.

When I went back out, everything seemed the same. Jade sat in the chair, looking at the gun. Marcus sat on the couch, smoking a joint, another joint. I stood there, looking, like I had been gone for a long time, like I wasn't really there in the room with them, and when I looked at my bag with my green jacket folded there, my jacket from Constanzia, Jimmy Henry's bag, Omaha, I had to lean against the wall, dizzy in my stomach and wanting something badly. Marcus looked at me smiling, and he held the joint out.

"No, thanks," I said.

I went back and sat next to him, in between him and my bag. He handed me the joint again, and I took it, and smoked it, and when I handed it back to him, he said, "No, go ahead."

COMING AWAKE, not opening my eyes, waiting, knowing where I was, on a couch in these kids' apartment in Omaha. It was hot. My neck ached, and my legs tingled numb and asleep, and my throat burned. Someone was moving, a soft noise.

The apartment was dark except for the streetlight coming in the window and a dark orange glow from the oven. I lay still. Blinking. My eyes fuzzy. Jade sat in the chair, almost invisible. She was watching me. She pointed the gun at me, and at her own head, going *click click* with her tongue.

THE ROOM was empty and cold when I woke up again, and gray daylight showed in the windows. The oven door was still open, cold and black. The cat Tangent sat in the chair, staring with flat gold cat eyes, its striped fur that same color. There was no sound except the heater ticked along the wall.

My head hammered with hurt when I sat up straight, and my elbow wouldn't unbend from being curled under me sleeping.

My hat was on the floor next to the couch. I put it on, and I pulled the strap of my bag onto my shoulder, my shoulder sore in that one spot, and I went out the door, up the cement stairs to the sidewalk, and away, any direction, away.

Rainy. Not raining, and early gray day. I walked fast, up the empty sidewalk, around a corner and another corner, fast away from the apartment down under the sidewalk. After a while I walked slower.

It was mostly empty places, painted-over windows of stores and nobody out walking around. Just me.

One place on a corner was open, with lights on inside, a drugstore, and a long counter inside, a guy reading a newspaper, a lady behind the counter being the waitress. They both looked at me when I pushed through the door. It smelled like bacon. A radio voice jabbered away somewhere, no music, just jabbering.

I said, "Hi."

The guy looked back at his newspaper. The waitress looked at me. I walked along the counter to a stool at the end away from the door and dropped my bag under the counter and sat down. The waitress picked up the coffee pot and came over.

"Coffee?" she said.

"No," I said. "No thanks. Can I get a BLT?"

She picked a menu out from behind a napkin holder, slid the menu on the counter in front of me, and she said, "There's the breakfast menu."

She walked away, put the coffee pot back, and leaned on the counter by the guy with the newspaper. She picked up a cigarette that was burning in an ashtray and smoked, looking out the window. It was raining now, rain streaking down the dirty window, and I wondered why the rain didn't just wash the window.

I looked at the menu, not reading. The aisles of the drugstore were empty. A guy in a white coat was behind a counter at the back.

"You going to order something?"

The waitress stood in front of me.

"French toast?" I said.

She turned around, to the stove, and she reached into a plastic bag of bread.

"Is there a bathroom here?" I said.

"Back by the pharmacy," she said, not turning around.

I dragged my bag out and went back through the aisles, past the toothbrushes and toothpaste. I looked at the toothbrushes, all hanging in rows, all different colors. I reached for a red one, a blue one, a green one. I picked one off a hook and went to the pharmacy counter. The guy in the white coat looked up at me over his glasses.

"Can I pay for this here?" I said.

"Ninety-two cents, with tax," he said.

The bathroom was warm and bright and clean. I dropped my bag onto the floor, shut the door behind me and locked it and slid to the floor, next to my bag, my eyes closed, just a moment, alone in the clean quiet bathroom. The water was hot, and I brushed my teeth hard until the toothpaste turned foamy pink. I washed my face with soap, Jimmy Henry's soap, the smell of it, the smell of him.

My hair stuck up all over my head. I put my hat back on and went back out.

There was a plate of French toast, two pieces, and two squares of butter not melting. I poured on syrup and ate part of one piece. The radio guy was still talking, selling cars maybe. Talking about traffic. He kept saying, "So, folks."

The waitress came back and put a piece of paper on the counter next to my plate. She started to walk away.

I said, "Can you tell me how to get to Belmont Street?"

"Sorry," she said, not turning around.

Not sorry.

When I went back out there were a few people walking fast in the rain. I stood in the doorway of the drugstore, and then I just went, out into the rain, rain on my hat, on my jacket. My feet were wet by the time I got to the first corner, and from there I saw the sign for the International House of Pancakes, and past it, down the hill, the bus station.

A BIG map of Omaha was on one wall, and along one side was a list of streets, alphabetical. I found Belmont Street. I found the bus station. They weren't very far apart. I unfolded the envelope and I drew a kind of map on the back, street to street, the bus station to Belmont Street.

Me to Tina Blue.

My heart was hurting from beating so hard, my whole self hurting from my heart beating so hard.

THE HOUSE was yellow, old, peeling, maybe white. There was a wide porch, and a screen door hanging crooked over the front door. I went up the two wide steps and knocked twice on the wooden edge of the screen door. I started to knock again when the inside door opened and a guy looked out.

"What is it?" he said.

He had short gray hair.

"I'm looking for someone," I said.

He said, "Who?"

"Tina Blue," I said.

"No one here named that," he said, and he started to shut the door.

"Wait," I said, a crack in my voice. "Wait."

He looked through the screen.

I said, "What about Christine? Blumenthal?"

"No," he said.

He shut the door.

The paint along the side of the door peeled up, yellow over gray, over tan. A plastic garbage bag next to the porch railing leaked something wet out the bottom. A three-legged chair sat in the corner. I went down the steps to the sidewalk and looked again at the number painted on the house. Fourteen twenty. The curtain at the window moved, and a face looked out. A different face. The face disappeared, and the front door opened again.

Her long hair was dark and gray.

My legs shook and my chest felt like it was opening up to the sky.

I said, "Tina Blue?"

My voice was some other voice, barely a sound, the street behind me, barely a sound. The screen door opened, and she stepped out onto the porch. Bare feet. The screen door slammed shut behind her with a loud crack, and my heart jumped inside me. She leaned back onto the door and crossed her arms over her chest.

"No," she said.

"Why are you looking for Tina Blue?" she said.

I said, "She's my mother."

Only those words on the empty street.

She came to the edge of the porch, came down one step, sat down there, looking at me. She had on blue jeans and a plaid shirt, old flannel. Silver earrings, big silver hoops.

"You don't look much like her," she said.

"You know her?" I said. "Do you know where she is? Is she here?"

"Nope," she said.

I couldn't move.

"She left about a year ago," she said.

"You don't know where she went?" I said in some weird, whispery voice.

"Nope."

She took a cigarette from a pack in her shirt pocket, lit the cigarette with a match, dropped the match to the step between her bare feet.

She said, "Why you looking for her?"

"She's my mother," I said.

"Yeah?" she said. "So?"

"Well, that's why," I said. "Did she used to live here?"

"Once in a while," she said. "She came and went."

"Did that other guy, in there, did he know her?" I said.

"That other guy in there doesn't like visitors," she said.

The rain started again, heavy cold drops. She stood up and stepped back under the porch roof, leaning there, looking at me.

"There's some stuff in here," she said. "It was hers. You want it?"

"Yeah," I said. "Yeah, I guess so."

She opened the screen door and went in, letting the screen door slam shut behind her. Slamming the inside door. I went up on the porch, out of the rain. I took out a cigarette and lit it, the match shaking in my cold wet fingers.

Gone.

The door opened again, and the lady came out holding a yellow envelope. She handed it to me, and I threw my cigarette out into the rain and took the envelope out of her hand.

"There was some more stuff, some books and shit," she said. "I don't know where it is."

I pulled out a folded paper. What I unfolded was a birth certificate. It said "Sarajean Blumenthal." It said "Mother, Christine Jeanette Blumenthal." It said "Father, John Doe."

"John Doe," I said. "Sarajean Blumenthal."

The lady looked at me and shook her head. The rain started to come down heavy and loud, pouring off the roof and splashing into a deep puddle at the corner of the porch.

There was a photograph in the envelope, a woman sitting on a couch, holding a baby wrapped in a blanket, the top of a small pink head poking out. There was a half a man sitting on the couch, and the edge of the photograph cut him off before his face.

"Is that her?" I said, holding the picture out.

She looked at the picture and shrugged.

"Hard to tell," she said. "Kind of looks like her. Not a very good picture."

I stared at the picture. I couldn't see the face. I couldn't see the face that was in the picture. I couldn't see the face that I couldn't remember.

The lady opened the screen door, and she looked back at me once more.

"Don't come back," she said.

Gone.

She came and went.

You don't look much like her.

THE FIRST time I called it sounded like Nancy that answered, and I hung up. The second time I couldn't tell, maybe it was Nancy, and I hung up. The third time it was some guy, and I said,

"Is JFK there?"

"Just a sec," the voice said.

And then, "Hello?"

"It's me," I said.

"Sarajean?" he said, and his voice went to a whisper in the telephone.

"She isn't here," I said. "She's gone. She's been gone a year."

"Sarajean," JFK whispered into the telephone. "You should come home. Jimmy Henry's not busted."

"Don't let anyone know it's me," I said. "Don't say Sarajean."

"Did you hear me?" he said. "Jimmy Henry's not busted."

"What do you mean?" I said.

"It wasn't cops," he said. "It was some dope guys. They wanted their money. They just messed him up."

"What do you mean, messed him up?" I said. "Dope guys?"

"Listen, you should come back," he said. "They all think you went to Los Angeles. Jimmy Henry says he's going to go there and find you."

"Los Angeles?" I said. "What do you mean, messed him up? Did they beat him up?"

"Well, yeah, sort of," he said. "He has a black eye kind of. His mouth is kind of smashed."

"They beat up Jimmy Henry?" I said. "Is he okay?"

"I knew you were leaving," JFK said. "Macaroni and cheese. Sure. Put on the macaroni water, she says. I have to go get my homework, she says."

"Jimmy Henry's going to Los Angeles?" I said. "Don't let him go to Los Angeles."

"Well, what should I say?" JFK said.

"Tell him I'm coming back," I said.

"You are?" he said. "Well, good, 'cause Lady Jane is a wreck, crying all the time. My mom had to work three shifts in a row."

The operator came on and asked for more money.

"I have to go," I said.

"Wait," JFK said. "When are you coming home?"

I hung up the phone.

THE BUS got to Indianola at ten o'clock in the morning, and the outside I stepped into was cool, with big, flat-bottomed clouds, and a smoky stink in the air.

The Indianola bus station wasn't really a bus station. It was the drugstore, Smithy's Drugstore, and a sign in the window said GREYHOUND BUS, with the Greyhound Bus greyhound. A bell jingled when I pushed through the door, and a guy behind the counter looked at me over the top of the glasses on his face. A fat lady was in an aisle by the door. She was looking at stuff like she wasn't looking at me.

I went to the counter.

"Where is the Rookery Bend Cemetery?" I said in a low voice.

"It's out east of town, out on Highway Twenty," the guy said out loud.

He looked at my green zipper bag.

He said, "You go about two miles after Blaine's Texaco, and then maybe another half a mile down Rookery Bend Road to the south."

East. South.

The guy said, "Go to your left on Fourth Street here, and you'll come to Highway Twenty. The old Iowa Road."

"Thank you."

I looked at the fat lady on my way out the door. She looked at my hat.

Right next to Smithy's Drugstore was a restaurant that said BARB'S on a red-painted sign over the screen door. A couple of old men sat at the counter in there, old men in baseball hats. They looked when I walked by the window, looked without moving their faces. Next was a big parking lot behind a fence with yellow and green tractors sitting out in the sun, in a shiny row. The sign said JOHN DEERE.

John Doe.

Mack Street was next, and little houses set back behind bushes, walkways leading carefully up to the front porch, and nobody around. Nobody looking out through pale white curtains pulled back inside each window like a bow. Nobody that I could see.

Jimmy Henry sitting at our kitchen table, in his tie-dye T-shirt, looking out our kitchen window, and him saying, "I don't think there's anyone there anymore."

The next street across Fourth Street was Euclid Street, and after Euclid Street the sidewalk ended.

Bumping my bag on my hip, switching to the other shoulder, I walked, watching my feet in the gravel along where the grassy weeds edged in. My hightop was rubbing on my ankle bone, a hot stinging spot every step. At the main road the sign on the corner said Iowa Road. Fourth Street ended, and across the Iowa Road the chopped yellow field went away in neat rows, up the hill of the field, and along the hills past that, and the flat-bottomed clouds filled up the sky as far away as the field went. There was a blue sign a little way up the road that said IOWA 20 WEST. Down the other way was a sign that said IOWA 20 EAST.

I dropped my bag onto the gravel and both of my shoulders ached. I untied my shoelace and tied it looser so it wouldn't rub so much on my ankle bone. I didn't want to hang the strap of my bag over my shoulder again, but I did, and I crossed the Iowa Road and headed east. Out east of town.

The little streets with houses were on one side of the Iowa Road, and the side where I walked was a grassy ditch, and a sagging line of wire fence, and then the field all cut down. The ditch was busy, and along the fence was rustling in the grasses, little black and yellow birds that never flew up, they hopped to the fence and the weeds and clumps of silvery stickers topped with purple flowers.

Blaine's Texaco was closed, and a sign said FOR SALE, and tall dead hollyhocks leaned up around the sign.

Then there was nothing, on both sides of the road. The gravel glittered with broken glass, and after a while the ditch had water in it, black water that showed the sky in a thin shine of oily color, and a breezy wind smelled like gas. There were trees along the far back edges of the fields. The trees ran in a straight line for a while, way off, and then ended, and the next field began.

"Always look at what's far away."

My shoulder burned where the strap rubbed, and I switched to the other shoulder again, and the burning switched to that shoulder.

Behind me, Indianola just sat there, houses and square buildings on the flat of the land, and the roll of the land spreading out, bigger than everything, going on and on under the sky.

The heavy clouds never moved through the sky, just hung there, dead still, like everything was dead still. Even the bird sounds didn't count somehow, never came up out of the ditch, part of the heavy quiet. The old men in the restaurant never moving their faces. The fat lady pretending I wasn't there.

Jimmy Henry. As quiet as this place was quiet. As quiet as sitting in his chair smoking Marlboros. As quiet as ever.

The only sound was the crunching of my feet in the gravel, sharp gravel through the bottoms of my hightops. I stepped out onto the blacktop, the blacktop leading away in front of me and behind me.

The trees at the far edges of the fields came out to Highway 20 East, and another road, a dirt road, led down under them. The ground under the trees was wet, water shining through in places. It was cooler, smelled cooler, and the branches reached over, closing off the clouds and the sky.

The dirt road was soft stepping, and quiet and dark in early day shade. The sun came down through the trees in broken shots, and swarms of tiny flying things hung in the air in crazy little clouds. A crow screeched, setting off echoes of cheeping and chirping and my heart inside me.

The cemetery was at the end of the road, at the end of the woods, at the edge of a low field. The field was full of still water and tall weeds, and there were dead standing trees broken and bare.

A log fence made a crooked square, and inside the square were the uneven rows of gravestones, standing, leaning, flat, stones of white gray and darker gray. The road led into the cemetery and faded to ruts of tire tracks in weedy grass. I dropped my bag off my shoulder, into the grass by the fence. The sun was full on the cemetery, hard flat light pressing down.

"Just some place on Earth they all go back to."

The sore spot on my ankle bone was a red watery blister. I took my shoes off and sat up on the log fence, and then I had to pick a splinter out of my hand. I pressed on my ankle blister and it squished under the skin.

There were square pieces of stone covered with bright green moss right along the log fence. And then a big carved cross, with a jar of pink plastic flowers set in front of it, said Mack on the cross, and little square markers spread out on each side of it, with a name on each, Sister Lucille, Brother Michael, Brother John. I got down off the fence and walked along all the little markers, all the Macks, Richard, Jeanette, Frances. The tall grass was soft and my feet ached, and the blister on my ankle bone burned, and grasshoppers hopped up out of my way.

A stone angel, sleeping, had "Susan" written under it, and the same date for born and died. There was a row of flat white pieces with the writing on them faded gone. A tall gray column was broken, the top part lying across the piece of grass it marked. The broken piece had "James Smithy" carved on there, and the part still standing said "Beloved Father."

A shiny silvery stone said "Blaine," with new green grass short and neat all around it.

There was another Smithy that said "Our Father," and old dates so that it must be the grandfather of the other Smithy. All the names were like "Dear Son," and "Wife of Samuel," and all those Mack brothers and Mack sisters, names and people connected to other names and other people, here, or not here, in Rookery Bend Cemetery, in Indianola.

Some other place on Earth.

The tire tracks curved around at the back of the cemetery. The log fence along the back was covered in white morning glory flowers with leafy vines and heart shaped leaves that reached along the ground to the uneven row of gravestones by the fence.

Jimmy Henry's people.

All the Henrys.

A curved stone, a flat stone, an Elizabeth with a cross. All Henrys.

A square stone of smooth gray and rounded corners said "Marie Anthony Henry," and the date. When Jimmy Henry was thirteen. The writing was carved deep, and I traced my finger in the words, in the cool jagged letters, touching something far away.

I sat in the grass there for a while, sat against the stone, and I looked out to the watery field. The light of the sun changed its weight, pressing down on the field, sinking into it.

A tall-legged bird stood there, so still I didn't see it for a long time, and when I moved, it lifted its wide wings and glided up into the low air over the field, around in a circle and then down again, to the same spot, to rest there again on its own long legs, perfectly still.